Some things just c...
Some plans c...
That's how it was ...
and Caitlin ...

SOON TO BE
BRIDES

Two bestselling authors deliver two
intense, emotional stories.

We're proud to present

MILLS & BOON

Spotlight

a chance to buy collections of bestselling novels
by favourite authors every month – they're
back by popular demand!

July 2008

Romancing the Crown:
Lorenzo & Anna

Featuring
The Man Who Would Be King by Linda Turner
The Princess and the Mercenary
by Marilyn Pappano

Soon To Be Brides

Featuring
The Marrying MacAllister by Joan Elliott Pickart
That Blackhawk Bride by Barbara McCauley

Aiugust 2008

Romancing the Crown: Max & Elena

Featuring
The Disenchanted Duke by Marie Ferrarella
Secret-Agent Sheikh by Linda Winstead Jones

One of a Kind

Featuring
Lionhearted by Diana Palmer
Letters to Kelly by Suzanne Brockmann

SOON TO BE BRIDES

The Marrying MacAllister
JOAN ELLIOTT PICKART

That Blackhawk Bride
BARBARA McCAULEY

⊚™ MILLS & BOON®
Pure reading pleasure™

This collection is first published in Great Britain 2008.
Harlequin Mills & Boon Limited,
Eton House, 18-24 Paradise Road, Richmond, Surrey TW9 1SR

SOON TO BE BRIDES © Harlequin Books S.A. 2008.

The publisher acknowledges the copyright holders of the individual works, which have already been published in the UK.

The Marrying MacAllister © Joan Elliott Pickart 2003
That Blackhawk Bride © Barbara Joel 2003

ISBN: 978 0 263 86105 1

064-0708

Printed and bound in Spain
by Litografía Rosés S.A., Barcelona

The Marrying MacAllister

JOAN ELLIOTT PICKART

JOAN ELLIOTT PICKART

When she isn't writing, Joan enjoys reading, gardening and attending craft shows with her young daughter, Autumn. Joan has three grown-up daughters and three fantastic grandchildren.

Dear Reader,

You are about to go on a trip to the enchanting land of China and you don't even have to worry about attempting to pack everything into one suitcase.

I hope you enjoy reading Matt and Caitlin's story as much as I did writing it. It gave me the opportunity to relive all the wonderful memories of my own trip to Hong Kong, Nanjing and Guangzhou when I adopted my three-month-old daughter Autumn in 1995.

As writers we sometimes wiggle facts around a bit to enable our characters to have their dreams come true. I wish to make it clear that Elizabeth's solution to Caitlin and Matt's dilemma and Henry's agreeing to take part in it would never have taken place.

But this book is fiction, where fairy tales are allowed to come true.

So sit back, put your feet up and travel the sometimes bumpy road to eternal love with Caitlin, Matt and two little China dolls who will hopefully steal your heart.

Warmest regards,

Joan Elliott Pickart

For my nifty niece
ALIDA ELIZABETH HUNT

Chapter One

"I warned you, MacAllister, but you refused to listen. Now? I'm going to punch your ticket."

Matt MacAllister glared at his longtime friend, Bud Mathis, who sat behind the desk in a masculinely decorated office. Matt was opposite the desk in a comfortable chair, one ankle propped on his other knee.

"Come on, Bud. Give me a break. Cut me some slack here."

"It's Dr. Mathis to you at the moment," Bud said, crossing his arms over his chest. "I already gave you a second chance. I told you a month ago that I'd hold off on faxing my report on your yearly physical to the board of directors at the hospital for thirty days to give you an opportunity to quit working such long hours, get proper rest, eat decently and on the list goes.

"Did you utilize that month to your advantage? Nope. You still have high blood pressure that is the cause of your frequent headaches, you're suffering from exhaustion and your ulcer is on the warpath."

"Being the public-relations director at Mercy Hospital is not a lightweight position, Bud," Matt said, dropping his foot to the floor. "Situations occur that simply can't be postponed because my doctor says I need to go home and take a nap."

"I heard this spiel a month ago. So cork it. I'm not giving you a clean bill of health so you can continue as you are. I am, in fact, going to inform the board that you're to take a medical leave for a minimum of a month and perhaps even longer."

Matt lunged to his feet. "Now wait just a damn minute."

"Sit," Bud said, meeting Matt glare for glare.

Matt muttered an earthy expletive, then slouched back onto the chair, his eyebrows knitted in a frown.

"I'll give you one week," Bud went on, "to bring the attorney the hospital keeps on retainer up to date on pending files, and you can use those same days to find a replacement to attend the fund-raising events that you said are scheduled on your calendar. After that, you're not to put one foot inside the hospital until you've cleared it through me.''

"Ah, man," Matt said, dragging one hand through his thick, auburn hair. "Some friend you are. I'll go nuts just sitting around. And if you tell me to go fishing or take up bridge I'll deck you.''

"I don't want you to even be here in Ventura," Bud said, "because you'll cheat, be on the phone every other minute to the attorney covering your spot.

"Marsha and I were talking about you last night, Matt. I told her it would be a very safe bet that you'd flunk your physical today. We came up with what we feel is a terrific solution to your situation."

"I bet you have," Matt said, rolling his eyes heavenward.

"Just listen...and keep an open mind. You know that Marsha and I have spent months completing the paperwork to adopt a baby girl from China.''

"Of course I know that. I'm going to be her godfather.''

"Yes, you are." Bud nodded. "Well, the adoption agency says the match pictures are on the way. It's finally happening, Matt. We're going to fly to the other side of the world and bring home our little miracle.''

Matt smiled. "No joke? That's great. I'm really

happy for you and Marsha.'' He paused and frowned again. ''But I don't have a clue as to what this has to do with your not allowing me to work at the hospital for the next month.''

''It's very simple. Marsha and I want you to come with us on the trip to China.''

''What?''

''It's perfect, don't you see?'' Bud said, flinging out his arms. ''If you're in China you sure can't pop into Mercy Hospital when no one is looking, nor pick up the phone to check on things every two seconds.

''You won't be under any stress during the trip because *you're* not the one who will be tending to a new member of the family. That awesome task is delegated to those of us in our group who are adopting the little ones.''

''But…''

''Hear me out.'' Bud raised one hand. ''We'll be over there for about two weeks as there are legal matters to attend to. However, the Chinese government schedules one meeting a day, leaving foreign visitors plenty of time to tour and spend money. To top it off, you'll be traveling with your own physician…me…and I intend to keep an eagle eye on you. Like I said…it's perfect.''

''It's nuts, that's what it is. You plan to just inform the adoption agency that a friend of yours is going to tag along for the ride? Yeah, right.''

"Yeah, you *are* right," Bud said, appearing extremely pleased with himself. "That's exactly what Marsha and I would do. One of the couples of the five families in our group is bringing the new grandparents along, and the one single mom has been advised to have a friend with her to help with luggage and what have you because there are no bellhops or redcaps in China.

"All the agency needs to know within the next few days is how many people are actually going so they can make arrangements."

"Oh," Matt said.

"Look, don't give me an answer now, but promise me you'll think about it. It's a win-win situation, Matt. You can't be tempted to sneak in some work time, plus you'll be sharing a very special event with Marsha and me and meeting your new goddaughter.

"This is Monday. The match pictures are winging their way west even as we speak. On Wednesday night everyone involved is coming to our house at six-thirty for a potluck dinner to receive the pictures...God, what a moment that will be...and to get instructions on dos and don'ts while in China so we don't offend anyone over there.

"It's called a culture training meeting and your cousin Carolyn will be conducting it. Carolyn isn't going on the trip because she's pregnant, as you know. Elizabeth Kane, the director of the agency, will be accompanying us.

"All I'm asking at this point, Matt, is that you attend the potluck at our house Wednesday night, having kept an open mind about possibly joining us on this trip. What do you say? Will you come Wednesday?"

Matt sighed. "Yeah, I guess so. It can't hurt to listen, I suppose, and I'll be able to see the picture of your daughter. But China? It's not exactly around the corner, Bud."

"No, it's a long, long way from Mercy Hospital in Ventura, California, my friend, which makes it a custom-ordered place for you to travel to. Hey, it beats going fishing."

"That's a very good point," Matt said, raising a finger. "I'll be at your house Wednesday night, but I'm not promising anything."

"Fair enough," Bud said. "There's something else that you ought to consider, too. A MacAllister going on a vacation is no big deal. But a Mac-Allister who is on a doctor-ordered medical leave? That's news and you'd be kidding yourself if you thought the press wouldn't get wind of it. If you stay in Ventura you'll be hounded by reporters wanting all the details regarding your health."

"The thought of that is enough to make my ulcer go nuts," Matt said, getting to his feet. "Do they have any forks in China? I have never been able to master the use of chopsticks. It's not going to do your reputation as a doctor any good if your patient starves to death while accompanying you to a foreign country, chum.''

Bud laughed. ''You can pack a fork in your suitcase just to be on the safe side of that question.''

''This isn't sounding like a thrill a minute, Mathis,'' Matt said, heading toward the door of the office. ''Yeah, yeah, I know, it beats going fishing. I'll see you Wednesday night.'' He opened the door, then turned to look at Bud again. ''Potluck. What should I bring?''

''An attitude adjustment.''

''Hell,'' Matt said, then strode out of the office.

By Wednesday night Matt's attitude was well on its way to being adjusted.

He parked his SUV behind the last car in the row in front of the Mathises' large ranch-style house, crossed his arms on the top of the steering wheel and glowered into space.

China, here I come, he thought. The last two days had been a study in frustration as he'd started the process of bringing the hospital's attorney up to date on the pending files that needed to be brought to closure. There was no doubt in his mind that the attorney would be calling him every two seconds to double-check something, causing him to want to march back over there and do it himself.

Stress to the max, that's what it would be, and his blood pressure would probably go off the Richter scale, making it impossible to get a passing grade on Bud's crummy physical.

Did he want to go to China and starve to death because he couldn't master the use of chopsticks? No. Was he in the mood for tours and sight-seeing trips with the typical bit about "On your left you will see…"? No. Did he feel like being surrounded by a slew of nervous new parents and babies who would no doubt wail their dismay at the sudden changes taking place in their lives? No.

Hey, he loved kids, which was a good thing since he was a MacAllister and was in proximity to the diaper brigade in vast numbers at every family gathering. But the scenario with *these* babies and *these* parents was far from the norm, and the new mom and dad's tension would be sensed by the munchkin and they'd all be wrecks.

Nope, he didn't want to go to China with this group, Matt thought as he rang the doorbell, but the opportunity was there and it certainly would put distance between himself and the attorney from hell. So be it.

The front door opened and a smiling Marsha Mathis greeted Matt. She was a tall, attractive blonde in her early thirties, who immediately kissed Matt on the cheek, then slipped one arm through one of his.

"I'll give you a quick introduction to everyone, Matt," Marsha said, "but if no one remembers your name the first time around don't take it personally, because we are coming unglued. Carolyn arrived just moments before you did and she's about to pass out the match pictures. I can hardly believe this is really happening after all these months."

"I'm very happy for you and Bud. That little lady waiting for you in China is a fortunate kiddo to be getting parents like you two."

"Oh, we're the ones who are counting our blessings," Marsha said as they entered a large family room beyond the living room. "Everyone, this is Matt MacAllister, who will hopefully be accompanying us on the trip. He's Carolyn's cousin-in-law, or some such thing."

"Hello, Matt," Carolyn said, smiling at him from across the room.

"Hi, Carolyn," Matt said. "How's Ryan?"

"Super."

"Okay, I'll make this fast," Marsha said, "so we can get our match pictures. Matt, that couple on the love seat is…"

Within seconds Matt gave up even comprehending what Marsha was saying, let alone being able to remember the names of the dozen-plus people, because she was rattling them off so fast it was a blur of sound. He just smiled and nodded, then nodded some more.

"And last but not least," Marsha said, "is our single mommy, Caitlin Cunningham. That's it. Find a place to sit, Matt." She hurried across the room to settle on a chair next to Bud and grab his hand.

Caitlin Cunningham, Matt mused, still looking at her where she was sitting on the raised hearth in front of the fireplace. *That* name belonging to *that* woman was now etched indelibly in his mind.

She was absolutely lovely.

With short, curly dark hair, delicate features and the biggest, most expressive eyes he'd ever seen, combined with a slender figure clad in pale blue slacks and a very feminine flowered top, Caitlin Cunningham was, indeed, worth remembering.

Matt made his way across the room and settled onto the hearth about three feet away from Caitlin, whose gaze was riveted on Carolyn. He slid a glance at Caitlin, and realized that she was clutching her hands so tightly beneath her chin that her knuckles were white. She drew a shuddering breath as Carolyn opened a large envelope and removed five envelopes containing the match pictures.

"The big moment has arrived, huh?" Matt said, directing his statement toward Caitlin.

She did not respond, nor give any indication that she had even heard him.

Way to go, MacAllister, Matt thought. He'd sure knocked her out with his good looks and charm. She was speechless with awe. Yeah, right.

He could tear off all his clothes and do a hip-swiveling dance worthy of a male stripper and he seriously doubted if Caitlin Cunningham would even notice.

Well, maybe he was being too hard on himself. After all, Ms. Cunningham was about to see a picture of her new child for the very first time. Nobody could compete with *that.*

Matt continued to scrutinize Caitlin out of the corner of his eye while being vaguely aware of the sound of excited reactions as well as sniffles in the background as Carolyn passed out the envelopes.

Carolyn moved to where Caitlin was sitting and gave her one of the coveted envelopes.

"Congratulations, Mother," Carolyn said, smiling.

With a trembling hand Caitlin took the envelope from Carolyn.

"Thank you, Carolyn," Caitlin said softly. "I… Thank you."

"Open the envelope." Carolyn laughed. "Staring at it like that isn't going to give you your first glimpse of your daughter. Okay, off I go. This is such fun."

"Well," Caitlin said, now gripping the envelope with both hands. "My daughter's picture is in here.

Oh, my goodness, *my daughter's picture is in this envelope.* This is wonderful and terrifying and...oh dear.''

Matt scooted about a foot closer to Caitlin on the hearth.

"Do you need some help opening that?"

"Aakk," Caitlin said, her head snapping around. "Who are you?"

"Matt MacAllister," he said, frowning. "Marsha introduced me when I came in. Remember? No, I guess you don't. This is quite a moment in your life. Go ahead. Say hello to your daughter."

"Yes, yes, I'm going to do that," Caitlin said, nodding jerkily. "Right now." She slid a fingertip under the flap of the envelope, lifted it, hesitated, then reached inside and took out two pictures. A lovely smile instantly formed on her lips and her eyes filled with tears. "Oh, look at her. Just look at her. She's the most beautiful baby I've ever seen. My daughter. This is my baby."

Matt craned his neck with the hope of getting a peek at the photographs but couldn't see them. He moved closer to Caitlin, just as she turned the pictures over to read what was written on the back.

"She's... Oh, I've forgotten every bit of math I've ever known. Okay, let's see. She's six months and...two, three...yes, six months and four days old." She looked at Matt. "Isn't she gorgeous?"

Matt chuckled. "I'm sure she is, but I haven't seen her yet."

"Oh," Caitlin said, turning the photos back over and holding them side by side for Matt to see. "Look, here she is."

A funny little sensation of warmth seemed to tip-toe around and through Matt's heart as he studied the pictures of the baby.

She had black hair that was sticking up in all directions, dark almond-shaped eyes that were star-ing right at the camera, a rosebud mouth and in both shots she was scowling with not even a hint of a smile. In one picture she was wearing a pink blanket sleeper and in another a faded red one.

Matt's palms actually began to tingle as he had the irrational urge to reach out, lift the baby from the photograph and nestle her close, hold her tight, tell her everything was going to be just fine.

"She's…" He cleared his throat. "She's a heart-stealer, Caitlin. Congratulations. Your daugh-ter is…well, she's really something. What are you going to name her?"

"I can't decide between Mackenzie and Madi-son," Caitlin said, gazing at the pictures again. "I think I'll wait until I actually hold her in my arms before I pick which one is right for her."

"Is everybody happy?" Carolyn said from across the room.

A chorus of affirmative replies filled the air.

"Some of you may have gotten more than one picture of your daughter," Carolyn went on. "There's never any rhyme or reason to what they send. I know you could spend the rest of the evening just gazing at those photos, but we have a lot to cover. Marsha, why don't we have our potluck supper, then we can get down to business. Let's take a few minutes to share the photographs with everyone before dinner."

"Okay," Marsha said, getting to her feet. "Matt, come see the picture of your goddaughter. She's eleven months old and she's standing alone in this photo. She's fantastic. Oh, I'm going to cry again."

Matt crossed the room and grinned when he saw the picture of Marsha and Bud's baby. She was wearing a dress that was much too large for her, was obviously not very steady on her feet, as she was holding her arms straight out at her sides, but had a broad smile on her face as though she knew that standing alone was a very big deal. She had a little fluff of dark hair on the top of her head and her smile revealed four teeth—two on the top and two on the bottom.

"Dynamite," Matt said, laughing. "You two better get your track shoes ready. This little lady is about to conquer the challenge of walking."

"Isn't her hair funny?" Bud said. "I love it. Just one wild plop on the top of her head. Hey, Grace,

I'm your daddy. Grace Marsha Mathis. How's that, Matt?''

"Perfect," Matt said. "Grace. That's nice. I like it. Caitlin is still undecided between naming her baby Mackenzie or Madison.''

"Oh?" Marsha said, raising her eyebrows. "Caitlin told you that?''

"Well, yeah, I was sitting right there and asked her what she was going to name her and… Marsha, don't start your matchmaking thing. Okay?'' Matt rolled his eyes heavenward. "I almost didn't survive that bit the last time you did it. Concentrate on Grace Marsha Mathis and forget about me.''

"What I want to know, ole chum," Bud said, "is whether or not you've made up your mind about going to China with us.''

"Count me in. I wouldn't miss it for the world. When do we leave?''

"I'm not certain. Carolyn may announce the date after dinner.''

"Dinner," Marsha said. "That's what I'm supposed to be doing.''

Marsha rushed off and Caitlin followed her to help put the potluck dishes on the dining-room table. The pictures of the babies were passed around, and Matt made no attempt to curb his smile as he looked at each one. They ranged in age from four months to two years.

"What made you decide to go with us on this trip?" Bud asked Matt.

"A lamebrain attorney. Well, that was the reason when I arrived here tonight. But now? This whole thing is awesome, Bud. Families are being created, kids are going to be brought out of crowded orphanages into loving homes and...I want to be there when you see Grace for the first time and Caitlin holds Mackenzie or Madison, whichever name she decides on and...I'm honestly looking forward to going on this journey. I'm...I'm honored to be included."

Bud nodded. "We're glad you're going to be with us, sharing it all." He paused. "I am now going to chat—not gossip—chat with you. Caitlin works with Marsha at the fashion magazine. Marsha is the assistant editor, as you know, and Caitlin is a copywriter. A very talented one, as a matter of fact.

"The way Marsha tells it, Caitlin wanted to hear every detail of what we were discovering about adopting from China since Marsha is unable to have kids. The Chinese government allows single women to adopt and Caitlin decided it was the perfect answer for her as well."

"Why?"

"That we don't know." Bud shrugged. "She just said that she hoped her approval came through at the same time as ours so we'd be traveling to-

gether to get our daughters. I believe a girlfriend
of Caitlin's is going with her to help out, like the
agency suggested for single moms. The friend must
have been busy tonight.''

"Interesting," Matt said. "I mean, hey, Caitlin
is a lovely young woman. Why isn't she married
and having a slew of kids herself? Why is she going the single-mom route?"

"Don't have a clue," Bud said. "I'm hungry."

"Who's hungry?" Marsha called from the doorway.

"I swear, my wife can read my mind, which is
a scary thought at times."

Matt managed to snag the chair next to Caitlin,
and Marsha and Bud sat across from them. The
pictures were placed carefully in front of plates
around the table. The food was delicious, the conversation centered on babies and the eagerly anticipated journey to the other side of the world.

"Attention, attention," Carolyn said as a three-
layer chocolate cake was being served for dessert.
"I'll talk so I won't be tempted to indulge in that
chocolate delight. Question. Has there been any
change in the number of people going along with
you?"

"Yes," Caitlin said. "My girlfriend who was to
accompany me to help with the luggage and what
have you broke her ankle while in-line skating with
her son. My mother and stepfather live in Italy and

my stepfather is ill, making it impossible for my mother to leave him right now. Other friends can't get vacation time on such short notice. So, I'm on my own.''

"We'll all help you, Caitlin," Bud said. "In fact, we're adding Matt to the list of who is going and he'll be free to assist you with your luggage. Right, Matt?''

"Sure," Matt said. "No problem."

"All things should be so easily solved." Carolyn laughed. "Okay, then, I have the final count so reservations will be made. You'll be called just as soon as everything is arranged and we have a date of departure. It will be soon, I promise. Matt, is your passport current?''

"Yes, ma'am. I'm ready to rock and roll."

"Excellent." Carolyn paused. "Finish your sinful dessert while I get the information packets I want to pass out to you."

"I appreciate your willingness to help me with my luggage, Matt," Caitlin said.

"It will be my pleasure," he said, smiling at her. "I'll just be hanging around tickling babies and taking in the sights."

Caitlin frowned. "I guess I don't quite understand why you're going on this trip. Have you always wanted to travel to China and the opportunity presented itself?''

"Well, not exactly."

"Before Matt says something that will make his nose grow," Bud said, "I'm squealing on him. As his physician I ordered him to stay away from his job as public-relations director at Mercy Hospital for a month because he's been working far too many hours for far too long. It was go to China with us, or be sent to his room for being a naughty boy."

"Thank you, Dr. Mouth Mathis," Matt said dryly.

"Well, it's true," Marsha said. "Work, work, work, that's all you do, Matt. This trip is just what the doctor, my sweet patootie, ordered."

"Whatever." Matt chuckled. "I happen to like my job, you know."

"More than anything else," Marsha retorted. "But we gotcha good, MacAllister. You can't drop by the hospital when you're hiking around China."

Caitlin laughed along with everyone else who had heard the conversation, but she sighed inwardly.

Oh, yes, she thought, the same old story. Here was another handsome and intelligent man who was pleasant to be with, but who was focused on his career above everything else. History seemed to repeat itself time and again for as long as she could remember. Men crossed her path who had priorities at opposite poles from hers. Well, hello and good-

bye to Mr. Matt MacAllister of *the* MacAllisters of
Ventura. So be it.

"Is something wrong, Caitlin?" Matt said.
"You look so serious all of a sudden."

"What? Oh. No. Nothing is wrong, Matt." She
smiled. "I was just doing a bit of reality check
time." She picked up the pictures of her daughter
and gazed at them. "But I'm fine now. We're going to be a terrific team, my daughter and I. Just
the two of us."

The woman on the other side of Caitlin spoke to
her, causing her to turn away from Matt. He looked
at her delicate fingers as they held the photographs
of the baby Caitlin would name either Mackenzie
or Madison.

*We're going to be a terrific team, my daughter
and I. Just the two of us.*

Caitlin's words echoed in Matt's mind and he
frowned.

Why? he wondered. Why was an extremely attractive, intelligent, I-have-a-lot-to-offer woman
like Caitlin Cunningham seemingly determined to
be a single mother, making no room in her life for
a husband for herself, a father for that adorable
baby girl?

Had Caitlin been deeply hurt by a man in the
past? Whoa. He didn't like the idea of that, not one
little bit.

Or...like Marsha, was Caitlin unable to have

children and felt that no man would want to marry her because of that?

Or... Hell, he didn't know.

She was an enigma, the lovely Ms. Cunningham, and for reasons he couldn't begin to fathom he wanted to unravel the mysteries, the secrets, surrounding her, discover who she really was, and why she had chosen the path leading to China and the baby who was waiting for her there.

Chapter Two

Everyone pitched in to clear away the dishes, and packed up their own containers to take home. Paper and pens were then produced to take notes on what Carolyn was going to say regarding the trip to China. She passed out a packet of papers.

"The information on these sheets," Carolyn said from where she sat at the head of the table, "touches on the high spots of what I'm going to tell you." She laughed. "Experience has shown that our new moms and dads can get a bit spacey on the night they receive their match pictures, so we put some of the data in print for you to read later."

Everyone laughed and Caitlin smiled at Matt, who was still sitting next to her.

"Do I look spacey to you?" she said.

She looked pretty as a picture, Matt thought, staring directly into her eyes.

"You're over the top," he said, smiling. "Totally zoned."

"I'm sorry I asked," Caitlin said, matching his smile.

"Fear not, new mommy. I'll take plenty of notes that will be at your disposal. Those plus the handout from Carolyn ought to cover it for you."

"Thank you, sir," Caitlin said, then redirected her attention to Carolyn.

Good grief, Caitlin thought, Matt MacAllister was so ruggedly handsome it was sinful. That auburn hair of his was a rich, yummy color like, well, like an Irish setter. And those brown eyes of his. Gracious, they were like fathomless pools of...of fudge sauce and... Oh, for Pete's sake, this was silly. Matt reminded her of a dog with eyes the color of an ice-cream topping? That was a rather bizarre description.

But there was no getting around the fact that Matt would turn women's heads whenever he entered the room. He was tall and well built with wide shoulders and long, muscular legs. He moved with an easy grace, like an athlete, a man who was comfortable in his own body.

He was charming, intelligent, had a way of listening that made a person feel very special and important. And when he looked directly into her eyes there was no ignoring that she felt a funny little flutter slither down her spine. Yes, masculinity personified was the drop-dead gorgeous Mr. Mac-Allister.

He was also one of the multitudes who was focused on his career to the exclusion of everything else in his life. No one was perfect and that was Matt's flaw, his glaring glitch. And she had no intention of allowing all his other attributes to make her forget it, not for one little second.

"Okay, first up," Carolyn said. "We ask that you don't wear jeans while in China. I know that must sound picky, but we're going into a country with a different culture than ours and we want to exhibit the respect due our hosts."

"But we can wear slacks?" Marsha asked.

"Yes," Carolyn said. "In any material other than denim."

"I'm writing this down," Matt said.

"Go for it." Caitlin laughed softly.

"You'll be spending one night in Hong Kong," Carolyn went on, "which we have found helps the jet-lag problem at least a little bit. The flight to Hong Kong is fifteen hours nonstop, so it's imperative that you get up, walk around the airplane and drink lots of water during the flight.

"After the night in Hong Kong you'll fly into Nanjing, China, and you'll be staying at a lovely hotel there. Cribs will be placed in each of your rooms for the babies."

"Oh-h-h," a woman named Jane said, "a crib."

Her husband Bill chuckled. "This is going to be a long, weepy trip, no doubt about it."

"Well, we've waited a long time to need a baby crib, honey," Jane said, sniffling.

"I know, sweetheart," he said, then kissed her on the forehead.

And they're sharing it all, together, every precious moment of it, Caitlin thought. No, no, she wasn't going to go there, wouldn't dwell on the fact that she was the only single mother making this journey. She'd thought and prayed for many months before making the decision to adopt a baby and it was right for her, just as it stood. This was the way she wanted it. This was the way it was going to be.

"Feel free to get all dewy-eyed about the crib in the room," Matt whispered to Caitlin. "Everyone else seems to be."

"I'm holding myself back. I'm saving up for when my daughter is *in* that crib."

"Good idea."

"On page two of your packet," Carolyn said, "is a list of suggested things to take for your baby. You will each be allowed one…I repeat…one suitcase. The laundry service in the hotels you'll be staying in is excellent, but you'll get tired of wearing the same clothes over and over. You're packing for your baby with your things tucked around the edges of that one suitcase.''

"This I've got to see," a man named Fred said, laughing. "Sally takes at least five suitcases for a weekend in San Francisco. One suitcase for a two-week stay in China? And the majority of the space is for our daughter? This is going to be a hoot.''

"Hush, Fred," Sally said. "I'll manage just fine, you'll see.''

"Yeah, right," Fred said, shaking his head and grinning.

Lots of diapers, Matt wrote on the paper in front of him.

"There are instructions on your sheets," Carolyn said, "about formula and how you'll need to cut it down with water because the babies aren't used to having such rich, nourishing food on a regular basis. You're going to be easing them into it slowly so they don't get tummyaches.

"As far as your tummies, you will be consuming some of the most delicious food you've ever eaten.''

"Do they have forks in China?" Matt asked, causing Bud to hoot with laughter.

"Yes, they have forks, Matt," Carolyn said. "They're used to fumble-fingered Westerners where you'll be staying and will provide you with utensils you're accustomed to.''

''That's very comforting,'' Matt said.

''Oh, before I forget,'' Carolyn added. ''The salt and pepper shakers are reversed from ours. Pepper has the big holes, salt the small ones. Write that down so that you don't ruin the fantastic food I'm raving about.''

''Write that down,'' Caitlin said, tapping the paper in front of Matt.

''Yes, ma'am,'' he said. ''I'm on it, ma'am.''

''You'll be in Nanjing about a week,'' Carolyn said, ''then you'll fly into Guangzhou, where our American consulate is located and the visas are issued for the babies. The adoptions will be final before you leave China and you won't have to readopt through our courts here when you get back.''

A buzz of conversation began around the table at that exciting news.

''This is all very interesting,'' Matt said, nodding. ''Fascinating. Just think, Caitlin, Madison or MacKenzie, whoever she turns out to be, will be your legal daughter when you two step onto U.S. of A. soil again. That's pretty awesome, don't you… Uh-oh, the crib didn't get to you, but this one did.''

''Ignore me,'' Caitlin said, flapping a hand in front of her tear-filled eyes. ''It's just the thought of leaving here as...as me, and returning as a mother with a daughter and...oh dear.''

Matt put one arm around Caitlin's shoulders.

''Tissue alert,'' he yelled. ''We need a tissue here. Marsha, didn't I see you go get a box?''

''Here it is,'' someone said, shoving it across the table. ''The container was full when Marsha brought it out here and it's half-empty already. We're all a mess.''

''You're all delightfully normal,'' Carolyn said, smiling. ''Be certain you have tissues with you for that moment when you see and hold those babies for the first time.''

''Oh-h-h,'' a woman wailed, and the tissue box went back in the direction it had come from.

''Okay now?'' Matt said, his arm still encircling Caitlin's shoulders.

She was so delicate, he thought, and warm and feminine. He'd like to pull her close, nestle her against his chest, sift his fingers through those silky black curls, then tip her chin up, lower his lips to hers and...

''I'm fine.'' Caitlin straightened her shoulders with the hope that Matt would get the hint that he should remove his arm. Now. Right now. Because it was such a strong arm, yet he was holding her so gently, so protectively. And it was such a warm arm, the heat seeming to suffuse her was now thrumming deep and low within her and... This

would never do. No. Matt had to move that arm.
"You can have your arm back."

"What?" Matt said. "Oh. Sure." He slowly
eased his arm away from Caitlin's shoulders.

"In Guangzhou," Carolyn said, snapping everyone back to attention, "you'll be at the White Swan
Hotel, which is a five-star establishment and the
one where visiting dignitaries stay. It is incredibly
beautiful. I'm not going to give you any more hints
about it because I want you to be surprised when
you get there."

Carolyn went on for another half hour with various information, answered questions, said she
would be available up until the time they left if
more thoughts came to them, then promised to call
each of them as soon as the departure date was set.

"It will be soon," she said. "Dr. Yang, our li-
aison in China, said your daughters are eager for
you to arrive and take them home." She laughed.
"Oops. Where did that tissue box go?"

Excitement was buzzing through the air as
everyone continued to chatter, then a few said it
was time to go as tomorrow was a workday.

"We've got to get a crib, Bud," Marsha said,
"and a changing table and... Goodness, we have
a lot to do before we leave."

"Plus I have to warn the two doctors who are
going to cover my practice that they are on red-
alert standby as of now," Bud said. "It's ironic,

isn't it? After all these months of paperwork, then waiting, then more paperwork, then waiting, and waiting and waiting, we're going to be dashing around like crazy at the last second. I just may sleep during that entire fifteen-hour flight.''

''Color me dumb,'' Matt said, ''but why aren't you more prepared as far as equipment goes? I mean, you don't even have a crib set up yet.''

''Well, you see, Matt,'' Marsha said, ''when you fill out the papers, you give the officials in Beijing an age range of a child you'd be willing to adopt. In our case we said newborn to three years old. We didn't know until tonight that Grace is eleven months and will need a crib.''

''Oh, I see,'' Matt said. ''That makes sense now.'' He looked at Caitlin. ''What about you, Caitlin? Are you prepared for Mackenzie or Madison?''

''No. I painted her room pale yellow and hung yellow curtains with a bunch of bunnies as the border print. I got a white dresser and matching rocking chair and bookcase for toys, but I don't have a crib. I also put newborn to three years on that form, so I didn't know if I'd need a crib or a toddler bed. I'm thrilled to pieces that Miss M. is so young. Six months and four days.''

''We're ecstatic that Grace is only eleven months old, too,'' Marsha said. ''We'll get to wit-

ness so many things that she does for the first
time.''

"Yeah," Bud said, laughing, "like leading us
on a merry chase when she takes off at a run after
mastering the walking bit.''

"Tomorrow evening we go shopping for a crib
and changing table," Marsha said firmly. "Then
come home and I'll watch you put them together,
Bud.''

"That's usually how those things go," he said.

"How about you, Caitlin?" Matt asked. "Could
you use some help assembling your stuff?''

"Oh, I couldn't ask you to do that, Matt. You've
already gotten roped into hauling my luggage
around once my arms are full of baby.''

"Believe me, I don't mind giving you a hand.
Thanks to Bud, who used to be my friend, I have
all my evenings free. I'm accustomed to putting in
those hours at the hospital. You'd be doing me a
favor by getting me out of the house, because I've
forgotten how to turn on my television set.''

"Well," Caitlin said slowly.

"It's perfect, Caitlin," Marsha said. "I'd suggest that the four of us go shopping together, but
we never know what time Bud will get home. You
two just go ahead and make your own plans. Oh,
jeez, I'm supposed to be doing my hostess duties
and seeing everyone to the door." She got to her
feet. "Wait, wait, Sally and Fred. Give me a

chance to be polite. Bud, get off your tush and come with me to execute socially acceptable behavior.''

''Whatever,'' Bud said, rising.

''Listen, try this idea,'' Matt said to Caitlin as Bud followed Marsha to the front door. ''We go out for pizza, shop for baby stuff, then go to your place and I'll put everything together. Does that work for you?''

Caitlin frowned. ''I don't think the big cartons that equipment comes in will fit in my car.''

''I have an SUV and the back seats fold down. Problem solved.''

''I don't have any tools.''

''I'll bring mine. Shall I pick you up at your place about six tomorrow night?''

''I...yes, all right. I appreciate this very much, Matt. I mean, you don't even know me and here you are willing to perform manual labor to help me complete the nursery. It's very generous of you.''

Matt picked up one of the pictures of Caitlin's daughter.

''This little lady deserves to have everything ready and waiting for her when she comes home. Man, she's cute. If she can grab hold of a person's heart when she's looking like a grumpy little old man, imagine what will happen the first time she smiles. Hey, Miss M., do you have any teeth in there to show off? How long are you going to make your mommy wait for that first smile, munchkin?''

"Her first smile," Caitlin said wistfully, then shook her head. "Don't get me started again. I think the tissue box is empty." She got to her feet. "I'll give you my address and I'll see you tomorrow night at six. Thank you again, Matt."

Matt stood. "I'm looking forward to it...very much, Caitlin."

After Matt had gotten Caitlin's address, he watched as she collected the dish she'd brought her contribution to the potluck in, hugged Carolyn, tucked the precious pictures of the baby in her purse, then bid Marsha and Bud good-night at the door. Carolyn said her goodbyes, then Matt wandered toward the front door himself.

"Need any help cleaning up?" he asked Marsha and Bud.

"No, we're fine," Bud said. "It's nice of you to give Caitlin a hand with the baby furniture, Matt."

Matt shrugged. "No biggie."

"Taking her out for pizza before you go shopping is a nice touch," Marsha said, beaming. "You're such a thoughtful guy, Matt MacAllister."

"No," he said, frowning. "I just happen to like pizza and haven't had any in a while."

"Mmm," Marsha said, batting her eyelashes at him.

"Don't start with me, Marsha. There is no room

for matchmaking in the middle of a baby boom, which is what this trip will be, so just forget it. Bud, control your wife.''

''Fat chance of that, chum,'' Bud said, laughing. ''Wow. It just hit me. I'm going to have a wife *and* a daughter. Talk about being ganged up on by females in my own home.''

''It makes my heart go pitter-patter,'' Marsha said. ''Women rule.''

''I'm outta here,'' Matt said, chuckling. ''Thanks for a great evening. I really enjoyed it. Ah, life is full of challenges. Good night, new mommy and daddy.''

''Oh-h-h, listen to that,'' Marsha said. ''I'm going to go find a fresh box of tissues.''

Caitlin propped the two pictures of the baby against the lamp on the nightstand, then wiggled into a comfortable position in the bed where she could gaze at the photographs.

''Hello, my daughter,'' she said, unable to curb her smile. ''Are you Mackenzie, or are you Madison, Miss M.? I just don't know yet, but I will when I see you, hold you, for the first time. Will you smile then? Or make me wait for that special moment?''

She kissed the tip of one finger, then gently touched each picture.

''I wish you knew that I'll be there very soon to

get you. Maybe an angel will whisper in your ear that your mommy is coming. You won't have a daddy, sweetheart, but we'll be fine, just the two of us, you'll see.''

Caitlin turned off the light, sighed in contentment and drifted off to sleep within minutes.

Hours later Matt was still awake, staring up at the ceiling. No matter how many lectures he gave himself to knock it off, he fumed, his mind kept replaying the entire evening at Marsha and Bud's over and over. He saw the beautiful expression of pure love on Caitlin's face when she'd looked at her daughter's photographs, and remembered the tears that had glistened in both Marsha and Bud's eyes as they'd gazed at the picture of Grace.

What an unbelievable night it had been for the people in that room. Dreams were coming true for those who had waited so long to have them fulfilled. Incredible.

Matt sighed and slid both hands beneath his head. He had been included in everything that had happened this evening but...not quite. Circumstances dictated that he stand on the edge of the circle of sunshine those match pictures had created, congratulate the new parents, wish them well.

But none of those photographs declared him to be a daddy because that wasn't *his* dream, his heartfelt desire, and he hadn't completed the tons of paperwork and waited the seemingly endless months as the others had.

He was grateful to have witnessed such happiness, such joy, was very honored to know he was to be Grace's godfather, was pleased he would be helping Caitlin, the lovely Caitlin, put the finishing touches on the nursery that would be waiting for Mackenzie or Madison when she arrived in her new home.

But...yeah, so okay, he was willing to admit that there had been flickers of chilling emptiness that had consumed him earlier. He'd been so aware of his...his aloneness, of the narrow focus of his life, had been forced to wonder if perhaps, just maybe, he was not only alone but might also be lonely.

"Ah, hell, come on, MacAllister, knock it off," he said, pulling his hands from beneath his head and dragging them down his face. "That's nuts."

The structure of his existence was of his making, his choice. He was centered on a challenging and rewarding career at Mercy Hospital that gave him a great deal of satisfaction. Granted, it was a tad rough on his physical well-being, but he'd get a handle on that, take control of that aspect of it.

Sure, he wanted a family someday, a wife, kids, a home bursting at the seams with love and laughter. He'd take part in the whole program...change diapers, teach each munchkin in turn to ride a bike, mow the lawn, take out the trash, help with homework and housework and read stories to sleepy bundles tucked safely on his lap. Yeah, he wanted all of that, plus a wife he'd love beyond measure and who would love him in kind.

Someday…but not now.

Hell, he was only thirty-two years old. He had plenty of time to join the rank and file of the MacAllisters who toted diaper bags to family gatherings. Plenty of time.

What had happened tonight at the Mathises' house was perfectly understandable. He'd been caught up in the emotions of the people there. He'd felt a momentary sense of aloneness and…okay… loneliness simply because he was odd man out in what had been a rather unusual situation.

There. He'd figured it all out. It had just taken a bit of logical thinking to get his head on straight again. He could now go on the trip to China, enjoy the entire thing, spend time with the very lovely Caitlin Cunningham, then return home and shortly afterward return to the hospital and the career that gave him everything he needed in his life now.

His reputation for being one of the best public-relations directors of a large hospital was rock solid across the country, and he had several awards framed and hanging on his office wall. The name Matt MacAllister meant something in his field and he would continue to maintain that level of expertise.

Matt rolled onto his stomach, closed his eyes, mentally patted himself on the back for his rather genius-level thinking that had solved the jumbled maze in his mind, then drifted off to sleep.

But through the night he dreamed of Caitlin. He was standing next to her in a room where they were surrounded by babies, each holding up little arms toward them, wanting to be held, comforted, loved. Wanting to be taken home.

Chapter Three

The next day was another long stretch of hours at the hospital as Matt once again dealt with Homer Holmes, the note-taking attorney. Matt finally glanced at his watch and inwardly cheered.

"Time to wrap it up, Homer," Matt said. "I have an important appointment to keep. In fact, we've covered everything that is pending. Starting tomorrow you're on your own."

"Listen, Matt," Homer said. "I've been admiring that miniature antique scale you have on the corner of your desk."

"The scale?" Matt said. "My grandfather gave that to me months ago. The workmanship is exquisite, don't you think? The chains holding the two small trays have the exact number of links, you can see the intricate scrollwork on the base...even the two gold coins in that one tray are antiques. It was a very special gift from a remarkable man, and I treasure it.''

''That's what I was getting at. It's obviously worth a great deal of money, and I'm afraid I might bump it, send it toppling to the floor, harm it in some way. Don't you think it would be a good idea to take it home during this time you'll be away from the hospital?''

Matt shrugged. ''I suppose I could but... No, I'll just move it to the bookshelves against the wall. I like to be able to see it, and this is where I spend the majority of my time.''

Matt picked up the scale, crossed the room and set it carefully on a shelf on the bookcase.

''There,'' he said. ''Feel better?''

''Much,'' Homer said, nodding. ''Is it a family heirloom?''

''No.'' Matt stared at the scale. ''My grandfather chose it especially for me. He selected special gifts for each of his grandchildren. I've heard the story behind some of the presents, the fact that our grandfather was delivering an important message to the recipient with the gift.

''In my case, there's no hidden message as far as I can figure out. It's just an extremely rare and

terrific present." He looked at his watch again.
"I'm out of here. Take good care of my baby while
I'm gone."

"Your...what?"

"The hospital. It's where I direct all my energies, like a parent would toward a child and...
Never mind. Bye."

Matt strode from the room, leaving a rather bemused Homer behind.

Caitlin frowned at her reflection in the full-
length mirror on the inside of her closet door.

Satisfied now? she asked herself. This was the
third outfit she'd tried on. Well, she wasn't changing her clothes again. Jeans, tennis shoes and a
peach-colored string sweater. That was it. Except...maybe the blue knit top would be better because...

"You are acting like an idiot, Caitlin Cunningham," she told her reflection, "and I've had
enough of this nonsense. This isn't a date, it's a
mission, the purpose of which is to complete the
nursery for your daughter."

Caitlin spun around, snatched her purse off the
double bed and left the bedroom. In the living room
she placed her purse on an end table and sank onto
the sofa.

Matt MacAllister, she fumed, had driven her
crazy the entire day. Every time she looked at the

match pictures she'd placed on the corner of her desk at work, the image of Matt inched its way into her mental vision.

In a way, that made sense. She needed to get the nursery ready.

Matt was going to make it possible for her to accomplish that, so when she gazed at the photographs of Miss M., it stood to reason that Matt would trek right in front of her mind's eye, too.

So, okay, it made sense...to a point. What didn't compute was why when she thought about Matt she got a funny flutter in her stomach and a sharp remembrance of Matt's strong-but-gentle arm encircling her shoulders last night. Thinking about that caused a strange heat to begin to swirl within her and... No doubt about it...Matt was driving her right over the edge.

Well, in all fairness to herself she was admittedly in the midst of an emotional upheaval because she was about to become a mother. After all these months, the hope, the dream, the prayer had finally come true. She was momentarily off kilter as she attempted to adjust to the wonderful, albeit a tad terrifying, news, and so she was overreacting to things she would normally just take in stride. Like Matt.

"Caitlin," she said aloud, "that was nothing short of brilliant the way you figured all that out. Thank goodness that mishmash is solved."

The doorbell rang and Caitlin jerked at the sudden noise, her heart racing as she hurried to the front door.

Matt stood on Caitlin's front porch and nodded in approval.

Nice place, he thought. Caitlin's home was small, as were the other houses on the block, but the neighborhood exhibited a great deal of pride of ownership. Caitlin's cottage...now, that had a nice ring to it...was painted country-blue with decorative white shutters edging the windows. The minuscule front yard was a lush carpet of green grass, plus a tall mulberry tree. When he'd pulled in to the driveway, he'd gotten a glimpse of a wooden fence enclosing the backyard. That was good. Miss M. would have a safe place to play. Well, so far, the outside of the house suited Caitlin. If she answered the door and let him in he'd get a glimpse of the inside.

Matt pressed the doorbell and a moment later Caitlin opened the door.

"Hi," Matt said. Oh, hey, what Ms. Cunningham did for a pair of snug jeans was something to behold.

Caitlin smiled as she stepped back to allow Matt to enter. "Come in, Matt." Matt MacAllister in jeans and a black knit shirt was causing that funny little flutter to slither down her spine again. Darn it. "How are you?" She closed the door.

"Fine." Matt swept his gaze over the living room. "Well, as fine as anyone could be after spending the day with an attorney who writes down everything, including what he had for lunch." He paused. "This is a very nice house, Caitlin. I like oak furniture myself and your colors are pretty...mint-green, and what would you call that? Salmon?"

Caitlin laughed. "I think I would call those colors a mistake for sticky toddler fingers. I didn't know when I made these selections that there would be a busy little girl living here. I'll worry about that later. Nothing can dim my excitement about becoming a mother."

"Good for you." Matt wandered across the room and looked at some of the titles of the books in a tall oak bookcase. "We have similar taste in authors, except I can't remember the last time I actually settled in and read a novel. There just aren't enough hours in the day."

"Perhaps you'll find the time while you're off work during this month or so Bud sentenced you to."

"Maybe, but I doubt it. I'll be in China for a couple of weeks, then when I get back I have a feeling I'll be on the phone more often than not with the guy who's taking my place for now. He doesn't exactly evoke a great deal of confidence in being able to handle what needs to be done. Man, when I think about the messes he could create while... Nope, erase that. I'm not supposed to think about it.''

''I imagine that's impossible for someone like you to do.''

Matt turned to look at her. ''Someone like me? Somehow that doesn't sound like a compliment.''

''I just meant that you're obviously focused on your job, dedicated to your career to the exclusion of just about anything, or anyone, else. To suddenly just shut off your mind and stop thinking about it would be extremely difficult, impossible, in fact.

''Putting thousands of miles between you and the hospital will help, but even so, I would guess that part of your thoughts will be at Mercy. You won't be totally there with all of us.''

Matt frowned. ''Is this the voice of experience I'm hearing? Have you been completely centered on your career in the past?''

''Me? Heavens no.'' Caitlin shook her head. ''I enjoy being a copywriter for the fashion magazine. It's very challenging and the work is continually fresh and new, but when I come home at night I don't think about it again until I report for duty the next day.''

''I see. The slight edge to your voice says you

don't approve of my 24/7 approach to my career, Caitlin.''

"I'm sorry if I gave you that impression, Matt. It's certainly not my place to approve or disapprove of the way you conduct your life. Goodness, I don't even know you.'' She paused. "I think it would be best if we changed the subject. Even better, why don't we go have our pizza.''

"Sure, we'll go for pizza, but let's change the subject first. Why did you decide to become a single mother?''

"Gosh, Matt, don't hold back, just ask me any personal question that pops into your head.''

Matt chuckled. "I'm sorry. I guess it *is* rather personal, isn't it? But I'm interested in why you came to this decision. Not that you're obligated to tell me, of course.''

"Let's just say that I believe this is the very best choice for me…personally. End of story. Subject closed. Shall we go?''

Matt nodded and followed Caitlin out the front door.

Oh, yes, he thought. The lovely lady did, indeed, have secrets that she didn't intend to share. So many questions surrounded Caitlin Cunningham, creating so many answers he intended to discover, one by one.

The pizza restaurant was popular and crowded, and Caitlin and Matt had a short wait before a booth became available. They decided on what toppings they wanted on their pizza and what they would drink, then Matt went to the counter to place their order.

"It'll be about fifteen minutes," he said, returning and sliding in across from Caitlin. "So. Have you made arrangements for day care for Miss M.?"

"I'm going to be working at home. I've already reached an agreement with my boss about it, and I've changed the third bedroom in the house into an office. Later, when Miss M. is ready to play with other children, I'll consider day care. Even if I had been matched with an older child, I planned to stay home with her at first because she'd have so many adjustments to make."

"Don't you think you'll get cabin fever working at home?"

"No, I don't believe so. I'll have my daughter with me, remember? Plus, she and I will be going back and forth to the magazine office to pick up and deliver work, connecting with other people. Once we get into a routine I should have a healthy balance during a given day."

"I hope it all goes the way you have it planned. Life has a way of throwing us curves when we least expect them at times. I'll keep my fingers crossed for you and Miss M. for smooth sailing ahead."

"That was a rather pessimistic statement." Caitlin frowned. "Life has a way of throwing us curves? Are you referring to yourself?"

"Me? No, no, not at all. My life is set up exactly the way I want it. I've hit a momentary glitch with this enforced-vacation bit, but things will get back to normal for me soon."

Caitlin nodded.

"The reason I said that about the throwing of curves," Matt went on, "is because I just saw a woman who reminded me of my cousin, Patty. She's going through a rough time right now and got more than her share of nasty curves, I'm afraid. I wasn't implying that anything would go wrong with your plans."

"Oh, I see." Caitlin paused, then looked directly at Matt. "You know, we seem to be just on the edge of getting into arguments no matter what topic we touch on tonight. There's a…I don't know…a tension between us that isn't very pleasant.

"If you'd rather not go shopping for baby supplies I'll certainly understand. We were all on such emotional highs last evening and… Anyway, we can have our pizza and forget about the other if you'd prefer."

Matt leaned forward and covered one of Caitlin's hands with one of his on the top of the table.

"No, Caitlin, I've been looking forward to this outing all day. I'm sorry if I've been short-tempered, or whatever. Hey, let's start over from right now.''

"I've been a bit brusque with you, too, and I apologize.'' She smiled. "All right. Hello, Matt, it's nice to see you again and I certainly thank you for your help with my grand endeavor this evening.''

"Hello, Caitlin,'' he said, not releasing her hand. "I'm glad to be of service.''

She had to get her hand back, Caitlin thought frantically. There was a tingling heat traveling up her arm and across her breasts, causing them to feel strangely achy as though needing a soothing touch. Now Matt was pinning her in place with his incredible brown eyes and her heart was beating like a bongo drum.

"That's our number,'' Matt said. "I'll be right back with a gourmet delight.''

Thank heaven for pizza restaurants that called out lifesaving numbers, Caitlin thought, drawing a steadying breath. Darn it, she had to get a grip on herself, stop this nonsense of being thrown so off kilter by Matt MacAllister's blatant masculinity. He touched her, she melted; he gazed at her, she dissolved. This would never do.

They were going to be together on a daily basis soon, and she couldn't fall apart every two seconds because Matt was close to her. Well, she'd probably be fine over there because she'd be focused on the baby. Her precious daughter.

Matt returned with a huge pizza and a pitcher of soda, then trekked back for plates, glasses and napkins.

"There," he said, sitting down. "I think I have everything we need...except..." He smiled at Caitlin.

"Except?" she asked.

"You don't happen to have the pictures of Miss M. in your purse, do you? I sure would like to see that munchkin again. She's already stolen a chunk of my heart. I'm going to be putty in her tiny hands when I actually see her. Do you? Have the pictures?"

Oh, Matt just didn't play fair, Caitlin thought as unexpected and unwelcome tears stung her eyes. Why did he have to be so sweet, so endearing, on top of everything else he had going for him in the plus column. How many men would ask to see baby pictures as he was? Not fair at all.

Focus on the minus column, she told herself. This was Mr. I Work 24/7/365. He wouldn't be caught up in cute pictures of babies and putting cribs together if he weren't being forced to take a vacation. Matt was just filling idle hours with anything available. *Remember that, Caitlin. Don't you dare forget it.*

"Of course I have the pictures." Caitlin smiled.

"I never leave home without them. I took them to work today and Marsha and I drove everyone nuts poking our photographs under their noses." She handed the two pictures to Matt. "Here she is."

"Hey, kiddo. You're just as cute today as you were last night. That is wild hair. Maybe we should take her some of the goop, that styling-gel junk, that people use."

We? Caitlin thought. *We* should take the baby some styling gel? Where had that *we* come from? Well, now, don't go crazy, Caitlin. Matt had been drafted into being her luggage handler or whatever his title was. Her partner, per se, because her friend couldn't go. So, it was natural that he'd see himself attached to her and the baby during the trip, in a manner of speaking.

Okay, she had that one figured out, but if she didn't quit analyzing and overreacting to everything that Matt said and did she was going to fall on her face from exhaustion. Food. She needed food.

"Food," she said, and reached for a slice of pizza.

Matt set the two pictures on the end of the table so both he and Caitlin could see them. They each ate a slice of pizza, and took a second one.

"This is delicious," Caitlin said.

"Mmm. You know, that one sleeper Miss M. has on looks okay, but the other one is really faded, worn. You can see how thin the material is in spots.''

''I know.'' Caitlin glanced over at the photographs. ''The orphanages in China have to make due with what they can get. Miss M. is healthy, so that means she made it through the winter months after she was born without getting seriously ill. The weather in China now is much like it is here…warm, sunny. That makes me rest a little easier about the condition of that sleeper.''

Matt chuckled. ''Maybe that's why she's frowning in both pictures. She's all girl and isn't satisfied with her wardrobe.''

''Oh, okay, I'll go with that theory, rather than one that says she's unhappy about something…like a tummyache or…oh, don't get me started. I'll worry myself into a sleepless night. I hope Carolyn calls soon and says we're scheduled to leave. I just want to go get my baby, my daughter. Marsha agrees with me that even though we've waited all these months, now that we've seen the pictures this is agony.''

''No joke. I wish she would have smiled in at least one of those photos. Nope. Whoa. We won't dwell on why she looks so grumpy.'' Matt narrowed his eyes. ''New topic. Sort of. Have you settled on a middle name yet?''

Caitlin nodded, raised one finger as she chewed, then swallowed a bite of pizza. ''Her middle name is going to be Olivia, after my mother. I not only love my mom but I also respect her more than I could ever begin to tell you. She conducted herself with such class and dignity through some very difficult years and, well, I thought that naming my daughter after her would really convey how I feel about her.''

''I think—'' Matt cleared his throat ''—I think that your mother must be very, very honored, Caitlin. I'd like to believe that I might have a daughter someday that thought that highly of me. What did your mother say when you told her?''

''She got all weepy, and Paulo, my stepfather, said it was a beautiful gift to give to her. My mother was a widow when she married Paulo last year. She met him during a trip she made to Italy, and it was a whirlwind courtship. Paulo is a delightful man who is crazy in love with my mother and they're so wonderful together. I'm thrilled for my mom. She deserves to have that kind of happiness.''

''You said your mother was a widow when she met Paulo.''

Caitlin nodded. ''Yes, my father died when I was sixteen.''

''Whew. That's rough. I'm sorry. Do you still miss him? Especially at a momentous time like this in your life when you're about to become a mother?''

"No. I don't miss him at all." There as a sudden sharp edge to her voice.

"Oh," Matt said, frowning slightly. Something wasn't quite on the mark here. There was a…a shadow hanging over the memory of Caitlin's father. Why? There he was again, stacking another question about Caitlin on the teetering tower. "You said last night that Paulo is ill?"

"Yes. They're running tests because they're not certain what is wrong and I'm very concerned about him. I'm praying he'll be fine and that he and my mother will be able to come to the States soon and meet Miss M."

"Who will be smiling by then," Matt said.

"Yes, she'll be smiling by then."

And then Caitlin and Matt were smiling as their gazes met, warm smiles, special smiles born of sharing the personal, meaningful story of why Caitlin had chosen the baby's middle name. The restaurant disappeared into a strange mist that surrounded them, the noise and the people simply no longer existed in the haze that swirled around them.

Their smiles faded as heat began to churn and thrum within them, pulsing, hot…so hot. They couldn't move, could hardly breathe, in the place they'd been transported to. It was so strange. And exciting. And terrifying. And…

"More to drink?" a voice said, snapping both

Caitlin and Matt back to reality with a thud. "It's all-you-can-drink night, refills free."

"It's who?" Matt said, staring at the young girl standing by their booth.

"Like...soda...ya know," the waitress said, pointing to the pitcher. "The drink? Free refills, like, twenty times if you want or whatever?"

"Oh. Sure." Matt nodded jerkily. "You bet. Fill it right up. Thank you. Nice of you to offer."

"Yeah, it's awesome," the girl said, snatching up the pitcher and eyeing Matt warily. "Back in a flash."

What had just happened between her and Matt? Caitlin wondered, fiddling with her napkin to avoid looking at him. She had never in her life experienced anything so...so unexplainable, so incredibly sensual and...

She wasn't going to address this. No. She'd just pretend that it hadn't happened. For all she knew, Matt hadn't even been aware of the strange... whatever it had been that had... It was over. Gone. Forgotten.

"So!" Caitlin said to a spot just above Matt's left shoulder. "Have you figured out how to pack enough for two weeks into one suitcase and..."

"Caitlin—"

"I've got to scrunch tons of diapers into my suitcase, along with baby clothes and bottles and... It certainly will be a challenge, that one suitcase, won't it? Yes, it definitely will and—''

''Caitlin—''

''What!'' she said much too loudly.

''I felt it. You felt it, I know you did. What... what was that?''

Caitlin plunked one elbow on the table and rested her forehead in her palm.

''I have no idea. And I don't care to discuss it, nor try to figure out what it was.''

''Why not?''

Caitlin raised her head. ''Why not? Because it was...was man-and-woman...stuff, and I don't want that in my life, complicating things. I am focused on mommy-and-baby...stuff, and that's all I can handle.

''I wish I could think of a more sophisticated word than *stuff,* but I'm a bit jangled at the moment. Whatever that was, Matt, it's in the past already, poof, gone.'' She lifted her chin. ''Please don't refer to it again.''

''You don't want me to refer to the fact that we're attracted to each other,'' Matt said, his gaze riveted on Caitlin. ''That there was suddenly such heated sexuality weaving back and forth between us that it's a wonder the pizza didn't burn to a crisp?

''You don't want me to tell you that during that strange moment out of time it took all the willpower I had not to come around this table, take you in my arms and kiss you until neither of us could breathe? Am I understanding you correctly?''

Caitlin opened her mouth to reply in the affirmative, only to discover she had no air in her lungs so she could speak. She nodded her head.

''I see. Well, I'll certainly respect your wishes on the above-mentioned subjects. But, Caitlin? That doesn't mean I won't be *thinking* about what just happened here. *Thinking* about what it would be like to kiss those very kissable lips of yours and—''

''Soda refill,'' the waitress said, plunking the pitcher onto the table.

''Oh, I am so glad to see you,'' Caitlin said to the young girl. ''I'm just delighted that you're here…right now.''

''Got it,'' the girl said slowly. ''I don't mean to be, like, rude or anything, but you folks are borderline weird. Bye.'' She hurried away.

Matt laughed. ''Borderline weird, is it?''

''At least she was more articulate than me saying *stuff*,'' Caitlin said, smiling. ''Oh, this is silly. Let's just finish up so we can get ready for Miss M.'s arrival. I am one hundred percent into my mommy *stuff* and I intend to stay there, Mr. MacAllister.''

Chapter Four

The crib and changing table were white to match the other nursery furniture Caitlin had purchased. Matt insisted on buying Miss M. a crib mobile with brightly colored, puffy felt clowns that pranced around in a circle to the tune of "Rock-a-Bye, Baby."

They loaded the large boxes into Matt's SUV, then trekked back into the mall to select blankets, crib sheets, sleepers, several two-piece outfits and a pretty, red dress.

Carolyn had said that it was traditional for all the children being adopted to wear red on their last night in China, as it was the Chinese color for health, happiness and prosperity. Matt refused to leave the clothing department until he found a pair of white socks with red bows to go with the dress.

The next stop was for diapers, bibs, bottles, formula and a pacifier that Carolyn had said the babies would need on the airplane because of the cabin pressure.

In each department Caitlin showed the saleswoman the pictures of Miss M. for advice as to what size to buy.

"It's a bit difficult to tell how big she is," one saleswoman said, "because no one is holding her for reference. She looks small for six months, I think, but better to have the clothes and diapers a little big than too small. Oh, she is so cute. What proud new parents you must be."

"Well, we're not..." Carolyn started.

"Not coming down off our cloud number nine for a very long time," Matt finished for her.

"Good for you," the woman said. "Now, let's get you what you need."

"Why did you allow her to believe that we're married and the parents of this baby?" Caitlin whispered to Matt as they followed the woman.

Matt shrugged. "That's what she assumed and it was easier just to go with it."

"Oh," she said, nodding.

That made sense, Caitlin thought as she placed packages of diapers in the cart. Why get into a lengthy explanation about how Matt was helping because her friend got hurt and couldn't make the trip and...yes, it was simpler to let it go. She and Matt looked the same as Marsha and Bud must as they were doing the same type of shopping, as well as the other people in their group.

The new mommies and daddies. Daddies and mommies. Daddies. Parents-to-be who were soon going to complete their family with a wonderful little daughter. Mommy, Daddy and Baby and...

Stop it, Caitlin, she ordered herself. She was getting caught up in the charade that Matt had put in place. Her daughter was getting a loving mother.

"Baby wipes," Matt said, dropping a box into the cart. "Great invention."

"You sound like an expert on the subject," Caitlin observed, pulling her thoughts back to attention.

"Hey, I'm a MacAllister. I've changed my share of diapers over the years. The MacAllister clan is very big on babies."

Caitlin laughed. "I've never changed a diaper in my life. I'm assuming it's not all that difficult. It isn't, is it?"

"I wouldn't say that. There's a definite technique to it. If you get a wiggly kid you can be in big trouble if you don't get that diaper on really fast. There's a lot of dexterity involved, wrist action, too."

"Oh, cut it out." Caitlin laughed. "You're making it sound like a person needs an engineering degree to do this.''

"That would help, yes," Matt said solemnly, then burst into laughter in the next instant. "I had you going there for a while, didn't I? You should have seen your face. No, Caitlin Cunningham, changing diapers is not tough. Now then, do you want to discuss methods of burping a baby?"

"Just hand me another package of those wipes."

Oh, this was a fun outing, she thought, and Matt was fun and funny. She felt so happy, carefree, so incredibly glad she was who she was. Well, that stood to reason. She was the one who was about to become a mother. But the extra gift of laughter that was accompanying this shopping trip was thanks to Matt MacAllister. She'd remember this evening because it was very, very special.

Back at the house, Caitlin insisted on washing all the baby clothes while Matt was assembling the crib and changing table.

"Don't forget to wash the diapers, too," he said, peering in his toolbox.

"Wash the...Matt, those are disposable paper diapers."

"See?" He grinned at her. "You know more about diapers than you thought you did. If you were a complete dunce about those nifty things you would have dumped them all in the washing machine. I'm just trying to boost your confidence, my dear.''

"You're cuckoo," Caitlin said, pointing one finger in the air.

"I know." Matt chuckled. "But I'm loveable. Ah, here's the screwdriver I want.''

Lovable, Caitlin thought as she left the room with an armload of clothes and blankets. Lovable? As in, Matt was a man who would be easy to love, fall in love with? No, that last mental babble needed to be split in two.

Yes, Matt probably would be a man who would be easy to fall in love with because he had it all at first glimpse—looks, charm, intelligence, a marvelous sense of humor, and on the list went.

But easy to love? To be a partner with, the other half of the whole? No. Matt the workaholic, the man so dedicated to his career that he had put his own health at risk, so focused on his position at Mercy Hospital to the exclusion of everything and everyone, would not be an easy man to be in love with.

It would, in fact, be impossible to be in a serious relationship with Matt because he wouldn't do his share, wouldn't help nurture the love. And like a flame of a candle struggling to stay warm and bright, that love would eventually be snuffed out, leaving the place where it had been in chilling darkness.

Caitlin frowned as she put the baby clothes in the washing machine, then held up the sweet little red dress before adding it to the load.

Where on earth, she thought, was all this heavy, nonsensical rambling coming from? She hardly knew Matt MacAllister. Yet she had jumped all the way from "How do you do, it's nice to meet you" to passing negative judgment on the man as a life partner. Ridiculous. Really dumb.

Caitlin added detergent to the wash, closed the lid on the machine, turned it on, then headed back to the nursery to see how the mechanic was coming along with the assembling of the crib for precious Miss M.

Matt finished his projects just as Caitlin was putting the last of the freshly washed purchases in the dresser.

"Done," he said.

"Me, too," she said, turning to smile at him. "Oh, this room looks perfect, Matt. Thank you so much."

"You're welcome," he said, then wound the mobile, causing the perky clowns to march in a circle as the music played. "Dynamite."

Caitlin laughed. "That mobile is so cute. It's a terrific gift for Miss M. and *she* thanks you, too. Now all we need is that telephone call from Carolyn saying it's time to pack our meager little suitcase and get ready to go. Oh, I get goose bumps just thinking about it.''

''Yep.'' Matt nodded. ''You know, I think 'Rock-a-Bye, Baby' is a waltz, of sorts. Ms. Cunningham, may I have this dance?''

''Are you serious?''

Matt closed the distance between them, drew Caitlin into his arms, then began to move her around the center of the room in time to the lilting music. Caitlin stiffened for a moment, then allowed Matt to nestle her close to his body.

And they danced.

They weren't in a huge ballroom dressed in their finery, with chandeliers twinkling above them as a band played. They were in a medium-size bedroom that had been transformed into a nursery decorated in yellow and white and that was waiting for a precious baby to arrive from the other side of the world.

They danced.

Not to the music produced by professional musicians in tuxedos, but to the tune accompanied by smiling clowns in brightly colored outfits who were keeping step to the music.

They danced.

It was a silly thing to do, yet it was the perfect thing to do, and Caitlin sighed in contentment as she savored the strength of Matt MacAllister, the aroma that was uniquely his, the feel of his tall, solid and nicely muscled body.

The music slowed, the clowns swung lazily around in their circle, then stopped as the last note played and a silence fell over the room.

The dance is over, Matt thought. He had to let Caitlin go and step away from her. But, oh, man, she felt fantastic in his arms, so delicate, so feminine, fitting against him as though custom-made just for him. She smelled like flowers and sunshine, and her dark curls had been woven from silken threads.

He had a feeling…oh, yeah, he knew…that he was going to remember this dance for a very, very long time.

Slowly and reluctantly, Matt eased Caitlin away from him, then dropped his arms to his sides. He nearly groaned aloud when he saw the dreamy expression on her face, the soft smile on her lips.

He wanted to kiss her, he thought. She was so beautiful, so womanly, and their dance had been so special and, damn it, he wanted to kiss her.

Don't do it, MacAllister, he ordered himself. Don't even think about it.

''Well,'' Matt said a tad too loudly. ''I guess I'd better be on my way.''

Caitlin blinked. ''Oh. Yes, of course, I… Would you like a dish of ice cream?''

No, Matt thought. He was treading on dangerous

ground, his desire for Caitlin liable to be stronger than his common sense. He was going to leave right now, get a solid night's sleep and be back to normal in the morning. Yes, that was exactly what he was going to do.

"Ice cream sounds great," he heard himself say, then glanced around quickly with the irrational thought that he would discover the source of his reply.

"It's mint chocolate chip."

"Sold," Matt said. To the jerk who should be walking out the door. "That's one of my favorites."

Why had she done that? Caitlin asked herself as Matt followed her to the kitchen. Why hadn't she escorted Matt to the door, thanked him again for his help with the nursery, then closed the door on his gorgeous face before she did something else as ridiculous as dancing in the middle of a not-even-here-yet baby's room?

That would have been the smart thing to do. But, oh, no, not her. She was now about to share a sinfully delicious dessert with Matt and prolong this unsettling evening even more. Where was her brain?

Caitlin sighed as she removed a carton of ice cream from the freezer.

Her brain, she thought, plunking the carton on the counter, had gone south the moment Matt had taken her into his arms. Well, all she could do now was shovel in the ice cream as quickly as possible, plead fatigue, then...finally and overdue...send Matt on his way.

"I'll serve that up if you like," Matt said. "How many scoops do you want?"

"One." Caitlin set two bowls next to the carton. "Just one. Small. A small one. I'm going to go check my answering machine for messages while you do that. I'll be right back."

Matt watched as Caitlin nearly ran from the kitchen, then he turned to open the carton of ice cream.

Caitlin was jangled, he thought. It made him feel a tad better knowing that she had been just as affected by the dance as he had. It fell under misery loves company, or some such thing.

But if she was struggling with desire as he was, why had she invited him to stay for dessert? He didn't know the answer to that one. Caitlin was definitely not the type who was inching toward enticing him into her bed after they'd had their snack. Not even close. He knew that, just somehow knew that.

"Matt," Caitlin said, rushing back into the room. "Oh, you won't believe this. Well, maybe you will, but *I* can't." She stopped by his side and pressed her palms to her flushed cheeks. "Can you? Believe it?"

Matt chuckled. "I don't have a clue if I can, or can't, because I don't know what you're talking about."

"Oh. Yes." Caitlin patted her cheeks. "I'm going over the edge." She drew a quick breath. "Okay. I'm fine. There was a message from Carolyn on my machine. We're leaving Sunday morning for China. This is Thursday, Matt, and we leave on Sunday. Oh, my gosh. I can't believe this."

Matt replaced the carton of ice cream in the freezer, then carried the bowls to the table at the end of the kitchen.

"Come sit down and have some of this before you either faint, or float away on your happy cloud." He paused and frowned. "Sunday morning? Whew. I'm scheduled to make a couple of speeches, attend some fund-raising events and... Homer just isn't cut out for going in there cold. This is very short notice to find people to take my place."

Caitlin slid onto a chair at the table. "It's wonderful notice."

Matt settled on the chair opposite her and took a bite of ice cream.

"Mmm. Great stuff," he said. "Are you going to be able to sleep tonight? You're so excited you're about to bounce off the walls."

"I know." Caitlin smiled brightly. "I can't stop smiling. In just a handful of hours I'll be on an airplane winging my way toward Mackenzie or Madison.''

"Take a bite of ice cream. You're eating for two now.''

Caitlin laughed. "That's true, in a way. I *am* getting closer and closer to being a mother. Oh, Matt, we leave on Sunday.''

Matt reached across the table, covered one of Caitlin's hands with one of his, and smiled at her warmly.

"I'm sincerely happy for you, Caitlin," he said. "I really am. Your excitement, joy, is contagious, too. I'm certainly looking forward to seeing Miss M. for the first time, instead of just looking at her pictures. That is going to be quite a moment." He released her hand and picked up his spoon again. "I'd better polish this off. After all, I'm also eating for two.''

"Pardon me?" Caitlin said, leaning toward him slightly.

Matt shrugged. "Well, think about it for a minute. I'm taking the place of your assistant, your girlfriend who flunked roller derby 101. So, for all practical purposes, as I take on the role she would have had during the length of the trip, I become Miss M.'s...surrogate father.''

Chapter Five

The hours until the group was to meet at the airport Sunday morning were filled with a flurry of activity for Caitlin.

Very early on Sunday morning Caitlin received a telephone call from Matt suggesting that he pick her up, as there was no point in both of them leaving their vehicles in long-term parking. To Caitlin's self-disgust she could not think of a reasonably reasonable reason why that wasn't a good idea and agreed to Matt's offer, reminding him that they'd have to put Miss M.'s car seat in his SUV.

When the group gathered at the designated gate at the airport, with everyone being much earlier than they needed to be, they were a very excited, emotional and exhausted bunch of people.

Elizabeth Kane, the director of the adoption agency, laughed when she saw them and said not to fear, because they were facing a fifteen-hour nonstop flight, which would give them plenty of time to catch up on their sleep. "And you'd better do just that," she said, beaming at them all, "because leisurely naps and undisturbed nights are soon to be a thing of the past."

"Oh, I know," one of the women said. "Isn't that wonderful?"

After what seemed like an endless wait, they boarded the plane, Matt having been assigned the seat next to Caitlin. Since Matt was to be Caitlin's extra pair of hands, Elizabeth explained, she thought by seating them together it would give them a chance to get to know each other better.

When the engines rumbled and lifted the huge aircraft off the ground, Caitlin closed her eyes.

"Are you afraid of flying?" Matt said, glancing over at her.

Caitlin opened her eyes and smiled at him.

"No, not at all. I'm just savoring the fact that we're on our way, actually on our way at long last." She paused. "Did you accomplish everything you needed to do at the hospital?"

Matt nodded. "It was down to the wire, but I did it. I haven't gotten more than a few hours' sleep in the last three nights, though. But as Elizabeth said, I can catch up during this flight. Fifteen hours. Man, that is grim. I plan to sleep, sleep, sleep during this trip. If I snore, just poke me.''

''I certainly will,'' Caitlin said, laughing.

Do not, Caitlin told herself, dwell on the image ''poke me if I snore'' evoked in her mind. Too late. She could feel the warm flush staining her cheeks.

During the flight the international dateline was crossed, and by the time the plane landed in Hong Kong in the early evening, no one was certain what day it was or how far off their physical clocks were.

They were transported to a nice hotel by a waiting van, checked in as a group by Elizabeth and arranged to meet again in the lobby in an hour to go out to dinner.

''We'll be going to a restaurant a few blocks from here,'' Elizabeth said, ''so we can walk, and I've made a reservation, so they're expecting us. My groups always eat there during this stopover in Hong Kong.

''I took the liberty of ordering for all of us, and there will be a multitude of dishes on a lazy Susan in the center of the table. You'll have the opportunity to sample all kinds of delicious offerings.''

On the third floor, where the entire group had been booked, Caitlin used a plastic key card to open the door to her room, settled her suitcase on the luggage rack, then snapped on a lamp. She frowned as the bulb remained dark. Moving carefully in the darkness she tried another lamp with the same result.

She inched her way back to the door and opened it to allow the lighted hallway to cast a dim glow over her room, then frowned.

She would, she supposed, have to find the telephone, wherever it was hiding in there, and call down to the desk to tell them the electricity wasn't working.

The door directly across from her opened suddenly and Matt appeared, his room brightly lit behind him.

"Problem?" he asked.

"I apparently don't have any electricity. None of the lamps work."

"Do you have your key card?"

"My...yes." Caitlin held up the card that was still in her hand.

Matt took it and slipped it into a slot on the wall by the door beneath the light switches. The lamps Caitlin had fiddled with immediately lit up.

"Let there be light."

"For goodness' sake. How did you know that was what to do?"

"I read the material the airline provided while

you were playing what must have been over a thousand games of gin rummy with the others.''

"Oh."

"May I see what kind of view you have from your window?" Matt asked. "I'm staring at the rear of the building behind us."

"Oh, well, sure, of course, go right ahead."

As Matt crossed the room, the door closed and Caitlin stared at it for a long moment.

Dandy, she thought. Now she and Matt were together in her room with the door closed. What if the others saw them come out when it was time to meet in the lobby? She'd spent as much time as possible, when she wasn't sleeping on the airplane, playing cards and visiting with the others instead of sitting by Matt as though they were a couple. The last thing she wanted was for rumors to start about a possible romance between her and Matt MacAllister.

So far she hadn't been aware of any speculative glances or sly smiles directed their way, but exiting her room with Matt would not be a terrific idea. She was hoping that the group would continue to remember that Matt was simply stepping in to help her out.

She had no intention, Caitlin thought, of using up any mental or emotional energy that should be directed toward her daughter denying queries about what was taking place between her and Matt. Especially since nothing was taking place between her and Matt. Nothing at all.

So what if she'd been aware of how peaceful he appeared when he slept, yet still had that aura of blatant masculinity emanating from him?

So what if she thought it was so endearing the way he rubbed his eyes with his fists like a little boy when he first woke up?

So what if there was a rugged earthiness about him that sent shivers down her spine when he needed a shave?

None of that was important. It didn't mean a thing.

"Las Vegas," Matt said from over by the window. "That's what Hong Kong reminds me of. Lots of neon lights, people crowding the sidewalks, noise, cars, the whole nine yards. Come look at this, Caitlin. See if this view doesn't remind you of Las Vegas."

"I've never been to Las Vegas," she said, staying by the door.

"Oh, well, come take a look anyway."

With a silent sigh, Caitlin crossed the room and joined Matt at the window. He slipped one arm across her shoulders, then pointed toward the street below.

"See? You'd never know you were in an Asian country. That is due, madam, to the fact that Hong Kong was under British rule for many, many years before once again being claimed by mainland China, and is very westernized, if there is such a word. However, when we arrive in Nanjing tomorrow, then later go on to Guangzhou, you will experience the real China of today.''

''Do tell.'' Caitlin managed to produce a small smile.

Matt had nestled her close to his body, she thought frantically. His big, strong, oh-so-warm body. Such heat. It was weaving its way from him into her, swirling within her, then pulsing low and hot. He was being so nonchalant about having his arm around her, acting as though it didn't matter, just happened to be where it had landed. Well, she could match him sophistication for sophistication, by golly. Unless she fainted dead out on her face first.

''I *am* telling you,'' Matt said, chuckling, ''so pay attention, because people pay tour guides *beaucoup* bucks for information like this.''

''I'm etching it all on my weary brain. I even got a bonus because now I know what Las Vegas looks like back in the States.'' She cleared her throat. ''Well, thank you for solving the mystery of the electricity. You were a hero to the rescue of a damsel in the darkness.''

Matt turned his head to smile at her, but his smile disappeared quickly as he realized that Caitlin was only inches away. His gaze swept over her delicate features, lingered on her lips, then he looked directly into her dark eyes.

"I don't think," he said, his voice husky, "that I'd be off base if I kissed you, Caitlin. After all, we *have* slept together."

Caitlin blinked. "We...we what?"

"Slept together. On the plane. Right there, side by side, we both were sleeping. So, therefore, we slept together. Sort of."

"That's the silliest—"

"No," he interrupted, lowering his head slowly toward hers, "it's not. And there is nothing silly about how much I want to kiss you, how long I've waited to kiss you, or about the fact that I'm about to kiss you."

And he did.

Caitlin stiffened as Matt brushed his lips lightly over hers, then shivered when he repeated the sensuous journey. He encircled her with his arms and pulled her close to his rugged body as he intensified the kiss, parting her lips to slip his tongue into the sweet darkness of her mouth.

Caitlin's hands floated upward to entwine behind Matt's neck, then her lashes drifted down as she savored the taste, the feel, the aroma of Matt.

She'd fantasized about this kiss, she thought hazily, dreamed about it, had been waiting, as Matt had, for it to take place.

Nothing more should, nor would, take place between them, she silently vowed, but this kiss was theirs to share, the memories of it to do with as they each desired.

Matt lifted his head just enough to draw a quick, sharp breath, then his mouth captured Caitlin's once again in a searing kiss.

Oh, Matt, Caitlin thought as she trembled in his arms. He had picked the perfect place for this to happen. Hong Kong was…was sort of in limbo, a place of bright colors and surging crowds, a mixture of cultures, the old, the new, creating an otherworldly aura.

It wasn't the reality of Ventura, nor of the China where her daughter waited. What happened between her and Matt here in Hong Kong was separate and apart from what truly existed. So be it.

Matt broke the kiss, took a rough breath, then eased Caitlin gently away from his aroused body.

"I should apologize for doing that," he said, his voice gritty with passion, "but I can't because I'm not sorry. I've wanted to kiss you from the moment I saw you, Caitlin. Before you decide to be mad as hell, remember that you shared these kisses, held nothing back."

"I'm not angry," she said, her voice unsteady. "I wanted that to happen as much as you did, Matt. The sensual tension between us has been building and building and… But that's over, now, done.

Nothing like this is going to take place between us again.''

Matt frowned and dragged a restless hand through his hair.

''I don't understand. We just shared kisses that were sensational, unbelievable. We also get along great together, have fun, laugh, talk. Something is going on here, Caitlin. Don't you want to know what it is?''

She took a step backward and wrapped her hands around her elbows. ''No, Matt, I don't.''

''Why in the hell not?'' he said none too quietly.

''Because,'' she said, dropping her hands to her hips and matching his volume, ''I am on this trip for one purpose. One. My daughter. She is all I'm focusing on. I certainly don't intend to fit a short-term affair in around the edges of my busy schedule over here. No, I'm not sorry about the kisses, but nothing else is going to... No.''

''You're making whatever this is between us sound cheap and tacky, Caitlin. I resent that.''

''Well, excuse me to hell and back,'' Caitlin said, plunking down on the edge of the bed. ''Okay, you don't like my short-term-affair description. Fine. What would you call it if we continue, end up in bed together?

''Tell me, Matt. Have you been struck by Cupid's arrow, fallen head over heels in love with me, intend to not rest until I agree to marry you?''

"Oh. Well, no, but give me a break here. That sort of stuff only happens in the movies or those romance novels that women read. Let's be realistic."

"I am being realistic. We're sexually attracted to each other, plus we have fun together, enjoy each other's company. However, since we're not in love with each other, taking this further would be nothing more than a short-term affair. I rest my case."

"I have never in my life," Matt said, a rather bemused expression on his face, "had a conversation like this one with a woman. Talk about analyzing something to death. I mean, I'm used to just letting things take their natural course and...then...later, down the road it's..." His voice trailed off.

"Aha." Caitlin pointed one finger in the air. "Down the road it's over, ending yet another short-term affair of which I speak."

"Would you cut that out?"

Before Caitlin could reply, a knock sounded at the door.

"Caitlin," came Marsha's muffled voice. "Are you ready to go down to meet the others for dinner? Caitlin?"

"Oh, good grief." Caitlin jumped to her feet. "That's Marsha."

Matt grinned. "Shall I get the door while you freshen your lipstick?"

"Don't you touch that door," Caitlin whispered. "Marsha's busy little mind will go nuts if she finds us in here together."

"Caitlin?" Marsha called. "Are you in there?"

"Yes, I'm here," Caitlin yelled. "Go on ahead, Marsha. I'll be along in just a couple of minutes."

"Okay. Have you seen Matt? He isn't in his room."

"Oh, he's around somewhere. Maybe he already went downstairs."

"Well, hurry up, because I am starving to death."

"I will. I just have to comb my hair."

"And freshen your lipstick," Matt said with a chuckle, which earned him a glare from Caitlin.

Caitlin ignored Matt to the best of her ability as she freshened up.

Matt folded his arms loosely over his chest and leaned one shoulder against the wall as he waited. Oh, Caitlin was something, he thought. The kisses they'd shared had been sensational. She was very sensual, very womanly and obviously was comfortable with her own femininity. She had returned his kisses in total abandon and he had been instantly aroused, wanting her, aching for her with an intensity like nothing he'd known before.

And Caitlin when angry? Dynamite. Her cheeks

became flushed and her eyes flashed like laser beams. She'd taken him on, toe to toe, and let him know what he could do with any ideas that he might be entertaining of a short-term affair with her.

Matt frowned.

Short-term affair. Caitlin had repeated that phrase like a broken record until he'd reached the point that he'd told her to put a cork in it. The problem was, she was right. He had nothing more than the now ever-famous short-term affair to offer her. He simply wasn't ready for a commitment to forever, a relationship that would inch toward marriage, hearth, home and Miss M. the baby.

Yeah, sure, he'd said he'd like to know what was happening between Caitlin and him because it was definitely…different somehow from his past experiences where casual dating was the order of the day and no one got hurt. No, there was more depth, intensity between him and Caitlin. But that didn't mean he was opening the door to a possible permanent future with her and the daughter she would see and hold for the first time tomorrow.

So, where did that leave him? Aching for Caitlin. Wanting to make love with her. Envisioning pulling her into his arms and kissing her senseless at every opportunity, which would no doubt result in her popping him right in the chops.

''Well, hell,'' Matt said under his breath.

He had volunteered to stick like glue to Caitlin to be ready to assist her in any way he was needed. He was the extra pair of hands, hands that would not be allowed to touch her again. This trip was suddenly losing its appeal. Big-time.

"I'm ready," Caitlin said, bringing Matt from his now-gloomy thoughts. "I'll go first, then you take the elevator after me. That way we won't arrive in the lobby at the same time and create a scenario ripe for rumor."

"Ripe for rumor?" Matt said with a burst of laughter. "I can sure tell you write for a living. You certainly have a unique way with words."

He paused and became serious. "Caitlin, I think you're making far too much of this business of us being seen together. Everyone is focused on their baby, that little munchkin waiting for them to arrive tomorrow. The last thing on the minds of anyone in our group is whether or not you and I are getting it on or... Well, I could have said that nicer, but you get the drift."

Caitlin opened her mouth to deliver a retort to Matt's statement, then frowned and snapped it closed again. A long, silent minute passed as she stared into space, deep in thought.

"You're right," she said finally, looking at Matt again. "I'm acting like an idiot. It's very self-centered of me to think that everyone would be in a twitter over what may, or may not, be going on between the two of us. I should be thinking about my daughter, too, not about how I felt when you kissed me, or how much I had wanted you to kiss me, or how long it seemed that I had been anticipating your kissing me, or…''

Caitlin's eyes widened and a flush stained her cheeks.

''I didn't just say all that,'' she said, shaking her head. ''Oh, tell me I didn't say all that. This is so embarrassing and… No, this is jet lag. Yes, that's what's wrong with me. I'm suffering from a severe case of jet lag. Food. Maybe food will help.''

Caitlin hurried to the door and flung it open.

''Let's go,'' she said. ''We're probably holding up the whole group. I need nourishment so my brain can start functioning like something I recognize again. Where's my key card?''

''It's still in the slot to turn on the electricity,'' Matt said, crossing the room slowly.

''I knew that,'' Caitlin said, pulling the plastic card free.

''You're sure we should ride down in the elevator together?'' Matt said, pulling the door closed behind them. ''I'll do whatever makes you comfortable.''

''Of course we'll go together,'' Caitlin said as they reached the elevator. ''You were the one who made me realize how silly I was being about all of this.''

"Mmm." Matt nodded. "Well, for the record, Caitlin, I felt as though I'd waited an eternity to kiss you, too, and I'm going to remember those kisses we shared. Oh, yes, ma'am, I certainly am."

As the elevator door swished open, Caitlin said, "The subject is closed."

"Hold the elevator," a man called as Caitlin and Matt stepped inside.

Matt pressed the proper button to keep the doors open, and another couple from the group hurried inside.

"Oh, I was so sure we'd kept the whole bunch waiting for us," the woman said, "but you're just going down, too. That makes me feel better. We wasted so much time trying to figure out how to get the electricity to work in the room."

"Really?" Matt said. "I read all about it on the plane."

"I was totally baffled," Caitlin said, "if that makes you feel better. I just stood there like an idiot wondering where the phone was so I could call for help. Matt came across the hall and poked the card in the little slot."

"Came across..." The woman paused. "Oh, that's right. You're not a couple, per se. It's so difficult to keep so many new people straight at the same time. You sat together on the plane and—"

"Honey," her husband said, smiling, "you wouldn't keep it straight if you had a scorecard to look at, because you are thinking about the baby, and everything else is just sort of floating on by you.''

Matt looked at Caitlin with a very smug expression. She rolled her eyes heavenward.

The addition of Caitlin, Matt and the couple with them on the elevator completed the group waiting in the lobby to go to dinner, except for a missing Elizabeth Kane.

Despite their jet lag everyone was in fine spirits and the chatter was lively and quite loud.

Marsha and Bud joined Caitlin and Matt and the four agreed they were looking forward to a meal that was not airplane food. Marsha reached up and swiped her thumb over the left edge of Matt's top lip.

''You should have freshened your lipstick before you came down here,'' she said, laughing merrily. ''I just removed the last dab. I mean, hey, either wear it or don't, whatever floats your boat.''

To Caitlin's amazement and delight, an embarrassed flush crept up Matt's neck and onto his face.

''Marsha,'' Bud said, chuckling, ''give Matt and Caitlin a break, would you? It's none of our business if they... Well, it's just none of our business.''

''Of course it isn't,'' Marsha said. ''But that doesn't mean I can just cancel being snoopy.''

''Changing the subject now,'' Bud said. ''I wonder what's keeping Elizabeth?''

As though she'd heard her name being called, Elizabeth emerged as the elevator doors swished open, and hurried across the lobby to join the others, glancing at her watch when she finally stopped.

"Only ten minutes late," she said, "but I'll still apologize for keeping you waiting. I was making my usual telephone call to Dr. Yang in Nanjing to confirm our plans. He'll notify the director of the orphanage that we're on schedule and good to go. Dr. Yang will leave a message for me at our hotel in Nanjing informing me of the time the vans will arrive to take us to the orphanage so you can meet your daughters.

"As you've been told, you'll have about an hour's visit with them tomorrow, then take them with you the next day when we go back to the orphanage to get them." She paused and laughed. "Uh-oh, there's no tissue box to pass around and some of you are getting weepy. Let's head for the restaurant before we flood this lobby."

Darkness had fallen and more neon lights had come alive when the group left the hotel and began the walk to the restaurant. The name Las Vegas was heard several times from the various conversations taking place.

Caitlin replayed in her mind the moment when Marsha had wiped the lipstick from Matt's lips and couldn't curb her smile. She should be totally mortified, she thought, but she wasn't. Matt had been so endearingly embarrassed, she'd wanted to give him a hug and tell him not to worry about what anyone might be thinking about the telltale clue, and to remember that he was the one who had said that new daughters were the main focus of the entire group, not the doings of Caitlin Cunningham and Matt MacAllister.

Elizabeth was greeted warmly when they arrived at the restaurant, and they were soon settled at a large round table with a lazy Susan in the middle.

Three waitresses appeared and began to place steaming hot, intriguing-appearing offerings of food on the turntable. Plates were soon piled high with the fragrant food, and they dug in.

"Did Dr. Yang say anything about the babies, Elizabeth?" one of the women asked. "Anything at all?"

"Only that they would be ready and waiting for you to see and hold them," she said, smiling.

"Oh-h-h," the woman said. "I can hardly wait. I hope the hours between now and then pass quickly. This is torture." She smiled at her husband. "Just think, Bill. Tomorrow we meet Emma Lin. Tomorrow."

"Yep," he said, matching her smile. "In the meantime, eat your dinner."

"Tomorrow," Caitlin whispered, staring into space.

Excited chatter erupted around the table centered

on the wondrous event that would take place the next day. Matt leaned close to Caitlin so only she could hear him.

"Tomorrow," he said, smiling at her when she met his gaze. "You'll meet your daughter. You'll hold her, look into her pretty eyes and know if she's Mackenzie or Madison. It will be one of those life-changing memories that will be etched in your mind forever."

"Yes," Caitlin said softly.

"And you know something, Caitlin? When I realize that I'll be right there to witness it all, I can honestly say there's no place else on this earth I'd rather be."

Chapter Six

Caitlin sat next to one of the windows on the rick-
ety bus that had picked up the group at the Nanjing
airport, her gaze riveted on the bustling crowds
within her view.

Nanjing, she decided, was absolutely enchanting,
an intriguing blend of the old and the new. There
were tall, modern buildings next to small, shanty-
type houses, and the number of people riding bicycles in the surging traffic seemed to outnumber
those in automobiles.

Some of the people were dressed in clothes she
might see in Ventura, while others were wearing
traditional dark pants and boxy jackets that she'd

seen so often in photographs of the Chinese populace. The weather was perfect, warm with a cooling breeze.

"Oh," Caitlin gasped as she witnessed yet another near miss of a car colliding with a bicycle. "It's dangerous out there. The people on those bikes are demanding equal space on the roads. Scary."

Matt leaned forward to look out the window, then immediately settled back again in his seat with a chuckle.

"I don't think watching that madness is good for my blood pressure. This makes driving in Los Angeles or New York City a leisurely outing. Whew."

"There are amazingly few accidents," Elizabeth said, overhearing what Caitlin and Matt were talking about. "It looks awful, but it's organized chaos, or some such thing. The majority of people can't afford cars, so the mode of transportation is most often a bike. There is a stiffer penalty for stealing a bicycle than a vehicle."

"Fascinating," Matt said, nodding.

"Caitlin," Marsha said from across the aisle, "you should be taking notes on some of this. I think with your talent for writing you could do some very interesting articles for the magazine from a fashion angle, make our readers feel as though they've actually visited China. It would be a nice way to add to your income while you're working at home, too.''

"In between changing Miss M.'s diapers.'' Matt chuckled.

"Babies do take naps, you know.'' Marsha frowned. "But I guess that's when you take one, too, or maybe get caught up on the laundry and what have you. I don't have a clue.''

"We'll find out very soon, sweetheart,'' Bud said. "You know, I have to admit I'm getting nervous about meeting Grace for the first time. What if I scare the socks off her? She's almost a year old, so I imagine she has definite opinions about things…like her father is terrifying.''

Marsha patted Bud's knee. "We'll just take it as it comes, give her space, time to get used to us. When we bring her back to the hotel tomorrow we'll let her call the shots. If she doesn't want us to hold her, we won't push it.'' She paused. "Oh, dear, now *I'm* getting nervous.''

Elizabeth laughed. "Just relax. If your new daughters sense that you're uptight they'll react accordingly. My years of making these trips allows me to say with confidence that you'll all be pleasantly surprised at how quickly your girls adjust to you and their new environment. They're extremely resilient little ladies.''

"Goodness,'' Caitlin said. "I never gave a thought to the idea that Miss M. might not…well, like me right off the bat. We've all fallen in love with our daughters by just looking at their pictures but...oh dear.''

''Don't get tense,'' Matt said. ''Miss M. will take one look at you and it will be love at first sight, Caitlin, you'll see. I don't believe in that stuff when it comes to adults, but babies? They know when they're connected to someone special. Everything will be just fine.''

As conversations started throughout the bus about what they were seeing out the windows, Caitlin cocked her head to one side and studied Matt, who looked at her questioningly.

''What?'' he said.

''You believe that babies are capable of experiencing love at first sight, but adults aren't?'' Caitlin asked. ''At what point in their lives do they change their view on the subject?''

''Well...'' Matt shrugged. ''I don't know. When we grow up and get worldly and wise, I suppose. Love at first sight? Give me a break. Love...adult, man-and-woman love...is something that grows over time, has to be nurtured, tended to, sort of like a garden that eventually produces beautiful flowers and... Jeez, I'm getting corny here.''

''No, you're not,'' Caitlin said quietly, looking directly into Matt's eyes. ''I think you expressed that very nicely, and I agree with you.''

''Which is why,'' Matt observed, switching his

gaze to the scene beyond the window, ''I don't see falling in love in my near future because I don't have time for the nurturing, doing my part in tending to the...well, to the garden.''

''I know,'' Caitlin said, then stared out the window again.

Well, Matt thought, he covered that topic very thoroughly, right on the mark. And for some unexplainable reason it had caused his ulcer to start burning with a hot pain as though voicing displeasure at what he had said.

Matt reached in his pocket, retrieved an antacid tablet and popped it into his mouth, frowning as he chewed the chalky circle.

''I saw that, MacAllister,'' Bud said. ''Whatever you're talking about over there, change the subject. Your doctor has spoken.''

''Cork it, Mathis.'' Matt glared at Bud.

The bus driver made a sudden sharp turn, and moments later they rattled to a stop in the circular driveway in front of a modern high-rise hotel.

''We have arrived,'' Elizabeth said. ''This is a lovely hotel, and you'll be very comfortable here. I'll check us in as a group again and hand out the key cards. It would be best if you'd wait in the lobby, though, while I telephone Dr. Yang and find out what time the vans are coming to take us to the orphanage. That will save me having to call each of your rooms to let you know. Okay?''

Elizabeth received quick, affirmative and excited answers to her request. The group was soon standing in the spacious, nicely furnished lobby with luggage at their feet and key cards in their hands as they waited to hear the outcome of her call.

They were all booked into the fourth floor, Elizabeth explaining that it kept crying babies from disturbing other guests. Matt glanced at Caitlin's key card, then his own, and nodded in approval that they were in side-by-side rooms.

Good, he thought. He'd be close at hand if Caitlin needed help with Miss M. She didn't have any experience with babies, while he had years of it due to being a MacAllister.

A MacAllister. Ah, yes, the powerful and well-known family of Ventura, the movers and shakers, the overachievers, who seemed to excel in whatever career choices they made. As each new generation came along, the pattern was repeated. Pick a subject? There was a MacAllister who did it…extremely well. Lawyers, doctors, architects, police officers, the list was endless. If you were a MacAllister, by damn, you'd better be top-notch at whatever you did or…

Whoa. Halt. Enough, he thought, frowning. Where was all this coming from? He was standing in a hotel lobby halfway around the world from Ventura and his clan. Why was he suddenly focusing on something that had hovered over him from the time he was a kid? A kid who wasn't good at sports in school, who had been an average student not a super brain, a kid who looked at the Mac-Allisters surrounding him and continually wondered why he fell short time after time after…

"Matt?" Caitlin said.

"What?" he said, looking at her.

"Do you have a headache? You're frowning and rubbing your forehead. Are you okay?"

"Oh, sure, sure, I'm fine." He forced a smile. "Just suffering from a bit of jet lag like everyone else." He paused. "Maybe I should figure out the time difference between here and Ventura and decide when I can call the hospital and see if everything is running smoothly."

Caitlin sighed. "I wondered how long it would take before you felt the need to do that. You're not focused on a new daughter like the rest of us. You're centered on your work."

"That's not true. I'm really eager to see Miss M., Caitlin, I told you that. Remember? I said there was nowhere else I'd rather be than—"

"Calling the hospital in Ventura," she interrupted, lifting her chin and meeting his gaze.

"Forget the call. I'm not going to do it. I'm not telephoning the hospital and checking up on things."

"Right." Caitlin rolled her eyes.

"I mean it. Cross my heart and hope to die, stick

a needle in my eye. Oh, hey, here comes Elizabeth.''

No one spoke as Elizabeth rejoined the group.

"Okay, we're on target," she said. "It's four o'clock. Go unpack and be back down here at five ready to go to the orphanage."

"Oh," Caitlin whispered. "Oh, my goodness."

Three new mommies-to-be burst into tears.

"Shoo, shoo," Elizabeth said, laughing and flapping her hands at them. "Go to your rooms. There. I sound like a stern old auntie. I'll see you all back down here in an hour."

Everyone collected their luggage, and Caitlin and Matt headed to their rooms.

Matt stopped as Caitlin poked the key card in the slot when they reached her room, then opened the door when the green light blinked on. She stepped inside the room far enough to hold the door open with her bottom and look back at Matt.

"I see the gizmo on the wall for the card so I can turn on the lights," she said, laughing. "I'm a quick study."

"Good for you, but maybe you should turn around and see what they've put in your room."

Caitlin frowned slightly in confusion, turned, then a gasp escaped from her lips.

"Oh. Oh, Matt, look. It's a crib. A port-a-crib. It's Miss M.'s crib where she'll sleep after I bring her back here tomorrow. Isn't that the most beautiful thing you've ever seen?''

Matt's gaze was riveted on Caitlin as he heard the awe, the wonder, the heartfelt emotion ringing in her voice.

''Yes, I'm looking at one of the most beautiful things I've seen.'' He cleared his throat as he heard the rasp of building emotions in his voice. ''I'll knock on your door when it's time to go back downstairs. Okay?''

'''Kay,'' Caitlin said absently, starting toward the crib.

The door swung free and closed in Matt's face with a thud. He stood statue still for a long moment, attempting to visualize Caitlin inside the room, maybe running her hand over the rail of the crib, or across the soft sheet on the tiny mattress, or perhaps just gazing into the crib and envisioning Miss M. sleeping peacefully there, where she belonged, with her mother watching over her.

He looked quickly in both directions to be certain that no one had seen him standing there like an idiot who was attempting to carry on a conversation with a closed door before trudging back to his room.

Everyone in the group was fifteen minutes early arriving in the lobby, but no one settled onto the comfortable-looking chairs and sofas, not having the patience to sit still.

"What time is it?" Marsha said to Bud.

"One minute later than when you last asked me," he said, smiling. "Chill, pretty wife, or you're going to pass out cold on your nose."

"Oh, right," Marsha said, frowning at him. "Like you're Mr. Cool, huh? Might I mention that you forgot to tie your shoelaces?"

"Well, cripe," Bud said, looking down at his feet.

Matt whopped Bud on the back as he bent over to tend to his laces.

"Little shook up, Daddy?" Matt said. "Mmm. Maybe we should check your blood pressure, Doctor. You're in a high-stress mode."

"Can it, MacAllister," Bud said, straightening and glaring at Matt. "Caitlin, do something about this man."

"Me? What man?" she said, laughing. "I'm such a wreck I'm having trouble remembering my own name."

"The vans are here," a woman said, more in the form of a squeal.

"So they are," Elizabeth agreed, joining the group. "Is everyone ready? Let me count noses." She did a quick perusal of the gathered people. "Right on the money. Let's go meet some new baby daughters."

The fifteen-minute ride to the orphanage was a total blur to Caitlin until they suddenly turned onto a narrow street lined with small, shabby houses made of a variety of nonmatching material. At the end of the street a tall, seven-story building could be partially seen.

"That's the orphanage," Elizabeth said. "It's big, as you can see, and filled to the brim with kids. There are infant floors, where the little ones sleep two and three to a crib at times, toddler floors, then older children have several floors where they sleep dorm-fashion until they are fostered out to work in the fields in rural areas.

"There is no heat in that building. They have to layer the kids in lots of clothes in the winter to keep them warm. A portion of the fees you paid for this trip will go directly to the orphanage for food, clothes, medical supplies, what have you.

"The vast majority of the children are girls, as you know. The few boys that are brought here have some kind of medical problem, or perhaps a birthmark that is too noticeable, or they might have been the second boy in the family, breaking the law about only being allowed to have one child, and there isn't a thing wrong with them. However, it's rare for boys to be in the orphanages.

"And," Elizabeth said as the vans drove around a circle driveway. "Here—" the vans stopped "—we are."

Matt reached over and squeezed one of Caitlin's hands, finding it ice cold.

"Calm down," he whispered to her. "If you touch Miss M. with hands that cold she'll have a screamer of a fit."

Caitlin nodded jerkily.

A beaming Dr. Yang greeted the group as they entered the building. He was a slightly built man in his mid-thirties with handsome features and dark, almond-shaped eyes that seemed to be actually sparkling.

"I feel as though I know you," he said, his English having only a trace of an accent, "because I've read all of your dossiers. Welcome to China. Welcome to Nanjing. Welcome to the humble place where your daughters are waiting to meet you. Our elevator is very small, so I'll ask that you go up to the third floor four at a time, please.

"We will go into a living room, then I'll tell the head of the orphanage that you are here and that the caregivers should bring the babies to where you are. My paperwork is upstairs that documents the matches." He laughed. "Same as always, Elizabeth. You bring me people who are too nervous to speak."

"Never fails," she said, smiling.

"But soon they'll be crying those happy tears we always see," Dr. Yang said.

"They've been practicing those already. Okay, folksies. Here we go."

The living room Dr. Yang had spoken of was quite large, but the furniture and carpeting was very faded and worn. The paint on the walls was a color somewhere between gray and yellow and was peeling in numerous spots. There was a dusty, plastic red rose in a bud vase on a shabby end table in one corner. No pictures adorned the walls.

Caitlin, Matt, Marsha and Bud settled onto a threadbare sofa. Bud wrapped his arm around Marsha's shoulders and she sat as close as possible to him. Matt fought the urge to do the same to Caitlin as she sat next to him, her hands clutched so tightly in her lap the knuckles were turning white.

Elizabeth and Dr. Yang left the room and a heavy silence fell as the minutes ticked slowly by. Then everyone stiffened as the pair reappeared followed by caregivers in white uniforms, some holding one baby, others with two.

Dr. Yang consulted a sheet of paper he was holding, then placed his hand on the shoulder of one of the caregivers.

"Sally and Fred Roberts," he said.

And so it began, the uniting of parents and their daughters, with happy tears flowing freely. Marsha and Ben were called and their Grace gurgled and smiled when Marsha lifted her from the caregiver's arms and held her close, laughing and crying at the same time.

"That's my goddaughter. Awesome. You have to be next," Matt whispered to Caitlin, "because you're the only one left. Are you ready?"

"Oh, I am so ready," Caitlin said, staring at the empty doorway. "Why isn't there another caregiver standing there. Where's Miss M.? I don't understand why—oh…my…God. Matt, look."

Matt's eyes widened as a caregiver stepped into the living room, a baby tucked in the crook of each arm. Without realizing he was doing it, he grabbed Caitlin's hand and got to his feet, drawing her up next to him.

"Caitlin Cunningham," Dr. Yang said, smiling. "Last, but certainly not least."

"I…" Caitlin said, making no attempt to free her hand from Matt's as she walked toward the caregiver on trembling legs. "There are two… The pictures I got of Miss M. were of two babies, not just two photographs of the same baby. Dear heaven, they're identical twins. Twins? I'm going to be the mother of twins? Did I know this? I didn't know this. Oh, they're so beautiful, so… Twins?"

Dr. Yang frowned and looked at the sheet of paper. "Yes, it says here that you have been matched with identical twin girls of six months of age. Is there a problem?"

"Let's just all stay calm," Elizabeth said

quickly. "Caitlin, you and Matt take the babies to the sofa while I speak with Dr. Yang and see what is going on here. Dr. Yang, we at the agency and, therefore, Caitlin, didn't realize she'd been matched with twins. Nothing came across my desk indicating that."

"Really?" Dr. Yang said. "Well, come with me, Elizabeth, and we'll telephone Beijing, where all these decisions are made and discover what is taking place. Our caregivers have so much to do so...Caitlin? Matt, is it? Would you please tend to the babies until we return?"

"Yes, oh, yes," Caitlin said, lifting one of the infants from the caregiver's arms. "Matt?"

"Sure thing," he said, accepting the other baby. "Hello, Miss M." He glanced at the baby that Caitlin held. "Hello, Miss M. Man, they are really identical, aren't they? And they're both scowling, just like in the pictures you got. Let's go sit down and see if we can get them to smile. Caitlin?"

"Twins," she said, staring at the baby she held. "That's two. One plus one equals two. Twins."

"Sitting down now," Matt said, shifting the baby to one arm and gripping Caitlin's elbow. "Right now."

On the sofa, both Caitlin and Matt propped the babies on their knees, having to support their backs as they obviously were unable to sit up alone. Tears filled Caitlin's eyes as her gaze darted back and forth between the little girls.

"Oh, my gosh, they are so fantastic, so incredibly beautiful, and wonderful and…"

"And twins," Marsha said. "Caitlin, what are you going to do? You're a single mother, for Pete's sake. I'm scared to death about tending to Grace with Bud's help and you'll be all alone with two?" She paused and smiled. "But, oh, they are so cute. Grace, look at your little friends."

"Twin friends," Bud said. "Holy cow."

Matt bounced the baby a bit on his knees, then made a clucking noise that sounded rather like a sick chicken. The baby stared at him for a long moment, then a smile broke across her face, revealing two little teeth on the bottom gums.

"She smiled at me," Matt said, beaming. "Caitlin, look at Miss M. She's smiling."

Caitlin sniffled. "My Miss M. isn't smiling. I think she's about to cry."

"No way," Matt said, leaning toward the other baby and making the same ridiculous noise. The baby grinned, and she had the same two teeth on the bottom. "There you go. We've been waiting for that smile ever since we saw the pictures of her looking so grumpy. Well, actually it was the pictures of both of them looking so grumpy, but…" He shrugged. "Now they're smiling."

"They're so beautiful," Caitlin said, unable to

halt her tears. "I can hardly believe I'm actually holding... Oh, but, Matt, Marsha's right. How can I possibly cope, tend to, care for, twins? But they're my daughters. I fell in love with the baby in the photograph. So, okay, I didn't know I was falling in love with two babies but... Oh, dear, my mind is mush."

Dr. Yang and Elizabeth returned and came to where Caitlin and Matt were sitting.

"Um...Caitlin?" Elizabeth said. "Dr. Yang has something he wants to say to you. Hear him out, please, and don't...don't overreact to what he says. You must remember this is a culture far different from ours."

"Yes, well, we spoke to the person we needed to in Beijing. It seems a new employee in the office checked the wrong box on the final approval sheet, indicating you wanted twins. So, the match was made.

"The officials in Beijing said you are certainly cleared to take both of the babies if you so choose, but if not..." He shrugged and smiled. "Well, that's fine, too. It was a clerical error on our part, and can be rectified by you simply picking the baby you want from the pair if you feel you can only raise one. That solves the problem."

Caitlin's eyes widened in horror, and a flush stained her cheeks. She opened her mouth to speak, but Elizabeth spoke first. "Caitlin, take a deep breath, count to ten, think before you say anything. We're guests in this country, dear, who are being allowed to adopt these wonderful children. We don't want to do anything to jeopardize the program in place. Dear.''

''Yes, I understand. Well, Dr. Yang, I think the officials in Beijing are being very…um…accommodating and I certainly appreciate being given the choices you've just presented to me.

''But, you see, I wouldn't dream of separating identical-twin sisters under any circumstances. It's a matter of…doing things just a teeny tiny bit differently in our country.

''So, sir, with heartfelt thanks, I accept being the mother of both of these girls and I'll love them to pieces and do the very best I can raising them.''

''Very good. I'll call Beijing right back and inform them of your decision.'' He turned and hurried from the room.

''Nicely done, Caitlin,'' Elizabeth said, letting out a pent-up breath. ''The Chinese people place little importance on twin girls staying together in these situations. Our emphasis that they not be separated baffles them. But you did very well. Are you certain you want to do this, though?''

''Yes,'' Caitlin said, raising her chin. ''I don't have a clue as to how I'll manage, but these are my daughters.''

"Okay, but we're not out of the woods yet," Elizabeth said. "We're going to run into problems at our own consulate in Guangzhou."

"Why?" Caitlin said.

"Let's not get into it now." Elizabeth smiled. "The clock is ticking away and this visit is so short. Enjoy your girls while you can today. We'll worry about the details later. I'm going to tour this room and tickle some tummies. Hello, Grace, aren't you a smiling little thing? Oh, and let me go see Emma Lin."

Elizabeth bustled off. Marsha and Bud got up to go greet the other babies, Grace waving merrily at nothing in particular as Bud carried her.

Caitlin drew a deep, steadying breath, then smiled at Matt. "Well," she said, "this is… interesting."

Matt laughed in delight. "That's a good word for it. Whew. What a shocker, huh? Hey, let's switch babies. As the official mother of twins, you've got to learn how to divide up your time and attention between them."

In a rather clumsy shuffle of blanket-sleeper-clad bundles, the switch was made.

"Hi, sweetheart," Caitlin said, smiling at the baby now on her lap. "My gosh, Matt, if it wasn't for the fact that this baby is wearing yellow and that baby has on green, I'd never know I was holding a different one from a moment ago."

"Yep," he said, narrowing his eyes as he peered at the infant on his lap. "They're identical, all right. And cute? I'm telling you, Caitlin, I thought the pictures of Miss M. were enough to steal a heart forever, but in person? Look at these munchkins. They are really something."

"I know." Caitlin blinked back fresh tears. "I'm thrilled. No, I'm terrified. No, I'm so happy I'm… No, I'm out of my mind. Oh, dear, I'm losing it. Matt, what do you think Elizabeth meant about there being problems at our own consulate?"

"I don't have a clue, but put it out of your mind for now. Elizabeth Kane obviously knows all the ins and outs of this stuff. She'll take care of whatever obstacle there might be in Guangzhou. I'm sure she will. Just enjoy seeing and holding your daughters in the time we have left. I will never forget this day, that's for certain."

Caitlin laughed. "Oh, it's etched indelibly in my mind, too." She smiled at the baby on her lap. "And my heart. Somehow, this is all going to work out just fine. I don't know how, but it will. I'm the mother of six-month-old twin girls." Her hold on the baby tightened. "Oh, dear heaven, I'm the mother of six-month-old twin girls. The *single* mother of said twins."

Matt laughed. "Yep, you are. Keep saying it until it really sinks in. No, maybe you'd better not right now, or you might get hysterical. Hey, look

at the bright side, Caitlin. You don't have to pick
between the names Mackenzie and Madison. You
need both of those names and it's just a matter of
deciding who is who.''

''Well, that's true, isn't it?'' she said, smiling.
''They're Madison Olivia and Mackenzie Olivia
Cunningham. Perfect.'' She sighed. ''The only
problem is how do I tell them apart?''

Chapter Seven

By the time the group gathered to have dinner in the restaurant in the hotel that evening, word had spread about Caitlin's twins. Some of the parents had been so engrossed in their own new daughter, besides dealing with raging emotions, that they had been oblivious. Everyone who had brought diapers that would fit the twins offered to give Caitlin as many as they thought they could possibly spare.

Elizabeth, who was starting to appear weary, spoke quietly to each couple and Caitlin, moving around the crowded table after saying she didn't have time to eat dinner. She asked them all individually if they were comfortable with the match, with their new daughter.

"Daughters, in your case, Caitlin," Elizabeth said, smiling. "I have to ask this question officially before you sign the adoption papers this evening. Do you wish to adopt the twin girls you were matched with?"

"Yes," Caitlin said, not hesitating for one second. "Oh, yes, Elizabeth, I do."

"Fine. I've been giving this some thought. My first reaction was to say that we would switch rooms around so I was next to yours and be available to help you...because you *are* going to need assistance during the next days and nights. However, that's not a viable idea because I have tons of paperwork to take care of each evening after we have taken one step, then the next, in the process we must follow here."

"I understand," Caitlin said, nodding.

"So, how's this?" Elizabeth went on. "Matt, I realize you were recruited to help Caitlin with her luggage and what have you, but it's apparent that you have experience with babies. I know you and Caitlin just met, but you do seem to be getting along just fine and...well, I spoke to the manager of the hotel and we can move the two of you to a suite with a living room and two separate bedrooms.

"If you're willing, Matt, you would be right there when Caitlin needs help. Plus, if you could put distance between the cribs, you'd have a fighting chance that the crying of one wouldn't wake the other. What do you think?''

"Fine with me," Matt said.

"Caitlin?" Elizabeth said.

Share a hotel suite with Matt? Caitlin thought, her mind racing. Yes, it was a great idea that would enable her to have an extra pair of hands when she had on her mommy hat.

But what about when she was wearing her woman hat?

Matt MacAllister sleeping on the other side of a wall? Matt sitting close by as she fed one baby and he the other? Matt functioning in the role of father as she was performing as a mother, giving the appearance that they were a true-blue family?

No.

No, this wasn't going to work, not at all.

She'd already shared kisses with Matt that had caused her to desire him, want to make love with him, with an intensity like none she'd ever known before.

She'd already daydreamed far too often about what it might be like to be the wife of a man like Matt, see him daily in his role of husband, and as the father to Mackenzie or…no, *and*…Madison.

She was already struggling to keep her confused emotions, her unsettled feelings about Matt at bay. She couldn't share a hotel suite with him. No.

"Excuse me," Bud said, bringing Caitlin from

her near-frantic thoughts. "I couldn't help but overhear what you said, Elizabeth, and I'm afraid I have to get into my doctor mode and object to that plan. Matt, you're on a medical leave of absence from your job. As your physician I have to voice my concerns about you being in a continual high-stress situation that twins produce by the simple fact that there are two of them."

"Now, wait a minute, Bud," Matt said.

"No, no, he's right," Elizabeth agreed. "I didn't know about your personal circumstances, Matt, and you must listen to your doctor." She shook her head. "Not only that, but now that I force my exhausted brain to work, I realize I'm running right over the top of you and Caitlin without thinking the situation through.

"There's a big jump from two people getting along together since the moment they met and that pair sharing a hotel suite, for heaven's sake. I apologize to you both. I'll figure out a better solution to this problem."

"May I have the floor?" Matt asked. "First of all, Bud, taking care of babies is not stressful to me. I'm a MacAllister, remember? I've been toting little ones around since I was a kid.

"I'm not saying that I'm eligible for the Father of the Year Award, because the needs of six-month-old infants are creature comforts, don't require the know-how of what to say to a child who, for example, got slugged by the bully at school. That part is out of my league.

"But help tend to Madison and Mackenzie? I can handle that without getting my blood pressure or ulcer in an uproar." Matt paused. "As far as sharing a suite with Caitlin? It makes more sense than being in rooms with a connecting door because it offers more space with the living room. I say we should go with the plan."

"You've convinced me," Bud said, then shifted his attention to Marsha, who was asking him a question.

"Caitlin?" Elizabeth said. "What do you think about this?"

"What? Oh, I was just mulling over what all of you said, Elizabeth. Matt's already on the other side of a wall, isn't he?"

"Pardon me?" Elizabeth said.

"Never mind. I agree to your plan, Elizabeth. Thank you for your willingness to help, Matt."

"No problem," he said, smiling.

Caitlin switched her attention back to Elizabeth.

"What did you mean, Elizabeth, when you said there was an obstacle at our embassy about the twins?"

"I'm the one who informs the embassy about how many visas we need for the babies to leave China. Since I didn't know about the twins, either, they're only prepared to issue you, a single mother, one entry visa. They will have gotten approval from our INS to do that and they have no authority to issue another visa because of the twins.''

"Oh, my gosh, what are we going to do?'' Caitlin asked.

"Not panic. I don't want to discuss the situation over the telephone with the man in charge, my longtime friend, Brian Hudson. I'd rather wait until I can plead our case in person when we arrive in Guangzhou in a few days. *Don't worry.* We'll find a loophole we can wiggle through somewhere.

"An emergency-need visa could be issued by Brian, but the stickler might be that you're a single woman requesting the INS to allow you to raise two babies at once. No one who is involved in international adoptions is allowed, as you've been told, to use any government-funded programs in the United States such as reduced-rate day care, free medical clinics, food-supplement distribution facilities and so on."

"I see,'' Caitlin said slowly. "So, our INS might view me as financially, or physically, unable to tend to the girls alone.''

Elizabeth nodded. "That's the hurdle we have to get over. But my mighty brain is working on it. Let me do the stewing. You and Matt get ready to pamper and please Mackenzie and Madison.''

Elizabeth paused and reached into her purse. "Oh, I almost forgot. I packed a bottle of nail polish to match my red dress for the big shebang we have the last night in China.'' She handed the bottle to Caitlin. ''This will save at least part of your sanity. Paint one of the babies' toenails or finger-nails red so you can tell them apart.''

''Thank you. What a fantastic idea.''

''Like I said,'' Elizabeth said, tapping one tem-ple with a fingertip. ''Mighty mind. I've got to dash. Dr. Yang is waiting for me to tell him every-one is happy with their match and he can bring the notary over tonight to take care of the next step in the paperwork. Bye for now.''

''Bye,'' Caitlin said absently. She sighed as she stared at the bright bottle of nail polish she was holding. ''Red. I only have one little red dress for the celebration dinner. How can I possibly pick one of the babies over the other to wear it?

''Oh, never mind. What a ridiculous thing to be stewing about when you consider everything I have to be concerned with regarding my daughters. For example, the matter of being one visa short.''

''Elizabeth will tend to that,'' Matt said. ''You go ahead and worry about little red dresses like a dedicated mommy should.''

A flash of anger consumed Caitlin and she glanced quickly around the table, seeing that no one was paying the least bit of attention to her and Matt before she spoke to him again.

''You know, Mr. Sunshine, your laid-back, look-at-the-bright-side, the-glass-is-half-full malarkey is starting to come across as very condescending, especially since I know that your life-is-just-a-bowl-of-cherries spiel is as phony as a three-dollar bill.''

Matt's eyes widened. "What?"

"You heard me," Caitlin said, lifting her chin.

"I'm condescending, and phony as a three-dollar bill?"

"At times." She nodded. "Well, ha to your nothing-bothers-me-so-quit-being-so-neurotic-Caitlin bit, because it is wearing thin.

"You seem to be forgetting that I know you are under Bud's care for stress and the symptoms thereof. You may put on a good front, but you obviously internalize what is bothering you. I may end up with more worry-wrinkle lines than you, but at least I'm healthy because I express my concerns.''

"Well, I'm just sorry to hell and back for attempting to relieve some of your anxieties, Ms. Cunningham,'' Matt said, his jaw tightening. "Okay, try this on for size and see if you like it better. I have a knot of fear in my gut the size of Toledo that Elizabeth won't be able to pull enough strings to get another entry visa, and you'll be forced to leave one those babies behind.

"And, Caitlin? If that happens, a part of my heart will be left here, too, because both of those sweethearts grabbed hold of it and won't let go. I can't even imagine how you, their mother, will feel if it actually happens that way. How's that for gloom and doom? Am I getting it? Do I pass the think-the-worst test?''

Matt shook his head. ''Man, if I ever have a son I'm going to tell him early on that he'll never understand women no matter how hard he tries.''

''Hey, Caitlin and Matt,'' Marsha said from across the table, ''what am I missing over there? You both look angry enough to chew nails. Care to share?''

''No,'' Caitlin and Matt said in unison.

''Marsha,'' Bud said, ''that's your cue to mind your own business.''

''It's perfectly understandable,'' one of the women said, ''that Caitlin and Matt, that any of us, for that matter, might be a bit touchy, edgy, at the moment.

''Between still having some jet lag and being on emotional overload about the babies, our nerves are just shot to blue blazes. Before we came down for dinner I snapped at Sam because he was channel surfing on the television and wasn't in the bathroom taking his shower so he could dress for dinner.''

''The clincher being,'' Sam said, laughing, ''I'd taken my shower and dressed before Mary Ellen did and she'd completely spaced out, didn't register it at all.''

"Right," Mary Ellen said. "I was sitting there going over every second of our time spent with our Holly at the orphanage and was totally unaware of what Sam was doing. So whatever you're fussing about, Caitlin and Matt, try to put it aside, because none of us are operating on all cylinders at the moment."

A flush of embarrassment stained Caitlin's cheeks and she dipped her head to smooth the napkin she'd placed across her lap.

Marsha laughed merrily. "I barked at Bud for putting the diapers in the drawer wrong side up, so they'd have to be flipped over when we use them. I mean, the man should go to jail for such a transgression, people. That was a major crime."

Laughter erupted around the table, with everyone joining in except Caitlin, who was staring off to the left, and Matt, who directed his attention in the opposite direction.

"Well, this was fun," Marsha said, pushing back her chair, "but I'm exhausted. After we're called to gather, and have signed whatever those papers are that Elizabeth was talking about, I'm going to go crawl in bed and finish the novel I packed and read most of on the plane. Good night, all."

The others nodded in agreement to being tired and got to their feet just as a man hurried to the table.

"Caitlin and Matt, please?" he said.

"Yes?" Caitlin said.

"Here are the key packets to the suite," the man said. "Your belongings have been moved for you already and another crib brought in to accommodate your twins."

"Thank you so much," Caitlin said, taking the packets and extending one to Matt without looking at him. "You're most kind."

"We are happy to please. The little girls you fine people are taking to America are lucky babies. Yes, lucky babies. Oh, and Ms. Elizabeth Kane asks that you all come to her room, which is number 419, at seven o'clock to sign documents. Thank you." He turned and bustled away.

"That gives us a half hour," Marsha said. "Bud, let's go into that little store off the lobby and buy some postcards."

"I thought you were exhausted," Bud said, following Marsha as she started away.

"Never too tired to shop, my sweet."

As the group started toward the door, Caitlin got quickly to her feet. "I'm going to the room and make certain that the diapers aren't upside down in the drawer," she said, then hurried after the others.

Matt sat alone at the table, absently drawing lines on the tablecloth with the end of a spoon, a deep frown on his face.

Well, he thought with a sigh, Caitlin could certainly be brutally frank when she got on a rip about something. He was condescending? Phony as a three-dollar bill with his cheerful-to-the-max persona? Talk about a pop in the chops.

But the thing was...she was right.

He had worked very hard over the years to master the technique of staying up, being the MacAllister cheerleader through the various crises the family faced. He'd fine-tuned that ability until it came naturally, just slid into place when he needed it.

And he did it better than any other MacAllister.

Exiting the restaurant, Matt wandered down the block, finally coming to a small park where he slouched onto a bench, crossing his feet at the ankles. He blanked his mind and watched the never-ending maze of bicycles versus automobiles in the street within his view.

Time lost meaning as he sat there aware only of the fact that he had never before felt so alone...and lonely.

After signing the papers as instructed, Caitlin went back to the suite that she and Matt would now be sharing with Mackenzie and Madison, fully expecting him to have returned by then. She intended to apologize to him for her rude and completely unreasonable remarks about him being so damnably cheerful about everything.

When she realized that Matt still hadn't come

upstairs, she sank onto the sofa in the living room and stared at the door, willing him to appear.

Dear heaven, she thought miserably, she hated, just hated, the fact that she and Matt were at odds, had had an honest-to-goodness argument...which was all her fault. She'd been so witchy. What kind of woman hollered at a man because he had a positive outlook toward life? A cuckoo woman, that's what kind.

She didn't blame Matt for not wanting to come to the suite in fear that she'd find some fault with him for...for what? Being willing to lose sleep and put out energy to help her with the babies?

Matt hadn't hesitated for even a heartbeat when he'd agreed to move into this suite and change his share of diapers. Oh, that was so sweet, so dear, so wonderful.

Caitlin's eyes filled with tears and she sniffled.

Matt was as worried as she was about the visa for the second baby, her mind rushed on. He'd said, in so many words, that Mackenzie and Madison had stolen his heart and he would be devastated if one of them had to be left behind. And he'd said that if *he* felt that way, he could only imagine how *she* must feel and...

He was so sensitive. So caring. So assured of his own masculinity that he had no qualms about expressing the fact that tiny babies had turned him into a puddle of putty. Not every man on this earth would be willing to do that. But Matt had.

And she'd told him he was as phony as a three-dollar bill.

"Oh-h-h," Caitlin said, "I can't stand myself. I'm an awful person, just awful. Matt, please come back so I can tell you how sorry I am. Please."

Caitlin sniffled again, stared at the door...and waited.

Just after midnight, Caitlin jerked awake, wondering where on earth she was. In the next three seconds she registered three facts—she had fallen asleep on the sofa in the living room of the suite, she'd been wakened by the sound of Matt opening the door and he was now walking slowly toward her.

Caitlin jumped to her feet, ran across the room, grabbed handfuls of Matt's shirt and looked into his wide-with-shock eyes.

"Oh, Matt," she said, "I'm so sorry for being so nasty. I apologize and I'm begging you to forgive me. To think I was criticizing you for having a bright outlook toward life and... There's no excuse for the terrible things I said to you. None.

"Your willingness to move into this suite and help me with the babies is so giving, so caring, and I should be thanking you a thousand times instead of...

"I don't care if the others were laughing about how crabby everyone is because we're all on emotional overload, that doesn't erase my need to tell you how wrong I was and how very, very sorry I am. Forgive me? Please?"

"I'll forgive you, Caitlin," Matt said, sliding his arms around her back, "on one condition."

"Just name it."

"That you forgive me."

"Forgive you? But you didn't do anything wrong."

"Yes, I did," he said with a sigh. "I've thought about this for hours as I sat in a little park near here. I tried to figure out a way to apologize to you without baring my soul, explain that I... But I finally came to the conclusion that there's no way to make it sensible without doing just that...bare my soul. Let's sit down."

They sat on the sofa, Matt shifting so he could take both of Caitlin's hands in his as he looked directly into her eyes. "Okay, here I go. The tale of woe of Matt MacAllister." He paused. "Caitlin, the MacAllisters are a fantastic family of overachievers who do things to the max and do them with excellence. While I was growing up I continually fell short. I wasn't as smart, wasn't as athletic, wasn't receiving awards for this and that. In my eyes, I didn't measure up."

"Oh, Matt, no, you're—"

"Let me finish, because this isn't easy for me to do."

Caitlin nodded.

"I'm not certain when I started doing it...maybe as far back as high school even, but I adopted a facade of go with the flow, give the appearance of always knowing that everything would be fine no matter what was going on, did my glass-is-half-full routine ad nauseam until I had it perfected. And it worked. I became known in the family as the one to go to with problems because good ole Matt just always seemed to make things better, sent you on your way with a pocketful of sunshine and a belief that all would be well.

"I was better at it than any other MacAllister, finally had something that set me apart, made me top-notch in an arena no one else could come close to matching."

"I understand," Caitlin said softly.

"The thing is," he went on, "I don't know how to turn it off when I should. Every woman I've ever been involved with has eventually complained that I don't really listen to what she is saying, I just wait for her to shut up so I can whip out one of my cheerful clichés and end the discussion.

"I dismissed those criticisms as being female logic I couldn't comprehend, the relationship would end, and I'd go merrily on my way. I finally got tired of arguments on the subject and haven't dated much in the past few years.

"I realized I was in another position to be the best, to measure up to MacAllister standards. My job at the hospital. So I dived into it, buried myself in that place, lived it, breathed it, until I wrecked my health. But what the hell, I was the best at what I did."

"Oh, Matt," Caitlin said, shaking her head.

"But tonight?" he went on. "When you, too, accused me of just glossing over problems, dismissing them with a breezy, corny platitude, I couldn't handle your being angry, disgusted with me, because you mean too much to me, Caitlin. I've never told anyone, not anyone, what I just revealed to you, but I hope that by your knowing you'll find it in your heart to forgive me."

Caitlin searched her mind frantically for the words that would express how deeply touched she was that Matt had shared what he had with her, how very special she felt, how consumed she was with a foreign warmth like nothing she'd ever experienced before. But those words stayed just beyond her reach.

She pulled her hands from beneath his, framed his face, then leaned forward and kissed him, hoping that somehow that kiss would convey her heartfelt emotions.

A groan rumbled in Matt's chest and heat rock-

eted throughout his body. Without breaking the
kiss, he scooped Caitlin onto his lap, wrapped his
arms around her and deepened the kiss, his tongue
delving into the sweet darkness of her mouth.

Caitlin shifted her hands to the back of Matt's
neck, inching her fingers into the depths of his
thick, dark auburn hair.

Matt cared for her, she thought hazily, just as
she cared for him. He'd cared and he'd shared his
innermost secrets with her. It didn't mean, oh no,
that he could, or would, change how he conducted
his life, but the fact that he wanted her to understand him, know who he was and why, was so important, so wondrous.

This night, her mind hummed in a misty place
of passion, was separate and apart from reality or
reason. She didn't want to think, to dwell, about
the right or wrong of her desire for Matt, nor give
one second of thought to the consequences she
would have to face at dawn's light.

All she wanted was Matt MacAllister.

Caitlin broke the kiss and spoke close to Matt's
lips, her voice trembling with need.

"I want you, Matt," she said. "I want to make
love with you. I've never done anything so brazen,
so... What you shared with me means so much and
it belongs to this night, this stolen night out of time.
Tomorrow doesn't exist, not now. There is only
this night."

"Ah, Caitlin," Matt said, his voice raspy. "Are you sure? I couldn't deal with your anger and I sure as hell couldn't handle your having regrets if we—"

"Shh. I promise. No regrets. It's one night. *Our* night."

But what about the nights yet to come? Matt's mind hammered. What about the strange yet awesome...whatever-it-was that was happening between them? Just this night, one night, was theirs? But...

"Do you want me, Matt?" Caitlin whispered. "Do you want this to be *our* night? Together?"

Matt captured Caitlin's lips in a searing kiss, pushing aside the raging questions in his mind, refusing to address them, to give them the power to diminish what he wanted, needed, was going to share, with Caitlin.

He lifted his head, got to his feet with Caitlin held tightly in his arms and crossed the room to one of the bedrooms where a soft light glowed from the lamp on the nightstand.

He registered absently that this was Caitlin's room as he saw her belongings. He set her on her feet next to the bed, swept back the blankets to reveal crisp white sheets, then looked directly into the depths of her fathomless dark eyes, drowning in them, savoring the sensation of somehow flowing into the very essence of who she was, holding nothing of himself back.

"I cherish you," he said, hardly recognizing the gritty sound of his own voice. "I respect and admire you. And, oh, Caitlin, how I want you."

As though standing outside of herself in a dreamy mist, Caitlin watched as her clothes and Matt's seem to float from their bodies, removed by a gentle, invisible hand. She saw herself smile, oh, what a womanly smile, as she drank in the sight of the magnificent man standing before her, and gloried in the heat of his gaze and the approval radiating from his dark brown eyes.

Matt reached up and drew one thumb over her lips, and Caitlin shivered from the sensuous foray, coming back into herself so as not to miss one exquisite moment of this night. Their night. Hers and Matt's.

He lifted her into his arms again, laid her in the center of the bed, then followed her down, catching his weight on one forearm.

They touched with caresses that were as soft as feathers, exploring, discovering, marveling in all that they found, all that would be theirs, given to them in total abandon and received with reverence. Where hands had trailed a heated path, lips followed, igniting flames of passion burning.

When Caitlin could bear no more, when a sob of need caught in her throat and Matt's name whimpered from her lips, he left her only long enough to take steps to protect her, then returned to her, having been gone far, far too long.

Matt moved over her. Into her. Filling her. Then began the rocking rhythm that built in intensity to a pounding force that caused them to cling tightly to each other as they were carried up and away, searching for the summit of their glorious climb, arriving there a heartbeat apart, shattering into a million brightly colored pieces of ecstasy.

"Matt!"

"Caitlin. *Caitlin.*"

They hovered, swaying, memorizing, drifting slowly back, so slowly, gathering the shards of the very essences of their being to become themselves again, whole yet changed, never to be quite the same again.

Matt shifted to Caitlin's side, then nestled her to him, sifting his fingers through her silky hair. She splayed one hand on the moist hair on his muscled chest, feeling his heart regain a normal rhythm beneath her palm.

Then their hands stilled as sleep crept over them like a soft, comforting blanket…and they slept.

Chapter Eight

Caitlin woke the next morning to the sound of water running in the shower in the connecting bathroom between her bedroom and Matt's. She turned her head to look at the pillow next to her that still held a slight indentation of his head.

Memories of the exquisite lovemaking shared with Matt the night before tumbled through her mind, and a soft smile formed on her lips.

She had no regrets about making love with Matt, she mused dreamily. None. It had been a stolen night, a gift to herself that she would always cherish. Granted, her actions had been very out of character, far from her normal behavior, but she didn't care.

Today, on this incredibly unbelievable day, she would officially become a mother of twin baby girls when she and Matt walked out of that orphanage carrying Mackenzie and Madison. Her life would be changed forever, and she could hardly wait to learn what time they were all going to pick up their daughters. Today she put on her mother hat, firmly anchoring it in place.

But last night? She had been wearing her woman hat and...how deliciously naughty...nothing else. She had experienced the most beautiful, awesome lovemaking of her limited experience and she intended to keep the memories of what she'd shared with Matt tucked safely away in a special chamber of her heart.

Her heart, Caitlin thought, frowning. She must remember, must not forget, that her heart belonged to her daughters. She cared for Matt MacAllister, she truly did, but she mustn't allow him to stake a claim on her heart, cause her to lose a part of it to him. No.

Matt had told her his most innermost secrets last night and she was deeply touched that he had.

But knowing what motivated Matt didn't mean that he intended to change his ways.

The water in the shower stopped, then Caitlin could hear Matt moving around the bedroom on the other side of the bathroom. A few minutes later he appeared in the doorway of her bedroom.

"Good morning," he said quietly.

Caitlin smiled. "Hello. Oh, Matt, this is it. The day I become a mother. I still have flashes of not really believing that my dream has come true. Well, I guess I'll believe it when both babies are here in the suite crying at the same time, or whatever. I wonder when we're going to go to the orphanage and—"

"Caitlin," Matt interrupted, no hint of a smile on his face.

"Yes?"

"You promised me that you'd have no regrets about last night," he said, shoving his hands into the pockets of his slacks. "I need...I need to know that you're really all right about what...about...you know."

Caitlin sat up, clutching the sheet to cover her bare breasts.

"I'm fine. I'm keeping my promise. I have no regrets about making love with you, Matt. None. It was beautiful, very special, and I intend to keep the memories of it in a...treasure chest, as corny as that may sound. So, please, don't give another thought to the possibility that I'm sorry about the step we took, because I'm not."

Caitlin flopped back onto the pillow and laughed.

"And today I become a mother of twins. Maybe you should take a peek at the door and see if Elizabeth taped a note to it about what time we're going to the orphanage. No, I suppose she'll call all of us when she knows. But, oh goodness, I hope we don't have to wait all day. You know, not go until this evening. I'll be a basket case if that's how it's scheduled.''

Matt raised one hand in a halting gesture. ''Wait a minute, Caitlin. Could we back up here a tad? I realize you're excited about getting the babies today, but I want to be certain that I'm understanding you correctly.''

''About what?''

''Last night.'' Matt stepped closer and sat down on the bed near the foot. ''What we shared is a distant memory already that you've put in some imaginary treasure chest? In this, the light of the morning after, it's old news and you're thinking only about the babies? Am I getting this right?''

''What you seem to be getting,'' Caitlin said, sitting up again, ''is angry. Why? I'm totally confused by how you're acting, Matt.''

Matt dragged both hands down his face and laughed, a strange sound that held no humor. ''So am I. Confused. You kept your word, you have no regrets, yet a part of me wants to say whoa, don't dust off what we shared so quickly, don't tuck it away, or whatever, because it was so sensational, so... There were emotions intertwined with the physical beauty of it, Caitlin, and I want to know what those emotions are, what they mean, and—''

''I don't. It was a stolen night, Matt. One night. Yes, it was wonderful. Yes, there were emotions involved, but there's no point in examining them closely because…well, there just isn't. This is a new day. This is the day I become a mother and I can't, won't, think about anything other than that. As centered as you are on your job when you're in Ventura, you can surely understand tunnel vision about something.''

"Sure," Matt said, forcing a lightness to his voice as he got to his feet. "I'll get out of your way and let you get ready to rock and roll and become a mommy. Do you want to eat breakfast downstairs, or shall we be indulgent and order room service?''

"Oh, let's go downstairs. Maybe some of the others will be there, or even Elizabeth herself, and we'll learn when we're going to go pick up the babies.''

"Right," Matt said, then turned and walked slowly from the room, pulling the door closed behind him.

Caitlin frowned as she stared at the closed door.

Matt was acting strangely, she thought. It was as though he wanted what they'd shared last night to stay front-row center in their minds.

Good grief, men were complicated creatures, she thought as she left the bed.

In the living room of the suite, Matt stared out one of the windows, not really seeing what was within his view.

What in the hell was the matter with him? he thought, frowning. Caitlin had kept her promise.

But the burning in his gut and the pounding in his head told him that he wasn't handling her behavior well at all. He was stressed to the max, wired, was being assaulted by an amalgam of emotions that were tumbling through his mind, twisting and turning, and driving him nuts.

What did he want from Caitlin? Would he have preferred that she greet him this morning with a dewy-eyed expression and the declaration that because their lovemaking had been so wonderful they must surely be falling in love with each other, had a future together, might even... Gosh, Matt, get married and raise the twins together? They could be a family, the four of them, and live happily ever after in Ventura and—

"No," Matt said, shaking his head.

No, that was *not* what he wanted to hear Caitlin say, because he wasn't ready for that lifestyle, that kind of commitment to hearth, home, babies and forever. Granted, he was going to have to ease up on his hours at the hospital, but his job there was still where he was centered, with room for little else in his existence.

Was this a disgusting male thing? he wondered. An issue of control? Did he want Caitlin to fall at his feet so he could go into testosterone overload and lecture her on how she had to keep her promise, that what they'd shared was over, done, finished, by golly, and no womanly fantasies of a wedding and instant fatherhood had any place in this scenario?

He'd declared the terms and she was to follow them, by damn. One night. No more. End of story. So, knock it off, Caitlin.

Oh, surely he wasn't that shallow, that caught up in flexing his male ego. No, what he was was terribly confused as to why he'd felt such a chilling emptiness, then anger, then hurt, then that hollowness again, as he heard Caitlin chatter on about today and getting the babies, while last night was already tucked away in a treasure chest or some such thing.

"You're losing it, MacAllister," he said aloud. "So find it and get it together. Right now."

By the time Caitlin emerged from the bedroom in blue slacks and a white blouse with blue flowers, Matt had managed to push aside the mangled mess in his mind and shift mental gears to match Caitlin's focus on the twins.

"I wonder," he said, "if we're supposed to take clothes to change the babies into before we leave the orphanage with them? I don't think they can afford to allow anything they have to be given away."

"That's a good thought," Caitlin said, nodding. "But I'm sure Elizabeth will tell us. She's done this so many times she probably can recite all the details without a second thought. Shall we go have some breakfast? I hope there's room in my stomach for food, because right now there are a whole bunch of butterflies fluttering around in there.''

Matt smiled. ''Let's go feed the butterflies.''

About half of the group had already eaten by the time Caitlin and Matt reached the lobby of the hotel. Others, including Marsha and Bud, were heading for the restaurant and Caitlin and Matt joined them.

The conversation at the table during the meal was about babies, rattled nerves, wondering where Elizabeth was, confessions of hardly being able to sleep the night before because of what would transpire on this day, and on and on.

''Have you figured out how you'll decide which of your girls is Madison and which is Mackenzie, Caitlin?'' Marsha said as they all lingered over one more cup of coffee.

Caitlin nodded.

''The caregivers will hand one baby to me, and one to Matt. The one I hold first is Madison.''

''Oh, I like that,'' Marsha said. ''It's as though you were giving birth to them. You know, the one who is born first is Madison. You're very clever, Caitlin.'' She paused and looked at the pitcher on the table. ''Do I want more coffee? No, better not. My nerves are edgy enough.''

It was as though Caitlin was giving birth to the twins, Matt mentally repeated. She wasn't, of course. But Marsha's statement had brought him full circle back to the night he'd met Caitlin and how he had wondered why she was taking the momentous step of adopting a baby from China and becoming a single mother.

It still didn't make much sense. Caitlin was an attractive, intelligent, fun to be with, and…yes, passionate woman that any man would be fortunate to have as his life partner, his soul mate, his wife and the mother of his children. He couldn't believe that Caitlin was here in China to gain the title of mother due to lack of opportunity to marry and have children in the conventional manner.

She skittered around the answer when he'd asked her why she'd chosen this path, had obviously not wished to share it with him.

Man, things were sure lopsided at the moment, he mused. He'd bared his soul to Caitlin last night, told her things about himself that no one, *no one,* knew. Maybe now, or at the exact right moment, she'd be willing to divulge *her* secret.

It was…okay…it was important to him that she trusted him enough to do that. Why? Hell, there was another unanswered question to throw on the towering heap.

"Headache, Matt?" Bud said, bringing Matt from his tangled thoughts. "You're rubbing your forehead."

"What? Oh, no, I'm fine. I had a little headache,

but the caffeine in the coffee is taking care of it. Bring on the babies. I'm ready.''

"Aren't we all?'' Marsha said. "I'll never survive if Elizabeth says we're not picking them up until tonight or something grim like that.''

"I already had that thought,'' Caitlin said. "What if Elizabeth is still snoozing away in her room because she knows nothing is going to happen this morning?''

"Elizabeth,'' Bud said, jumping to his feet and nearly knocking over his chair. "I just caught a glimpse of her in the lobby.''

"Well, my goodness,'' Marsha said, rising. "Don't you dare say another word about me being wound up to the point of ridiculous. You just scared the bejeebers out of all of us.''

Bud laughed. "Sorry about that. I've never been a father before, and today is the day I become one. This, people, is scary stuff.''

"You're going to be a super dad.'' Marsha kissed him on the cheek.

"And I'm going to be a super temporary daddy,'' Matt said, getting to his feet and extending one hand to Caitlin. "Feel free to call on me for advice as needed, Bud.''

Caitlin rose and smiled up at Matt, who was still holding her hand. "On behalf of Madison and Mackenzie who would otherwise be left to my inexperienced mercy,'' she said, "we are eternally grateful for your baby expertise, Mr. MacAllister.''

"I live to serve," Matt said, matching her smile.

They continued to look directly into each other's eyes, suddenly oblivious to those around them. Heat from their clasped hands traveled up and through them, igniting the embers of desire that still glowed from the previous night.

"Um," Marsha said, stifling a giggle, "I hate to interrupt, but are you two ready to go into the lobby and see if Elizabeth is still there and if she has any news?"

"What?" Matt said, dropping Caitlin's hand. "Oh, sure thing."

"Yes, of course," Caitlin said, spinning around. "Off we go."

In the lobby Elizabeth welcomed those emerging from the restaurant, then narrowed her eyes as she looked at the entire group. "Okay, good," she said finally. "Everyone is here. I just spoke with Dr. Yang, and the vans are on the way to pick us up to go to the orphanage. This, as they say, is it."

Excited chatter broke out, gaining volume until Elizabeth raised one hand for silence.

"You'll be bringing your daughters back here in their clothes from the orphanage, but we need to return those clothes later, as they can't be spared. Please have them laundered by the service here in the hotel, then you can bring them to my room when they're fresh and clean again.

"We have no appointments scheduled for today, so you can spend the hours getting to know the newest member of your family. By the time we get back, pitchers of hot water will have been brought to your rooms so that you can make formula.

"I urge you to talk to your daughter as much as possible so she gets used to the sound of your voice, which will have a very different pitch than what she's used to.

"If she fusses if you hold her for any length of time, don't be upset. You must remember that these babies haven't been held a great deal as there simply aren't enough caregivers to go around at the orphanage. Sometimes, though, they come to enjoy being held so much they pitch a fit when you put them down. You just never know. Any questions?"

"Only about a million," Bud said, smiling. "But I guess the bottom line is…we wing it."

Elizabeth laughed. "That's right on the money. Just do the best you can. If you feel there is a medical problem, call my room and we'll take it from there." She glanced over her shoulder. "The vans are here. Is everyone ready to go?"

Caitlin patted her cheeks. "No. Yes. No. Oh, I'm a wreck."

"Me, too," Matt said as the group started across the lobby. "I'm not going to say everything is going to be just fine, because I'm suddenly very intimidated by the image of Madison and Mackenzie in my mind. They're about to run our show, Caitlin. They are definitely going to call the shots."

"Thank you for admitting that you're as nervous

as I am. It's very honest of you, real, and…well, thank you.''

''Honest, real and overdue.'' Matt frowned. ''Wait until my family gets a load of the new me. They'll tell me something gloomy and I'll say, 'Wow, that is really lousy. If I were you I'd be totally bummed.' They'll fall over from shock.''

''At first maybe, but I think they'll come to appreciate the new you as much…well, as much as I do.''

''Time will tell,'' Matt said, then followed Caitlin into one of the vans.

As Caitlin settled in her seat with Matt next to her, she glanced up at him quickly.

Matt really was changing, she mused. He was dropping the phony everything-is-always-rosy facade and expressing his true feelings about things.

If he could make a major adjustment like that after so many years of behaving as he had been, couldn't he also adopt a better balance in his existence between work and his personal life? If he really wanted to, couldn't he own more than one hat?

Caitlin, stop it, she ordered herself and focused on the drive to the orphanage. The streets were the usual maze of bicycles and cars, and it seemed to her that the drive was taking forever. But at last the tall structure came into view and she clutched her hands tightly in her lap.

Inside the building, they once again entered the

elevator in small numbers, then were finally all gathered in the living room where they'd been the day before. Dr. Yang appeared, smiled at everyone, then disappeared again with Elizabeth. Everyone sat statue still, hardly breathing, gazes riveted on the doorway.

"Breathe," Matt whispered in Caitlin's ear. "In. Out. Inhale. Exhale."

A funny little bubble of laughter escaped from Caitlin's lips, then she drew a deep breath.

"What's taking so long?" she said, her voice hushed.

"It's been two minutes and twenty seconds," Matt said, looking at his watch.

"It's been two years and twenty hours," she said, smiling up at him.

"Close, very close. Man, this is torture."

Elizabeth and Dr. Yang suddenly reappeared with a group of caregivers visible behind them.

"Mommies and daddies," Elizabeth said, beaming, "your daughters are ready to go home with you. Bless you all."

Names were called in the same manner as the previous day and precious bundles placed in welcoming arms.

"Caitlin Cunningham," Dr. Yang said.

Caitlin and Matt got to their feet and crossed the room. A caregiver placed a baby in a faded yellow blanket sleeper in Caitlin's arms and another in a very worn pale green sleeper in Matt's. Tears filled

Caitlin's eyes as she looked at the infant who was staring up at her.

"Hello, Madison," she said. "Hello. I'm your mommy." She gazed at the baby Matt was holding. "And you are Mackenzie. I'm your mommy, Mackenzie." She sniffled. "Who is falling apart. Oh, Matt, aren't they wonderful?"

When Matt didn't answer, she looked up at him. Her breath caught and her heart seemed to skip a beat as she saw the tears glistening in Matt's eyes.

"Yeah," he said, his voice gritty. "They're really something. We're holding miracles, Caitlin. Do you realize that? There aren't words to express… Whew.

"Let's go sit down and see if we can get these little ladies to smile at us again. What do you say, Madison and Mackenzie? Do you have smiles to share with your mommy and your…well, I qualify for now. How about a smile for your daddy, too?"

Chapter Nine

At midnight that night *no one* in the Cunningham-
MacAllister suite in the hotel was smiling.

The day had flown by and Caitlin couldn't remember when she'd been so consumed with pure
joy as she and Matt worked side by side tending to
the babies.

She painted Madison's toenails with the bright
red polish, then she and Matt bathed the girls, sup-
porting their backs so they could sit up in the tub
and splash to their heart's content, resulting in the
adults having to change into dry tops.

After consuming bottles down to the last drop of
the formula Caitlin prepared, the babies took long

naps in the cribs that were standing end to end in the living room.

At dinnertime Matt ordered room service, and he and Caitlin ate while watching the twins as they lay on their tummies on a blanket on the floor. They could both hold their heads up and reach for the small toys Caitlin had tucked along the edges of her suitcase.

They played with the babies after dinner until they began to fuss, then changed them into blanket sleepers, fed each a bottle and put them in the cribs, where they fell instantly asleep.

Exhausted but happy, Caitlin bid Matt good-night, then went to her room, leaving the door open halfway so she could be certain to hear the infants if they cried. Matt watched *Casablanca* on television with the characters all speaking Chinese in voice-overs that didn't match the movement of their mouths, which he found strangely entertaining, then headed for bed about ten o'clock.

At 10:32, only seconds apart, both girls began to cry. Caitlin nearly flew into the living room, wearing a full-length white granny nightgown, and Matt came barreling out of his room after pulling on his slacks but not stopping long enough for a shirt.

Diapers were changed. Bottles were offered and firmly refused. The twins wailed on, louder and louder. Caitlin and Matt began to walk the floor, each patting an unhappy bundle on the back and

speaking in soothing tones. Madison and Mackenzie cried, and cried and cried.

At midnight, Caitlin sank onto the sofa with
Mackenzie in her arms and continued to pat her on
the back. Matt settled next to her with a weary sigh,
Madision matching her sister's volume of distress.

"Oh, my gosh," Caitlin said, loud enough to be
heard above the din. "What on earth can be the
matter with them? They were fine all day, Matt.
Are they sick? In pain? How can they cry so hard
for so long and not run out of oxygen? What's
wrong with them?"

"I don't know," he said, rubbing Madison's
back as he propped her against one shoulder.
"Don't even have a clue."

"I thought you were the expert on babies."

"That doesn't include reading their minds."

Caitlin got to her feet again and resumed her
trek, jiggling Mackenzie.

"Please, Mackenzie, don't cry," she said, then
sniffled. "Oh, I feel so helpless, so inadequate.
What if I was home right now and trying to do this
alone? Aren't I supposed to be able to figure out
what's the matter with my own daughters?" Tears
filled her eyes. "Oh, good, Caitlin, now I'll cry
right along with them, which will solve absolutely
nothing."

"I may start wailing any moment myself," Matt
said, chuckling. "This is nuts. We're two intelli-

gent adults and we're reduced to stressed-out mush by two tiny little girls.''

''It's scary, isn't it?'' Caitlin laughed in spite of herself. ''They are really pushing our buttons.''

Matt got up, gripped Madison around the chest and held her high in the air.

''Hello up there,'' he said to the screaming infant. ''Care to share what's wrong with you?''

Madison drew a wobbly breath, then threw up curdled formula all down the front of Matt's bare chest.

''Oh, man,'' Matt shouted, holding Madison straight out in front of him. ''Oh, hell. Oh, yuck.''

Madison kicked her feet, gurgled, then produced a big smile.

''She stopped crying,'' Caitlin said as Mackenzie wailed on. ''She had a tummyache all this time. I bet that's what's wrong with Mackenzie, too. I diluted the formula, but it was still too rich for them. Oh, poor babies.''

''Poor babies?'' Matt said none too quietly as he kept Madison at arm's length. ''What about me? This junk is rank, really gross.''

''True. You smell rather... Never mind. Look at the bright side, which you do so well. At least you aren't wearing a shirt that has to be laundered. You have a very nice build, by the way. Very nice. I don't think I told you that when we... Changing the subject now. Would you consider holding Mackenzie up in the air like you did Madison so she might…''

''Don't even think about it,'' Matt said, narrowing his eyes.

''Just thought I'd ask.''

Mackenzie suddenly burped. It was a loud, very unladylike belch. Then she shivered, sighed and laid her head on Caitlin's shoulder. A blessed silence fell over the room.

Matt laid Madison in her crib and she lifted her feet and grabbed her toes with her tiny hands as she made funny little noises and blew bubbles. Caitlin eased Mackenzie from her shoulder and put her in the other crib. Her lashes drifted down and she fell asleep.

''Don't make any sudden moves,'' Matt said, his voice hushed. ''Okay, Madison, let go of the piggies and take a snooze. That's it. You can play with your toes tomorrow. Good night, good night, good night.''

Madison blinked slowly several times, then drifted off in a peaceful slumber.

Caitlin and Matt peered in the cribs, hardly breathing, then looked at each other.

''What do you think?'' Caitlin whispered.

''I think that if I don't go take a shower in the next three seconds I'm going to lose my dinner, too. Who invented this formula junk?''

Caitlin clamped a hand over her mouth to stifle a laugh.

"It's not funny."

"No, it isn't," Caitlin said, attempting and failing to curb a smile. "But you're the hero in this awful scenario. If you hadn't held Madison up in the air like that she probably wouldn't have... Well, you know."

"Yeah, I know." Matt chuckled. "Well, we survived our first baby crisis together. I'm off to take a shower."

"Matt," Caitlin said as he started across the room. "Thank you. I don't know what I would have done without you. You were wonderful. So patient and...well, all I can say is thank you."

"Hey," he said, turning to face her, "we're in this together. We're a team, Caitlin. There's nothing to thank me for. Okay?"

"Okay," she said, smiling at him warmly.

"By the way, do you always wear a granny gown to bed?"

"What? Oh, no. I sleep in a T-shirt at home. I bought this nightie for the trip because I didn't know how cool the nights would be, and I didn't have room in my suitcase for a robe, and I figured I'd be getting up in the night with the baby...which turned out to be two babies and..." She glanced down at her gown. "It's awful, isn't it?"

"Yes, it is. But not entirely, because I know

what's beneath that grim creation. That gown is sort of like the bulky wrapping on a hidden gift that is actually extremely exquisite. Just thought I'd mention it.''

Matt turned and strode away, disappearing into his bedroom.

"Oh. Well,'' Caitlin said, looking down at her nightie again. "Fancy that.''

She shook her head slightly to dispel the sudden, sensuous pictures in her mind of when both she and Matt had stood naked before the other, then reached out and…

Don't go there, Caitlin.

She went to the cribs where Mackenzie and Madison were sleeping peacefully, covered each with a soft blanket, then went back to the sofa and slouched onto it, staring at the ceiling.

She was exhausted, Caitlin thought. The time spent trying to soothe the crying babies had seemed like an eternity. She'd felt so helpless, so inadequate, so useless.

Caitlin raised her head and wrapped her hands around her elbows.

If it hadn't been for Matt, she thought miserably, her daughters would probably still be crying, suffering from tummyaches caused by the formula she'd prepared.

Two tears slid down Caitlin's cheeks.

What was she going to do without Matt? She

would miss him. He'd become very important to her, very quickly. She cared for him deeply, she was willing to admit that. No, no, she wasn't in love with him, wouldn't be so foolish as to lose her heart to a man who was centered so completely on his career. She'd had enough pain in her life due to a man like that. But she *did* care for him very, very much.

When she and the babies were back in Ventura, they'd get into a workable routine, she mentally rambled on. She'd learn how to take care of them to the best of her ability and hope and pray that would be good enough. If they both cried at the same time like tonight she'd just…she'd just weep right along with them and wait for a fairy godmother to show up, wave her wand and fix whatever was wrong with Madison and Mackenzie.

Two more tears slid down Caitlin's face, but she ignored them.

Go to bed, she ordered herself. Get some sleep, much-needed sleep, while the babies were doing the same. But she didn't seem to have the energy to move, to get to her feet, shuffle into the bedroom and crawl into bed. All she was capable of doing at the moment was just sit and cry.

"Hey," Matt said.

Caitlin jerked at the sudden sound of Matt's voice, then dashed the tears from her cheeks as he sat down next to her and encircled her shoulders with one arm.

"Tears?" he said gently.

"I...I'm just tired, and I guess I'm frightened, too, Matt, because I'm so overwhelmed right now with the realization of what a momentous task I've taken on. I failed miserably tonight. I couldn't soothe or comfort them, couldn't figure out what was wrong with them or... They'd still be crying if I'd been taking care of them alone, I just know they would be."

"And you're projecting that into when you'll be home with them in Ventura."

Caitlin nodded.

"Your fears are understandable, but what I can't get a handle on is why you were determined to become a single mother in the first place."

"You're a perfect example of why I made the decision I did."

"What do you mean?"

"Suppose, just pretend for a moment that you and I fell in love and got married. This is hypothetical, of course, but you're a classic case, so I'm using you to explain my position."

"Mmm," Matt said, frowning.

"The truth of the matter would be," Caitlin went on, "that you really wouldn't be married to me but to your job, your chosen career. I lived that nightmare, Matt, and I won't do it again, nor will I allow Mackenzie and Madison to be subjected to it.''

''But...''

Caitlin got to her feet, then turned to look at Matt, wrapping her hands around her elbows.

''I won't drag the pain of my past into my present and future, relive that agony, that chilling loneliness, helplessness.'' Tears filled Caitlin's eyes and threatened to spill onto her pale cheeks. ''I won't.''

''What are you talking about?'' Matt said, staring at her intently.

''My father was a doctor, a highly respected heart surgeon. People came from across the country, the world, to be his patient, to receive his expertise.

''Oh, God, I remember staring out the window waiting, waiting for him to come home to celebrate my birthday, or to go to the school play I was in, or to take me to the zoo like he promised...but he didn't come. Time after time he didn't come because one of his patients needed him and they were always more important than me, than my mother.

''And my mother? I can still see her, Matt, in her pretty, new dress, standing by the door waiting for my father to arrive so they could go out to celebrate their anniversary, or *her* birthday, or because he'd promised her that this time nothing would keep him from being there for her. But he didn't come.

"I'd hear her, Matt," Caitlin said, weeping openly, "crying behind her closed bedroom door, her heart broken yet again, just as mine was so many, many times. We never came first with him. His patients were more important. His almighty career, reputation, the power and prestige, came before his wife and child.

"He died of a heart attack when I was sixteen and I didn't even cry. Why would I? He was a stranger I hardly knew. A man who was gone before I got up in the morning and didn't return home until I was sound asleep at night. He was a shadowy figure who broke promises, made me cry, made my mother weep as he chipped away at her heart and her love for him until there was nothing left.

"Oh, I knew that all men aren't like my father, but every man I've dated put his career at the top of the list of importance."

"Ah, Caitlin."

"That's why I decided to become a single mother and adopt my child from China. Oh, sure, I daydreamed about finding a man who would put me, his children, first, have the proper balance in his existence between work and family, but I never found him. I still haven't. But I vowed I wouldn't be cheated out of my dream of being a mother, too.''

"I...I don't know what to say to you.''

"There's nothing to say, nothing,'' she said, shaking her head. "I've got to get some sleep. I'm tired, so very tired. Good night, Matt. Thank... thank you again for your help with the babies.''

Caitlin hurried to her bedroom.

Matt drew a deep breath, let it out slowly, then rose and went to the cribs. He smoothed the blankets on the sleeping babies, then dragged both hands down his face.

Well, he thought, as they said in courtrooms, the question was asked and answered. He now knew Caitlin's secret, the reason she had been determined to become a single mother. She'd even used him as the perfect example of the type of career-oriented man she would never marry, nor allow to be a father to her daughters.

Caitlin had looked so...so sad as she'd poured out her heart to him. He'd wanted to take her into his arms, comfort her, tell her that not all men were like her father, that he, Matt MacAllister wasn't. But he'd been frozen in place, words of assurance beyond his reach.

Visions of arriving late time after time at family functions had flashed before his mind's eye, as well as when he hadn't gotten there at all because he was still tied up at the hospital. He'd seen himself finally showing up, then being so exhausted he'd added nothing to the conversations taking place.

But how did a man become the very best in his chosen career without that kind of devotion to duty? How did he continue to meet the high MacAllister standards?

Matt sighed and a few minutes later was in bed, hoping sleep would claim him quickly and give him a reprieve from the cacophony of voices in his beleaguered mind.

His thoughts floated back to the screaming crisis of earlier with Mackenzie and Madison. He'd been focused totally on Caitlin and the unhappy babies, had given the situation his complete concentration just as he did when he was working at Mercy Hospital. But how did a man give one hundred percent of himself to two completely different parts of his life?

That was the question asked and not yet answered.

But tonight? he thought, smiling into the darkness. Tonight he'd been right in there pitching with those little munchkins. Had stood by Caitlin's side as an equal partner.

His contribution to the crisis had been important, it mattered, and he'd even solved the dilemma by accident. Granted, having a six-month-old baby throw up all over him wasn't a thrill a minute, but it had done the trick and he'd felt about ten feet tall. Smelly but victorious.

He'd given Caitlin a hard time about her granny gown, he mentally rambled on, but the truth of the matter was she looked adorable, made him want to just scoop her into his arms and kiss her until they both couldn't breathe. Plus, there was the fact, as he'd told her, that he knew how exquisitely feminine she was beneath those endless folds of material.

Ah, yes, this had been a night to remember. A night that made him realize what it would be like when he got married, became a husband and father. But when would that be? When would he figure out how to balance two worlds so that no one got shortchanged? Other MacAllisters seemed to be able to do it, so what was the secret formula? What if he was never able to get a handle on it? God, what a bleak picture of his future that thought painted.

Well, forget it for now. He was in China with Caitlin and those precious babies and they had his full attention. He'd zero in on the big picture of his life when he got home.

But, damn it, he had a big enough challenge facing him when he returned to Ventura. He had to continue to excel at his job, be the best, without further damaging his health. That was going to take his full concentration as he learned to delegate, cut back on his hours a little…okay, more than a little…while still maintaining his reputation as being top-notch, one of the leaders in his field.

"Enough of this," Matt said. "I'm just going in mental circles here. Mind…shut up."

Minutes later blessed slumber claimed him.

The following four days and nights in Nanjing flew by as the new families formalized their adoptions. The pending issue of the visa for Caitlin's second baby rose to the fore again on the day the passport photographs were taken, but Elizabeth told her to stay calm, have pictures done of both girls and they'd tackle the visa situation when they arrived in Guangzhou.

Once the official business was taken care of for the day, they went on wonderful sightseeing trips, with the babies taking it all in stride. Everyone scurried to buy more and more film as they attempted to record everything they were experiencing.

Caitlin's adjustments in Madison and Mackenzie's formula resulted in the girls eagerly devouring their bottles with no tummyaches following. They woke once in the night to eat and Matt and Caitlin got up together and fed them, chatting quietly as they each held a hungry bundle about what they had seen and done that day.

It was memory-making fun. It was smiles and

laughter, sunny skies and perfect weather. It was buying so many souvenirs that Elizabeth made arrangements with the hotel to help the shoppers box up their purchases and mail them to their addresses in Ventura. It was people who had dreamed of being parents for so long glorying in their new roles, with Bud declaring that this father business was even better than he'd ever imagined it would be.

It was Caitlin and Matt spending endless hours together with the twins. And each night it became more and more difficult to leave the other and go to their own rooms, where they tossed and turned until sleep claimed them.

They all shared a delicious dinner at a fancy restaurant on the last night in Nanjing, raising their glasses in a toast to the fact that the adoptions were final, their daughters were officially theirs... forever.

The next day they flew to Guangzhou and checked into the White Swan Hotel, which was like something out of a fairy tale, complete with a towering waterfall that flowed from three stories up in the center of the enormous lobby.

The suite assigned to Caitlin and Matt was even larger than the one they'd shared in Nanjing. By unspoken agreement they left both cribs in the living room despite the fact that a crying baby woke her sister. Neither Caitlin nor Matt wished to give up the time they spent together in the middle of the night sitting and feeding the girls. Besides, Caitlin rationalized, it was easier to have the twins on the same schedule. Once she was home and tackling their care alone, she'd work out a system to assure that each of her daughters was held in equal allotments of time.

On the morning of the third day in Guangzhou, Elizabeth found Caitlin, Matt and the twins as they were emerging from the dining room after breakfast.

"Well, this is it," Elizabeth said. "We have an appointment with Brian Hudson, who issues the visas, in half an hour. We can walk from here and it takes about fifteen minutes. Do you want to go to your room and change the babies before we leave?"

Caitlin nodded. "Yes, and we'll bring along a bottle for each." She sighed. "Oh, I don't want to go. I've been burying my head in the sand, pretending the problem of the second visa doesn't exist. What if... No, I can't bear the thought. No."

"We'll figure out something," Elizabeth said, unable to produce a smile. "Hurry along now. I'll wait for you down here."

In the suite Caitlin and Matt changed the babbling babies' diapers, then Matt put them in their cribs while Caitlin packed some supplies in a tote bag. After dropping bibs three times before she could tuck them in the bag, she sank onto the sofa.

"I'm terrified, Matt," she said, struggling against threatening tears.

"Me, too. Come on, Caitlin, we have to go downstairs. We're in enough trouble without being late for the appointment."

"Could you do your sunshine thing?" she asked, looking up at him. "Tell me that everything is going to work out just fine, and I shouldn't worry, and every glass you ever met in your entire life was half-full?"

Matt chuckled. "No."

"Oh."

Brian Hudson was a portly gentlemen in his early sixties, who greeted Elizabeth with a hug and smiled warmly at Caitlin and Matt and the twins. His smile, however, was replaced by a deep frown as Elizabeth explained the situation surrounding Caitlin and the babies. He tossed his pen on the large desk he sat behind and leaned back in a worn and creaking leather chair.

"Elizabeth, you know I have no authority to issue a second visa. I can only document the number that the INS is aware of for your group. Caitlin was approved, as a single mother, to adopt one child. The INS felt she had the financial, physical and emotional ability to do that. But a single woman suddenly saying she's adopting two babies?''

Brian shook his head. ''She's not allowed to use any government-funded agencies for assistance or...'' He looked at the girls who were being held by Caitlin and Matt. ''They sure are cute, aren't they? The thought of separating them, leaving one behind is...I don't have a magic solution to pull out of a hat like a rabbit.''

''I can't leave one of my babies behind. I won't. They're my daughters and I love them, don't you understand? Oh, please, there has to be a way to solve this.''

''We're not getting on a plane without both of these babies,'' Matt said, narrowing his eyes.

''I'm not the bad guy here.'' Brian threw up his hands. ''These aren't *my* rules, but I have to follow them. If I did issue a visa without INS approval it wouldn't be valid.''

''But,'' Caitlin said.

''Everyone, calm down,'' Elizabeth said firmly. ''Now, Brian, listen to me. Remember five years ago when we discovered at the last minute that one of our couples in the group who had adopted a baby girl was told in a casual remark by a caregiver that their daughter had a four-year-old brother still at the orphanage who was blind?''

''Oh, yes.'' Brian chuckled. ''That was quite an experience once you got the bee in your bonnet to help those folks get that boy. I think we wore out our fax machine sending documents to the INS assuring them that the couple would finance all special training for the youngster, were emotionally prepared to deal with his handicap and... You were awesome in action, my friend.''

''And the INS allowed you to issue the second visa,'' Elizabeth said, leaning forward in her chair. ''My couple adopted both of those kids and they all flew home at the same time.''

''So they did,'' Brian said, nodding. ''Then I took a very long nap.'' He paused and narrowed his eyes. ''Okay, Elizabeth Kane, what sneaky little plan do you have up your sleeve *this* time?''

''Elizabeth?'' Caitlin asked, her heart starting to race.

Matt popped two antacid tablets in his mouth.

''All right,'' Elizabeth said. ''Caitlin's application to adopt one child as a single mother was approved months ago, months and months ago. But, you see, since then her circumstances have changed.''

''Is that a fact?'' Brian smiled and shook his head. ''And just what has occurred in Ms. Cunningham's life that would make her unquestionably eligible to be the mother of twins?''

Elizabeth beamed. ''Caitlin got married. She is now—ta-da—Mrs. Matt MacAllister.''

Chapter Ten

Brian Hudson, Caitlin thought, from what seemed like a faraway place, was wearing a very attractive tie. He no doubt knew where the best places were to shop in Guangzhou due to the fact that he lived here. Then again, maybe he had family in the United States and someone had sent him the tie for his birthday or...

She had gotten married and was now Mrs. Matt MacAllister?

"What?" Caitlin said in a squeaky little voice that she immediately decided couldn't be hers.

"Could you," Matt said, staring into space. "Could you run that by me again? I don't believe I heard you correctly."

"Everyone just stay calm," Elizabeth said, patting the air with flattened hands. "It's brilliant. It will work. Brian, you know as well as I do that the people at the INS who handle international adoptions are just as thrilled about these kids getting a chance at a decent life as we are. I know that because I've spoken to them personally."

Brian laced his fingers over his ample stomach and nodded, an expression of deep concentration on his face.

"They have to follow the rules and regs regarding paperwork," Elizabeth rushed on, "so we supply them with paperwork. You're authorized to marry people, so you perform the ceremony for Caitlin and Matt.

"Then you fax the INS a letter stating that you're simply updating Caitlin's file and informing them that she is no longer a single woman, because she has a husband. It isn't necessary to reveal how long she has had said husband.

"You also tell them that due to a glitch in Beijing, the fact that Caitlin—oh, and Matt—were matched with twins didn't come to light until we got here, but that's fine because they're a couple, wife and husband, mom and dad, and blah, blah, blah, and perfectly capable of taking care of the girls on all levels…physically, financially and emotionally."

Brian nodded. "It could work."

"It *would* work," Elizabeth said. "You request permission to issue another visa and we're home free. There. That's settled. My goodness, I amaze myself sometimes when my mighty mind kicks into action."

"Excuse me," Caitlin said, raising one finger. "This…um…wedding ceremony that Mr. Hudson would perform…is it legal and binding in the United States, or only official here in China?"

"Oh, it's for real everywhere," Elizabeth said. "Brian's status at the consulate gives him the power to do all kinds of nifty things. You and Matt can have the marriage quietly annulled once you return home, of course, but we're concentrating on getting that second visa and this is the way to do it.

"We're not breaking the law, we're just wiggling around it…sort of. The INS will be happy because they'll have the paperwork they need, and you get to take both girls with you when you leave." Elizabeth paused. "Matt? Any comments?"

"I'm just wondering if Bud would agree to be my best man."

Caitlin's head snapped around and her mouth dropped open for a moment as she stared at Matt. "That's what's on your mind?" she said, nearly shrieking. "Whether Bud will stand up with you? Matt, these people are talking about us getting mar-

ried. As in…I do, and in sickness and health, and
better or worse, until we croak and…'' She pressed
one hand on her flushed forehead. ''I'm losing it.
But, dear heaven, this is insane.''

''This,'' Matt said firmly, ''is the solution to our
problem. Elizabeth, you are to be commended for
coming up with this plan.''

''Thank you,'' she said, obviously pleased with
herself. ''I admit that I'm rather proud of myself.''

''But,'' Caitlin said, then mentally threw up her
hands.

''Having Marsha and Bud as your witnesses is
fine,'' Elizabeth said, ''but we won't tell the rest
of the group what has taken place. We're not breaking rules, we're just bending them, but the fewer
people that know the better.''

''No problem,'' Matt said.

''But,'' Caitlin started again, then realized she
was not capable of stringing words together to
make a coherent sentence.

''Well,'' Brian said, getting to his feet, ''let's do
the deed. You don't have that many days left here
in Guangzhou, and we need that permission to issue another visa pronto. The sooner I can fax them
the new data the better. I'll go get the forms needed
so I can marry you folks.''

''Now?'' Caitlin said, jumping to her feet and
startling Madison, who began to cry.

"The sooner the better," Brian said, then left the room.

"I'll call the hotel and see if Bud and Marsha are there," Elizabeth said, rising. "If they went sight-seeing we'll just have to settle for witnesses from the staff here. I'll go find a phone."

As Elizabeth hurried from the room, Caitlin soothed Madison, then placed her in a playpen that had been provided for the little ones. Matt laid Mackenzie on her tummy next to her sister. Caitlin sank back onto her chair as her trembling legs refused to hold her for another moment. She glared at Matt.

"Why are you so calm about this?"

Matt smiled. "My doctor told me that stress is bad for my health."

Caitlin leaned toward him. "Read my lips. You are getting married. Today. To me."

"Yep," he said, nodding. "That's what's happening, by golly. Elizabeth is something, isn't she? Think about it, Caitlin. We don't have to face the heartbreak of leaving one of the girls behind. God, I can't even imagine that scenario, I really can't. But Mackenzie and Madison are both going home. You should be smiling, not looking like the dentist just announced that you need six root canals."

"Yes," Caitlin said slowly. "Yes, of course, you're right. I was just so stunned by... But my focus should be on the babies, and the fact that everything is going to be fine, and Mr. Hudson will issue the visa and… We'll just cancel the marriage after we get back to Ventura. Sure. Okay.''

No, Matt thought suddenly. Cancel the marriage? Erase it? Pretend it never happened? Caitlin was certainly quick to get that laid out on the table. Hello, husband. Goodbye, husband. Thanks for your help. Have a nice life. Buzz off, MacAllister.

What if he didn't want to cancel the marriage, as Caitlin put it? He was…oh, God, he was in love with this woman, and he loved those babies, and once Brian did his thing they would be a family. An honest-to-goodness family. What if he didn't want to be erased?

Whoa, Matt thought, getting to his feet and beginning to pace. Where was his mind going? Yes, he loved Caitlin, had actually fallen in love with her. But marry her? Now? All that hearth-and-home stuff was for later when he figured out how to be the best in two arenas and…

But later, somewhere in the future, Caitlin might have married someone else, fallen in love and vowed to stay by that man's side until death parted them. Mackenzie and Madison would have a father who wouldn't be him.

Somewhere in the future he would still be alone and so damn lonely it sent chills down his spine just thinking about it.

Matt stopped his trek and looked at Caitlin, who

was staring at her hands that were clutched tightly in her lap.

He was going to marry the woman he loved, Matt thought. The timing was off from his master plan but so be it. He'd have some major adjustments to make in his work schedule, but he'd deal with that…somehow.

Matt frowned.

What he should be zeroing in on was the dismal fact that while he was about to marry the woman he loved, the woman he was about to marry didn't love him. She was already talking about canceling him out of her life before they'd even tied the knot. Just undo the knot and ship him off to Buffalo. Hell.

Matt shoved his hands in his pockets and resumed pacing.

Married, Caitlin thought, with a weary sigh. This should be such a happy day in her life, but the reality of the situation could not be ignored. The wedding ceremony that Brian Hudson would perform was a sham, a means to an end, which would guarantee that both of her daughters could go home to Ventura.

It was a marriage of convenience, per se, which was about as romantic as stale bread.

Focus, Caitlin, she ordered herself. She must concentrate on the purpose of this marriage, the fact that without it, she would be forced to leave one of her precious daughters behind when she left, and that was totally unacceptable.

She'd blank her mind during the necessary ceremony, repeat her lines by rote, knowing they meant nothing, not really. She could only hope that Brian Hudson whizzed through the exchanging of vows and got it over with as quickly as possible before she burst into depressed tears.

If she did think at all it would be about Mackenzie and Madison and the realization that she was doing this for them and for herself when she was wearing her mother hat. It had absolutely nothing to do with her woman hat. Nothing.

Caitlin's tormented thoughts were interrupted by Elizabeth and Brian reentering the room followed by a breathless Marsha and Bud. Caitlin got to her feet and was immediately hugged by a beaming Marsha.

"Isn't this exciting?" Marsha said. "It's awesome, it's wonderful, it's—"

"It doesn't mean a thing. This wedding ceremony, Matt and I getting married, is for the single purpose of making it possible to get the second visa, Marsha. It's a temporary situation that will be undone…for lack of a better word…once we return to Ventura."

Marsha grabbed Caitlin's arm and hauled her to the end of the room. "But you and Matt care for each other," Marsha said, her voice hushed. "More than care, from what I've witnessed going on between the two of you. Personally I think you two are in love with each other.''

"Don't be silly,'' Caitlin said, averting her gaze from Marsha's. ''We haven't even known each other very long.''

"What difference does that make? When you meet your soul mate—blam—that's it. When you two are together there is so much...something... crackling through the air between you it's a wonder there aren't visible flames dancing around.''

"Lust is not love,'' Caitlin said, lifting her chin. ''You're misinterpreting what you're seeing. I care for Matt. I'll admit that. But I would never marry a man who is as dedicated to his career as he is, no matter how I felt about him. Which is not to say that how I feel about him is of any great significance at this point in time. Am I making myself clear?''

"Honey, you and Matt have been making yourselves clear from the get-go.''

"Darn it, Marsha, I—''

"Are we ready to proceed?'' Brian said.

No, Caitlin thought.

"Yes,'' she said.

Elizabeth peered into the playpen. ''The kiddies are going to miss the whole shebang. They're sound asleep.''

"Rings," Bud said. "I'm the best man. I'm supposed to hand Matt a ring to put on Caitlin's finger."

Caitlin crossed the room with Marsha right behind her.

"Forget about rings, Bud," Caitlin said. "This is not a wedding in the normal sense of the word. Right, Matt?"

Matt didn't answer for so long that Caitlin looked at him questioningly.

"Matt?"

"Oh. Right. This is a marriage—"

"Of convenience, to use a Victorian term. We say 'I do' so Mr. Hudson can say, 'I do hereby issue a second visa.' End of story."

"I don't think so," Marsha said in a singsong voice.

Caitlin glared at her, then directed her attention to Brian.

"Shall we proceed?" she said. Before she started to cry and couldn't stop, because she was hating this, really hating this. "Please?"

"Certainly," Brian said.

Everyone took their places and Brian opened a book, flipping through the pages.

"Okay, here it is," he said. "We are gathered here today to unite this man and this woman in holy matrimony. Do you, Matt, take Caitlin to be your lawfully wedded wife, to love her, cherish her, through…''

Caitlin forced herself to tune out what Brian was saying as tears misted her eyes.

She couldn't do this, she thought frantically. Yes, she could. She had to.

''I do,'' Matt said, his voice ringing with conviction that caused everyone in the room to stare at him.

''Thought so,'' Marsha said.

''Do you, Caitlin,'' Brian went on, ''take Matt to be your…''

Two tears slid down Caitlin's pale cheeks and Elizabeth pressed a tissue into Caitlin's hand. Matt encircled her shoulders with one arm and eased her close to his side.

''Caitlin?'' Brian said.

''What?'' she said, dabbing at her nose. ''Oh. Yes. I do.''

''By the power invested in me,'' Brian boomed, ''I now pronounce you husband and wife.''

Forever, Matt thought fiercely. There were a million hurdles blocking the path to that forever but somehow, somehow, he'd plow them down, one by one. He was in love with Caitlin and she was now his wife. Oh, man, that sounded so terrific. And he was Mackenzie and Madison's daddy and… He was about to begin a battle for his future happiness, for his very life…with Caitlin. The war was on and he intended to win…somehow.

"Temporary wife," Caitlin said.

"Shh," Matt said. "That's not written in the book."

"You may kiss the bride," Brian said.

"Oh, well, that isn't necessary," Caitlin said, "because…"

Matt framed Caitlin's face with his hands, then claimed her mouth in a kiss that was so soft, so gentle, so reverent that fresh tears spilled onto her cheeks.

"Oh-h-h," Marsha said. "I just love weddings." She sniffled. "This is so romantic, so… Oh-h-h."

Matt lifted his head and smiled at Caitlin.

"Hello, Mrs. MacAllister," he said.

The sudden sound of a crying baby saved Caitlin from having to respond to her new title.

"That's Madison," she and Matt said in unison.

"Well, well, well," Elizabeth said, "we know which baby is crying without looking, do we? That's a true sign of a dedicated mommy and daddy. I'd bet that you both can tell them apart by now, too, without looking for the fingernail polish on tiny toes."

"Sure can," Matt said.

"Are we finished here?" Caitlin said, her voice quivering.

"There are papers to sign," Brian said. "Caitlin,

since the adoption documents show the twins with the last name of Cunningham, sign the marriage certificate as Caitlin Cunningham. The INS won't blink an eye at that. They'll just assume you're an eccentric couple who gave the babies their mother's name and the mother kept her name and…whatever. My cover letter will assure them that you all are, indeed, the MacAllister family.''

Amen, Matt thought. Forever.

For now, Caitlin thought miserably. Only for a tick of time.

In a foggy blur, Caitlin signed her name where Brian indicated, then went to the playpen and lifted a still-crying Madison into her arms. Mackenzie slept on.

''Marsha, Bud,'' Matt said after signing the documents, ''are you going back to the hotel? Can you help Caitlin with the babies? I have something I need to do.''

''Sure,'' Marsha said. ''We left Grace with Jane and Bill because our sweetie was due to eat, then sleep. We can tote as many babies as need toting.''

''We only have two,'' Matt said, laughing. ''Which is quite enough…for now.''

''For now?'' Marsha raised her eyebrows.

''Figure of speech, I'm sure,'' Caitlin said quickly. ''Mr. Hudson, I can't begin to thank you for all you're doing to assure that the twins will be able to stay together. I hope you know how grateful—''

"We are," Matt interjected, reaching out and pumping Brian's hand. "On behalf of all members of the newly created MacAllister family I sincerely thank you, sir."

"My pleasure. Elizabeth, I'll be in touch and keep you informed as to how we're doing with the flurry of faxes that is about to start between here and the INS in the States. The minute I receive permission to issue that second visa I'll call you at the hotel."

"Splendid," Elizabeth said, then kissed Brian on the cheek. "You're a dear for doing this."

"No, I just know better than to argue with you when you get a bee in your bonnet, Elizabeth. Well, best of luck to all of you."

"I'm gone," Matt said. "I'll see you back at the hotel, Mrs. MacAllister." He strode from the room.

"Stop calling me that," Caitlin said, shaking her head.

"Why?" Marsha said, taking Madison from Caitlin's arms. "That's who you are now, Caitlin."

"She's also exhausted," Bud said. "That's the doctor part of me talking. Caitlin, you are stressed to the max. I hereby prescribe a nap for you. Marsha and I will tend to your girls for the next two hours. You are to march yourself back to the hotel and stretch out on the bed."

"Oh, but—"

"Go," Bud said, pointing to the door.

"Thank you," Caitlin said, her shoulders slumping with fatigue. "I feel as though I need to concentrate just to put one foot in front of the other." She glanced around the room. "This was quite an experience. I—" A soft cry interrupted her. "Mackenzie is awake."

"I'll get her," Bud said. "Ah, there's the tote bag with all the treasures needed to keep little ladies fed and dry. Goodbye, Caitlin."

"Thank you. I'm sure I'll be as good as new after I rest a bit. I don't know why I'm so exhausted, so drained."

"Well, it's not every day that a person gets married, you know," Marsha said, then cringed when she saw Caitlin's stricken expression. "Forget I said that. Go take a nap."

With one last long look at Mackenzie and Madison, Caitlin left the room, then the building. She walked slowly along the tree-lined sidewalk, oblivious to the people around her and the usual battle of bicycles versus cars taking place on the road.

Oh, my, she thought. She was doing her half-and-half thing again. Part of her was so thankful, so relieved that a solution had been found regarding the second visa.

But it was that very solution that was causing her to feel so...so sad. A woman's wedding day, the ceremony where sacred vows were exchanged with the man of her heart, a pledge made to stand side by side until death parted them, should be one of the happiest days of her life.

But she was miserable.

Her marriage to Matt was nothing more than a charade. That was about the crummiest wedding day imaginable.

Focus on Mackenzie and Madison, Caitlin told herself over and over like a mantra.

When she finally reached the hotel suite, she slipped off her shoes and stretched out on the bed in her room.

She wished she could pour out her tale of woe to her mother, Caitlin thought, but that wouldn't be fair because her mother was worried enough about Paulo's health without having a weeping daughter calling long distance.

No, she'd share the news of the twins after returning safely to Ventura. Maybe she'd never tell her mother about having been Matt's wife to accomplish the goal of obtaining the second visa. What was the point of sharing that newsflash when the marriage would be over as quickly as the paperwork could be completed?

Her mother didn't need to know that along with coming home from China with two beautiful daughters instead of one, she'd also arrived back

in Ventura with a heart that was struggling frantically not to fall in love with the wrong man, a man
who would shatter that heart into a million pieces
that could never be put back together again.

Chapter Eleven

When Matt returned to the hotel he found a note from Bud and Marsha taped to the door of the suite. They were going on a sight-seeing tour, they said, and with the help of others in the group were taking Mackenzie and Madison along for the fun. They would probably be gone longer than the originally planned two hours, and Caitlin and Matt were not to worry about the twins.

"Bless you," Matt said, removing the paper. "I need all the time I can get for this."

He entered the suite, then frowned when he saw that Caitlin was not in the living room. He went to the open doorway of her bedroom and stopped, his gaze riveted on Caitlin where she lay sleeping. He set the bag he was carrying on a chair and went to the side of the bed, drinking in the sight of...

"My wife," he whispered.

And, oh, God, how he loved her.

While he'd been wandering the streets of Guangzhou after leaving the consulate, he'd realized that people were staring at the tall American who was striding along the sidewalk grinning like an idiot.

But he couldn't help smiling as the sense of pure joy, of being complete, whole, overflowed to show itself on his face. He was married to the woman he loved, the only woman he had ever, would ever love.

So, okay, maybe she didn't love him...not yet. But the kernel of caring was there within Caitlin, he just knew it was. If she'd give it a chance to grow, blossom into the wondrous love he felt for her, they could have a together together with their fantastic little girls.

Ah, Caitlin, Matt thought, still gazing at her. Give me a chance. Give *us* a chance. Please, my love.

As if sensing his presence, Caitlin stirred, then opened her eyes. Still foggy from her deep sleep, she registered only the fact that Matt was there. The man she must *not* fall in love with but who was, just for now, her husband.

"Hi," Matt said quietly. "Marsha and Bud took

the twins on a sight-seeing tour. I need to talk to you, Caitlin. Are you awake enough to listen to what I have to say?''

Caitlin stared at Matt for a moment. ''All I know right now,'' she finally said, her voice slightly husky with sleep, ''is that this is our wedding day. This is another one of those stolen times apart from reality.'' She lifted her arms toward Matt. ''Just say it once more, Matt. Call me Mrs. MacAllister, then make love to me, your wife.''

''But I want to tell you that I—''

''Shh. No. Just say, 'Hello, Mrs. MacAllister.'''

A bolt of heated desire rocketed through Matt and the heartfelt words, the declaration of his love that he wanted Caitlin to hear floated into oblivion as his want of her consumed him.

As she slid off the bed to stand before him and remove her clothes, he tore at his own, tossing them to the floor, then reaching for her eagerly because she was just too far away.

They tumbled onto the bed, their lips meeting in a searing kiss. Matt finally raised his head to look directly into Caitlin's eyes.

''Hello, Mrs. MacAllister,'' he said, his voice gritty with passion.

''Hello, Mr. MacAllister,'' she whispered.

Matt felt as though his heart would burst with love as he kissed her again, gently this time, with a sense of awe and wonder at how quickly and intensely he'd fallen in love with this exquisite woman. His wife.

His wife, his mind sang, as though a chorus of angels was announcing it to the world.

They'd made love before, but this, he knew, was special and new, the consummating of their marriage, the sealing of the bond, the commitment to forever as husband and wife.

Caitlin loved him, *she did,* because she had wanted to hear him say, "Hello, Mrs. Mac-Allister," have those words entwine with her reply of "Hello, Mr. MacAllister," words that warmed his heart, his mind, his very soul.

Caitlin sank her fingers into Matt's thick hair and urged his mouth to claim hers once again.

They kissed and caressed, hands never still, lips and tongues tasting and savoring, hearts racing and breathing becoming labored.

Matt raised above Caitlin, then filled her with all that he was as a man and she received him with all that she was as a woman. The perfectly synchronized tempo of their rocking bodies was wild and earthy. They clung tightly to each other as they were carried up and away, then were flung into the brightly colored place they had yearned to go to.

It was ecstasy. It was so beautiful it defied description in its splendor.

Hello, Mr. and Mrs. MacAllister.

Matt collapsed against Caitlin, his energy spent,

then mustered enough strength to move off her. He tucked her close to his side. They were silent as their bodies cooled and hearts quieted.

"Caitlin," Matt said finally, breaking the dreamy silence in the room, "will you listen to me now? I want, I need, to tell you something."

"Mmm. Yes. All right."

Matt shifted just enough to enable him to look directly into Caitlin's eyes that still held the lingering smoky hue of desire. "I...Caitlin, I love you. I've fallen deeply and forever in love with you. And I love Mackenzie and Madison and...I believe, I hope and pray, that you love me, too."

"No, don't say that you love me." Tears filled her eyes. "It's difficult enough for me to... No."

"Caitlin, I know that you care for me, may even be in love with me although you won't admit it," he said, his voice raspy with emotion. "Everything could be perfect. Just perfect. We're already married. We're husband and wife and the parents of the two most fantastic babies in the world.

"I want to spend the rest of my life coming in the door at night and saying, 'Hello, Mrs. MacAllister.' We'll be a family, the four of us. Ah, Caitlin, I love you so much. I'm a husband, a father, you're my wife and—"

"No." Caitlin pressed her hands on Matt's chest to gain her freedom from his embrace, then left the bed and began to gather her clothes. "No."

Matt sat up and stared at her. "Why? Why are you doing this? We both love our daughters and—"

"They're *my* daughters," she said, clutching her clothes and ignoring the tears that spilled onto her cheeks. "It doesn't matter what my feelings for you might or might not be. This marriage will be over just as soon as the proper steps can be taken to end it when we return to Ventura."

Matt stood and gripped Caitlin's bare shoulders. "Why won't you give us a chance to have a future together?"

"Because you're him," she yelled. "You're him. You're just like my father, Matt. Your career comes first to the point that nothing else matters. Oh, yes, you'd be so sorry that you missed the twins' birthday party, or didn't get home in time to keep the reservation at the restaurant where we were going to dinner to celebrate our anniversary. So very sorry.

"But you'd do it again and again and again. Always so sorry, but telling me, telling the girls that we should be able to understand that what you do for a living is vitally important and... No. I made a vow years ago that I would never marry a man who was centered on his work, had tunnel vision about his career.

"And then here you were, attempting to steal my heart. But I won't be your wife and you won't be the father to Mackenzie and Madison. I won't re-live the heartache I grew up with, saw my mother suffer through, nor will I subject my daughters to it. *My daughters.* They're mine, Matt, and I'm going to protect my heart and theirs from you.''

''No, no,'' Matt said, a frantic edge to his voice. ''I'll change. I have no intention of putting in the kind of hours I did before at the hospital. I'll delegate and…I swear to you that my focus will be on you and the babies, us, our family. I *will* change, Caitlin, I promise you that.''

Caitlin closed her eyes for a moment and her shoulders slumped with fatigue and defeat.

''No, you won't change,'' she said, hardly above a whisper. ''Oh, I believe you intend to, actually believe you're capable of doing that, but I know better.''

''Damn it, Caitlin,'' Matt said, dragging a restless hand through his hair. ''I am not your father.''

''No, you're not,'' she said. ''Nor will you be Mackenzie and Madison's father, or my husband. I can't live in the world you would bring to our lives. I can't. I won't.''

''Don't do this to me, to us, to the twins,'' Matt said, holding out one hand toward her. ''Ah, please, Caitlin, give me a chance to prove to you that I—''

''No, no, no.''

''Don't do this,'' Matt said, his voice choked with emotion.

"I have to."

Caitlin turned and walked into the bathroom, closed the door, then seconds later the sound of water running in the shower could be heard.

Matt splayed one hand on his chest.

His heart hurt, he thought. It had nothing to do with his blood pressure or any of the other things that Bud had jumped on his case about. It was an emotional pain that was spreading, he could feel it consuming him, gripping his mind, his soul, in an icy fist.

Damn it, this wasn't fair. He was being judged and found guilty because of the sins of her father. Well, he wasn't her lousy dad, he was Matt MacAllister who…

Matt MacAllister who had pushed himself so hard executing his chosen career he'd nearly blown his health beyond repair. But, by damn, he had to be the best at what he did, have a flag to wave just like all the other MacAllisters.

But he understood that now. He'd been wrong. It had taken Caitlin to make him realize that. Caitlin and those babies. He was going to change. When they returned to Ventura, Caitlin would see that his promise was going to be kept. She'd see.

Oh, really? a nasty, niggling voice whispered in Matt's mind. How was she going to *see* when she had no intention of letting him come near her when they were home?

"I'll figure that out later," Matt said, beginning to gather his clothes.

Caitlin emerged from the bathroom in the clothes she'd been wearing earlier. "You'd better shower and dress," she said, not looking at him. "We don't know for certain when Marsha and Bud are going to bring the babies back, so..."

"Yeah, okay." Matt scooped up the last article of clothing from the floor. He straightened and looked over at Caitlin, who was smoothing the bed linens. "I love you, Caitlin. I want to spend the rest of my life with you, with our babies. And you love me, or at least you're damn close to it. This isn't over yet, not by a long shot."

Matt waited for her to reply, then when she didn't he went into the bathroom and closed the door.

"Yes, it *is* over, Matt," Caitlin said to the empty room, covering her face with her trembling hands. "It is."

When Matt came into the living room, having showered and dressed in clean clothes, he found Caitlin sitting on the sofa, flipping through a magazine. He went into her bedroom and returned with the bag he'd placed on the chair.

"Caitlin?" he said, standing in front of her.

"Hmm?"

"I went shopping when I left the consulate," he said quietly. "I got this."

Caitlin raised her head slowly, then her breath caught when she saw Matt take a tiny red dress from the bag.

"I didn't think it was right that one of the girls would have a red dress for the farewell dinner," he went on, leaning forward and placing the dress on her lap. "So, I... Then I saw this..." He drew a bundle of silk from the bag. "It's for you to wear that night. It's white but it has red flowers down the front. See? You'll be wearing red, too, and I bought myself a bright red tie. I pictured us all in my mind in our red finery, the MacAllister family." He put the blouse on top of the red dress.

"Oh, Matt," Caitlin said, shaking her head as fresh tears threatened. "This...all of this is so sweet, so thoughtful and..."

"Will you wear the blouse that night?"

"Yes, of course I will. Thank you. And thank you for buying the second red dress. I forgot all about the fact that I only have one with me and... You're a very—"

"Dedicated father," he said, a slight edge to his voice, "but I don't get any lasting points for that, do I?"

"Matt, don't. Please...just don't."

"Yes, ma'am," he said, saluting her. "Whatever you say, ma'am. After all, you're obviously running this show. You put me on trial, found me guilty, sentenced me to a future without you, without my daughters, without giving me an opportunity to defend myself, prove to you that I—

"Hell, forget it. You're not hearing what I'm saying. You've made up your mind about me. I'm a carbon copy of your father. Case closed." He paused. "I'll be in my bedroom practicing smiling until Marsha and Bud bring the girls back."

Matt strode into his bedroom, closed the door, then sank onto the edge of the bed. He reached into the bag he was still holding and took out a small box covered in flocked red satin. He opened it, then stared at what was inside through tear-filled eyes.

Wedding rings, he thought. Matching. Gold. With Chinese lettering that said love and happiness. Shiny rings that represented a bright future for a man and woman who planned to be together as husband and wife. Forever.

Matt snapped the box closed, the sound seeming to strike him like a physical blow that caused a moan to rumble in his chest. He looked at the box, the trash can next to the bed, then back at the box.

No, damn it, he thought fiercely. He wasn't throwing these rings away. They represented his future with Caitlin. He wasn't giving up on what he knew in his mind, his heart and soul, that they could have together.

He was going to fight for it, for her, for their daughters, with every breath in his body.

Chapter Twelve

Caitlin sighed as the airplane gained altitude and the last glimpse of the land below was covered by a marshmallow cloud. She sank back in her seat.

"I'm eager to return home," she said, "but I hate to leave China, too. It's so beautiful and intriguing and I'll never see it again."

Wrong, Matt thought. He'd already decided that a trip back to this country was in order when the twins were teenagers so they could learn more about their heritage, their roots. They'd all come, the MacAllister family, including the children he and Caitlin had created together. Yep, that was on his mental agenda.

"It's a nice place, but I wouldn't want to live there," he said pleasantly. "I'm looking forward to drinks with ice in the glass, mayonnaise on my sandwiches, and eating a meal that doesn't include a fried egg. Besides, I'll never master using chopsticks. Ventura, here I come."

Matt leaned forward and peered in the bassinets that were mounted on the bulkhead in front of them.

"How about you two Miss M.'s?" he said, switching his gaze back and forth between the twins. "Ready to become California surfers?"

The babies kicked their feet and waved tiny fists in the air.

"Right on," Matt said. "You're learning how to do high fives like pros." He chuckled, settled back in his seat again and took a magazine from the side pocket.

Caitlin slid a glance at Matt from beneath her lashes, then looked out the window of the plane again as though fluffy white stuff was the most fascinating thing she had ever seen.

She did not, she thought, understand Matt MacAllister, not even close. After the emotional scene in the hotel suite when she'd said that she would not, could not, marry him, she fully expected him to brood, be angry, hurt, whatever. She was dreading the remainder of the stay in Guangzhou as she anticipated an ever-growing tension between them.

But none of that had taken place.

When Marsha and Bud had returned the twins to the suite, Matt had been cheerful and smiling and hadn't dropped his life-is-grand facade since.

They'd gone on sight-seeing tours with the others, shopped in a quaint marketplace and continued to take endless photographs.

The wonderful news had been delivered by Elizabeth that the INS had approved the issuing of the second visa and off they'd gone to the consulate to meet with a beaming Brian.

They'd dressed in their red finery for the farewell dinner the previous night, with Matt insisting that Bud take several pictures of Matt, her and the twins together.

Oh, yes, Matt was acting very weird, Caitlin mentally rambled on. How could a man who had declared his love to a woman, proposed to her, been turned down flat, be so darn happy?

Was Matt slipping back into his old, the-glass-is-half-full demeanor that had been in place when she'd met him? No, she didn't think so. The way he was behaving now was different in an unexplainable way. It was unsettling, to say the least, and her nerves were shot.

She was sad, too. She refused to look deep within herself to determine if she was in love with

Matt because it was so hopeless. She had to some-how, *somehow,* get on with her life with the twins without Matt, never see him again, and if anyone looked at her crooked she'd burst into tears.

"Caitlin?" Matt said, bringing her from her gloomy thoughts.

"What," she said much too loudly.

"Jeez, did I wake you?"

"No, I'm sorry. I didn't mean to bark at you. What did you want to say?"

Matt shrugged. "I was just going to chat, com-ment on the fact that Elizabeth has covered every detail by having Carolyn bring an extra baby car seat to the airport so we can transport these little critters home." He paused. "You're short one crib, though."

"Well, I'll worry about that later. The girls are small enough to both fit in the one crib until I can get another one."

"Try this. I'm still on leave from the hospital, you know. Why don't I go to the store the day after we get back and buy another crib to match the one we bought. I'll bring it over and put it together for you."

"Oh, no, I don't think—"

"Do you have a better plan?"

"Well, no," Caitlin said, "but—"

"That settles it then. I'll get some more diapers, too. What else do you think you'll need? Food for yourself? Well, sure, that makes sense. You must have cleaned out your refrigerator before leaving for so long. While we're on this flight, start making a list that lasts thirty-two days and I'll grocery shop for you.''

''Why are you doing this?'' Caitlin said, leaning toward him.

''Doing what?'' he said, an expression of pure innocence on his face.

''Being so...so nice to me.''

''I happen to be a nice person, Ms. Cunningham,'' Matt said.

''You're a confusing person,'' Caitlin said, slouching back in her seat again.

Matt faked a cough to cover the burst of laughter that escaped from his throat.

Caitlin was rattled, he thought smugly. Big-time. And he was exhausted. It was taking every bit of his acting ability, such as it was, to present the appearance that he was doing just fine, thank you very much.

But he wasn't.

He had a cold fist in his gut that refused to go away, a chilling dread that no matter how hard he tried, no matter how hard he fought to prove to Caitlin that he would be a dedicated husband and father, she wouldn't believe it. He would fail.

He was going to change his lifestyle, and he'd figure out ways to be certain that she *did* see that it was happening. He couldn't lose her. He couldn't lose his family. His future. His everything. No.

Caitlin yawned and Matt looked at her and frowned.

"You're tired," he said. "Why don't you snooze for a while?"

"Not while the babies are awake. They might decide they want a bottle or a dry diaper."

"Which I am perfectly capable of tending to. You have the little pillow and the blanket that were on our seats. You can curl up and use the middle seat here, plus yours." He patted his right thigh. "You can plop your pillow on my leg if you want to and have even more room."

No way, Caitlin thought. She wasn't about to snuggle up to Matt like that. No, no, no.

"If you're certain you don't mind if I take a nap. I will."

Matt patted his thigh again. "Go for it."

Caitlin propped the pillow on the upper part of her seat next to the window, turned her back on Matt and curled up into a ball.

"Nudge me if you need help with the twins," she said, her voice muffled.

That, Matt thought, staring at Caitlin's back, had *not* gone well.

He sighed, folded his arms on his chest and glowered into space. He had to hang in there, not give up, just keep chipping away at Caitlin's defensive wall until it crumbled into dust.

Caitlin stirred, opened her eyes and wondered foggily why her nose was smushed into a lumpy, minuscule pillow. Realizing where she was as the last of the misty curtain of sleep dissipated, she unfolded her legs and cringed as she stretched her stiff muscles. She turned her head and her eyes widened.

Matt was feeding Mackenzie a bottle while she lay on his thighs, and had another bottle poked into Madison's mouth where she was tucked next to him on her back in the vacant seat separating Caitlin from him.

"You're feeding them both at once? Why didn't you wake me? Why didn't I hear them crying?" She glanced at her watch. "I slept for two hours? What kind of mother sleeps through the wailing of her babies when they're hungry?"

"They didn't wail. They fussed, complained a bit, so I made up two bottles, asked the flight attendant to warm them, and here we are, doing fine."

"Well, I'm awake now so I'll finish feeding Madison."

"There's no need to disturb her. They're both about to drain the last drop and they're starting to doze already. They need to catch up on their sleep, too, after the big party last night at the hotel. We put them down for the night later than usual, you know.''

"They must need dry diapers.''

"I changed them while the bottles were being warmed.''

"Oh. Well. You certainly have everything under control, Matt.'' Caitlin laughed. "I feel like a fifth wheel, or a fourth wheel in this case.

"That's a very clever way to feed both of them, too. I figured I'd have to take turns propping one of their bottles, but I think you have a sixth sense when dealing with the babies. You're a natural-born father. I'll probably end up keeping my mothering manual close at hand when I get the girls home.''

"No, you won't,'' Matt said, easing the bottles out of the twins' mouths. "I've been there with you for many hours as we cared for these guys. Your instincts are right on target, Caitlin.''

"You're forgetting about the tummyache episode.''

"Believe me, I have not forgotten about the special delivery made to my bare chest the night of the tummies.'' He chuckled. "That will be a great story for me to tell them when they're older. They'll love hearing how Dad got plastered with formula when....'' Matt's voice trailed off and he looked at Caitlin.

A chill coursed through Matt as the menacing voice in his mind tormented him with the message that he might not be a part of the twins' lives when they were old enough to recognize the humor in the events of what would, by then, be a long-ago night.

"Ah, Caitlin, I…" He shook his head and stared at Mackenzie, who was sleeping peacefully.

It took all the willpower that Caitlin possessed to keep from reaching out and placing her hand on Matt's shoulder, telling him that she was certain the girls would enjoy the funny story he would relate to them at some point in the future.

She'd heard the anguish in his voice when he said, "Ah, Caitlin," saw it on his face and in the depths of his dark brown eyes. She wanted to erase his pain, push it into oblivion where it couldn't reach him.

But she couldn't do that, Caitlin thought, because there was no future for them. And *that* pain was hers to bear. They were in the countdown of hours now as they flew in the direction that would take them back to Ventura.

Ventura, California, where she would raise her daughters…alone.

The flight seemed endless.

All the babies in the group appeared to somehow sense that they were being held captive in that metal capsule and became cranky. Marsha and Bud took turns walking up and down the aisles with a whining Grace, and unhappy wails erupted from various parts of the airplane.

Caitlin told Matt that she felt sorry for the passengers who were not connected to them and were no doubt not pleased to have their attempts to sleep interrupted by a crying baby.

"No joke," Matt said. "I think I'd tell the flight attendant to stop and let me off of this flying daycare center. You and I aren't in a position to complain because Mackenzie and Madison are adding their two cents' worth to the racket. Oh, well, there are only about four more hours to go."

Caitlin looked at her watch. "Yes. Four hours."

And then? she thought. Oh, Caitlin, don't go there. She was torturing herself with the image in her mind of Matt driving her and the babies home from the airport, then leaving them in her cozy house, turning his back and walking away.

Granted, she would see him when he brought the second crib and put it together. But once that chore was done, he would leave again. Probably for the last time.

Mackenzie began to cry, and Caitlin scooped her out of the bassinet. "I'll walk with her for a bit."

Matt stood to allow Caitlin to reach the aisle, then sank back onto his seat. As if aware that her

sister was receiving attention that she wasn't getting, Madison cut loose with an ear-splitting wail.

Matt lifted her from the bassinet and plopped her
on his lap, facing him. "And what is the nature of
your complaint, madam?" he said.

Madison stopped crying as suddenly as she had
started and smiled at Matt.

"Spoiled rotten to the core," he said, laughing.
"You ladies sure learn how to push a guy's buttons
at a very early age." He looked up and his smile
faded as he saw Caitlin in the distance. "But I love
you anyway."

When the captain announced that they were beginning their descent into Ventura, Caitlin stiffened
for a moment, then snapped on her seat belt as
instructed. They would arrive at approximately
3:00 p.m. California time, the captain went on to
say, and the weather was warm with a slight breeze.

"Home," Caitlin said. "I remember that I could
hardly believe it when we were told we were about
to land in Hong Kong, and now I'm having as
much difficulty believing we're back in California." She paused. "I feel like I should say something profound like this is the first day of the rest
of my life as a single mother of twins."

"Mmm," Matt said, frowning.

"Never mind." Caitlin waved one hand in the
air. "I'm so tired I don't think I'm up for profound.

Did the captain say what day of the week it is? Crossing the international dateline certainly is confusing. I...ignore me, I'm blithering.''

''Are you nervous about tending to the twins on your own?'' Matt said quietly, looking over at Caitlin.

''Yes, I am,'' she said, meeting his gaze. ''But one of the first things I'm going to do is to call my mother and tell her that surprise, surprise, I came home from China with two daughters instead of one. My mother said not to call until I was back in Ventura so she could picture me with the baby in our home. I thought that was so sweet. I'm also hoping she has good news to share about Paulo.''

''Especially because she was so unhappy while married to your father. Right?'' Matt said.

Caitlin nodded.

''Don't you think you deserve happiness like that, too?'' he said.

''It's not that easy to find, Matt. Maybe it's there for me years from now. I'll meet a man who is retired, isn't focused on a demanding career and... Oh, I don't know. I'm just going to concentrate on being a mommy.''

''Caitlin, I love you,'' Matt said, his voice hushed so no one else could hear him, ''and I believe that you love me. If you'd just give us a chance, give *me* a chance to prove to you that I'm going to change and—''

"Don't," she said, shaking her head. "There is no point in getting into all that again, Matt. What happened between us belongs to the memories of China. All my physical and emotional energies must be focused on Mackenzie and Madison now."

Matt sank back in his seat and sighed. "Right."

When the airplane bumped onto the runway a cheer went up from the passengers and several babies began to cry.

"Ready?" Caitlin asked, looking at Matt as the plane door was opened and the people around them began collecting their belongings.

"Yep," he said, feeling that cold fist in his gut tighten even more. "Grab a kid, I'll take the other one, and let's get off of this machine."

As they made their way up the tunnel leading to the arrivals area in the airport, Caitlin frowned. "Look up ahead there. Am I just punchy exhausted or are there very bright lights by the doorway?"

"I don't know," Matt said, attempting to quiet a fussing Mackenzie who was squirming in his arms.

The bright lights were not a figment of Caitlin's imagination. They emerged from the tunnel to find a camera crew filming and an attractive woman with a microphone approaching the people with babies and speaking to them.

"What's all this?" Caitlin said as Madison started to cry. "Shh, sweetheart. It's okay."

"Matt MacAllister?" the woman with the microphone said, stepping in front of him. "This is an extra bonus for my story for the six o'clock news about these babies being adopted and brought here to Ventura. People know who you are and… Terrific.

"But, you son of a gun, I've interviewed you so many times regarding news at Mercy Hospital and you never mentioned that you were married. And now you're a daddy?" She looked quickly at Mackenzie and Madison. "Of twins? Fantastic. Why didn't you tell me you had a wife and that you planned to go to China and—"

"You never asked about my personal life, Sophie," Matt said, with a shrug. "But we're exhausted, the babies are getting hungry and—"

"Just a little footage," Sophie said. "Jerry, bring the camera and lights over here."

Caitlin said, "Oh, I don't think—"

"I'll make it quick," Sophie interrupted, then turned to face the camera. "And here is a familiar face to those who live in Ventura. Matt MacAllister, the highly respected public-relations director of Mercy Hospital.

"When we got the call from one of the new grandparents waiting for this group telling us that they were arriving today, we didn't know that Matt

MacAllister and his wife were among those bringing a baby home. In this case, two babies. Identical
twins. Matt, your daughters are darling. How does
it feel to be the father of twins?''

"I've enjoyed my role of daddy to these girls
while we were in China.''

"I bet you did," Sophie said, beaming. "Would
you introduce your wife to our audience?''

"This is the mother of the twins. Caitlin.''

"And how do you feel about your bundles of
joy?'' Sophie said, pushing the microphone in front
of Caitlin's face.

"I'm...I'm thrilled," Caitlin said.

"Is Matt a helpful daddy?''

"He has been totally involved in their care.''

"Matt, when did you get married and why did
you keep it such a secret? Plus, why didn't you let
us know you were making this momentous trip?''

Mackenzie had had enough of this nonsense and
began to wail at top volume as she stiffened in
Matt's arms.

"Sorry, Sophie," Matt said, edging around her,
"but these babies need to eat and be put to bed
without the sound of airplane engines roaring in
their ears. Good to see you. Bye.''

Matt strode away with Caitlin scrambling to
reach his side again.

"Why did you do that?'' she said, glancing
quickly around to be certain no one was listening.

"She thinks we're married and you didn't set her straight."

"Caitlin, I wasn't about to put our personal business on the six o'clock news. And if you think back over what I said, and how I phrased it, I never said that we are married. I'm a PR man, remember? I think very fast on my feet. Sophie assumed that we were married but I did *not* confirm that fact."

Caitlin frowned. "Oh. No, I guess you didn't, did you?"

"No. Hey, Carolyn, come meet Mackenzie and Madison."

Carolyn hurried toward them carrying a car seat. "Oh, they are so beautiful. Congratulations, Caitlin. Your daughters are exquisite. All the babies are gorgeous, aren't they? I love meeting these planes when they arrive. But you two look like what I'm used to seeing. Exhausted. Go. Shoo. Get those girls home so you can put your feet up. Remember what we told you, though, you should stay up as late as possible this evening to take care of your jet lag as quickly as it can be done."

In a flurry of activity, Caitlin nestled Madison into the car seat, then they headed for the baggage-claim area, seeing several of the people from their group already going that way at a brisk clip.

Caitlin glanced over her shoulder to make certain that Sophie with her menacing microphone wasn't following them to get more footage for the news.

Maybe the interview Sophie had done with Matt would get edited out because of Mackenzie starting to cry, not being a picture-perfect baby at that moment.

Yes, okay, Matt had fielded the questions about his wife with slippery expertise, but would the average person watching the news realize that Matt never did say he was married, was the twins' father? Oh, forget it. She didn't have the energy to think about this. She just wanted to go home.

After luggage was collected, hugs were exchanged with the others from the group as well as promises to get together just as soon as their lives settled into sensible routines.

Marsha told Caitlin she'd telephone tomorrow, or maybe this *was* tomorrow for all she knew.

Madison and Mackenzie wailed their displeasure at being confined to the car seats during the entire drive to Caitlin's house.

"I fantasized about this moment." Caitlin raised her voice so Matt could hear her over the babies as they entered her living room. "You know, walking into my house carrying my baby, having her look around as though she knew she was finally home where she belonged and… Never mind. They're both so unhappy." She glanced at the ceiling. "I wonder if the plaster will crack from this noise. Gracious."

"Dry diapers and bottles are called for here. Let's do it, then I'll bring in your suitcase."

"Oh, Matt, you're as exhausted as I am, as the twins are. I can't ask you to stay and help me change and feed them."

"You're not asking, I'm volunteering. Don't argue the point. I don't have the energy to debate the subject."

A half hour later, the babies were changed, fed and wearing fresh sleepers taken from the dresser in the nursery. Caitlin and Matt tucked them into opposite ends of the crib. They wiggled a bit, then closed their eyes and slept.

"Oh, blessed silence," Caitlin said, then smiled up at Matt. "Look at them. They're here, Matt. They're honest-to-goodness here. Home. I don't believe it." She laughed. "I'll believe it the next time they wake up, that's for sure. Well, I'm going to take a leisurely bubble bath while I have the chance."

"I'll get your suitcase, then hit the road."

Matt strode from the room and Caitlin stood for another long moment gazing at the sleeping babies.

"Welcome home," she whispered. "I'm so very glad you're here, my darlings. I love you so much."

She turned and walked slowly from the room. Matt reentered the house and set Caitlin's suitcase by the front door.

"Well, I'm outta here," he said, not looking directly at her. "I'll get the second crib tomorrow and pick up some groceries for you. I'll phone you before I come over, to be certain it's a convenient time for you."

"Let me give you some money for the crib and food."

"Don't worry about it, Caitlin. We'll even up later." Matt paused. "So. We did it. We got those munchkins home safe and sound and... Hey, you know, if you need an extra set of hands just give me a shout and... No, I guess you won't do that, will you? Well, I'll pop in tomorrow with the crib and... Goodbye, Caitlin."

"Matt, wait." Caitlin closed the distance between them. "Thank you for everything. I don't have any idea how to express my gratitude for your help, for... All I can say is a simple thank-you knowing it isn't enough."

"I enjoyed every minute of it." He looked directly into Caitlin's eyes. "You know I did. Those girls own a chunk of my heart, always will, and you... Well, there's no sense in going there again, is there? I'll see you tomorrow."

Matt turned and left the house, closing the door behind him with a gentle click. Caitlin wrapped her hands around her elbows and stared at the door, aware of how very quiet it was, how empty somehow, despite the fact that two babies were sleeping down the hall. Aware of how much she already missed Matt MacAllister. Tears filled her eyes and she blinked them away, shaking her head in self-disgust.

''Go take a bubble bath, Caitlin,'' she said, starting across the room. ''And while you're at it, get your act together.''

During Caitlin's absence her neighbor, Stella, a widow in her mid-sixties, had collected Caitlin's mail, placed it on the desk in the bedroom she used for an office and watered the plants as needed.

After her very relaxing bath where she had actually been able to blank her mind, Caitlin checked on the still-sleeping twins, then stood staring at the pile of mail on her cluttered desk.

Forget it, she thought, she wasn't plowing through all this now. Her mother had made her promise to telephone when she, the mommy, arrived home and neither the new grandma nor the grandpa would care one iota what hour it was.

Caitlin's address book was, thank goodness, tucked safely in the top drawer of the desk, and moments later she was sitting in the chair and pressing the long list of numbers to make the international call. Caitlin's mother answered on the first ring.

With Paulo listening on an extension, Caitlin delivered her fantastic news. The three-way conversation was a babble of excited asking and answering of questions, sniffles of joy and the grandparents' heartfelt wish that they were there to see and hold the babies as well as give Caitlin a helping hand.

"When do you think you'll be able to visit?" Caitlin asked finally. "What is going on with your tests, Paulo?"

"Oh, nothing fancy," Paulo said. "I need double-bypass surgery, which is a walk in the park these days. What will hold up our getting on the plane is that it turns out I'm anemic and they are building me up before they operate. I'm afraid we can't put our finger on a date on the calendar at this point, sweetheart, so send us lots of pictures of our granddaughters."

"But you're going to be fine?" Caitlin said, frowning.

"As good as new," Paulo said.

"That's wonderful," she said. "I'll just have to be patient then, and wait until you two can make the trip."

"But how will you manage alone with two babies?" Olivia said. "As far as that goes, how did you manage on your own in China?"

"I had...I had help in China," Caitlin said quietly. "There was a man, Matt MacAllister, who is a friend of one of the couples and who knows all about babies and... Well, Matt was my...my partner, per se, in tending to the girls while we were over there.''

"I see," Caitlin's mother said slowly. "And?"

"And…what?"

"Caitlin, I'm your mother. I know you as well as I know myself. Something changed in your voice when you mentioned Matt MacAllister's name. There's something you're not telling us.''

Oh, it's no biggie, Mom, Caitlin thought miserably. It's just the fact that she might very well have fallen in love with Matt, with the wrong man, while halfway around the world. But she wasn't about to tell her mother and Paulo that as they would only worry about her, and they had enough to deal with concerning Paulo's health.

"Caitlin?" her mother said.

"What? Oh, I'm sorry, Mom. The something I'm not telling you is that I'm falling asleep sitting here because of jet lag. They told us to stay up as late as we could tonight to get back on schedule but… Anyway, you're up to date on my news. Exciting, isn't it? Almost unbelievable.''

Goodbyes were exchanged, more sniffles echoed across the telephone lines, then Caitlin hung up the receiver. She leaned back in the chair and sighed.

The sound of a crying baby reached Caitlin and she jumped to her feet, the addition of a second wailing infant causing her to run from the room and down the hall toward the nursery. She came to a halt next to the crib where the unhappy twins were voicing their displeasure at the top of their lungs.

"I'm here. Mommy is here," she said above the din as she scooped up Mackenzie. "Don't cry. Everything is under control."

And her nose was going to grow, Caitlin thought, placing Mackenzie on the changing table as Madison cried on. Just like Pinocchio.

Chapter Thirteen

Matt flung back the blankets and left the bed. As he strode toward the bathroom, each heavy footfall was accompanied by his earthy expletive.

What a lousy night's sleep that had been, he fumed as he stood under the stinging water in the shower moments later. He'd stayed up, per instructions, as late as possible the night before to hopefully conquer his jet lag. When he'd begun to nod off in his favorite recliner he had given up the battle and gone to bed.

Yeah, sure, he'd fallen right to sleep, only to jerk awake an hour later positive that he'd heard Mackenzie and Madison crying. That had proven to be part of the dream he'd been having about Caitlin and the twins. He'd repeated that performance two hours later, then two after that until he was so stressed his head was pounding and his stomach burning. Enough was enough.

So here he was, Matt mentally rambled on as he pulled on jeans and a knit shirt, all dressed and nowhere to go because it was 6:16 in the morning.

Toting a mug of freshly brewed coffee Matt settled in the recliner and glowered into space.

He missed Caitlin, he thought. He loved her, he missed her, he wanted to be with her instead of sitting here alone...and lonely. And he missed Mackenzie and Madison, too, damn it.

Matt took a sip of coffee and narrowed his eyes.

Look at the bright side, MacAllister, he told himself. Okay, he would...except what was it? There wasn't one bright and sunny thing about the fact that the woman he loved and who, yes, darn it, loved him in kind refused to allow him to be part of her present and future.

Okay, so he'd see Caitlin and the babies today when he delivered the crib and groceries. But even if he moved as slow as molasses, it wouldn't take him more than an hour to put the crib together. One crummy little hour. Hell.

If he even lasted long enough to get through that hour without exploding into a zillion pieces from tension-building frustration.

The store where he would buy the crib to match the other one didn't open until nine o'clock. There was no way on earth he could sit here that long without going straight out of his mind.

He would go to the hospital and kill some time, just wander into his office and see how things were with ole Homer at the helm. He'd make it clear he wasn't there to work, was just passing by and decided to say howdy. It wasn't a great plan but it was all he had.

Matt had only gotten about three feet from the elevator when his secretary, Linda, spotted him and rushed to stand in front of him, blocking his way. Linda was in her mid-forties but appeared haggard and thoroughly exhausted.

"What are you doing here so early?" Matt said.

"I can't remember if I went home last night. Thank the stars you're back. This place is a zoo, Matt. Are you really standing before my very eyes or are you a figment of my imagination that has willed you to appear?"

"I'm here, but I'm not. What I mean is, I'm not reporting for duty. I just dropped by to say hello."

"You can't leave again," Linda said, grasping one of Matt's hands with both of hers. "We're in the midst of a crisis, a full-blown disaster, I tell you."

"Where's Homer?"

"He had an emergency appendectomy yesterday morning, and no one is running this show. I swear, Matt, everything that could go wrong has gone wrong.

"Would you believe we have a man suing the hospital for emotional distress because they cut his shirt off in the E.R. to jump-start his heart? His wife gave him that shirt for their anniversary, and he's despondent that it was shredded.

"And there's some royal somebody in for heart surgery and he brought his own cook and the health department says no way is that guy cooking in the hospital kitchen.

"And a woman is having her attorney get a court order to allow her to have her poodle sleep with her in her hospital bed the night before her gall-bladder surgery.

"And—"

"Whoa. Halt. Stop," Matt said.

"But that's just the tip of the iceberg. There is a stack of files on your desk that you wouldn't believe."

"Okay, look. I'll donate a couple of hours and put out the worst of the fires, then I'm out of here, Linda. I have a baby crib and some groceries to buy, and I intend to do that."

"Which reminds me that I'm furious with you for not telling me you got married. Why keep it a secret, as well as your plans to adopt a baby from

China? I saw you on the news last night. Twins? They are so cute, Matt, but my feelings are hurt to think—''

''Things are not always what they seem to be,'' Matt said. ''I'll explain about the marriage and the twins later. Right now I need to get to work here, but I meant it when I said I'm only putting in a couple of hours.''

Just before nine o'clock that night Matt pulled in to Caitlin's driveway and turned off the ignition to the SUV. He rotated his neck back and forth in an attempt to loosen the tight muscles, then gave up the effort as futile. He chewed two antacid tablets, then got out of the vehicle.

Ridiculous day, he fumed, striding to the rear of the SUV. He hadn't had a thing to eat, his stomach was on fire, his head was holding a convention for bongo-drum players and he was many hours later getting to Caitlin's than he'd intended to be.

Matt opened the rear hatch of the vehicle and wrapped his arms around two packed-to-the-brim grocery bags.

Each time he'd reached for the phone to call Caitlin and tell her he hadn't forgotten his promise to get the crib and groceries, his hand had stilled. He'd been so afraid he'd call at the exact time when Caitlin was managing to take a nap because the twins were also sleeping.

Matt rang Caitlin's doorbell with his elbow, then cringed as he heard the chimes inside the house, envisioning the noise waking the babies, which would result, no doubt, in Caitlin popping him right in the chops.

"Who is it, please?" Caitlin's muffled voice asked from beyond the door.

"Matt."

"Matt who?"

"Caitlin, come on. I know you're probably upset with me because I didn't get here earlier, but I'm holding grocery bags, and if you keep me standing here you're going to have a front porch that is decorated in melted raspberry sherbet."

A silent second ticked by, then two, then three.

"Caitlin?"

Matt heard the snap of the lock as it was released, then the door was opened to reveal a frowning Caitlin.

"Let me get the sherbet into the freezer, then I'll explain why I'm so late. Okay?"

Caitlin stepped back and swept one arm through the air. She didn't speak, nor did the stormy expression on her face soften one iota.

Matt entered the house and hurried to the kitchen. He placed the bags on the counter and began to unpack them, glancing at Caitlin as she sat down at the table.

"How are the twins?"

"Fine."

"Good. Did you get along all right today with the two of them?" he said, putting the sherbet in the freezer.

"Yes."

"Was it fun?"

"Yes."

"Do you think you could add a little more to this conversation than one-word answers, Caitlin?"

"No."

Matt shoved lettuce, tomatoes, cucumbers and bean sprouts into the refrigerator then crossed the room and sat down opposite Caitlin.

"Look, I'm really sorry I'm so late getting here. I started to call you a half-dozen times but never did it because I was afraid I'd wake you if you'd managed to catch a nap when the babies were sleeping. I fully intended to be here hours ago but—"

"Let me guess," Caitlin said, crossing her arms on the top of the table and leaning toward him. "You decided to stop by the hospital just to say hello, see if things were running smoothly without your expertise. And lo and behold, there was some kind of a crisis, or emergency, or whatever, that you just had to tend to while you were there. How am I doing, Matt? Have I hit the nail on its ever-famous head?"

"You're making it sound like I did something

totally unreasonable. Cripe, Caitlin, the guy who was covering for me had emergency surgery and things were piling up and—''

''And nobody could fix it all but you,'' Caitlin said, getting to her feet. ''And, of course, that hospital, what you do there, is far more important than buying a second crib and filling my Mother Hubbard cupboards.''

''That's not true,'' Matt said, lunging to his feet.

His chair fell over and toppled to the floor with a crash. He and Caitlin froze, straining their ears for the sound of...

Mackenzie began to cry. Then Madison began to cry.

''You—'' Caitlin pointed at him ''—are a dead man.''

She spun around and stomped out of the kitchen.

Matt set his chair back into place. ''You're doing just dandy so far, MacAllister. Men have been murdered for waking a sleeping baby and I woke up two. I'm scoring points all over the map.''

Maybe he could redeem himself, he thought, hurrying after Caitlin. He'd step in and lend a hand with the now-wailing babies, be useful, needed. Oh, yeah, that was it. He could show Caitlin that she needed him there to help her, if she'd forget for a second that he was the one who woke the girls in the first place.

When Matt arrived at the open doorway of the

nursery, the twins were quieting and the clowns hanging from the mobile were dancing in a circle to the lilting lullaby. A night-light cast a soft, golden glow over the room.

"Shh," Caitlin was saying. "You're all right. Mommy is right here. That was a loud noise, wasn't it? But everything is fine. Go to sleep, my darlings. Mommy is here."

And so is Daddy, Matt's mind yelled.

"May I see them?" he said quietly. "Please?"

Caitlin turned her head to look at him, then finally nodded. Matt went to the crib and stared at the babies who had drifted back to sleep.

"Hello, little munchkins. I missed seeing you guys today, I really did." He shifted his gaze to Caitlin, his heart seeming to skip a beat when he found her looking directly into his eyes. "I missed you, too, Caitlin. I know I blew it by being so late getting here but... Ah, Caitlin, I love you so damn much."

"Don't." She shook her head as her eyes filled with tears.

Caitlin hurried from the room and Matt followed slowly behind her. In the living room he found her standing by the sofa, her hands wrapped protectively around her elbows.

"Caitlin," Matt said, stopping across the room from her, "we can have it all, don't you see, if you'll only give me a chance to—"

"To repeat what happened today?" she said, tears spilling unnoticed onto her cheeks. "Over and over and over again? Promises made, promises broken? No. I grew up with that kind of heartache, watched my mother be destroyed by inches by it, too. I won't do that to myself, not again, nor will I allow it to happen to my daughters.

"Leave us alone, Matt. It isn't going to work between us, not in a million years. It's too painful to have you here, in my home." A sob caught in her throat. "I might be in love with you, I don't know, but I don't like how you view life, your priorities, what you believe is more important than..." She shook her head as tears choked off her words.

"But—"

"No. No, no, no."

Matt's shoulders slumped and an achy sensation gripped his throat, making it impossible to speak.

This was it? he thought. The end? He would never see Caitlin Cunningham again? He wouldn't be here to watch the twins learn to crawl, then take those first, wondrous wobbling steps? He'd never hear those little girls call him Daddy? Oh, God, no. He couldn't bear the thought of a future without the woman he loved, without his Caitlin. Without his family.

"I..." Matt started, then realized he didn't know

what to say as a jumble of tangled, confusing thoughts flooded his mind.

"Please go," Caitlin said.

"Yeah," he said, nodding. "Okay. But I intend to put the crib together first, Caitlin. You can go to your bedroom or whatever. I'll work here in the living room and you can pull the crib into the nursery in the morning."

Caitlin nodded jerkily, dashed the tears from her cheeks, then left the room. Matt watched her go, and with a weary sigh headed outside to bring in the boxes containing the crib and mattress.

An hour later Matt shut his toolbox, then wound the knob on the clown mobile that he'd bought to match the other one. To the sound of the pretty song that he had once held Caitlin in his arms and danced to, he left the house, closing the door on his happiness.

A week later Matt slid into the booth in a busy café and immediately raised both hands in a gesture of peace as he looked at his glowering twin sister, Noel.

"I know, I know, I'm guilty as sin," he said.

"Got it in one," Noel said, narrowing her eyes. "You've been avoiding the whole family since you returned from China, haven't returned our calls or… For crying out loud, Matt, we saw you on the news last week. I am the official MacAllister representative, buster, and you're not leaving this restaurant until you tell me what's going on.''

"Can we order lunch first?" Matt said, attempting to produce a smile that fizzled.

"Make it snappy," Noel said.

They ordered hamburgers and fries, then Noel tapped the fingers of one hand impatiently on the table. "Speak," she said. "And this better be good. Oh, by the way, you look like hell."

"I haven't been sleeping well. Plus I've been putting in long hours at the hospital and—"

"Wait a minute," Noel said. "You're not even supposed to be back at work yet...according to Bud's orders."

"It can't be helped. The guy who was taking my place had his appendix out and... I've been trying to put in decent hours at the hospital, Noel, but every night when I get ready to leave something comes up that needs my attention. Caitlin was right about me. I'm not fit to be a husband and father. I can't have it all and it's tearing me to shreds."

Their lunches were put in front of them and ignored.

"Back up, back up," Noel said. "Start at the top. There's nothing we can't solve if we put our genius-level minds together."

"Not this time. It's hopeless. *I'm* hopeless. And, oh, God, Noel, I love Caitlin Cunningham and those babies so much I can't even begin to express it to you in words. They're...my life, my..." He shook his head.

Noel covered one of Matt's hands with one of hers on the top of the table.

"Start at the beginning," she said gently. "You decided to tag along on the trip to China with Bud and Marsha and..." She gave Matt's hand a little squeeze. "And?"

And Matt began to talk, pouring out his heart to his sister, his twin. They had been more than just sister and brother since they had been born on that same day thirty-two years before. They were best friends.

But even Noel hadn't known Matt's deepest secret of why he was so driven to succeed in his career, the inner need to be the best at something just as all the MacAllisters were.

"Oh, honey," Noel said, shaking her head as Matt revealed the truth. "We've always been so close. Yet you kept this churning inside you."

"I told Caitlin this while we were in China," Matt said. "She made me realize that I didn't need to be Mr. Sunshine all of the time, plus the fact that I needed to change the pattern of how I was living. No, correct that. Not living...just existing."

Noel nodded.

Matt continued his story, his voice often raspy with emotion.

"I was going to be a macho MacAllister, fight

the toughest battle of my life and win, prove to Caitlin that I could change, that I was worthy of her love, of being her husband and the father to our daughters.

"But, Noel? I didn't win. I won't win. Not now. Not in the future. Not ever. Because this past week has shown me that Caitlin is right about me. I can't change. God knows I tried, but…" Matt's voice trailed off.

"You've created a monster."

"And his name is Matt MacAllister," he said with a sharp bark of laughter that held absolutely no humor.

"No, sweetie," Noel said. "Its name is Mercy Hospital."

"What?" he said, obviously confused.

"Oh, Matt, don't you see?" she said, leaning toward him. "It's the people at Mercy who need to change. They're not willing to allow you to delegate. Can you reprogram all of them? Of course not. But don't you dare say that *you* can't change your ways."

Matt picked up a very cold fry, looked at it for a long moment, then tossed it back onto the plate.

"You're dealing in semantics, Noel," he said, leaning back in the booth. "The bottom line is still the same. It's hopeless. I've lost Caitlin. I've lost my baby girls."

Noel shook her head. "You're wrong. What you

need to do is right there in front of your nose, Matt.''

''That's news to me,'' he said, frowning. ''Would you care to share this what-any-idiot-should-be-able-to-see answer to my dilemma?''

''No. I'm sorry, Matt, but no. You've got to figure it out on your own. It has to come from your mind, your heart, your very soul so that you own it, make it truly yours.

''I'll give you a clue, though, because you're a man and your species is generally dense.''

''I used to like you, Noel.'' Matt sighed. ''Okay, lay it on me. The clue.''

''Okay. Here it is. Take another look at the gift you received from Grandpa.''

''The scale? My gift didn't have a hidden meaning like so many of the others he gave to his grandchildren. It's a beautiful object, but it doesn't have a message I'm supposed to figure out.''

''Doesn't it?'' Noel slid out of the booth, came around the table and kissed Matt on the forehead. ''I love you, my brother. Go look at the scale again.''

Chapter Fourteen

At ten o'clock that night Matt leaned back in the chair behind his desk at the hospital with a weary sigh. He squeezed his temples between the fingers of one hand, hoping the pressure would lessen the pain of his throbbing headache. It didn't.

Matt got to his feet and crossed the room to retrieve his suit coat from the clothes tree in the corner. As he slipped on the jacket his gaze fell on the antique scale that was still sitting on the bookcase where he had placed it to humor Homer Holmes.

Well, Matt thought wearily, if he'd been that accommodating for a nerdy, fussbudget attorney, he at least owed Noel the courtesy of *looking* at the scale again...which was a total waste of time.

Matt scooped the two coins off the left tray of the scale, dropped them into his pocket, then picked up the scale and left the office.

At home, Matt set the scale on the table next to his favorite chair and laid the two coins by it.

When his grandfather had given him the gift of the scale, he mused, the two coins had been held in place in the left tray by a narrow strip of tape. He'd removed it when he took the scale to his office, leaving both coins in that tray.

Matt placed one coin in the left tray, then hesitated before doing the same with the other one. He stared intently at the scale, the coin in his hand, then the scale again.

Every muscle in his body seemed to tense and he had to remind himself to breathe. Acutely aware that his hand was trembling, Matt put the second coin in the right tray, causing the saucer-shaped disks to move, then still in perfect side-by-side balance.

"Oh, my God," Matt said aloud. "Noel was right."

There *had* been a message connected to the gift that his grandfather had given him, he thought, his mind racing. There was the answer right in front him. Balance. That was what was sorely missing in his existence. An equal and healthy balance between his career and his personal life. Noel was a very smart woman. And his grandfather? Oh, what a wise and wonderful man was Robert MacAllister.

"Caitlin and the babies," Matt said, his voice ringing with emotion. He gently touched the coin in the left-hand tray with one fingertip, then switched his gaze to the other coin. "My job at Mercy. In proper balance."

You've created a monster. Its name is Mercy Hospital.

Noel's words echoed suddenly in Matt's mind, causing his heart to race. Time lost meaning as Matt continued to stare at the scale.

Very early the next morning Matt telephoned Noel.

"Do you know what time it is?" she said, nearly yelling.

"I'm sorry I woke you," Matt said, "but I have to talk to you. I need your help, Noel."

Three days later in the early afternoon Caitlin sat cross-legged on the floor of her living room next to a blanket where the twins were on their tummies, picking up, then discarding, a variety of brightly colored toys. A yellow envelope was in her lap and she was staring at a photograph that was one of many in the envelope containing the developed pictures of the trip to China.

Tears stung her eyes as she continued to gaze at the photograph she was clutching.

There they all were, Caitlin thought, swallowing past the lump in her throat. This picture was taken at the celebration dinner on the last night in China. There they all were—Matt, Caitlin, Mackenzie and Madison. They were dressed in the traditional red, and they were all smiling.

Like a happy family.

"Oh, Matt," she said, then sniffled. "There's nowhere left for me to hide from the truth. I love you, Matt MacAllister, so very, very much. If only... No, I'm not going down the 'if only' road. There's nothing to be gained from that. But, oh, if only..."

The doorbell rang and Caitlin nearly cheered aloud that something had pulled her back to reality and reason. She got to her feet and hurried to the door.

"Hello," a woman said, smiling, after Caitlin opened the door.

"Hello," Caitlin replied, producing a small smile. "May I help you?"

"You don't know me, Caitlin, but I feel as though I know you. And Mackenzie and Madison. I'm Noel. Matt's sister. May I come in for a second?"

"Oh...well...sure," Caitlin said, stepping back to allow Noel to enter the house.

"There they are," Noel said, laughing in delight. "Oh, Caitlin, your daughters are sensational, just adorable."

"Thank you."

"I hope you don't mind that I brought them a little gift," Noel said, handing Caitlin a glossy pink bag.

"This is very kind of you. Please, sit down."

"Thanks," Noel said, glancing at her watch as she settled onto the sofa.

Caitlin sat down on the opposite end and took the tissue out of the top of the bag. She pulled out two pink T-shirts and two pink seersucker bib overalls.

"Oh, thank you, Noel. This is so lovely of you, especially since you don't even know me."

"Like I said," Noel said, looking quickly at her watch again, "I feel as though I know you and the babies. Matt told me all about you three."

"Really?" Caitlin said, making a production out of folding the new clothes, smoothing them, then placing them on the coffee table. "How...how is Matt?" She turned her head slowly to look at Noel.

"Oh, you know," Noel said, flipping one hand in the air. "Matt is Matt."

Caitlin frowned. "In other words, he's back to his old routine of working ungodly hours at the hospital."

"I was thinking more in the terms of his being

a handsome, loving, caring and sharing, thoughtful and kind, intelligent man.''

"Who is working ungodly hours at the hospital again, right?''

Noel looked at her watch. "Oh, my. Oh, my. Look at the time. I don't mean to be a rude guest but there's a press conference starting in about a minute or so and it's going to be televised. Would you mind if I watched it?''

"No, I don't mind.'' Caitlin picked up the remote control from the coffee table and pressed a button to bring the television to life. "What channel do you want?''

"The Ventura station. This is a press conference being held here.''

"Oh,'' Caitlin said, then found the proper station. "I'll go heat some bottles for the babies while you're watching this.''

"No,'' Noel said none too quietly.

Caitlin jerked in surprise at her visitor's outburst.

"What I mean is—'' Noel beamed "—I really believe you'll find this press conference very... informative.'' She glanced at the babies. "Your sweeties are content at the moment.''

"Well, okay,'' Caitlin said, deciding that Matt's sister was a tad strange.

"Here we go,'' Noel said as the words *special bulletin* appeared on the television screen.

The next image was of an attractive woman speaking into a handheld microphone.

"This is Sophie Spencer," the woman said, "reporting to you live outside of Mercy Hospital here in Ventura. Matt MacAllister, who is a household name in our city, has called a press conference that will begin any minute now. We have no idea what this pertains to."

Caitlin's eyes widened, her gaze riveted on the screen. Mackenzie began to whine.

"I'll get her," Noel said, moving to the blanket and picking up the fussing infant. "Not now, kiddo. Your mommy is busy."

"I don't need to watch this news conference," Caitlin said, rising. "I'll go warm the bottles."

"Caitlin Cunningham," Noel yelled, "sit back down on that sofa and don't move."

Mackenzie began to cry and Noel patted her on the back.

"Noel…" Caitlin said, obviously having had enough of Noel's weird behavior.

"Look," Noel said, pacing back and forth in an attempt to pacify the unhappy Mackenzie. "I'm doing a lousy job here, but I don't exactly do this for a living, for heaven's sake. Please, Caitlin, just do it. Please? Sit down and listen to what Matt has to say."

Caitlin sank back down on the sofa with a sigh of defeat. Matt MacAllister was about to arrive

smack-dab in her living room, Caitlin thought frantically. She would hear the rich timbre of his voice,
drink in the sight of his wide shoulders, his thick,
auburn hair, those mesmerizing fudge-sauce-
colored eyes of his. He would no doubt smile at
some point while making the announcement about
whatever it was he was making the announcement
about and…

Madison began to cry.

"Oh, dear," Caitlin said, landing back in reality
with a thud.

"Fear not," Noel said, heading in the direction
she assumed would lead her to the kitchen. "I can
handle this. Two bottles coming right up, little cut-
ies."

"And here is Matt MacAllister now," Sophie
said as a door of the hospital opened behind her.

There were three other reporters besides Sophie,
who were stringers for the national news stations.
Their bosses would determine whether what was
covered should be added to the evening newscast.
Four microphones were tilted in Matt's direction.

Oh, look at him, Caitlin thought. He was so
handsome. But he appeared to be exhausted, had
dark smudges under his eyes.

Noel returned to the living room, plunked Mackenzie in Caitlin's lap and handed her a bottle, then
scooped up Madison from the floor. She tucked
Madison next to her on the sofa, retrieved Mac-

kenzie from Caitlin and popped bottles into mouths.

"Matt fed them that way on the plane one time," Caitlin said, "so I could get some sleep."

"MacAllisters know their stuff when it comes to tending to babies," Noel said. "Shh. Listen to Matt."

"Thank you for coming, ladies and gentlemen," Matt said. "The board of directors and I agreed that this is the most efficient way to get this known. I have," Matt went on, "turned in my resignation letter for the position of public-relations director at Mercy Hospital."

"What?" Caitlin whispered, inching to the edge of the sofa and staring at the television with wide eyes.

"Shh," Noel said.

"I've enjoyed my many years here at Mercy," Matt said, "but it's time for a change, time for *me* to change. Not just talk about it, but actually do it, and I am. There is more to life than a fancy title, a record of excellence and a plush office inside a tall building."

"What are your plans, Matt?" Sophie asked.

"I'm going to open my own public-relations firm," he said. "It won't be the biggest, nor the most well-known operation, but it will allow me to have a proper balance in my existence between work and my personal life.

"My replacement here at Mercy will be Homer Holmes, who is a fine attorney and who will do a superb job of stepping into my shoes. He's already had some experience here while I was away recently."

"I don't believe this," Caitlin said, flattening her hands on her cheeks.

"Shh," Noel said.

"Matt," Sophie said, "I know that all of Ventura wishes you the very best in your new endeavor and I'm certain your public-relations agency will be a huge success."

"Thank you, Sophie," Matt said, smiling.

"One more question," Sophie said. "There seems to be some confusion about whether or not you are married and are the daddy of those adorable adopted babies we saw you with at the airport. Could you clear that up for our viewers? Do you have a family, or not? Are you a husband and father?"

Caitlin's breath caught and she pressed trembling fingertips against her lips.

"I'm not avoiding answering your question, Sophie," Matt said, "nor do I mean to sound mysterious, or whatever. It's just that I honestly don't know. I'm not the person to answer that." He shifted his gaze from Sophie to look directly into the camera. "Caitlin? If Noel came through for me, and she always has in the past, then you're watching this. Am I married, Caitlin? Do I have two beautiful daughters?''

Caitlin extended one hand toward the television as tears filled her eyes. ''Yes. Oh, yes, Matt.''

''Oh, jeez,'' Noel said, sniffling, ''this is so romantic I'm falling apart.'' She reached past the babies and took a piece of paper from her purse that was on the floor next to the sofa.

''Here.'' She handed Caitlin the paper. ''This is Matt's cell-phone number.''

Caitlin snatched up the telephone receiver on the end table next to her and punched in the numbers. She heard it ring in her ear and on the television screen at the same time. Matt retrieved the phone from his jacket pocket but didn't speak as he pressed it to his ear.

''Hello, Mr. MacAllister,'' Caitlin said, smiling through her tears.

She replaced the receiver on the base.

''That's it?'' Noel said. ''You didn't tell him that—''

''Shh,'' Caitlin said.

''Yes,'' Matt said, punching one fist in the air.

''Yes…what?'' Sophie said. ''Matt, I'm still confused.''

''Gotta go,'' Matt said, grinning. ''I'll call you later, Sophie, and give you the details. Bye.''

Matt disappeared off the screen and the camera zoomed in on Sophie.

"This is Sophie Spencer," she said, laughing, "a confused Sophie Spencer, reporting live from Mercy Hospital. We'll give you more details on this story as we get them. We now return you to your regular programming."

"She thinks *she's* confused," Noel said. "Caitlin, does your saying 'Hello, Mr. MacAllister' to Matt mean we're getting a happy ending here?"

Caitlin pressed the remote to turn off the television and smiled at Noel.

"Oh, yes, very happy and very forever," Caitlin said. "Matt understood what I meant by my saying what I did. He's on his way over here right now."

"I'm gone," Noel said. "The babies are asleep. Let's get them into their cribs." She frowned. "'Hello, Mr. MacAllister'? I just don't get it."

The twins were tucked into their beds, Noel hugged Caitlin, who thanked Matt's sister for her wonderful performance, then Noel rushed out the door.

Five minutes after Noel left, Matt pulled in to the driveway, patted his suit coat pocket to be certain once again that the rings he'd bought in China were safely there and seconds later was sprinting toward the front door of Caitlin's house. She flung open the door, her eyes brimming with tears and a lovely smile on her face. Matt stepped into the room, pushed the door closed, then framed her face in his hands.

"Hello," he said, his voice husky with emotion and his dark brown eyes glistening. "Hello, Mrs. MacAllister."

He lowered his head and kissed her, softly, reverently, lovingly. It was a kiss that sealed their commitment to a life to be spent together, in proper balance.

They were Mr. and Mrs. MacAllister, father and mother to Mackenzie and Madison, husband and wife, from now until forever.

* * * * *

That
Blackhawk Bride

BARBARA
McCAULEY

BARBARA McCAULEY

has written more than twenty novels. She lives in Southern California with her own handsome hero husband, Frank, who makes it easy to believe in and write about the magic of romance. Barbara's stories have won and been nominated for numerous awards, including the prestigious RITA® Award from the Romance Writers of America.

One

_____

"Clair, for heaven's sake! How will Evelyn ever get this done if you don't stop fidgeting?" Josephine Dupre-Beauchamp glanced at the gold Rolex watch on her slender wrist, sighed, then frowned impatiently at her daughter. "Now stand up straight, dear, and goodness, keep your chin up. The wedding is only three days away and this has to be *perfect*."

Josephine, with her willowy figure and stunning dark looks, was herself a picture of perfection. Some said that her daughter looked just like her, though Clair was three inches taller and her eyes were blue instead of Josephine's brown. "From our French ancestors," Josephine had always proclaimed when anyone commented on her daughter's striking eye color.

While Josephine circled, Clair sucked in her stomach, gritted her teeth against the pins sticking in her bust and waist, then rolled her shoulders back and lifted her chin.

She couldn't breathe, couldn't move, and an annoying, persistent itch stabbed the center of her back.

Three days.

As if Clair needed her mother, or anyone else for that matter, telling her that her own wedding was only three days away.

To be precise: seventy-eight hours, forty-two minutes and—she looked up at the wall clock in the exclusive bridal shop fitting room—thirty-seven seconds.

Clair swallowed the lump in her throat. From the triple mirrors in front of her, three identical young women dressed in white satin and Italian lace stared back. It was odd, Clair thought, that the reflecting images didn't really look like her at all.

Didn't *feel* like her.

"She's lost weight." Evelyn Goodmyer, the hottest and most sought after couturier in all of South Carolina, pinched the seam under Clair's arm and frowned. "She was a perfect size six when we measured four weeks ago and her bust was a 34B. How can I possibly—"

"Ohmigod, Jo-Jo!" Victoria Hollingsworth burst into the fitting room, waving a newspaper. "Wait until you see *this!*"

Momentarily distracted by the triple reflection of herself in the mirrors, Victoria tucked a short red curl behind her ear, then smoothed a hand over her ecru raw silk trousers.

"*Vickie.*" Josephine crossed her arms and arched an impatient brow.

Victoria dragged her gaze from the mirror, then

snapped open the newspaper and thrust it under Josephine's nose. "This morning's *Charleston Times*," she said, smiling brightly. "Society section, center page."

Victoria had not only been Josephine's college roommate at Vassar University, she was also Clair's godmother. And—Clair felt her heart skip as she glanced at the clock again—in seventy-eight hours, thirty-nine minutes and twenty-six seconds, Victoria would become her mother-in-law, as well.

Clair craned her head slightly to get a view of the paper, but could only see the picture of a charging bull running amuck in a china shop on the back page.

Victoria quickly snatched the newspaper back and started to read, "'Oliver Hollingsworth and his fiancée, Clair Beauchamp, photographed while attending a charity ball last week in support of the new children's wing at St. Evastine's Memorial Hospital, will wed this Saturday at Chilton Cathedral.'"

Josephine brushed an imaginary piece of lint from her beige linen jacket. "That's it?"

"Of course not, silly." Victoria cleared her throat. "'Ms. Beauchamp, twenty-five, daughter of shipping magnate, Charles Beauchamp III and Josephine Dupre-Beauchamp, longtime residents of Rolling Estates in Hillgrove, is a summa cum laude graduate from Radcliffe University. Oliver, twenty-six, son of Nevin and Victoria Hollingsworth, also residents of Rolling Estates, recently received his M.B.A. from Harvard after graduating Phi Beta Kappa from Princeton. He is currently manager of accounts at Hollingsworth and Associates accounting firm in nearby Blossomville.'"

Victoria's eyes filled with tears and her voice wavered. "My little boy's all grown up, Jo-Jo. And Clair, our beautiful, precious Clair—"

Both Victoria and Josephine looked at Clair and sighed.

Stop! she wanted to yell at them. Stop, stop, *stop!* Between her mother and godmother these past few weeks, Clair had seen more female tears than a boy band concert.

When Evelyn jammed another pin into the pearled bodice of the wedding dress and hit skin, Clair felt her own eyes tear.

"Shame on you, Vickie, you're making her cry, too." Sniffing, Josephine took the newspaper from Victoria and folded it. "You can read this later, Clair. We've got to hurry if we're going to make our eleven thirty lunch reservations at Season's."

Clair opened her mouth, but before she could speak, Evelyn cut her off.

"I can't possibly finish that quickly," the couturier insisted. "And she still needs to try on the shoes you've ordered. She can meet you there when we're done here."

"I suppose that will be all right." Josephine stepped close to her daughter and pressed a kiss to her cheek. "I'll send Thomas back to pick you up, dear. Call me when you're on your way and I'll order for you."

While Evelyn walked Josephine and Victoria to the front of the shop, Clair turned back to the mirrors and stared.

This time, the tears that burned her eyes had noth-

ing at all to do with sharp pins. She looked at the
clock again.

Seventy-eight hours, twenty-nine minutes and
twelve seconds....

Jacob Carver was in a hell of a bad mood. He supposed the ninety-degree heat and one hundred percent
humidity inside his car might be the reason. Or perhaps it was because he'd driven twelve hours straight
through from New Jersey last night and hadn't seen
a bed in twenty-four hours. Or quite possibly his foul
disposition had something to do with the fact he'd
been sitting across the street from this fancy bridal
store for two hours, sweating his butt off, without so
much as a glimpse of the woman.

What the *hell* could she possibly be doing in there
for two hours?

Not that he really wanted to know, Jacob thought
as he reached for another bottle of water from the
foam ice chest on the front seat of his car. There were
areas where he preferred to maintain his ignorance.
Anything connected to weddings was at the top of the
list and a female shopping was a close second. The
less he knew about those things, the better.

He guzzled half the bottle of water, then tossed it
back in the cooler. The upside was that the mother had
left a half hour ago with another woman. Since he'd
had explicit instructions from Lucas Blackhawk that he
was to approach Clair Beauchamp only if she were
alone, Jacob figured his window of opportunity would
be opening any minute now. Based on the tight leash
the Beauchamps kept on their only daughter, Jacob also
figured he might not get another opportunity.

And Lord knew, if Mommy and Daddy Beauchamp
caught sight of a long-haired private investigator

speaking to their precious little girl, they'd probably call the cops and have him locked up faster than he could say Jack Daniels. It wouldn't matter that he hadn't broken any laws, either. The rich had their own set of rules, their own laws.

And he had his.

But he had no intention of going to jail. Not for anyone, or any amount of money. He'd do what he'd been paid to do, then he'd hit the road again. Because he specialized in the most difficult, or most touchy, location of missing persons, his referral work took him all over the country. It kept him on the road more than at his apartment in New Jersey, but that was fine with him. Jacob liked to keep moving, and he liked to move fast.

And he had the car to do it in—a '68 Charger 426 Hemi, stroked and bored to 487 cubic inches. Restored meticulously by his own hands, his baby was all muscle and speed. On the open road, she could do a quarter-mile in 10.6.

He just might see if he could break that record after this job was done. Maybe he'd head down to Miami for a couple of weeks, find a warm, sandy spot on a beach and share a pitcher of margaritas with…what was that waitress's name he'd met last year when he'd been staking out a con artist at a resort hotel? Sandy—that was it. Blonde and buxom and happily divorced. He smiled at the memory, realized he'd been working too many hours for way too long. All work and no play had indeed made Jacob a very dull boy.

But all that was about to change.

Jacob sat abruptly when the woman came out of the bridal shop. She carried a shopping bag in one

hand and a small clutch purse in the other. The sun
shimmered off her baby-blue silk tailored pantsuit and
picked up the strands of red in her shoulder-length
dark hair. He watched as she slipped on a pair of
sunglasses, then stood in front of the shop, glancing
in the direction of oncoming traffic.

Damn, but she was a looker. She was tall for a
woman, he thought, probably around five foot seven
or eight, very slender, with long legs and a delicate
bone structure. Her face was heart-shaped, with high
cheekbones and finely arched brows.

And her mouth, Lord. Wide and lush and curved
at the corners.

He sighed with disappointment. She was business,
he reminded himself, not pleasure.

But hey, he thought, snatching his keys from his
ignition. A guy can look, can't he?

He slipped out of his car, careful not to make eye
contact with her as he casually stepped off the curb.
It appeared that she was waiting for a ride and he'd
have to move fast or she'd get away. He was halfway
across the street when she turned suddenly, then
walked quickly in the opposite direction and disappeared around the corner.

Dammit!

Had she seen him? he wondered. He didn't think
so, and even if she had, she couldn't possibly know
he was coming for her. He sprinted to the corner, then
looked down the street. There were people out walking, business men and women headed for lunch and
shoppers coming out and going into stores, but no
sign of Clair Beauchamp.

What the hell? Had she gone into another store?
Clenching his jaw, he was about to head for the clos-

est shop, Maiman's Jewelers, when he spotted the arched brick walkway leading to an inner court. The scent of grilling hamburgers and freshly made pizza drifted from the corridor.

Letting instinct lead him, Jacob ducked into the walkway and followed it into an inner, open-air court-yard heavy with ferns and fountains. Lunch diners sat at wrought-iron tables and chairs in the center of the shaded court where vendors served everything from sandwiches to hot dogs.

Gotcha.

She stood in front of a corner cart where a freckled-faced young man was too busy staring at his pretty customer to pay attention to the money she was counting out. When she looked up at the moon-eyed kid, he turned bright red, then handed her a plump hot dog smothered in ketchup and mustard. Jacob shook his head with amusement, then ducked behind a fern when she glanced over her shoulder in his di-rection. He watched as she walked a few feet away and stood with her back to him.

"Show time," Jacob muttered under his breath.

He came up behind her, stopped three feet away to give her a little space. "Clair Beauchamp?"

She jumped, and without turning around, pitched the hot dog into the trash can. Puzzled, Jacob watched as she straightened her shoulders and turned.

"Yes?"

Damn. She might be business, but his pulse still leaped when she faced him. He thought she'd looked good from across the street, but close up she was lethal.

"Miss Beauchamp, I—" He paused, then looked at the trash can and frowned. "Why did you do that?"

"Do what?"

Annoyed, he gestured toward the trash can. "Throw a perfectly good hot dog away."

"I have no idea what you're talking about." Lifting her pretty chin, she slid her sunglasses down her nose. "Do I know you?"

Oh, she was good, Jacob thought. Just the right amount of disdain in her soft Southern voice and impatience in her piercing blue gaze to put him in his place without being overly rude. What the hell. What did he care if she'd tossed the damn hot dog? No skin off his nose.

"My name is Jacob Carver." He pulled out his P.I. badge and flashed it at her. "I've been hired by a lawyer's firm in Wolf River, Texas, to contact you."

She leaned closer and took a look at his badge, then slid her sunglasses back up. "Whatever for?"

"Can we sit?" He nodded at an empty table a few feet away.

"I'm afraid not, Mr. Carver. I'm already late for a lunch meeting." She flipped open the catch on her purse, then smoothly retrieved a card and handed it to him. "If you call this number, my mother's secretary will set up an appointment. Now if you'll excuse me—"

"Miss Beauchamp." He moved and blocked her path, watched her lips press together in annoyance. "My employer insists that I speak to you and only to you."

"And I insist that you let me pass."

"I only want five minutes." He smiled and spread his hands. "You don't need to be afraid. I'm not here to hurt you."

"I'm not afraid," she said icily. "I'm in a hurry."

But the fact was, Clair thought, she *was* afraid. And though she was used to people approaching her, usually for a donation to a charity or a request for an endorsement, it wasn't every day a man sneaked up behind her, caught her completely off guard, then cornered her.

And he wasn't just *any* man, she thought, holding her purse tightly to her chest. He had to be the most *rugged* man she'd ever seen. The navy-blue T-shirt he wore hugged his muscular upper torso, while faded denim stretched across his long legs. He'd neglected to cut his dark hair for some time and his face—a face that had made her breath catch when she'd first turned around—hadn't seen the sharp end of a razor for a couple of days, either. His eyes were almost as dark as his hair, his nose bent at the bridge and his mouth—her gaze dropped there now—his mouth had a devil-take-you arrogance that made her throat go dry.

Straightening her shoulders, she tried to push past him. "I'm sorry, but I really can't—"

Once again he blocked her. "Have you ever heard the names Jonathan and Norah Blackhawk?"

"No. And I would appreciate—"

"What about Rand and Seth Blackhawk?"

She faltered, had to blink back the unexpected and sudden pain behind her eyes. She'd never heard any of those names before, she was certain she hadn't. And yet...

Rand and Seth...

She shook her head. "Why would I?"

"Because—" Jacob leaned down and inched his face closer to hers "—Jonathan and Norah Blackhawk are your real parents, and Rand and Seth are your brothers.''

She stared at him for what felt like an eternity, then started to laugh. ''That's the most ridiculous thing I've ever heard.''

But he didn't smile, just kept that dark, somber gaze locked on her face. ''Jonathan and Norah were killed in a car accident in Wolf River twenty-three years ago. Their three children were in the car, as well, but they survived the accident and were split up. Rand, age nine, was adopted by Edward and Mary Sloan in San Antonio. Seth, age seven, was adopted by Ben and Susan Granger, in New Mexico. Elizabeth Marie, age two, was adopted by Charles and Josephine Beauchamp, from South Carolina, but living in France at the time. You and Elizabeth, Miss Beauchamp, are one and the same.''

The smile on her lips died, and the pain behind her eyes intensified. ''This is either a bad joke, Mr. Carver, or you're a bad private investigator who's made a very big mistake.''

''This is no joke,'' he said, shaking his head. ''And I don't make mistakes. You were born Elizabeth Marie Blackhawk, adopted illegally by the Beauchamps while they were living in France. When Charles and Josephine returned to the States a year later with a three-year-old baby girl and told everyone you were their daughter, no one questioned their story.''

White spots swam in front of her eyes, and the sounds of people talking and laughing suddenly seemed very far away. ''I—I don't believe you.''

''Come, sit down.'' His voice was gentle as he touched her arm. ''Just for a minute.''

Dazed, she let him lead her to a table where he

pulled a chair out for her. She started to sit, then shook her head. "No. This is *ridiculous*." She jerked her arm from his hand. "I *do not* believe you!"

Heads turned. Clair didn't look at them, didn't care. What did it matter if a hundred people stared? A thousand? The man—Jacob—reached into his back pocket, pulled out some folded papers, then handed them to her.

"I realize you need some time to think about this, Miss Beauchamp. These documents will explain what happened. Read them, ask your parents for the truth. Call me when you're ready."

The papers in his hand might as well have been snakes. She couldn't touch them, *wouldn't* touch them.

With a sigh, he slipped them into her shopping bag. Her heart pounded in her chest and the pain behind her eyes became unbearable.

She had to get out of here. Now.

She turned and ran...and did not look back.

"Clair, darling, please open the door. Please, baby."

Clair lay on her bed inside her locked bedroom and ignored her mother's persistent knocking. She'd been standing in the hallway for fifteen minutes, pleading, threatening, even crying, but Clair had refused to answer.

"I know you're in there, sweetheart. Talk to me. Tell me what's wrong. Your daddy and I will fix it."

Holding the papers that Jacob Carver had given her, Clair stared at the ceiling. The documents were from a lawyer named Henry Barnes: a copy of a birth certificate, a newspaper article describing the car accident, a photograph—enlarged and scanned—of Norah Blackhawk in a hospital bed holding a new-born, surrounded by her smiling family: a handsome husband and two little boys.

Clair had stared at the photograph for the past hour. Norah Blackhawk looked so much like herself, she thought. The same hair, the same high cheekbones, the same blue eyes.

And the most damning evidence of all, a copy of a contract between a lawyer named Leon Waters in Granite Springs and Charles and Josephine Beau-champ, a vague agreement to exchange an undis-closed amount of money if a certain "package" met with their approval.

Clair had come straight home after the P.I. Jacob had sucker punched her with this information. She hadn't believed anything the man told her, she *still* didn't believe it.

How could it be possible? How could any of this have happened? And why would her parents have done such a thing?

"Oh, Charles, thank God you're here," Clair heard her mother say on the other side of the door. "She was supposed to meet Victoria and me for lunch, but she never showed so I called the house and Tiffany said that she came in over an hour ago, looking as if she'd seen a ghost. She wouldn't speak to Tiffany or Richard, just went straight to her room and now she won't open the door."

"Clair, this is your father!" A heavy knock rattled the walls. "Open this door at once! I haven't time for this nonsense."

With a sigh, Clair sat. She knew she wouldn't be

able to hold her father off for long. She was going to have to face her parents and it might as well be now.

A knot twisted in her stomach as she stood, and she stared at the papers still in her hand.

Jonathan and Norah Blackhawk are your real parents...killed in a car accident...Rand and Seth...

Rand and Seth. Those names meant something to her. Something important.

She sucked in a breath and swallowed hard. Whatever the truth was, whatever it was that happened twenty-three years ago, she had to know.

"Clair Louise! Open up immed—"

Her father's fist was in the air, ready to knock again, as Clair opened the door. Wide-eyed, her mother rushed forward.

"Clair, baby!" Her mother hugged her.

"What's happened?" her father demanded.

Her body stiff, Clair pulled away from her mother's embrace, then stepped aside. "Mother, Father. Come in and sit down, please."

It amazed Clair how calm her voice sounded, how calm *she* actually felt.

"What's gotten into you?" Charles frowned. "Your mother dragged me away from a meeting, insisting you were ill. I demand to know what's going on."

"Stop yelling at her, Charles." Josephine waved a dismissive hand at her husband. "Can't you see she's already upset?"

"Mother—"

"Clair, sugar." Josephine reached out and cupped Clair's face in her hands. "All brides are nervous before their wedding. It's perfectly normal. Charles, run and get my sedatives from the medicine—"

"No!"

Charles and Josephine both went still. Clair had never spoken to her parents in that tone of voice in her entire life. She couldn't even remember if she'd ever said no to them.

"Clair, you're frightening me." Her mother clasped a hand to her throat. "What is it? What's—"

"Wolf River."

"Wolf River?" Josephine whispered, then glanced at her husband.

And in that second, in that space between heart-beats, between breaths, Clair knew it was true.

Dear God.

Josephine's deep-brown eyes filled with panic. She made a move toward her daughter, but Clair held out a hand and shook her head.

"It's true." Clair felt her heart slam against her ribs and her pulse pound in her head. "I *am* adopted."

Charles pressed his mouth into a firm line. "Where did you hear such a thing?"

For the past hour, she'd been praying that someone had been playing a horrible joke on her, or that the private investigator had made a mistake.

I don't make mistakes, he'd told her.

Based on her parents' expressions, it appeared that he was right.

Her throat felt like dust, and when she finally found the words to speak, her voice was barely a whisper. "A man named Jacob Carver, a private investigator hired by a lawyer from Wolf River, approached me when I came out of Evelyn's. He gave me a news-paper article about the car accident and a photograph

of my birth parents and two brothers.'' Clair held up
the papers in her hand. "He also gave me a copy of
a document, an agreement between you and a man
named Leon Waters.''

Josephine gasped, then reached for her husband's
arm to steady herself. "Clair—"

"He told me my name—my real name—is Elizabeth Marie.'' Clair moved to her bedroom window,
stared out at the sprawling front lawn of the estate
where she'd been raised. It was green and lush, surrounded by neat rows of thick azaleas and tall crepe
myrtles. The house, a two-story brick tudor, with ten
bedrooms and a grand, sweeping staircase guaranteed
to present the most proper, the most elegant, and the
most impressive entrance to any party, was the largest
in the wealthy neighborhood.

"My...parents' names were Jonathan and Norah
Blackhawk. Jonathan was Cherokee and Norah was
Welsh.''

"Please, come sit down," Charles said tightly.
"We need to talk about this.''

Clair turned sharply from the window. "You
bought me. Just like one of your ships or houses or
cars.''

"For God's sake, Clair." Charles shook his head.
"You're overdramatizing. It wasn't like that at all.''

She held the papers to her stomach as if they were
a shield. "Then why don't you tell me what it *was*
like?''

"Charles, please, let me." Josephine looked up at
her husband and squeezed his arm. When he nodded,
she turned her gaze back to her daughter. "Shortly
after your father and I were married, his business partner in Paris offered to sell his interest in the company.

Though it meant moving to France for a few years and being away from the States, we both knew it was an opportunity we couldn't let pass. It was a busy time for your father, and I was alone a great deal of the time. Two years later, when we found out I was pregnant, we were both thrilled.''

Josephine moved to Clair's bed and sank down on the edge. "I miscarried at five months. There were complications. I...I had to have a hysterectomy when I was only twenty-eight.'' Josephine closed her eyes. "I thought my life was over.''

Through her own cloud of confusion and anger, Clair's heart ached for her mother. She moved to the bed and sat beside her. There were tears in Josephine's eyes when she opened them again.

"When your father brought you home to me—'' Josephine reached up and tucked a loose strand of hair behind Clair's ear "—I didn't ask how he found you. I didn't care. All I knew was that you were the most beautiful child I'd ever seen, the most perfect little girl in the whole world, and you belonged to me. You were three when we came back to the States and since we'd been gone for over four years, there were never any questions.''

"Mr. Carver said the adoptions were illegal.'' Clair looked at her father. "That a lawyer named Leon Waters sold me to you.''

"That vile man,'' Josephine said with a shudder. "I never would have known his name if he hadn't called six months after you came to live with us. He threatened to take you away from us if we didn't give him more money. We gave him what he wanted, and then your father told me the truth after everything. About Wolf River and how your family had died.''

"Mr. Carver said my brothers didn't die." Clair handed the photograph of her birth family to her mother. "That they live in Texas and they want to meet me."

Josephine shook her head. "That's not true. There were death certificates on record for your brothers. Your father told me he saw them."

"But the newspaper—" she drew in a deep, steadying breath "—the article said that the *entire* Blackhawk family was killed."

"The lawyer assured me that was an error by an incompetent reporter," Charles stated firmly. "Waters knew that I wanted to adopt without going through months—if not years—of paperwork, so when you were brought to him, he didn't bother to correct the newspaper. He called me, I flew to the States, then I brought you back to France with me."

"Clair." Josephine took her daughter's hand. "This man, this Jacob Carver, is lying about your brothers. He must have found out what happened and he wants money. That's the only explanation why after all these years this has come to the surface."

Clair shook her head. "He didn't ask me for money."

"Not yet, but he will." Josephine's face was ashen, her voice trembling. "A scandal like this three days before your wedding? He knows we'd do anything to keep this quiet for now. Promise me you won't speak to him again."

"I, I don't know. I'm not—"

"Sweetheart." Josephine's chest rose on a sob. "Even if I didn't carry you in my womb, you're my little girl and I love you so very much. Please, Clair, forgive us for keeping the truth from you, and please,

please tell me you won't speak to that awful man again.''

Maybe she's right, Clair thought. Considering everything she'd just learned, she supposed it was possible that Jacob Carver was lying, that he was looking for some easy money. The P.I. *had* been a bit rough around the edges. And even though he hadn't appeared to be a blackmailer, you certainly couldn't look at a person and know what was going on inside.

She, of all people, knew how true that was.

Numb, Clair settled into the warmth of Josephine's embrace. This was the only mother she knew, the mother who'd played dress-up and dolls with her when she was little, brought her soup when she'd been sick, then tucked her in bed every night. The mother who'd fussed over her first date, cried at her high school and college graduation, worried when she came home too late.

Sooner or later, Clair knew that she would have to deal with the overwhelming reality of being adopted and the fact her parents had lied to her. It was too big, too *huge,* to be avoided or ignored.

And so was the fact that in seventy-six hours, thirty-three minutes and twenty-one seconds, Clair Louise Beauchamp was getting married.

Arms crossed, Jacob leaned against a thick marble column in the back of the one-hundred-eighty-five-year-old cathedral. Huge sprays of white and pink roses filled the church. A quartet played Handel's water music while at least two hundred smiling, murmuring people sat watching a blond bridesmaid dressed in satin turquoise float down an aisle long enough to land a Cessna.

Jacob wondered what those two hundred people would be murmuring if they'd seen Blondie and Oliver slipping out of the Wanderlust Motel at 1:00 a.m. for the past two nights. Most likely they'd be wishing they hadn't had their present engraved.

It had been completely by coincidence that Jacob had discovered Clair's husband-to-be's little peccadillo. Since Jacob hadn't been able to get close to Clair's gated estate, he'd decided to follow her fiancé instead, hoping the prospective groom might somehow lead him to Clair.

Only it wasn't Clair that Oliver Hollingsworth met at the seedy motel just outside of town. It was Blondie. Out of habit, Jacob had snapped a few pictures, but he'd have no use for them. He wasn't here to catch a philandering fiancé or husband. He was here to convince Clair to speak with her brothers, or better, to meet with them.

He'd thought for certain that she would have called him after he'd given her the documents proving his story was true. Though he'd just met her, and barely spoken to her for more than a few minutes, there was something about Clair that made him think she was different from that rich, snobby crowd her family ran with. When she hadn't known he was watching her, there'd been something in her eyes, something in her expression, that set her apart.

Obviously he'd been wrong.

At the sound of the quartet playing the "Wedding March," Jacob straightened. Two hundred heads turned in the direction of the door where the bride would be entering the cathedral.

Damn. So much for catching the bride alone for five seconds. Once she walked down that aisle, it would be days, probably weeks, before he'd be able to get close to her again.

Damn, damn.

He watched the side door at the back of the church open, then, for one long, heart-stopping moment, he simply couldn't think at all. Like a white cloud, Clair Beauchamp floated toward him, her face covered by her veil.

Oliver Hollingsworth might be a two-timing jerk, Jacob thought, but he was one hell of a lucky two-timing jerk.

Clair might have kept her carefully paced stride steady and even, might have kept her shoulders straight and her chin level, might have even remembered to breathe—if she hadn't seen Jacob Carver leaning casually against a marble column when she'd come out of the bride's anteroom.

He wore black—T-shirt, jeans, boots—and Clair thought he looked like the devil himself. When he grinned at her and touched two fingers to his temple, her step faltered and her icy hands clutched desperately at the elegant bouquet of white roses.

How dare he show up here! At her wedding, with two hundred guests in attendance. And how dare he look at her with such accusation in his eyes, such reproach.

So she hadn't called him. Why should she? After twenty-three years, what difference did it make now that she'd been adopted? Her parents loved her. Oliver loved her. They had a wonderful, happy life ahead of them.

Only a few feet away, her father held out a hand to her. She glanced at him, then at Oliver, who stood at the front of the church, watching her, smiling calmly, waiting.

Oh, God.

Her heart pounding fiercely, Clair stepped up to her father and looked into his eyes. "Daddy, I—I'm sorry."

With a sigh, Charles dropped his chin, then nodded. "It's all right, baby." He leaned forward and kissed her on the cheek. "Do what you have to do."

"Thank you," she whispered through the lump in her throat, then handed the bouquet to her father and hugged him. "Tell Mom I love her."

She heard the murmur from the pews behind her as she turned and walked briskly toward Jacob. Lifting her chin, she met his dark gaze with her own.

"Mr. Carver," she said politely. "May I trouble you for a ride?"

Two

While the sun rode low on a silver-streaked horizon, they drove in silence. Past sprawling, two-story colonial estates. Past a thoroughbred farm with long, white fences and sleek, shiny horses grazing in thick, green grass. Past a restored antebellum mansion that was now a hotel and spa.

Clair stared straight ahead, back perfectly straight, her long, elegant neck held high. She clasped her slender hands tightly together in her lap. Between her billowing skirts and the fountain of sheer white netting that covered her head, she literally filled the front seat of his car. The sweet, delicate scent of roses still clung to her gown.

Jacob checked his rear view mirror for the tenth time, was relieved to see that no one had followed them. Pushing her skirt out of his way, he shifted gears and pulled down a quiet, tree-lined neighbor-

hood of old, but elegant brick homes, then parked his
car under the shade of a spreading magnolia. He shut
off the engine, rolled down his window, then reached
across Clair and rolled hers down, as well. She didn't
flinch, didn't move. Didn't speak.

On the same side of the street, a white-haired gen-
tleman strolled toward them with a Pekinese on the
end of a leash. Both man and dog glanced over as
they approached, and the old guy's eyes went soft
with admiration as he stared at the vintage car. When
he caught sight of Clair, the man lifted a curious brow
and then shrugged and moved on.

Clair didn't even notice.

"Clair."

He said her name gently, shifted his body in his
seat and looked at her. She sat stiff as a preacher's
collar, unblinking, her lips pressed into a thin line.

"Clair."

His gaze dropped to her chest to see if she was
breathing. Based on the shallow rise and fall of her
breasts, he determined she was. And because he was
only human, he took a moment to appreciate the view
before he said her name more sharply.

"*Clair.*"

She blinked. Her blue eyes wide, she slowly turned
to look at him.

"You want to tell me what happened back there?"
he asked.

"I—" She stopped, swallowed, then glanced away.
"I just ran out on my fiancé, my parents and two
hundred guests."

He'd pretty much figured that part out. Now to ask
the next, most logical question. "Why?"

"I didn't love him." Her voice quivered. She

turned back and leveled her gaze with his. "I…didn't *love* him."

The second time she said it, her voice was stronger and didn't waver. Jacob leaned back against his car door and studied her, decided that maybe his first assessment of her had been right, after all. Maybe there *was* something different about Clair.

"And you just realized that now?"

She stared at the sparkling diamond on her hand. "I've known Oliver most of my life. Our families spent holidays together, celebrated birthdays and anniversaries. It made my parents so happy when he proposed. It never occurred to me to turn him down."

"Until today."

"My entire life has been a lie." She slipped the ring off her finger and laid it in the palm of her hand. "My parents lied to me. I lied to myself and to Oliver. All because we were afraid to tell the truth, afraid of the consequences. When I walked out and looked at all those people sitting in the church, then saw you, I knew it was now or never."

Her fingers closed around the ring. "They'll never forgive me."

He'd liked to tell her that she'd made the right decision, that her fiancé had been doing the mattress mambo with one of her so-called friends. But he could see the cold fear in her eyes, the heavy guilt. He sure as hell didn't want to be the one to add to the woman's grief.

And besides, Clair Beauchamp's love life wasn't his problem. He'd been hired to find her, not rescue her.

"My parents confirmed everything you said about my birth family." From a pocket at her hip, she pulled out a white silk handkerchief, folded the ring inside, then tucked it back into the dress. "Except they told me that my brothers were dead, that they died in the accident along with my parents. My father saw the death certificates for Rand and Seth."

"The death certificates were phonies," Jacob said. "And so was yours."

She swiveled a look at him, blinked. "Mine?"

Jacob nodded.

"I see." Frowning, she touched a shaking hand to her temple and shook her head. "No, actually, I don't see at all. How could this be possible? How could a family be separated like we were and adopted out, legal or illegal? Why didn't anyone know?"

"The lawyer in Wolf River will explain everything." Jacob pulled his cell phone out of his shirt pocket. "You can talk to your brothers and—"

"No."

He stopped dialing and looked up at her. "No?"

"No. Not on the phone."

"All right." Jacob set the phone down. "I'll drive you to your house, you can pack a few things, then I'll put you on a plane to Dallas. Wolf River is about three hours from the airport and someone will—"

"Mr. Carver, the last place I'd go right now is home. And I have no intention of getting on a plane."

Clair wasn't certain when she'd actually made that decision. Maybe two seconds ago, or maybe the moment she'd seen Jacob in the church. Either way, it didn't matter.

She was *not* going home.

"First of all," he said on an exhale, "why don't you just call me Jacob?"

Clair felt her breath catch when his gaze slid slowly

over her. Something in those dark eyes of his sent a strange shiver up her spine.

Good Lord, it was hot in his car.

"Second…" His gaze came back up to meet hers. "Just in just you forgot, you're still in your wedding dress."

"I assure you, Jacob, *no one* could *possibly* be more aware of what I'm wearing than me." The dress had been made to fit like a glove and it was squeezing the breath out of her. It was squeezing the *life* out of her. "But I'm not going home."

"Oookaay." He draped an arm over his steering wheel. "And your plan is?"

"Quite simple, really." It had taken her mother fifteen minutes to get her veil anchored to her head in the church dressing room. It took Clair two seconds to rip it out. "You'll drive me to Wolf River."

He stared at her for a full five seconds. "Excuse me?"

"I said—" she did her best to ignore the horrific itch between her tightly bound breasts "—I'd like you to drive me to Wolf River."

"Not possible." He shook his head. "I was hired to find you and make contact. I'm sorry, but my job is finished now."

"Then I'm rehiring you." She rolled her shoulders back, but it did nothing to relieve the unbearable itch. "What's your fee?"

"You're actually serious?" His laugh was short and dry. "It doesn't matter what my fee is. I'll take you to the airport and get you on a plane, but that's all I can do."

"I'll double it."

She saw the hesitation in his eyes, the slight lift of one eyebrow, but then he shook his head again.

"Look," he said slowly, "I can appreciate you're a little upset at the moment and you're not thinking clearly, but—"

"Stop." She leaned in closer to him and narrowed her eyes. "Just stop right there. *You* show up three days ago and tell me my entire life has been a lie. I just walked out on the only family I've ever known, not to mention my fiancé and two hundred wedding guests. Do *not* tell me you can appreciate what I'm feeling or thinking at this moment. You can't possibly have a *clue* what's going on inside me right now."

Clair pressed a hand to her stomach, stunned that she'd actually raised her voice. Stunned to realize that it *felt good* to raise her voice. Still, a lifetime of strict manners and proper behavior had her quickly backtracking.

"I apologize." She straightened her shoulders and did her best to ignore the increasing itch across her chest. "That was rude of me. I'm sure we can discuss this in a calm manner."

"There's nothing to discuss."

When his gaze dropped to her breasts and lingered there, Clair felt a thrill lurch in her stomach. Good heavens, but the man was brazen! Even Oliver would never have stared so blatantly at her. She resisted the urge to cover herself with her hands. And scratch.

When his gaze did not lift, the thrill Clair had felt faded and turned to indignation. "Mr. Carver," she said, forcing a cool tone to her voice, "if you stopped staring at my chest, perhaps you could at least hear me out."

"Sorry. But that wasn't there a few minutes ago."

"What wasn't where?"

"That."

Clair glanced down and gasped. On her chest, spreading upward from her décolletage, was a trail of dime-size bright red splotches. Damn this miserable dress!

"That's gotta itch," he said.

"It's nothing," she lied. Her cheeks were as hot as her chest when she grabbed her veil and covered herself. She *wouldn't* scratch. "Mr. Car—Jacob—I need to go to Wolf River, but I also need a few days to absorb everything that's happened. I may not have any money on me at this moment, but I assure you, I have access to personal funds. Name your price."

Damn, but Clair Louise Beauchamp–Elizabeth-Marie Blackhawk was a haughty priss, Jacob thought. He couldn't decide if he was amused or annoyed. Maybe a little of both. But one thing was certain, she was one gorgeous haughty priss.

When she'd tugged her veil away from the sophisticated knot on top of her head, several strands of shiny dark hair had escaped and tumbled down her long, slender neck. Tear-shaped pearls dripped from her earlobes and a matching necklace hugged the base of her throat. She had eyes that flashed blue fire one minute and cold ice the next, and a mouth that could tempt a saint.

He was no saint.

"Look, Clair," he said impatiently. "Maybe you're right. Maybe you do need some time to think all this over. I could check you into a quiet resort somewhere, incognito. In a few days—"

"I have no desire or intention to hide away in a resort." She lifted her chin. "I know what I want.

Maybe for the first time in my life. I'll *triple* your fee.''

"I—" He stumbled mentally as her offer sank in. "Triple?"

"Please." She leaned across the seat, laid her fingers on his arm. "Jacob, please."

Her hand on his bare skin was as smooth and warm as her plea. He told himself the sudden drought in his throat was caused by the late-afternoon heat building inside his car. He watched her lips part softly as she stared imploringly at him and felt a jolt of desire slam into his gut.

Pressing his lips tightly together, he pulled away and shook his head. "No. I'm sorry, but you'll have to—"

When Clair started to ring, Jacob realized his cell phone was somewhere underneath the thick cloud of her gown. She gasped when he burrowed his way through the yards of stiff tulle, then pulled his phone out from under her bottom. "Carver here."

"Jacob Carver, you son of a bitch!" a man said at the other end of the line. "I demand you return my fiancée to the church immediately!"

Jacob raised a brow and casually asked, "To whom am I speaking?"

"You know damn well who you're speaking to," Oliver Hollingsworth yelled. "Get back here now!"

"I'm a little busy at the moment," Jacob drawled. "How 'bout I get back to you?"

Oliver's response had Jacob raising both brows. Clair chewed nervously on her lip.

"I won't be humiliated like this," Oliver screamed into the phone. "You'll return Clair this minute or I'll have your license revoked. I'll sue you for every

penny you have. I'll have you arrested and thrown
in—''

''I've got your number.'' Jacob cut him off.
''Room 16 at the Wanderlust Motel. Nice little place,
though the walls are a little thin, don't you think?''

There was a long, tight silence at the other end of
the line, then Oliver said quietly, ''Look, Carver, I'll
make it worth your while to keep that little bit of
information between us. Say twenty-five thousand?
Return Clair to the church immediately and there'll
be another twenty thousand on top of that. After the
ceremony, you and I can talk man-to-man and—''

Jacob hung up on him, then shut his phone off.

I'll make it worth your while. The bastard hadn't
even asked about Clair, Jacob thought irritably.
Hadn't asked if she was all right, or even to speak to
her. Hollingsworth just wanted her back at the church
so he wouldn't be humiliated.

''Who was that?'' Clair asked anxiously.

''No one you know,'' Jacob said almost truthfully
and watched her relax.

''Jacob, if you would just please reconsider my offer and—''

''Fine.''

''Fine?''

''I'll do it.''

''You will?''

''I said I would, didn't I?'' he said tightly. ''But
we'll do this my way, you got that?''

''Of course.''

She smiled at him so sweetly, with such innocence,
he felt another slam of desire in his gut.

Dammit.

"We'll stop when I say, where I say," he added. "And I don't want a lot of chitchat."

Pressing her lips firmly together, she nodded.

"Buckle up."

She snapped her seat belt on—not an easy task, considering that dress of hers—then leaned back in the seat and stared straight ahead.

He looked at her—her perfect profile, her serene smile, her stunningly beautiful face—and thought he was looking at an angel.

Clenching his jaw, Jacob started the car and headed back toward the highway. If he was going to keep his hands off Clair—and he *would,* dammit—he needed to get to Wolf River as fast—and with as few stops—as possible.

For the next forty-five minutes, Clair did her best not to think about what she'd left behind. Though she had no regrets she hadn't married Oliver, she felt terribly, horribly guilty for leaving like she had. Even if he had never been especially romantic or passionate with her in the two years they'd formally dated, he still hadn't deserved to be abandoned at the altar.

She had no idea if he or Victoria would ever forgive her, or even speak to her again. Strange, but she was most upset at the thought of Victoria never speaking to her again than she was Oliver.

Clair knew her parents would weather the scandal, though certainly those seas would be rough for a while. Knowing she had her father's approval gave her comfort, but there was still her mother to contend with, to appease. The thought made the incessant itch on Clair's chest intensify. She squeezed her fingers into fists, did her best to concentrate on the passing greenery of the countryside and the wail of Aretha Franklin blasting from Jacob's car stereo.

She'd managed not to speak since Jacob had turned onto the highway, hadn't even asked him where they were going. He'd made no effort to speak at all, either. She'd tried counting red cars, then blue cars, then cars with four-doors versus two-doors, but she simply couldn't distract herself from what was currently, and most immediately, on her mind—

The overwhelming, overpowering, all-consuming need to scratch.

Damn, this miserable rash! She knew it was only nerves, but that certainly didn't ease her misery. She'd felt it spreading to her back, and with the way her dress seemed to be shrinking, her entire torso would be covered before long.

She wouldn't scratch…she wouldn't scratch…she wouldn't scratch…

"Stop the car!"

Jacob snapped his head around. "What?"

"Stop the car," she hissed through her teeth. "Now."

Frowning, he pulled off the highway and parked behind a stand of cypress trees. "Sweetheart, if you've changed your mind, then you're on your—"

She unbuckled her seat belt and turned her back to him, pressed a hand to her chest and felt the burning heat there. "Unbutton me."

"What?"

"Hurry!"

Under a more "normal" situation, a woman asking him to unbutton her dress and be quick about it would have been a compliment and a pleasure to Jacob. With Clair, however, the situation was anything but normal.

"Jacob, *please!*"

"All right, all right." Jacob stared at the back of Clair's dress. There were five tiny pearl buttons to release before the zipper could be pulled down. She wiggled under him while he struggled to unbutton her, and when he pulled the zipper down and the garment loosened around her, she let her head fall back and expelled a soft groan of delight.

"Now the corset."

His heart slammed against his ribs. *Oh, no...bad, bad idea...* "I don't really think I should be—"

"I can't do it myself." She squirmed, making the dress gape wider. "I swear I'll scream if I don't get out of this contraption immediately!"

Terrific. The last thing he needed was to be parked off the highway with a half-naked screaming woman. He reached for the top hook, then loosened each one until the stiff lace underwear fell away.

"Bless you," she sighed breathlessly, then sagged sideways against the seat.

Jacob winced at the sight of the red marks on her bare lower back. Her skin was blotchy, like her chest had been, and there were deep impressions from the too-tight corset. Without thinking, he reached out and laid his hand on her back. She jerked upright at the contact and stiffened.

"Relax," he said, lightly rubbing his palm over her hot skin. "I think I can manage to control myself, Clair. Just tell me where it itches."

"Right there." Her voice was strained, but she did settle back against the seat. "Everywhere."

Gently he moved his hand over her lower back, felt her slowly relax under his touch. When he slid his hand upward, she moaned softly and arched her spine against him, Jacob bit the inside of his mouth to hold back the threatening swear word.

Her skin felt like warm silk and he felt his own hand itch to explore, to slip deeper inside the dress and curve around her narrow waist. To slide his palm upward over her flat belly and feel the firm weight of her breast in his hand.

Her back, long and slender, was completely exposed to him. He felt an overwhelming desire to press his mouth to one smooth, bare shoulder and taste her, to nip at her warm skin.

"That feels wonderful," Clair breathed and snuggled against the car seat.

Clair had never experienced anything quite so relaxing—or *erotic*—in her life. Jacob's large hands moving slowly over her back were the most exquisite feeling in the world. His palms were rough, his fingers strong, yet gentle. Her entire body tingled at his touch, her skin felt unusually tight. Warm shivers of sheer pleasure coursed through her veins.

She felt as if she'd been drugged, or as if she'd just wakened from an intensely sensual dream and she was still trapped between fantasy and reality. Her limbs felt heavy, her mind sluggish.

It shocked her that she would allow this man she barely knew to touch her in such an intimate manner. Shocked her that she *wanted* him to touch her, to keep touching her, not only on her back, but other places, too. Her breasts ached to be touched, her nipples tightened. And lower, between her thighs, she felt a heavy warmth and a dull throb.

When his hands slid up her waist and his fingertips were no more than an inch from the underside of her breast, she felt her heart skip a beat, then start to pound furiously. She knew she should move away, but she couldn't. She *couldn't.*

Breath held, eyes closed, she felt him lean closer, felt the warmth of his breath on her shoulder...

And then, just as suddenly, he pulled her dress back up to cover her shoulders and moved away.

"Better?" he asked.

Too embarrassed to turn around and look at him, she simply nodded.

He said nothing, but she heard him open the car door, then step out. Thankful for the moment alone, she covered her face with her hands and groaned. She could only imagine what he must think of her. Not only had she begged him to unhook her dress, she'd allowed—no, *welcomed*—his touch.

She heard him rooting around in his trunk, and when he slammed it shut and came back around the car, she reached behind her to hold her dress together.

He stood outside the driver's door and tossed some clothing into the front seat. "Put these on for now. We'll find something more suitable when we stop for the night."

Clair glanced at the gray sweatpants and plain white T-shirt and looked up at Jacob. "I—thank you."

"You've got five minutes to change, then I'm getting back in this car whether you're dressed or not. I suggest you hurry."

He closed the door, then leaned up against the driver's door, arms crossed. Clair stared at his stiff back for a full ten seconds, then looked at the clothing. They'd be huge on her, but anything was better than this miserable dress.

Five minutes he'd given her, then he was getting

back in the car. Realizing she'd already wasted twenty seconds, she scrambled out of her wedding dress and corset and tossed them in the back seat, yanked the T-shirt over her head, then kicked her satin pumps off. She'd barely tugged the sweatpants over her hips when Jacob climbed back in the car and started the engine.

A plume of dirt sprayed behind them as he headed back to the highway. He held the steering wheel in a death grip and squealed onto the road as if the devil himself were on his heels. When he shifted gears and gunned the motor, the car leapt forward like a beast loosened from its cage.

With the church and her wedding behind her and the long road ahead, Clair felt a giddy sense of freedom she'd never experienced before. Smiling, she snapped her seat belt on, settled back, then mentally sang along with an Eagles' tune blasting from the radio.

Take It Easy...take it easy...

Three

It was nearly eight o'clock when Jacob pulled into the hamburger drive-thru stand. He was hungry, tired and in one hell of a bad mood.

He was used to traveling alone. He *liked* traveling alone. It hadn't mattered that Clair had managed to keep quiet for the entire time they'd been on the road. He couldn't relax, couldn't concentrate with a one-hundred-twenty-pound bundle of female sitting next to him. He'd kept his eyes off her and on the road, but he'd felt the energy radiating from her, felt her excitement, her nervousness, her anxiety.

And if that wasn't enough to drive him crazy, he could smell her. That incredible, tantalizing scent that kept reminding him how soft her skin had been under his hands, how smooth. Reminded him how much he'd wanted to touch her all over. With his hands and his mouth and—

"Welcome to Bobby Burgers in the beautiful town of Lenore, South Carolina. My name is Tiffany," a perky teenager bubbled through the speaker static of the drive-thru stand. "May I take your order, please?"

He dragged a hand through his hair, then stuck his head out of the window. "We'll have three Big Bob's, two fries and two—"

"Wait, wait, wait." Clair unbuckled her seat belt. "Let me look."

"What's to look at?" he said irritably when she scooted across the seat.

Pleasure lit her eyes as she stared at the menu. "Chili fries," she said with reverence. "I want one of those, please."

Shaking his head, Jacob turned back to the speaker. "Make that a—"

"Wait, wait, wait." She leaned over him, placed a hand on his arm. "With extra cheese. Oh, and a chocolate shake."

She was practically in his lap. He could feel the warmth of her body, and the knowledge she had no bra on under his T-shirt had Jacob grinding his teeth. "Is that all?"

"Maybe some extra pickles and mayonnaise on the hamburger. Oh, and some of those little green spicy things, too, please."

"Jalapeños?"

She smiled brightly and nodded. "That's it. On the side."

They picked up their order, then he pulled the car into the hamburger stand's parking lot and handed Clair her cache. She pulled several napkins out of the greasy brown paper bag and spread them over her lap.

Jacob watched with interest as she opened her burger and took a small, delicate bite. She closed her eyes with a sigh and smiled.

"I take it you like Bobby's Burgers," he said, and tore into his own hamburger.

"This is my first." She pulled out a jalapeño and stuck it between the meat and her bun.

"Your first Bobby's Burger?" He stared at her in disbelief. "They have twenty-five thousand franchises in fifty states," he quoted the sign. "*Everyone* has eaten a Bobby's Burger."

"I haven't." She took a bite, then sucked in a breath as she waved her hand in front of her mouth. There were tears in her eyes.

Grinning, he handed her the chocolate shake she'd ordered. She took a long sip, then settled back in her seat and reached for a chili-covered French fry.

"My mother had a very specific list of foods our chef was allowed to prepare." She ate the French fry as delicately as her burger. "Hamburger was on the forbidden list."

"So that's why you pitched the hot dog in the trash can." He reached for his soda. "You thought I was one of your mother's spies."

"Something like that." Clair chewed thoughtfully. "My mother worries."

"About hamburgers and hot dogs?"

"You don't even want to know." She sighed, then stared thoughtfully at another French fry. "Sometimes she's a little overprotective."

"A *little* overprotective?" Jacob snorted and took a gulp of soda. "That's like saying Shaquille O'Neil is a little tall."

Clair lifted her chin. "It's only because she loves

me. I was—am—her only child. I'm sure your mother worries about you, too.''

''My mother worried so much she left me and my younger brother with an alcoholic father when I was nine,'' he said without emotion. ''She did manage to show up at my dad's funeral when I was eighteen, but only because she'd found out she was the beneficiary of a small life insurance policy. She collected her money and I haven't seen her since.''

''I'm sorry,'' Clair said quietly, lifting her gaze to his. ''It appears we come from two extremes.''

''Sweetheart—'' he raised his drink to her ''—that's the understatement of the century.''

They finished their meal in silence, and he had to admit he was more than a little surprised that Clair managed to polish off the food she'd ordered, including the peppers.

He watched her long, slender fingers smooth and fold the paper from her burger, flatten the foam cup her fries had been in, then place everything back in the brown paper bag. It was like watching a ballet, he decided. She moved with the grace and fluidity of a dancer, and the fact she was dressed in an oversize T-shirt and baggy sweats didn't detract from her elegance in the slightest.

Still, no matter how well she wore his clothes, he realized she would need something more suitable for their trip, not to mention a few personal items.

There was no getting around it, Jacob thought with a silent groan. He was going to have to do something he *dreaded*. Something he *swore* he'd never do.

His palms started to sweat at the very thought of it.

He was going to take a woman shopping.

* * *

Two hours later, Clair sat in the middle of her motel room floor and pulled her treasures out of the plastic Sav-Mart shopping bags. A pretty pink cotton tank top, a short denim skirt, a mint-green button-up blouse. She hadn't tried anything on, but she had bags and bags of clothes in front of her. Smiling, she picked up a soft lavender sweater and held it to her cheek.

Every single item she'd chosen completely by herself. She'd never been in a Sav-Mart Department store before, though she'd heard of them. After all, they were the largest discount department store in the country. But Josephine Beauchamp would never have been caught dead in a Sav-Mart. If she knew that her daughter had not only gone to the huge chain store, but bought an entire wardrobe off the racks, she would be hyperventilating. And if she'd seen what her daughter had *worn* to go shopping there—a man's T-shirt, sweatpants and satin pumps—Good Lord, she'd need smelling salts to recover.

Though certainly Clair had felt more than a little self-conscious about her attire when she'd first entered the store, she'd quickly forgotten her discomfort once Jacob had grabbed a shopping cart and headed for the women's section. She'd followed along behind him, trying to keep up with his long strides, while taking in the experience at the same time.

Everything about the warehouse-style shopping had absolutely fascinated Clair. Aisles that seemed as long as a football field, heavily stocked six-foot-high shelves. Huge bins filled with a fascinating assortment of discounted items. Bicycles, trash cans, pet food,

patio furniture, books—everything under the same
roof.

Jacob stopped at the women's section, folded those
muscular arms across that broad chest of his, assumed
a sour expression, then told her to be quick about it.

Clair had always shopped in exclusive specialty
stores with designer labels and tailored, custom-made
clothing. But here there were racks and racks of
ready-to-wear clothes. Dresses, blouses, skirts, underwear, night wear, shoes. Jacob had complained that
she'd grabbed at least one of everything, but he'd paid
for everything with his credit card, and she'd assured
him that he would be reimbursed in full.

She'd filled the cart with clothes, spent another
thirty minutes in the toiletries-and-cosmetics section,
where she'd also bought nearly one of everything,
including a jar of iridescent glitter body cream and a
tube of sparkling, liquid blue eye shadow. Jacob had
driven to the motel when she'd finished shopping, and
she'd waited in the car while he registered them for
two rooms. Grumbling and growling the entire time,
he'd grabbed her shopping bags and the suitcase she'd
picked out, then helped her into her room. Clair was
certain he hadn't said more than three words since
they'd left the store.

She couldn't imagine what his problem was, and
at the moment she really didn't care.

She was too busy having fun.

Dizzy with delight, she reached for the bag filled
with the assortment of underwear she'd picked out.
She'd been thankful that Jacob had occupied himself
with a sports magazine on the other side of the register while she'd emptied the shopping cart onto the
register conveyer belt. If it hadn't been embarrassing

enough to watch the young male clerk pick up and scan her undergarments, he'd also had to yell at another employee for a price check on one of the bras. Clair had forced herself to stand there calmly, though inside she'd wished that the floor would open up and swallow her whole.

Amazingly, she'd survived, and now, sitting cross-legged, she laid everything out in front of her: bras and panties in black lace and white silk and flowered satin. Push-up, sheer, embroidered, strapless—she'd shown no restraint.

And last, but not least, she pulled her most daring purchase of the evening out of the bag—one leopard-print thong panty.

She couldn't wait to try it on.

Gathering everything into her arms, she stood quickly and started for the bathroom. Halfway there, she paused at the first rumble of pain in her stomach.

The knock on the door came at the same time the second pain hit. Sucking in a breath, she set the lingerie on the bed, then carefully, slowly moved toward the door and opened it. Jacob stood on the other side.

He looked at her, then furrowed his brow. "You okay?"

"I—" The pain eased off, though the nausea lingered. "Yes. I'm fine."

"You look a little pale."

"Just a twinge in my stomach. Nerves, I'm sure," she said, drawing in a deep breath. "I'm all right now."

"You sure?"

"I'm fine. Really."

"Good." He held out a sweet-smelling pink box and opened the lid. "I bought some doughnuts across the street. I figured you might want one now or in the morning.''

If she'd been pale a second before, Clair's face turned sheet-white as she stared at the box. Jacob watched her clamp a hand over her mouth, spin on her bare heels and dash for the bathroom. She slammed the door behind her.

Uh-oh.

So much for doughnuts.

He snagged a maple bar for himself, then moved into her room and closed the door behind him. There were bags and articles of clothing everywhere, which hardly surprised him since he'd not only had to suffer the shopping ordeal, he'd hauled all the bags into her room. You'd have thought she was going on a six-month cruise, he thought, taking a big bite of the sugary doughnut. He lifted a brow at the undergarments she'd tossed on the bed. Her choice of lingerie had been the more interesting part of the shopping trip, though he'd pretended not to notice one way or the other what she'd thrown into the Sav-Mart basket. But, hey—he took another bite of doughnut—a guy couldn't completely ignore racy black lace bras and skimpy matching panties, now, could he?

Stepping beside the bed, he picked up the leopard print and nearly choked on his last bite of doughnut.

Good Lord, she'd bought a *thong.*

His heart skipped, then raced as he stared at the tiny scrap of silk. The last thing he needed was an image of thong underwear on Clair. For that matter, he didn't need—or want—an image of Clair in *any* underwear.

No, wait—he shook his head—that wasn't what he meant, either, dammit.

Thankfully the sound of the toilet flushing was like ice water on his wandering thoughts. He dropped the thong back onto the bed, licked the sugar crust off his thumb, then moved to the bathroom door.

"You okay?" He knocked lightly.

"I'm fine," she said weakly. "Go away, please."

Ignoring her request, he opened the door and stepped into the bathroom. She sat on the cool, white tile floor, her back against the tub, her forehead resting on her bent knees. He pulled a washcloth off the towel rack, ran it under cold water, then handed it to her. "Here."

Glancing up, she took the damp cloth and pressed it to her cheeks. "Thank you. Now if you don't mind…"

He sat down beside her. "So what do you think? Was it the chili fries, the chocolate shake, the jalapeños or maybe—"

"*Stop,*" she said on a groan. "I don't need you to tell me it was stupid. I learned that all by myself, thank you very much."

Smiling, he took her chin in his hand and lifted her face. Her skin looked like chalk. "You need to learn to pace yourself, Clair, that's all. Maybe inch out into the cold water, instead of just jumping in. Walk before you run."

"I've been inching and walking my entire life, Jacob," she said softly. "I don't care if the water is cold, I don't care if I fall. I've already missed out on so much. I'll make mistakes, but whatever they are, they'll be mine."

"So the life of a pampered princess is not all it's cracked up to be, is it?" he asked, cocking his head.

"I won't make excuses for who I am, or how I was

raised," she said defensively, then closed her eyes and exhaled slowly. "Or who I thought I was anyway."

He'd been around spoiled, wealthy women who thought the world should revolve around them. But there was something different about Clair. An innocence that unnerved him, made him want to get in his car and drive away as fast and as far as he could.

For a moment, he considered doing just that, then swore silently and scooped her up in his arms instead. She gasped, then stiffened at his unexpected maneuver.

"Well, Miss Beauchamp," he said evenly, "since you don't want to 'miss out' on anything, I suggest we get you in bed."

Her eyes popped open wide. "I never said, I mean, I certainly wasn't implying that I wanted to, I mean, that we should—"

He carried her to the bed. "Relax, Clair. I meant to *sleep*. We've got a long couple of days ahead of us before we get to Wolf River. But hey—" he dropped her on the squeaky mattress "—thanks for thinking of me."

Her cheeks turned scarlet against her still pale skin. "Oh," she said somewhere between a croak and a squeak.

She looked so lost lying on the bed, so…disappointed?…that Jacob considered "jumping in" himself. He stared at her, saw the outline of her soft breasts against his white T-shirt, the faint press of hardened nipples, that long expanse of legs covered by his sweatpants. A jolt of lust shot through his blood.

"Get some sleep," he said through the dryness in

his throat as he turned. "We'll hit the road around nine."

He walked through the connecting door to their rooms, closed it tightly behind him, then groaned.

This, he thought miserably, was going to be one long trip.

It was dark when Jacob woke. He wasn't even certain why he *had* awakened, especially considering it was—he slitted a glance at the red dial of the nightstand clock—*5:46 a.m.*? Good God, it was still the middle of the night.

And was that coffee he smelled? He breathed in the wonderful scent and nestled his head back into his pillow. He'd have to get himself a cup when he finally did wake up in a couple of hours.

But there was another smell, he realized dimly. A light, fresh scent of…peaches? Where was that coming from?

He heard her whisper his name at the same time he felt the mattress dip on the other side of the bed. When he bolted upright, muttering a swear word, she gasped.

"What's wrong?" He could see her outline in the early dawn seeping through the closed drapes, but he couldn't make out her face. She'd already jumped up from the edge of the bed and stood a safe distance away, holding a mug of coffee in her hands. "What's happened?"

"Nothing's happened." Her voice broke, and she cleared her throat. "I wanted to talk to you."

"At five forty-six in the morning?" he hissed.

"It couldn't wait."

"The hell it can't." He pulled the covers up and turned his back to her.

"I have a plan." She came around the bed, flipped on the bedside lamp, then set the steaming mug of coffee on the nightstand.

He winced at the stream of light, was almost enticed by the coffee, then shook it off and growled, "Go away, Clair, or I won't be responsible for anything that happens."

Folding her arms, she looked down her nose at him. "What's *that* supposed to mean?"

He rose on one elbow, let the covers slide down his bare chest and narrowed a look at her. Her hair, still damp from the shower she'd obviously just taken, curved around her pretty oval face and touched the top of the sleeveless button-up pink blouse she wore. She'd pulled on slim-fitting black capris that showed off her long legs and narrow hips. Her feet were bare, her toenails painted with pink glitter polish.

Dammit. He wanted to consume her whole. He fisted the covers in his hands to keep himself from dragging her into his bed and *showing* her *exactly* what he meant.

But he wouldn't. Not only was she a client, she was trouble. With a capital *T*. Clair Beauchamp was complicated. He preferred simple when it came to sex and women.

"Wasn't going into naked, strange men's motel rooms on your mother's forbidden list?" he snarled.

He saw her hesitation, then she squared her shoulders. "Well, that's partly what I want to talk to you about."

Once again she'd caught him off balance. Another reason to keep his distance from this woman. "You want to talk to me about strange, naked men in hotel rooms?''

''Of course not.'' She rolled her eyes. ''I want to talk to you about my plan.''

On a groan, he slid back under the covers. ''Have you always been this big a pest?''

''That's the point, Jacob.'' She sank down on the floor and sat on her heels. ''I've never been a pest. My entire life I've always been expected to, and always have, behaved in a certain manner. It never occurred to me there was an option.''

''You're telling me you never rebelled, even when you were a teenager?'' Even for a socialite priss like Clair, that was hard to believe. He thought about all the foster homes he'd been through, the hell he'd raised through his most difficult years. ''*Every* kid drives their parents nuts at least once.''

''I gave the term PC a whole new meaning.'' She stared down at her clasped hands. ''For me it was Perfect Child. More than anything, I wanted my parents' approval.''

''Not an easy job, I gather,'' he said.

She looked up sharply, a snap of fire in her blue eyes. ''I wasn't the poor little rich girl, if that's what you're thinking. My parents have always been wonderful to me. Have always done what they thought was best for me. They were protective, yes, overly, yes, but only because they loved me. And because I loved them, I wanted to please them.''

At the cost of pleasing herself, Jacob realized. It didn't take a shrink to figure out she'd lost one family and was afraid she'd lose another if she wasn't—in her mind's eye—the ''Perfect Child.'' Even though she'd only been two when her birth parents had died, the memory was locked in her little brain and stayed with her.

But this was hardly the time for Psych 101.

On a sigh, he sat and dragged both hands through his hair. "So what's your plan?"

Smiling, she picked up the coffee mug and handed it to him. "My plan is no plan."

"Excuse me?"

"I've had my whole life mapped out for me, like a paint-by-number. For just a little while, I want to be spontaneous. Impulsive. Irresponsible."

Bad idea, he thought, but who was he to tell her what to do? She'd had enough of that in her life already. He took a sip of coffee. "Fine. I'll get you to Wolf River and you can do and be whatever you want from that point."

"I mean *before* I get to Wolf River. I want to take the long way there. See things I've never seen. Do things I've never done. Experience as much as I can along the way." Her eyes were as bright as her smile. "And I want you to drive me."

"Me?" Coffee sloshed over the sides of his cup. *Very* bad idea. "No way."

"Jacob, I'll pay you for your time." She rocked forward off her heels and laid her arms on the edge of the bed. "What's another three or four days?"

The heat of her body and the scent of peaches drifting off her smooth skin sent his blood racing. Could she possibly be so oblivious not to realize the effect she had on him? Or was she manipulating him to get what she wanted?

Either way, he felt the slow rise of anger. He set the coffee mug down, then startled her when he took hold of her shoulders and brought her close.

"Let me spell it out for you, Clair," he said narrowing his gaze. "Client or no client, I don't trust myself to keep my hands off you for the next two days, let alone another three or four."

She stared at him, her eyes wide. "I trust you," she said quietly.

He didn't *want* her to trust him, dammit. Didn't want that kind of responsibility.

"You want spontaneity? You want impulsive?" he said through gritted teeth. "Fine. You got it."

He dragged her closer and covered her mouth with his, felt the shock wave course through her body. He was shocked, as well, not only at the raw intensity of his own need, but the fact she didn't pull away. He parted those incredible lips of hers with his tongue, then dived inside.

And still she didn't pull away.

She was every bit as sweet as he'd imagined. He tipped her head back and deepened the kiss even more, felt her shiver of response and her low, soft moan. Her lips molded to his, then tentatively she met his tongue with her own.

It was the shimmer of innocence that had him yanking his head back. He stared down at her, watched her thick lashes slowly rise. There was confusion in her eyes, and desire. Definitely desire. Her lips were still parted and wet from his kiss.

He'd expected her to slap him, or at the very least, to tell him off. The fact that she did neither nearly had him dragging her back to him again.

He wanted to, dammit. His body ached to bring her to his bed.

But he wouldn't. Somehow, somewhere, he knew there'd be a price he wasn't willing to pay.

"Don't trust me," he said dryly and released her so suddenly she fell back on the floor. "Get yourself another man."

She sat there staring at him, then slowly, as unexpected as everything else was with this woman, she started to laugh.

"What's so damn funny?"

"Whatever on earth made you think I'm looking for a man?" she said, crossing her arms over her stomach. "Good heavens, the *last* thing I need or want right now is a man."

"Is that so?"

"Don't take offense, Jacob." Tucking her hair back behind her ears, she sat down on her heels again. "I mean, that kiss was very nice and all, but I assure you I wasn't looking for anything more than a ride to Wolf River with a few detours along the way."

His kiss was *very nice?* He frowned darkly. He'd show her *very nice...*

But she was already up on her feet and moving toward the door. "I'm sorry you don't want the job," she said over her shoulder. "I'll send you a check for your time and expenses. Thank you for everything you've done for me and if you—"

"Just stop right there."

She paused at the connecting door and looked back at him. "Yes?"

"What do you think you're doing?"

"I'm going to pack, then call a rental car company to come pick me up."

"You're going to drive yourself?" he asked incredulously.

She turned and lifted a brow. "I don't believe that's any of your business."

"Well, I'm making it my business, dammit." He grabbed the sheets, then wrapped them around him as he slid off the bed.

Damn fool woman.

Her eyes widened when he stomped across the room toward her. "We'll leave in fifteen minutes and you better be ready. Until I've had at least three cups of coffee, don't speak to me. Got that?"

"All right," she said demurely.

"Now unless you want an eyeful," he snapped, "I suggest you get the hell out of my room."

She moved quickly across the threshold, then shut the door tightly behind her. Jacob stared at the closed door for a full minute and wondered what the hell had just happened.

You lost your mind, Carver, he said, swearing hotly. *That's what happened.*

The No-Plan, Plan, my ass.

Still swearing, he headed for the shower and decided it was going to be a cold one.

Four

Clair suspected that Jacob kept the volume on his CD player high to deter conversation from her as much to enjoy the music. She didn't mind, not only because she enjoyed the diverse selection of rock he played—Dave Matthews, Beatles, Stones, Springsteen, Zeppelin—but because she needed a little time alone with her own thoughts at the moment, as well.

She glanced at Jacob, watched his thumbs move to the beat of "Jumpin' Jack Flash," and wondered if he knew he hummed along with most of the songs and even occasionally, under his breath, sang a line or chorus. But then he'd catch himself and sink back into that brooding silence of his. It was obvious he was used to being alone in this big car, and he wasn't happy about anyone invading the sanctity of his space.

They'd left Lenore three hours ago and at her request, stopped for bottled water in a town called Don't Blink, then crossed the state line into Georgia. The day was hot and humid, and Clair was thankful that Jacob's car had an air conditioner powerful enough to keep a penguin cool.

Or a woman whose body was still on fire after being thoroughly and completely kissed.

Jacob's kiss had sizzled her brain and scorched her body clear down to her toes. Even now, her lips still tingled and her stomach fluttered. Her entire life, Clair had been taught how to behave with poise and grace. To be calm and composed in every situation. One kiss from Jacob, and she'd nearly melted into the floor.

She'd nearly begged for more.

Oliver's kisses had been…polite compared to Jacob. Pleasant. Controlled. Tepid. Jacob's kiss had been wild and reckless. *Hot.*

He'd told her he didn't think he could keep his hands off her, and though his words had made her heart skip and her breath stop, she didn't believe him. A man like Jacob couldn't really be interested in an inexperienced, bluenose stiff like herself. She knew he'd only said that, then kissed her to intimidate her, to change her mind about taking detours on the way to Wolf River.

But his intentions had not made the kiss any less thrilling. If anything, he'd proven to her that there was a whole world waiting to explore, to experience. And while she might not be ready for the Jacob Carvers of the world, she was definitely ready for a little excitement, a little adventure.

While she pretended to be engrossed in the lush greenery of the passing farms and hillsides along the highway, she cast a sideways glance at him. The black T-shirt he had on fit snugly over his broad chest and muscular arms. He wore a day-old beard and a pair of sunglasses. A small, jagged scar over his right eyebrow reminded her of a bolt of lightning. His jaw was strong, his nose slightly crooked, his mouth—her breath caught just thinking about his mouth—was bracketed by lines on either side.

Even though *she* wasn't looking for a man at the moment, she could only imagine that Jacob had more than his share of interested females. The man exuded the kind of raw masculinity that would have women dropping at his feet.

She yanked her gaze away, disgusted at her line of thinking. In a meadow beyond a white rail fence, she saw two little boys running through knee-high grass, pulling red and yellow kites high in the air behind them. Long, blue streamers swirled from the bottom of each kite.

"I've never done that," she said absently, watching the kites dip and soar with the air current.

He lowered the music. "What?"

She turned in her seat, still staring out the window as the car passed the meadow. "I've never flown a kite."

"Never?"

She felt silly now that she'd said it. Leaning back in her seat, she looked over at Jacob. "Have you?"

"Of course."

"What color was it?"

He furrowed his brow. "Color?"

"Your kite."

"Oh. Orange, with the number O1."

"Why, 01?"

He looked at her as if she knew nothing. "The General Lee."

"General Lee?"

"You know. *The Dukes of Hazard.* Bo Duke, Luke Duke, Daisy Duke."

"The TV show." Understanding finally dawned. "I've heard of it."

"But you've never seen it?" he said in disbelief. "Jeez, you *did* lead a sheltered life."

"More like a scheduled life." She thought of all the after school lessons, the Saturday recitals. "Ballet, piano, Cotillion."

"Cotillion?"

"Formal dances for young people," she explained.

Jacob shuddered. "I'd rather drive nails through my toes."

She laughed. "Sometimes it felt like that if you got the wrong partner. But we learned proper etiquette and social graces."

"Yeah? Like what?"

She sat very straight and lifted her chin. "Introductions, for one. 'Mr. Carver,'" she said in a very stuffy voice. "'May I introduce you to Mrs. Widebottom. Mrs. Widebottom, Mr. Carver.'"

He tilted his head down and glanced at her over the top of his sunglasses. "You're kidding, right?"

"Absolutely not. Then, Mr. Carver, you would ask Mrs. Widebottom if she would like a glass of punch. 'Why, yes, Mr. Carver, I'd love a glass of punch.'" Clair batted her eyes. "After you fill the punch glass for her, you then ask if she'd like a cookie. Once you have punch and cookies, you have a conversation."

"You mean you can't just eat the cookies?"

"Heavens, no. You have to talk first. Engaging

your partner in polite conversation is required. 'Mr. Carver, that's a very nice T-shirt you're wearing. Is it Tommy Hillfiger, by chance?'''

One corner of his mouth lifted. '''Why, no, Mrs. Widebottom, it's Sidewalk Sam.'''

'''I'm not familiar with that designer,''' Clair said with a sniff. '''New York, or Paris?'''

'''Lower East Side. Sam's on his corner from noon to six every afternoon. Three shirts for twelve bucks, but if you tell him you know me, he'll cut you a deal.'''

It was the first time Jacob had truly heard Clair laugh, and the sound rippled over his skin. The smile on her lips faded when she turned back to the window and stared out.

"Did you ever wonder," she said thoughtfully, "what your life would be like if your mother had never left?"

He had from time to time. But he knew what she was really wondering about was how different her own life would be if her birth mother hadn't died. He shrugged, then focused his gaze back on the highway. "You can't change your life. It is what it is."

She shook her head. "It's not that I want to change it, I just want to make it better."

"You already did that yesterday, when you walked out of that church. That took guts, Clair."

"I hurt a lot of people," she said quietly.

"And if you'd married Oliver?" Jacob shifted gears, then changed lanes and passed a ten-wheeler. "Who would you have hurt?"

She turned back from the window. "Me."

"Damn straight." He smiled at her, noticed a sign along the road announcing Ambiance, population two

thousand, three hundred and forty-six. Five miles
ahead. The next sign was a twenty-foot billboard ad-
vertising Doug's Delicious Dogs.

He glanced over at her, saw her staring at the billboard.

"Ms. Beauchamp," he said ever so politely. "May
I interest you in a Doug's Delicious Dog?"

Smiling, she looked at him and dipped a hand to
her chest. "Why, thank you, Mr. Carver." She laid
the Southern drawl on heavy. "If it's not too much
trouble, I would adore one."

They pulled into the town of Plug Nickel around
seven-thirty that evening. While Jacob checked them
into The Night Owl Motel, Clair stretched her legs in
the parking lot. Though she'd ridden in airplanes for
long periods of time, she'd never traveled or taken
vacations by car. Her mother had thought a car too
confining and uncomfortable for trips.

Clair loved it. She loved the feel of speed on the
open highway, the power of the big car's engine, the
passing and ever-changing scenery. She ran her hand
over the smooth paint of the shiny black car. Maybe
she'd buy one of these vintage cars herself. Nothing
this large, of course. Something more compact and
sporty. A Mustang or a Corvette.

Definitely a convertible.

Drawn by the country-western music drifting from
the restaurant next door to the motel, Clair wandered
across the weed-spotted parking lot. A yellow neon
sign over the front entrance blinked Weber's Bar and
Grill. Arms wrapped around each other, a young couple came out, bringing the scent of barbecue and cig-
arette smoke with them.

Clair looked back at the motel office; through the glass front window she could see Jacob still waiting at the counter. The clerk had not yet appeared, and even from this distance, Clair could see the tug of annoyance on Jacob's face.

A black, dusty pickup drove by and a wolf whistle pierced the hot evening air. Clair stiffened indignantly, prepared to icily ignore the gauche behavior, when she realized she hadn't been the object of attention. A platinum-blond in a short, black leather skirt, red halter top and black stiletto heels had appeared from the convenience store next door. The woman was probably around Clair's age, though it was hard to tell under the heavy makeup. The blonde lifted a haughty brow as she passed, adjusted the V of her top to increase her already bulging bustline, then went into the restaurant.

Fascinating.

Clair had never been in a place like this before, had never even been *close* to a place like this. She was dying to see what it looked like inside. She looked down at what she was wearing, the black capris, pink tank top and flip-flop sandals, and thought she should probably change into more appropriate clothes, but she didn't have any clothes like the blonde. Besides, she only wanted a peek. She glanced back over her shoulder at Jacob, saw him pacing the motel office.

She'd just pop inside for a minute, she told herself, look around, then pop back out again.

The interior was blissfully air-conditioned, though extremely dark, lit only by the colorful neon beer signs on the walls. Clair waited a moment for her eyes to adjust to the dim light. Sawdust and peanut shells littered the concrete floor. People, mostly young, crowded the bar to the left and filled the pine tables in the center of the room. Between the din of conversation, a baseball game on a television over the bar and a jukebox blasting out a country song about a girl named Norma Jean Riley, it was nearly impossible to hear. Cigarettes were lit at the bar, but where the food was being served, it appeared to be smoke-free. The tangy scent of barbecue sauce hung heavy in the air, reminding Clair she hadn't eaten since they'd stopped in Ambiance for hot dogs.

No one at the tables seemed to notice her, but several heads, male and female, swiveled from the bar area and stared. *Time to go,* she decided. She turned and ran smack dab into a tall, dark-haired man entering the bar.

"Whoa." He put his hands on her shoulders to steady her.

"Pardon me." She attempted to step out of his hold, but he held on and grinned at her.

"What's your hurry, beautiful?" he asked in a voice that sounded like he had rocks in his throat. His white T-shirt said Mad Dog Construction.

He was a nice-looking man, Clair thought, but she didn't care for his hands on her. "I'm terribly sorry. If you'll excuse me, I was just leaving."

"I'll accept your apology if you come have a drink with me."

"Thank you." She smiled cooly, attempted unsuccessfully to slip from his firm grasp. "But I'm afraid I already have plans."

"You can be a little late," he coaxed, still holding her. "It's healthy to keep a guy waiting once in a while."

"Not healthy for you," a deep voice said from behind them.

Mad Dog dropped his hands from Clair and turned around to face Jacob. "Hey, sorry, man." The construction worker shrugged. "Can't blame a guy for trying."

Jacob moved beside Clair and took her arm. "Try somewhere else."

"Sure," the other man said, though he couldn't resist one last look at Clair as he moved past her.

Clair released the breath she'd been holding and looked up at Jacob. "Thank heavens you—"

"Are you crazy?" He hauled her up against him. "What the hell were you thinking, coming into a place like this by yourself?"

"What's wrong with this—"

"Obviously you weren't thinking," he snapped. "God knows what would have happened if I hadn't looked up and seen you sneak in here."

"I didn't sneak in anywhere." She pressed a hand against his rock-hard chest and pushed. She might as well have shoved at a brick wall. "And nothing would have happened. That man was perfectly nice."

Jacob frowned at her. "You call a strange man putting his hands on you 'perfectly nice?'"

"I wasn't watching where I was going and I ran into him." She narrowed her eyes. "And *you* have your hands on me, in case you didn't notice."

Oh, he noticed all right. A twitch jumped in the corner of his left eye. It had been a long day cooped up in the car with Clair. A long day forcing himself to concentrate on the curves of the road instead of the curves of the sweet-smelling woman sitting beside him. A long day keeping his hands on the steering wheel instead of where he really wanted them, which was all over Clair.

He let loose of her, then started to turn. "Let's get out of here."

"I want to stay."

He froze, then swung back around. "What?"

"We're already here." She folded her arms and lifted her chin. "The food here looks and smells wonderful. Give me one good reason we shouldn't eat here."

He could have given her at least ten reasons, all of them sitting at the bar checking her out. He knew if he'd been sitting at the bar, he'd be checking her out, too.

When he'd walked in and seen that guy with his hands on Clair, Jacob had come much too close to punching him out, which could have turned ugly, considering "Mad Dog" obviously had a pack of buddies at the bar, and they probably would have felt it necessary to intervene on their friend's behalf.

Fortunately for everyone, the construction worker appeared to be more of a lover than a fighter and had backed off.

"There's a coffee shop down the street," he said tightly. "It's quieter and—"

"Table for two?" A petite brunette holding menus bounced up and had to yell to be heard over a song about beer and bones.

Clair nodded at the waitress, then followed her through the crowded restaurant to a table in the center of the room.

Damn this woman. Grinding his teeth, crunching peanut shells under his boots, Jacob strode after her.

"Tri-tip and baby back combo is the special tonight.'' The waitress laid the menus on the table. ''What can I get you to drink?''

Jacob dropped down in his chair. ''Black and Tan and a cola.''

Clair sat primly. ''*Two* Black and Tans, please.''

He frowned at her when the waitress left. ''Do you even know what a Black and Tan is?''

She picked up the menu. ''No, but I hope it's cold. I'm very thirsty.''

Jacob sighed and prayed for patience.

They ordered two specials when the waitress returned with their drinks and a complimentary basket of deep-fried cheese balls. Jacob settled back in his chair and watched Clair delicately pick up her glass, then lift it cheerfully toward him. He raised his to her, as well.

She took a big sip, then froze, an expression of utter disgust on her face.

''Sometimes you have to chew it a little to help it down.'' He smiled and took a gulp of his own dark, thick beer. ''You'll get used to the taste after a few sips.''

She pressed her lips into a thin line, then closed her eyes as she swallowed.

If only he'd had a camera.

Enjoying himself now, Jacob glanced around the restaurant. For a Monday night, the place seemed unusually crowded, but he supposed there wasn't much else to do in Plug Nickel. At the far back of the restaurant, two pool tables had games going, and in the front of the room, a bald-headed deejay was setting up his equipment on a small stage.

The waitress placed two heaping plates of food on the table while a bus boy delivered two glasses of ice water, then nearly spilled it he was so busy staring at Clair. When Clair smiled at the smitten pup and thanked him, he grinned awkwardly, then tripped over his own feet backing away. Too busy washing away the taste of the beer, Clair didn't notice.

Was she really that oblivious to her effect on men? Jacob wondered. He realized she'd lived in a confined community of culture and privilege, that her life had been arranged right down to the man she would marry, but still, how could she be so unaware of her looks? He knew from his report that her birth father was Cherokee, her mother Welsh. The combination had created an exotic appearance, a dark sensuality that could make a monk forget his vows.

He watched her take another sip of her beer, shudder, then dig delicately into her food. An expression of sheer pleasure, something that bordered on sexual, washed over her face as she chewed. The bite of tri-tip Jacob had taken turned to cardboard, and his throat went dry. The blood from his brain went south.

The woman had to be playing him for a fool, dammit. She *couldn't* be as innocent as she appeared.

He kept his eyes and attention on his food, determined not to let her get to him. When the deejay announced it was karaoke night, Jacob was happy for the distraction, even though the first volunteer who sang Wynonna Judd's "Why Not Me?" had a voice like a slipping radiator belt. Fascination lit Clair's big blue eyes as she watched the different singers belt out an assortment of country and pop tunes.

"You should try it," she yelled over the music. "You have a nice voice."

He gave her a look that said, *not in a million years.* Smiling, she pushed her plate aside and stood. He thought for a moment she was going to go up and sing, but she excused herself and headed for the ladies' room. He watched the sway of her hips as she made her way through the crowded room, frowned when he noticed that several other men were watching her, as well.

He stabbed a bite of meat. What the hell did he care if other guys stared at her? It wasn't like he was *with* her, or they were on a date or anything. Hell, even on those rare occasions when he'd been dating a woman on a regular basis, he'd never gotten himself worked up if another man looked. So why should it matter with Clair?

It didn't matter. Not at all.

He watched a man sing his own rendition of Garth Brooks "Friends in Low Places," then a woman who did a pretty good job with an old Patsy Cline song. He'd finished his meal, a second beer and still no sign of Clair. He told himself he wasn't worried, he was simply annoyed. Extremely annoyed.

Frowning, he paid the bill, then headed in the direction of the ladies' room. Honest to God, he was going to have Lojack installed in the woman.

He relaxed a little when he found her standing with another woman, watching a pool game between Mad Dog and one of his buddies. Based on the amount of cheers and whistles, there was some heavy betting going on.

Clair's companion, a blonde in a short leather skirt, red halter top and high heels you could pick ice with, was busy talking and gesturing toward the pool table while Clair listened intently. When Jacob came up behind them, the blonde saw him first. She was dressed to catch a man's eye, exposing more skin than fabric. He returned the smile she threw him, though more out of habit than interest. She was a fine-looking woman, but standing next to Clair, the blonde paled.

He slipped an easy arm around Clair's shoulders, as much to lead her away as to establish who was with whom. Somehow he doubted that Clair's Cotillion lessons had included singles bars and lounge lizards. He felt her stiffen, then saw the indignation in her narrowed eyes when she turned to see who had dared manhandle her. She frowned at him, but did not step away.

"Jacob," Clair said over the noise, "this is Mindy Moreland. Mindy, Jacob Carver."

Jacob nodded; Mindy lifted her beer glass to him and smiled wider.

"Mindy is head of housekeeping at The Night Owl," Clair said as if it were the most fascinating job on earth. "We met in the rest room and I told her we're staying there."

Loud groans and cat calls drew their attention back to the pool game which had just ended with Mad Dog as the victor. Mindy ran over to throw her arms around the construction worker, and the loser ordered pitchers of beer for everyone. From the opposite end of the restaurant, a man was struggling through Roy Orbison's "Pretty Woman."

Jacob had to get out of here. Now.

Tightening his hold on Clair, he leaned down and whispered in her ear, "Let's go."

"You go ahead."

He stared at her blankly. "What?"

"I'm going to hang around a little." She waved a hand, as if to dismiss him. "I'll see you in the morning."

I'll see you in the morning?

Like *hell.*

"Dammit, Clair," he said tightly, "this isn't the kind of place a nice girl hangs around alone."

"Mindy's nice, and she's alone. We're going to play a game of pool."

Jacob looked at Mindy, watched her give Mad Dog a big, wet kiss. Mindy was an *exceptionally* nice girl, he thought, but knew better than to give Clair his opinion of the woman.

"Fine," he said through clenched teeth. "*I'll* play you a game of pool. If I win, we leave."

"All right. But if I win—" she hesitated, thought carefully, then smiled "—you have to sing. And I pick the song."

Like *that* would ever happen. "Absolutely not."

She arched a brow. "So you think I'll beat you?"

He heard the challenge in her voice and knew he should walk out. Just leave her. It was no skin off his nose if she wanted to hang out in a bar and play pool. She was a big girl, for God sakes. Isn't that how she'd learn? By making mistakes?

But he couldn't do it. He felt a…responsibility. Her brothers had paid him to find her, Clair was paying him to bring her to Wolf River. He had an obligation to see she got there safe and sound.

And besides, he'd never turned down a challenge in his life. He put his nose to hers. They'd be out of here in ten minutes tops.

"You're on."

They snagged a table and two pool cues, then Mindy, excited over the game, racked the balls. Jacob considered offering the break to Clair, maybe even setting her up for a shot or two.

Then he watched Mad Dog come over to wish her luck, and Jacob felt his lip curl.

No mercy.

"Lag for break," he barked. When Clair stared at him in confusion, Mindy explained the term. Whoever banked off the far end of the pool table and came closest to the opposite cushion took the break.

Jacob took his shot, grinned confidently when he came with three inches. Clair took her shot and came within two.

Luck, he thought, but wasn't worried. She'd need more than luck to win the game. When she leaned over and wiggled her hips to get in position, it was all Jacob could do to keep his mind on the game and his eye on the table.

When Clair broke and sank three balls, two solids and a stripe, he narrowed a gaze at her.

Damn lucky.

"What do I do now?" Clair asked her new best-buddy Mindy.

"Pick solids or stripes," the blonde said.

To Jacob's annoyance, a crowd had gathered around. When Clair chose stripes, clearly giving him the advantage, he scowled at her.

In perfect form, she sank the fourteen ball, then the twelve.

Sweat broke out on his brow when she sank the nine ball.

Nobody was *that* lucky. Son of a *bitch*. He set his jaw so tight he could have cracked a molar.

Little Miss Innocent had set him up.

He got a break on the next shot when the sound of shattering glass from the bar distracted her. No fool, he made every shot count. He sank four balls, then just missed the one ball on a double bank. He'd pick it up next turn.

He never got the chance.

He watched in disbelief as one after the other, she sank her remaining balls, then smoothly popped in the eight ball.

She'd beat him. She'd actually *won.*

There were cheers and whistles around the table. Mindy hugged Clair and Mad Dog gave her a high-five. Jacob stared at the surreal scene, then leveled a gaze at her. "You've played pool before."

She shook her head. "Only snooker with my father. He's very good."

Very good? Jacob lifted a brow.

Clair handed her cue to Mindy, then came around the table. "You aren't going to welch on our bet, are you?"

He set his teeth. "Let's just get this over with."

Clair supposed she could let Jacob off the hook. In a way, she *had* hustled him. She'd played snooker since she was a child and was better than good at it. Though the rules and strategy were completely different from standard pool, the basics of how to strike a ball were the same. She also knew that because he hadn't expected her to beat him, she'd caught him off guard and he hadn't played to his ability.

It hardly seemed fair or proper to compel him to make good on their bet, she thought. After all, wasn't it enough she'd actually won? Shouldn't she be the gracious victor and allow him a little dignity?

She glanced at his scowling face.

Nah.

Slipping her arm through his, she dragged him up to the deejay.

He glared at her while she scanned the list of songs. Dylan, Sinatra, Manilow—he'd *hate* that one—Morrison, Stewart...

Bingo.

She made her selection and handed it to him, then hurried off to find a seat before he could grab her by the throat. To Clair's pleasure and Jacob's disgust, it seemed that every person in the place had gathered around to watch.

The music started. Jacob gulped down a swallow of beer Mad Dog offered him from his front row seat, then handed it back and stepped to the microphone.

When he yanked down a lock of dark hair from the center of his forehead, narrowed his eyes and swiveled his hips, the women went wild.

"Love me tender..."

Five

Clair woke the next morning to the sound of "Jail-house Rock" playing in her head. After "Love Me Tender," the crowd had insisted on another Elvis tune. Jacob had done his best to refuse, but he'd been outnumbered. If he hadn't sang another song, the women might not have let him out alive.

Every woman in the place had melted when he'd sang the first song, then screamed when he'd sang the next. By the end of "Jailhouse Rock," he'd had everyone in the entire restaurant and bar up on their feet, singing and dancing along.

Jacob Carver was quite a package. Not only of surprises, but of contradictions, as well.

He'd made it clear to her that he wasn't her baby-sitter, yet he'd stood guard over her last night from the moment he'd found her in the bar with David— or Mad Dog, as Jacob called him. She'd seen him narrowing that dark gaze of his at any male who looked at her in a way he didn't like. Clair wasn't certain if she was annoyed or relieved that the men had kept their distance. Probably a little of both. Fund-raisers and ladies' luncheons had not exactly prepared her for the wild and raucous beer-drinking singles crowd.

Still, she couldn't remember when she'd ever laughed so hard, or when she'd had so much fun. Just thinking about it now made her smile. She'd been relaxed. No social niceties to worry about, no restraints.

Her smile faded. And still she hadn't felt as if she'd fit in. Not there.

Not anywhere.

All the ballet, the dance, the Ivy League schools. The charity balls and formal dinners, the afternoon teas. She'd never felt as if she completely belonged. She'd never felt as if she were a part of the whole.

It certainly wasn't for lack of love. Her parents loved her deeply, and she loved them, too.

But something had always been missing. Something she couldn't put a finger on. Something as elusive as a scent carried on a breeze, or a dream she couldn't remember.

She'd taken child development in college. She understood that all memories from childhood, even the actual process of being born, were retained and stored in the brain. Feelings, textures, smells, images. Everything was there. Nothing truly forgotten.

With a sigh, she stared at the acoustic ceiling over her head. She'd spent the first two years of her life with a different family. Mother, father, two brothers.

A different house, yard, environment. She wanted to remember *something*. Even *one* little thing.

She squeezed her eyes shut, took a slow, deep breath and let her mind drift.

Pink clouds floated by…smiling blue eyes, eyes so like her own. Clair felt the warmth of the woman's arms around her. They were outside…so many people, laughing and talking. Two little boys ran in circles around her…

The image melted away, too, and though she tried, Clair could not pull it back up.

Was that her family? Had she simply invoked the images because she wanted so badly to remember even one little thing from her past? Or had they been real?

Her heart beat faster at the thought. Her hands shook as she dragged on a short cotton robe, then flew out of bed.

When Jacob heard Clair knocking at the connecting door, he groaned and pulled his pillow over his head. The woman woke up too damn early.

"Go away," he shouted.

He heard the sound of the door opening and burrowed deeper into his bed. "So help me, woman—"

"Jacob, I'm sorry." Her voice bounced with excitement. "I just have to tell someone."

"Go tell the janitor," he growled. "He was banging on the air conditioner outside my door a minute ago. I'm sure he'd be more than happy to hear about how you hustled me last night."

She dropped down on her knees beside the bed. "I let you win the second game, didn't I?"

"*Let* me win?" He popped his head out from under

the pillow. "The hell you say. I beat your butt fair and square."

"Okay," she said affably, which only aggravated him all the more. "But that's not what I want to talk about. I remembered something."

"You woke me up to tell me you *remembered* something?" He fisted his hands in his pillow, rather than her pretty little neck, then did his best to think about how easy it would be to drag her into his bed with him and relieve the ever-growing tension in his body. "You know, for a woman who's supposed to be so well-mannered, that's damn rude."

"It's about my family." Though still heavy from sleep, her eyes sparkled in the early morning light. "My birth family."

"Your birth family?" He furrowed his brow, rose up on one elbow. "You remembered something from when you were two years old?"

"Just a fragment," she said breathlessly. "A fleeting image."

He sat, dragged a hand through his hair. "Clair, considering everything, it would be easy for your imagination to—"

"It *wasn't* my imagination," she insisted. "I know it sounds strange, but we were outside with lots of other people, there were pink clouds, a woman with eyes like mine, two little boys. It was *real,* Jacob. I know it was."

Pink clouds?

Interesting.

Though Jacob knew quite a bit about little Elizabeth Blackhawk and her family, he'd been asked not to tell Clair any more than necessary. Her brothers had decided they wanted to give her details and share their memories with her.

But he felt she needed to know about this. That it was important for her to know.

"You were at a county fair with your family the day of the accident." Her gaze met his. "They sell cotton candy at fairs."

"Pink clouds," she whispered, then dropped her forehead down on the edge of the bed. "My brothers," she said raggedly. "Rand and Seth?"

"What about them?"

"Were their names changed, too?"

"Since they were older when they were adopted, only their last names are different. Instead of Blackhawk, it's Rand Sloan and Seth Granger."

"Blackhawk," she murmured the name, then lifted her head. "It's so familiar. It feels—" she put a hand to her heart "—so right."

He watched her blink furiously at the sudden tears in her eyes and look away.

"Hey." He took her chin in his hand and turned her face back toward him. "What's this for?"

"I—" Swallowing hard, she whispered, "Jacob, what if they don't like me?"

"What are you talking about?"

She wiped at a tear that slid from the corner of her eye. "What if I don't fit in with them? What if after they meet me, I'm not the sister they remember?"

Who the hell cares? he wanted to say, but he realized that she did. Very much. Something shifted in his chest as he stared at her, something completely foreign to him. He didn't like it one little bit.

He had a sudden, fierce urge to take her to his bed, to make nothing else in her world matter. Sex could do that. Make a person forget everything, if only for a little while. They would both find pleasure there, he knew. Just looking at her, with that tousled hair and those liquid eyes made his blood boil. The thought of her long legs wrapped around him, imagining what it would feel like to bury himself deep inside her, made him instantly hard.

Grating his teeth, he held back the threatening groan. He'd never taken advantage of a woman's vulnerability before. And dammit, he sure as hell didn't plan to start now.

With something between a sigh and a swear word, he reached for her. She stiffened at his touch, but he tugged insistently until she sat on the bed beside him.

"Relax, Clair." He pulled her into his arms. "I'm not going to jump your bones."

"I've heard *that* one before." But she did lay her head on his chest. "Usually a minute or two before, 'I just want to hold you.'"

Jacob smiled, remembered using that line a time or two in high school. "I *am* just going to hold you. If I was intending to do more, you'd know."

"I would?" she said quietly.

"If I was doing it right, you would."

Chuckling softly, she relaxed against him. "I know I'm being silly, worrying if Rand and Seth will like me, if they will want me to be a part of their lives. It's just that I've always wanted a sister or a brother."

"Maybe you should worry if you'll like them," Jacob told her, tucking a strand of hair behind her ear.

"Maybe."

The warm breath of her sigh whispered over his

chest, and when she slid her hand up his arm, Jacob felt his heart slam against his ribs.

This was a bad idea, he thought.

Her fingers moved back and forth on his shoulder.

A *really* bad idea.

Her lips lightly brushed his collarbone.

Dammit, dammit, *dammit.*

He knew there were reasons he shouldn't just give in to what they both wanted. Good reasons. But with her touching him like she was, knowing she wasn't wearing much under that little robe, and that he wasn't wearing anything at all, he was having a hell of a time remembering what those reasons were.

And in roughly two seconds, even if he did remember them, he wouldn't give a damn.

Setting his teeth, he took hold of her arms and held her away. ''We should get going.''

Her eyes, heavy-lidded and filled with the same need he felt burning in his veins, lifted to his. ''What?''

''It's late, Clair,'' he said tightly. ''We need to get on the road.''

''Oh.'' She blinked, then her cheeks flushed bright pink. ''Of course. I'll just…go get ready.''

''Good idea.''

She slid off the bed, hesitated, then turned and headed for her room.

''Clair?''

From the doorway, she glanced over her shoulder.

''You didn't really let me win last night, did you?''

She smiled slowly. ''Of course not. Like you said, you beat me fair and square.''

He frowned at the door she closed behind her, then said loudly, ''I *did* beat you, dammit.''

He heard her laugh from the other side of the door. Swearing, he tossed the covers off and stomped to the bathroom, wondering what he'd ever done to deserve the likes of Clair Beauchamp.

An hour later, while Jacob checked them out of the motel, Clair stood in the parking lot with Mindy and said goodbye.

Dressed in a simple black skirt, white cotton blouse and plain black flats, The Night Owl's head house-keeper looked like a different woman from the sexpot Clair had met at Weber's Bar and Grill the night before. Clair actually thought Mindy looked more beau-tiful without the heavy makeup, and younger, too.

"Maybe you can call me after you get to Wolf River," Mindy said after Clair explained briefly why she and Jacob were driving together to Wolf River. "I can't wait to know what happens."

"I'm a little nervous to meet my brothers," Clair admitted, "but excited, too."

Mindy grinned. "I'm not talking about your broth-ers, though I can't wait to hear about them, too. I'm talking about you and Jacob."

"Me and Jacob?" Clair felt her stomach do a back flip. "There's nothing between us."

"Right." Mindy gave a snort of laughter. "That's why he couldn't take his eyes off you last night, un-less it was to warn off every other guy that you were already taken."

"We weren't—aren't—together that way," Clair insisted. "We have a business relationship."

"I don't know if you're trying to convince me or yourself," Mindy said with an arched eyebrow, "but

I know when a man's interested, and trust me, he's definitely interested."

Clair glanced toward the motel office where Jacob stood at the counter paying the bill. Yesterday, when she hadn't considered him being attracted to her, he'd kissed her and told her he didn't think he could keep his hands off her. Then this morning, when she'd practically thrown herself at him, he'd rejected her.

The man completely confused and frustrated her.

Shaking her head, Clair looked back at Mindy. "I think he sees me as a responsibility, like a package to be delivered. One that has Fragile stamped all over it."

"Well, then maybe you need to rewrap that package, honey," Mindy drawled. "Show him you won't break so easy."

Clair laughed at the idea, watched Jacob come out of the motel office, slip his sunglasses on, then head toward them.

"Damn," Mindy muttered as Jacob approached. "That is one fine man."

Clair couldn't agree more. His dark, rugged looks and tall muscular build were enough to make a woman's breath catch, but add that dazzling smile along with his easy, confident stride, and the effect was deadly to any female within fifty yards.

"You ready?" He pulled his keys out of his pocket.

Clair turned to Mindy and gave her a hug while Jacob started his car. The engine roared to life, then rumbled, like a caged beast waiting to be released.

They waved goodbye to Mindy, bought coffee and French toast strips at a fast-food drive-thru, then left the town of Plug Nickel and headed for the Interstate.

"What's your whim today, Miss Beauchamp?" Jacob sipped on his coffee. "You have a town that calls to you?"

Clair dipped her French toast strip in a tiny plastic vat of maple syrup, took a bite, then dragged her map out of the glove box. While she chewed, she studied the crisscross of cities and towns. The names flew at her: Raccoon, Rainbow, Yazoo, Picayune.

Tapping the map, she looked up at Jacob and smiled. "Liberty, Louisiana."

"You got coolant coming out of the water pump. Probably a failed seal." Odell, the gas station mechanic, stared down under the open hood of Jacob's car. "Lucky thing for you the engine didn't overheat."

Frowning, Jacob stood beside the middle-aged mechanic and bit back the swear word on the tip of his tongue. *Lucky* would hardly be the word he would have used. After driving all day, stopping at every little town along the way that caught Clair's attention, they'd been ten minutes out of Liberty when the temperature gauge had started to rise. By the time they'd pulled into town, a cloud of thick steam had begun to seep out from under the hood of the car.

"How long?" Jacob glanced in the direction of the gas station office where Clair had gone in search of a restroom, then looked back at the mechanic.

"Wellll…" Odell stretched the word out. "It's already two, but I can try to pull the pump this afternoon."

Try? Jacob ground his teeth. "And you think it might be done when?"

"Hard to say." Odell scratched the back of his

neck. "Maybe tomorrow. Can't promise, though. Gordon, my helper, went fishing this afternoon. I'm all by myself, and I've got a bad back."

"What if I help you?" Jacob suggested. Clair had spotted several antiques stores she'd wanted to browse through when they'd drove down the main street in the small town. Jacob not only welcomed the opportunity to avoid shopping of any kind, he was nervous about letting anyone work on his car beside himself.

Odell gave Jacob a dubious look. "You know how to reverse directions on a rachet?"

"I restored her myself from the ground up, dropped the drive train in the chassis and added ram air induction."

"426 or 440?"

"426 Hemi."

Odell nodded with approval. "Grab yourself a pair of overalls from the office, son. Just ask Tina."

The afternoon was hot and muggy; the deep blue sky laced with white clouds. The smell of motor oil and warm asphalt hung heavy in the air, but when Jacob opened the glass office door, an icy blast of air-conditioning and the scent of lemon deodorizer rushed out to meet him.

No sign of Clair, but behind the counter of a small convenience store area, a pretty woman probably in her early thirties sat reading a Hollywood entertainment magazine. Everything about her was red. Her short, spiked hair, her lips, her long nails. Even her low-cut, wraparound top was the color of a fire engine.

"Tina?"

She looked up, then slowly slid her gaze over him. "That's me, sugar."

"Odell said I should get a pair of overalls from you."

One hopeful brow shot up. "You working here now?"

"Just helping out for the afternoon."

"Too bad." The clerk laid her elbows on the counter and leaned forward with a provocative smile. "No fair you know my name and I don't know yours."

"Jacob." He would have had to been dead not to notice—and appreciate—the cleavage the redhead seemed determined to show him. "Jacob Carver."

"Tina Holland." She stood, gave her spandex-clad hips an extra swing as she moved to a closet at the back of her cubicle, then glanced over her shoulder and sized him with her eyes. "Large or extra-large?"

When her gaze lingered on his crotch, Jacob shifted awkwardly. "Extra-large."

"Of course you are." Smiling, Tina pulled out a pair of clean overalls and moved back toward him. "So are you just passing through Liberty, or do we have some time to get to—"

"Hello."

Jacob turned at the sound of Clair's voice. She'd just walked around the corner from the ladies' room. Even though the weather was humid and they'd been driving most of the day, she still looked crisp and cool in her pink tank top and denim skirt. Her timing had been so perfect just now, he wanted to kiss her.

Hell, he just wanted to kiss her.

That's all he'd seemed to be able to think about the entire day. Kissing Her. Touching her. Wondering if she was wearing the white lace bra and panties she'd bought at the department store.

Or the leopard thong. He thought a lot about that leopard thong.

He swore he was losing his mind.

"Clair, hi," he said, but hesitated when the two women looked at each other. "Ah, Clair this is Tina Holland. Tina, Clair Beauchamp. Tina works here."

Oh, for God's sake.

He'd not only just made a formal introduction between the gas station clerk and Clair, he'd made a ridiculously obvious statement.

He was definitely losing his mind.

"I'm going to be working on my car all afternoon," he said more roughly than he intended. "You'll have to find something to do on your own."

Clair watched Jacob snatch up the overalls and leave the office. She stared after him, wondering why he'd suddenly been so gruff, then realized she'd interrupted his conversation with Tina. Had he been trying to hit on the woman? Clair wondered. He'd been staring at the clerk when she'd walked around the corner, and with the ample amount of bossom the pretty redhead displayed, why wouldn't he? He'd also seemed flustered, she thought, and definitely in a hurry to leave.

Clair looked back at the clerk. Was this the kind of woman that attracted Jacob? When he'd first met Mindy, Clair was certain she'd seen interest in his eyes, too.

It was all she could do not to stare down at her own plain clothes and her uninteresting B cup. Even the new makeup she'd bought had been conservative compared to Mindy and Tina.

Maybe you need to rewrap the package, Mindy had said. Clair glanced over her shoulder, watched as Jacob tugged on the overalls, then jumped in his car, closed the hood and drove it into the gas station garage.

"Can I help you with anything?" Tina asked.

Clair blinked, then turned back to the clerk. "Yes," she said and smiled slowly. "I believe you can…"

Six

She was late.

For the tenth time in twenty minutes, Jacob stared at his watch and frowned. It was nearly seven o'clock. Clair had left a message on his motel room phone for him to meet her at Pink's Steak House at six-thirty.

So where the hell was she?

Not that he was worried. Liberty seemed to be a quiet, friendly town, and Jacob had spotted several Liberty County sheriff cars driving around this afternoon. Since Clair had told him she was going shopping on the main thoroughfare through town, and the motel they were staying at was on the same street, as well, there was no reason to be concerned.

She *did* have a knack for getting herself into situations, though, Jacob thought. All alone for the afternoon, in a strange town, a woman as naive as Clair could probably find trouble. He thought about her go-

ing into that bar last night by herself and running into
Mad Dog. Though the construction worker had turned
out to be a nice guy, he could have just as easily been
not so nice.

Jacob's frown darkened. He stared at his watch
again and signaled the cocktail waitress to bring him
another beer.

He *wasn't* worried, dammit.

Tapping his fingers on the tabletop, he glanced
around the dimly lit restaurant. A single pink rose in
a cut glass vase and a flickering votive graced every
linen covered table. Nice place, he thought, yet he
still felt comfortable in his jeans and the black button-
down shirt he'd pulled on after he'd scrubbed the
grease from his hands and showered.

It had felt good to get his hands dirty again. He'd
been so busy these past few months he'd had no time
to even pick up a wrench, let alone tinker with his
engine. Usually he found working on his car calmed
him down, eased the stress of a difficult, and sometimes dangerous, job.

But today he'd been too distracted to relax, had
found his mind drifting and his concentration shot to
hell. He'd scraped his knuckles on an alternator
mount and burned the inside of his forearm on the
radiator. All because of Clair.

Even while he'd been covered with grease, drip-
ping with sweat, bending over a one-hundred-twenty-
degree engine, he'd had thoughts about Clair. Lurid,
scandalous, erotic thoughts.

How the hell was he was going to last another three
or four days? The woman was driving him crazy.
Killing him.

The cocktail waitress, a shapely blonde, set another

beer in front of him, gave him a lingering smile, then left. He watched her walk away, then mentally shook his head and groaned. Last night Mindy, this morning Tina, now this waitress. Pretty women all around him, women who were clearly experienced with the opposite sex. Women he normally would have at least flirted with, maybe even more if the situation were right.

He lifted his beer and took a sip. Clair had never been the type of woman he'd been attracted to before. Naive, innocent, conservative—

Sexy?

The sip of beer in his mouth nearly went flying out as he caught sight of her moving toward him. He gulped to swallow it, then choked.

Good God, what had she done to herself?

The tight, black skirt skimming her slender hips had to be illegal in some states. Though it was well past her knees, the slit up the side seemed to expose leg all the way from the tips of her shiny black high heels clear up to her neck. Her lips were full and glossy wet, the same deep burgundy color as the sheer, long-sleeved blouse she wore. Her hair, normally straight, fell in loose, soft curls around her face and shoulders. Her eyes smoldered; her skin glowed. She kept that smoky gaze on him as she approached, exposing bare thigh with every stride.

A waiter carrying a tray of drinks caught sight of her and bumped into a chair, nearly spilling his load. His jaw slack, Jacob noticed that the rest of the men in the restaurant were staring, as well.

What the hell was she trying to do? Start a riot?

His hand tightened on his glass when she slid smoothly into the booth across from him.

"Hi," she said as if she were out of breath.

Hi? He narrowed a gaze at her. She'd walked in here looking like some kind of a sultry sex goddess and all she could say was "hi?"

He caught her scent and drew it slowly into his lungs. Dammit, she *smelled* sexy, too. Exotic and seductive.

"Sorry I'm late. I got caught up shopping this afternoon, then dropped into the hair salon and told them I wanted a new look." She pulled at one loose curl brushing her neck. "What do you think?"

What did he *think?* That it would be so easy to slide his hand up that slit in her skirt, even easier to slip off her underwear and be inside her in a matter of—

"Good evening." A pencil-necked waiter with short blond hair appeared from nowhere and gaped at Clair. "My name is George and I'll be your server this evening. May I get you something to drink?"

"Hello, George." Clair pursed her lips while she thought. "Maybe a glass of wine."

"We have a house chardonnay that's very nice." George pulled a wine list from his pocket. "And a 1995 pinot from Chile that I'm sure you'll find quite crisp and light."

Gimme a break. Jacob resisted the temptation to roll his eyes.

"Something more robust, I think," Clair breathed. "And full-bodied."

When the waiter's gaze dropped to Clair's breasts, Jacob felt a tick jump at the corner of his eye.

George blinked, then visibly swallowed. "Ah, perhaps a merlot or a cabernet?"

Clair smiled. "You pick."

"Thank you." The waiter blushed, then cleared his throat. "Yes, I will. Pick something nice, I mean."

Jacob decided that if the man didn't stop gawking at Clair, the only thing he'd pick would be his teeth from the back of his throat. When the waiter hurried away, Jacob narrowed a gaze at Clair. "I thought you were shopping for antiques today."

"I changed my mind." She shrugged a shoulder, drawing attention to the outline of a black bra under her sheer blouse. "One of those spur-of-the-moment, impulse things."

He kept his eyes on her face so he wouldn't stare at the soft swell of her breasts peeking out from the vee of her blouse. "Part of your No-Plan, Plan?"

"Absolutely." George brought her wine, but left quickly when Jacob shot him a warning look. Clair picked up her glass and sipped. "You must be hungry. What looks good on the menu?"

What looked good to him wasn't on the menu, he thought. And he was hungry, all right, but the hunger wasn't in his stomach. He would have gobbled her whole if he could have. Just watching her wet lips touch her glass made his groin ache. Made him think of other places he wanted that luscious mouth, and where he wanted his mouth on her, which was everywhere.

He'd always taken pride in his control, in his ability to take charge of a situation. It irritated the hell out of him that Clair Beauchamp could have him rolling over like a puppy wanting his tummy scratched. He'd never met a woman who could make him beg yet, and he wasn't about to start with Clair. He'd made a vow to keep his hands off her, and dammit, that's what he intended to do.

Determined that every man in this place knew she was off-limits, as well, he scanned the restaurant, saw several heads turn away when he curled his lip and all but growled. Satisfied, he buried his nose in his menu as if it were a shield of armor.

Clair glanced cautiously up at Jacob, considered telling him that his menu was upside down, but the hard set of his mouth and the twitch in the corner of his left eye warned her off. Heavens, but he was in a mood.

Not exactly the reaction she'd been hoping for.

The waiter returned and they ordered their food, then Jacob excused himself and headed toward the rest rooms.

Thank heavens.

Clair sank back in the booth on a heavy sigh of relief, then took a long sip of her wine. Her insides were still shaking from what she'd hoped would be her grand entrance. The new hairstyle and makeup had been difficult enough, but wearing a sheer blouse and skirt with a high slit had nearly caused her to hyperventilate. If ever she'd been grateful for the years of poise and self-assured composure continually pounded into her, it was now. She'd been amazed herself that she'd been able to hold her head high and that her knees hadn't crumpled under her.

What had seemed like a courageous, daring plan to gain Jacob's attention now felt silly and foolish.

Tina, from the gas station, had recommended The Head to Toe Salon and when Clair had told Bridgette, the hairdresser, that she wanted a look sexy enough to attract a man, the woman had taken on the project with the tenacity of a bulldog. The salon Clair had always gone to in Charleston, Jean-Lucs, was sub-

dued, conservative. They served Perrier and iced mint
tea while they permed and cut, played Beethoven and
Bach while they colored and weaved. The Head to
Toe played a country-western radio station which
could barely be heard over the phones ringing, blow-
dryers buzzing and the hairstylists talking over one
another. It was gossip central, and in the few short
hours she'd sat in the chair, Clair had learned about
two affairs, three divorces and four pregnancies—one
with a heated debate over who the father really was.

The afternoon had flown by. Clair's hair had been
trimmed and curled, her fingernails and toes polished
in WildBerry Wine. Smoke Me Blue eye shadow and
RazzleDazzle lip gloss completed her makeup, then
Suzie, the owner of the clothes boutique next door,
brought over outfits and everyone in the place gave
their opinions on what was right for Clair to catch a
man. There'd been much discussion between the
ladies, but they'd all finally agreed that the sheer
blouse, the black, slit-up-the-side skirt, and high heels
were guaranteed to bring the toughest, most hardheaded man to his knees.

So much for guarantees.

But there had been a few moments, she thought as
she took another sip of her wine. When she'd walked
into the restaurant, her heart pounding and her palms
sweating, she'd have sworn she'd seen Jacob's mouth
drop open. There'd been more than interest in his dark
gaze, there'd been lust. She'd felt her hopes soar and
her pulse race.

Then she'd slid into the booth and he'd been nothing but abrupt and cross.

Maybe she wasn't giving this enough of a chance,
she thought. Maybe his mind was still on his car, or

maybe he was hungry. She'd waited twenty-five years to seduce a man, surely she could give him a few more minutes before she...what was the term he'd used before? Oh, yes. Before she jumped his bones.

Clearly she'd gone about this all wrong. She'd been too subtle. Women who were confident, who knew what they wanted and went after it, were direct. She loosened one more button, then adjusted her blouse to expose the slightest edge of black lace. If he needed direct, then fine, she'd give him direct.

He walked back to the table at the same time their food arrived. She saw his stride falter as he looked at her, then he sat back down into the booth and dug into his food.

She took a bite of her chicken. "This is so tender," she said on a soft moan. "Would you like a taste?"

The piece of steak he'd had halfway to his mouth froze, then he glanced up at her and scowled. "No, thanks."

"Are you sure?" She took another bite, gave another sigh of pleasure. "You won't know what you're missing if you don't try it."

"Fine," he said tightly. "I'll try it."

Smiling, she speared a bite and held it out to him. Her heart all but stopped when he closed his mouth over her fork.

As strange as it seemed, that was the most erotic thing she'd ever done. Her pulse began to skip and her throat turned dry as dust.

And she could swear she'd gotten a reaction from Jacob, the kind she'd wanted. His eyes narrowed and darkened and his nostrils seemed to flare.

"So what do you think?" she asked, amazed she had any voice at all.

He stared at her for a long moment, then shrugged. "It was fine."

"That's it?" Determined to shake him up, she leaned closer, arched one eyebrow and curved her lips. "Just fine?"

His gaze dropped to the black lace she'd exposed, and he visibly swallowed. "Maybe a little better than fine."

Dammit, but the man was hardheaded. What did she have to do to break through his wall of indifference? Take her blouse off and jump on the table?

Like hell she would.

All her life she'd molded herself to suit other people, to be the person she thought someone else wanted her to be. Her mother, her father, Oliver.

And now Jacob.

She might be a fool, but she wasn't stupid.

"Thank you for meeting me for dinner, Jacob." She forced a smile. "But if you'll excuse me, I'm a little tired. I think I'll go back to the motel."

He started to push his plate away, but she shook her head. "You go on and finish your dinner. I'll see you in the morning."

"I'll just get the—"

"Don't worry about me." She slid out of the booth. "I can get myself back. You just take your time."

She quickly walked away, head held high. This time, her knees didn't tremble and her palms didn't sweat. In spite of her disappointment, she felt lighter, more comfortable in her own skin than she'd felt in her entire life.

She was almost at the front door when she heard a woman call her name. Clair saw Bridgette waving frantically from a darkened corner of the lounge area. She was with a small group of men and women.

Why not? Clair thought. She could go back to the motel, get into her pj's and watch TV, or she could spend the evening with Bridgette and her friends. She thought about the empty motel room, her empty bed, and it wasn't a difficult choice.

Smiling, she turned and walked into the lounge.

Where the hell was she?

Jacob paced irritably from Clair's motel room into his own, then back again. After he'd wolfed down the rest of his meal and paid the bill, he'd been no more than ten minutes behind her. The motel they were staying at was across the street and three doors down from the restaurant, so she couldn't have made a wrong turn.

He stared at his wristwatch, then clenched his jaw. She'd said she was tired, that she was going back to the motel. She should have been here long before him.

Dammit.

What if someone had followed her out of the restaurant? Or approached her on the street? The way she looked, she would have easily stopped traffic, not to mention caused an accident or two.

Didn't she realize the trouble she could get into dressed like that? He stomped to the motel window and looked out at the well-lit parking lot.

Nothing.

His gut twisted into a knot.

Hell, it wasn't that he hadn't liked the way she'd looked. He'd have to be dead not to appreciate the sensuality she'd radiated. What man wouldn't, for crying out loud?

But what possible reason could she have to completely change her look from cool and calm into hot and wild? And why here, in Liberty? Who would she want to impress with a new style in this small town?

He was on his way to the phone to call the front desk when it hit him like a sucker punch to the gut.

Good God, but he was an idiot.

He would have kicked himself all the way back across the street to the restaurant, but it would have taken longer for him to get there if he did. He had a pretty good idea where he'd find her.

The question was, did she *want* to be found?

"...and the kid says, 'No problem. Hillary took my backpack.'"

The crowd busted out in laughter at Bridgette's joke and Clair joined in. They'd been on a jokefest for the past ten minutes and what had started out as a small group had doubled in size, with each new member contributing a joke, a few of them risqué enough to make Clair's cheeks warm.

After Jacob's indifference to her, it felt good to be welcomed into Bridgette's group of friends. She knew a couple of the men were working their way into position to make a move on her, and while it raised her self-confidence, it didn't raise her interest.

There was only one man on her mind; only one man she wanted to be with.

Old habits died hard, she realized. She'd changed her clothing, her hair, her makeup, even the way she walked, just so Jacob would see her as a desirable woman. A woman he would want to make love to.

But as embarrassing as it was to realize she'd made
a complete fool of herself, the lesson she'd learned
was invaluable. From now on, she would let her heart
and her gut tell her who the real Clair Beauchamp
was. She would not change to please someone else,
most especially a pigheaded, dim-witted private investigator from New Jersey.

While Bridgette's fiancé Pete began telling a joke
about two men who had slept in a country barn for
the night, Clair sipped on the drink Bridgette had insisted on buying her, something called Ride 'Em
Cowboy. She'd never heard of the concoction of coffee liqueurs and vodka; she rarely drank alcohol and
her parents and Oliver only drank wine or martinis.

Maybe she should let herself get a little tipsy, she
thought. If only for tonight, it might get her mind off
Jacob. She watched a band setting up on the other
side of the lounge. Why shouldn't she dance and have
some fun?

No. With a sigh, she set the drink down. She'd only
regret it later if she had too much to drink, then made
an idiot out of herself. She refused to have any regrets. Tonight, tomorrow or the day after. Whatever
she did, she'd go into with her eyes wide open. Whatever mistakes she made, that was fine. They'd be *her*
mistakes.

"...so the guy says," Pete continued, "'I don't
mind at all. She died and left me a million dollars.'"

Between a mixture of groans and laughs, the cocktail waitress took new drink orders while the band
announced over the microphone they'd be playing in
a few moments. Steve, Pete's brother, offered to buy
another drink for Clair, but she politely declined the
good-looking Liberty fireman's offer. There was no

point in encouraging him, not when she knew she was leaving this bar alone.

Going back to her room alone.

Still, in spite of that fact, she was ready to go back to the motel. The room would be quiet and lonely, but she'd at least have the comfort of knowing Jacob was next door.

How pathetic was she? she thought, reaching for her purse. Her only consolation, and it wasn't much, was that she knew she wasn't the first woman, and most certainly wouldn't be the last, to make a fool of herself over a man.

"Lord, have mercy." Her eyes wide, Julie, Bridgette's sister, looked over Clair's shoulder. "I think I'm in love."

"Stand in line, girlfriend," Julie's friend, Christie, gasped and stared, as well.

Clair turned and saw Jacob standing at the entrance to the lounge. His dark, narrowed gaze slowly scanned the room.

Her heart skipped a beat. Was he looking for *her?* Or was he just here, *looking* for a woman in general?

Either way, she didn't want to know. She certainly didn't need anymore rejection from Jacob, and the last thing she wanted was to see him pick up another woman.

She turned her back to him and scooted down in her seat, hoping he wouldn't spot her in the dimly lit corner. "He's coming this way." Julie sucked in a breath and leaned close to Julie and Clair. "Remember, I saw him first."

Dammit. Clair clutched her purse and clenched her teeth. If he thought he could lecture her in front of

Bridgette and her friends, he had another think coming. She refused to let him bully her or—

"Clair!" He moved beside her, put his hands on her shoulders and pulled her out of her chair. "Thank God I found you!"

While everyone looked on, Jacob dragged her close and smothered her in a hug.

"Sweetheart, I've been so worried." He laid his big hand on the back of her head and pushed her face flat against his chest. "Little Jake has been asking where his mommy is and the baby won't stop crying."

Little Jake? The baby? What in the world was he talking about?

She tried to pull away, but with her arms captured at her sides, she couldn't move. Couldn't breathe, for that matter.

"Who the hell are you?" Steve asked, starting to stand.

"Her husband." Jacob squeezed her tighter when she squeaked at his answer. Steve quickly sat back down.

"She never mentioned a husband." Bridgette eyed Jacob suspiciously. "Just that she was driving to Texas with some guy."

"We're on our way to see a specialist there for Clair's myopsia infarction," Jacob said over the music from a three-man band that had just started to play a jazzy instrumental. "When she takes her medication she can control it, but when she misses—" he shook his head sadly "—well, she forgets things."

What! Clair pushed harder to break away from Jacob's grip, but she might as well have been pushing against a brick wall.

"She forgets she has a husband and children?" Julie asked with disbelief.

Clair managed to yank her head back an inch. "Jacob, for God's sake, will you—"

He smashed her against his chest again. "Our car broke down and I had to go to the garage. I took the kids with me, and when we didn't come right back, she obviously got confused. Clair, sweetheart—" he thrust her out at arm's length "—I've been sick with worry."

She sucked in a lungful of air, ready to lambaste him, when he pulled her close again and dropped his mouth over hers. Shocked, all she could do was hold on.

It didn't seem to matter that he was simply trying to shut her up. Or even that there were several pairs of eyes watching them. All that mattered was the hot press of his lips on hers, the moist brush of his tongue.

Her pulse raced, excitement shimmered over her skin. Her fingers curled into his arms....

Dammit!

Smoothly she twisted her foot and stepped on his insole with her high heel. She felt, more than heard, the growl in his throat. He yanked away from her, his brow furrowed in pain.

"Jacob. Oh, sweetheart, I remember now." She touched his cheek tenderly. "I got sick right after you lost your job at the fertilizer plant."

"Right," he said through gritted teeth. "Now we really should get back to the kids, in case they wake up."

"And then the explosion at the fireworks plant." Clair glanced at everyone as she leaned in and whispered, "Would you ever guess he has a glass eye?"

"Never," Julie breathed, staring openmouthed at Jacob. "Which one?"

"The right one," Christie said, narrowing her gaze at Jacob.

Jacob's hand tightened on her arm. "We *really* should go now, *sweetheart*."

"Of course." Clair picked up her purse and did her best not to smile at the sympathetic expressions on everyone's faces as they all said goodbye.

His face set tight, Jacob dragged her through the crowd, then out the front door. The night air was cool, heavy with the scent of steaks grilling from the restaurant inside, and the muted sound of Santana's "Smooth" drifted from the lounge.

She tried to break loose from his grip, but he held on tight.

"Let go of me!" she yelled at him when they hit the sidewalk.

"No." Pulling her along, he started across the street.

"How dare you say no!" With no other option, Clair stumbled behind him. "Are you crazy?"

"Obviously." When she managed to yank free, he twisted around and grabbed her by the waist, picked her up and tossed her over his shoulder.

"Jacob Carver, put me down this instant!"

"No, again," he said calmly and walked to the motel.

"You're fired," she shouted. "Terminated. Discharged. Canned. I don't ever want to—"

When he dropped her hard on her feet at his motel door, her teeth rattled.

"—see you again," she finished as he shoved his

key in the door. "You're insane. Deeply disturbed. A lunatic. Unbal—"

"Will you just shut up?" he said, then pulled her into his arms and covered her mouth with his.

Seven

If she'd had time to think, Clair might have been able to defend herself against the thrilling jolt of pleasure that slammed against her senses when Jacob's lips swept down on her own. But she couldn't think, couldn't breathe; she could only *feel*. Her arms curled around his neck, her hands moved upward and plowed into his hair. He yanked her closer, deepening the kiss as he forced her back against the door. Her entire body came alive, every nerve ending tingling with the impact of his mouth on hers. Heat coursed through her rushing blood.

She strained against him, would have climbed inside him if it were possible.

He dragged his lips from hers and blazed a trail down her neck. With a moan, her head fell to the side, offering more.

"What were you saying?" he murmured, biting the base of her earlobe.

"You're...deeply...disturbed," she said between ragged breaths.

"Very deeply." He nibbled on her throat.

"Insane." She dug her fingers into his scalp.

"Certifiable." He slid his hands around her waist, then jerked her closer.

Clair's eyes opened wide at the intimate press of his arousal against the v of her thighs. "Unbalanced," she gasped.

"Completely." He reached behind her, twisted the doorknob and they stumbled into the room.

The nightstand lamp cast shadows across the soft beige carpet and the blue floral bedspread. The tangy scent of lemon wax filled the room, and from the corner, an air conditioner hummed, lifting the ends of the sheer white drapes covering the window.

He kicked the door shut behind him and dragged her close again.

His kiss was hot and hungry, urgent. Need shivered through her. She held onto his shoulders and rose on her tiptoes, wanting more.

He'd kissed her before, but this was different. This was no-holds-barred. This was out of control.

This was pure, unbridled *passion.*

Her heart sang with the joy she felt. When he pulled his mouth from hers and moved away, left her standing alone, her eyes shot open and she felt a moment of fear that he'd changed his mind. She swayed on weak knees, watched him take two long, quick strides to the drapes and snap them closed.

Then he was back again, his arms around her, his heat seeping into her, his tongue sliding over her parted lips, then rushing inside. She met him eagerly, opened to him, felt her blood pounding through her veins.

As one, they moved toward the bed.

This time when he kissed her, he slowed the pace a bit, lingered on the corner of her mouth, a leisurely exploration. While one hand fisted into her hair at the back of her head, the other slid down her arm, then slipped inside the high slit of her skirt.

She trembled.

"I've wanted to do that from the first moment I saw you walk in the restaurant," he said hoarsely, skimming the outer skin of her thigh with his fingertips.

Why didn't you? she wanted to ask, but she couldn't think, couldn't speak. Intense arrows of pleasure shot through her. She felt dizzy and hot. And then he cupped her buttocks, pulled her closer to the hard bulge at the front of his jeans, and every thought flew out of her head.

She rose up on her toes, pressing against him, then lowered herself slowly down.

He moaned.

"Clair," His voice was ragged and hoarse. "Are you sure about this?"

"Yes," she whispered, wondered how he could even ask.

"Look at me." He cupped her face in his hands. "No doubts?"

She shook her head, laid her hands on his broad chest, felt the rapid beating of his heart. "No doubts."

"Good."

Her knees hit the edge of the bed and they tumbled

backward, sank into the mattress. While his mouth tasted the base of her throat, he dipped under her skirt again and slid his callused palm down her thigh. Whimpering, she lifted her hips upward. He tugged her zipper open, then slid the garment away.

She reached to slip her heels off, but he took her hand and held it down on the bed. "Leave them on a minute. I want to look at you."

Clair felt her cheeks flush, but the look in Jacob's eyes as his gaze slid from her black lace underwear, slowly down her bare legs, all the way to the tips of her black high heels, excited her beyond anything she could have ever imagined.

When his hand followed the same path as his gaze, her heart skipped, then raced.

Closing her eyes, she laid her head back and let herself savor the rough slide of his fingers over her skin. Fire raced up and down her entire body. One by one, her heels dropped to the floor. Then his hand moved back up, over her calf...her thigh. He hesitated at the lacy edge of her underwear, brushed the tips of his fingers back and forth, moved upward again. Breath held, heart pounding, she felt him unbutton her blouse. When the sheer fabric parted, he flattened his hand over her bare belly. She quivered at his gentle touch.

"You're so smooth." His voice was rough. "So soft."

Sensation after sensation swirled through her. Ribbons of bright colors, a tapestry of textures. The scent of man and woman and passion.

And then his hands closed over her breasts.

On its own, her body bowed slightly upward as she pressed herself more fully into him. Her breath came in short, ragged gasps as he kneaded her soft flesh. A fever built between her legs, a pulsing, throbbing pressure that demanded release. She wanted more, was certain she'd die if he didn't hurry.

When she reached for the buttons on his shirt, he smiled and shook his head. "Not yet."

Jacob knew he'd lose it completely if he didn't keep some kind of barrier between them. He wanted to take his time, to make this last, though he wasn't so certain he could. Not with those soft little sounds of needs she was making, and the way her long, tempting body kept squirming under him.

When her fingers slid down his chest and moved toward the snap of his jeans, he snagged her wrist and lifted it over her head, then captured her other wrist and pulled it over her head, as well. If she touched him, it would be all over.

He wanted more.

With his free hand, he flicked open the front clasp of her black lace bra and bared her breasts.

Then he did nearly lose it.

She was perfect. Her breasts were full and firm, her skin flushed, soft as rose petals. Her chest rose and fell rapidly. Fire raced through his blood, pounded in his temple.

He wanted like he'd never wanted before. He lowered his head to take.

When his mouth closed over the pebbled, rosy tip of her breast, she arched upward on a gasp. He pulled her deeper into his mouth, slid his tongue back and forth over her nipple. It grew harder.

So did he.

Ignoring the insistent ache in his groin, he kept his attention on Clair, tasted her sweetness. She moaned deeply, moved restlessly under him. When he moved to her other breast, she whimpered. He suckled her, flicked his thumb over the damp nipple he'd just abandoned, felt the bud tighten even more under the rough texture of his skin.

"Jacob, *please.*" Clair choked out the words.

"Not yet," he murmured.

He released her hands, then moved down her belly. He heard her breath catch in her throat, then her fingers drove into his hair. He wasn't certain if she were trying to tug him back up or hold him still.

He didn't care.

He slid his hands under her hips, blazed kisses over her belly, explored the curves and valleys with his tongue. Then he moved lower still.

He felt her body tighten, tremble with need and uncertainty. He nipped at the edge of black lace, then slid the thin swatch of fabric down her hips, down her legs. He caressed her with his hands, nibbled on her hipbone. Then lower.

Her body felt like liquid fire. When he dipped into the sweetness of her body with the tip of his tongue, the breath she'd been holding rushed out on a deep, low moan. He stroked her, made love to her with his mouth. Mindless, she lifted her hips, rolled her head from side to side on a deep moan.

"*Jacob!*" She twisted under him on a sob. "*Now.* Please now."

"Yes." He moved quickly, knowing he couldn't last. He practically tore his shirt away, barely got the rest of his clothes off. He kneed her legs apart, took her hips in his hands, then entered her fast and hard.

He heard her cry out, hesitated, but when she wrapped her legs and arms around him and moved

against him, he couldn't think at all. He moved inside
the tight, hot, velvet glove of her body. Never had he
felt anything so intense, so exquisite. So perfect.

She met him thrust for thrust, dug her fingernails
into his back. They strained together, desperately,
wildly.

He felt her climax shatter through her in violent
waves of heat and pleasure. Her arms came tightly
around his neck, held on.

He let himself go, groaned as his own body found
release. He thrust deeply, shuddering, then fell over
the edge with her.

Amazing.

Sprawled across the bed, across each other, Clair
waited for her heart to slow and her breath to even
out.

She couldn't move.

Unbelievably amazing.

Jacob had rolled to his side, but he still had one
arm and one leg draped over her. His skin was damp,
his breathing as erratic as her own.

"Damn," he muttered.

She smiled, deciding that the single swear word
was a compliment.

"I didn't get that blouse off you," he said, his
voice thick and hoarse. "I really wanted to get that
blouse off you."

He shifted, pulled her snugly against him, stroked
her hair away from her face, then pressed his lips
lightly to her temple. A moment passed, long and
silent, then Jacob finally spoke. "You could have told
me, Clair."

She laid her hand on his chest, felt the heavy thud of his heart against her palm. "That I was a virgin?"

"No. That you have a freckle in the shape of a poodle in the middle of your back."

She yanked away from him. "I most certainly do—"

"For God's sake, I'm kidding." He pulled her back into his arms. "Yes. That you were a virgin."

"I was afraid you wouldn't—that you might not—" Her gaze dropped. "That you wouldn't want me."

His chuckle rumbled deep in his chest. "Sweetheart, of all the things to be afraid of, trust me, that's not one you need to concern yourself with."

"Then it wouldn't have mattered to you?" she asked. "Given you one more reason to stay away from me?"

"Maybe." He kissed each cheek, then the tip of her nose. "But sooner or later, this would have happened even if I had known. One more day in the car with you and I think I would have pulled off the road, dragged you in the back seat and taken you right there."

Just the thought of him doing that made her pulse pick up again. "Really?"

"Really. When you walked into the restaurant tonight, I nearly swallowed my tongue."

Though her cheeks warmed, pleasure swelled in her chest. She slid her hand to his arm and brushed her fingers back and forth over his muscular biceps. "I was hoping I'd get your attention."

He sighed, then rolled to his back, pulling her on top of him. "You didn't need to change a thing about yourself to get my attention. You've had my complete attention from the second you stepped out of that bridal shop.''

''The bridal shop?'' Her eyes widened in surprise. ''But I was engaged, practically married. You didn't know me at all.''

''Practically married is not married,'' he said, shaking his head in disbelief. ''And you're not *that* naive, Clair, to think a man has to know a woman to fantasize about taking her to bed.''

He'd fantasized about her? The idea made her stomach flutter. Folding her arms over his chest, she gazed down at him. ''No, I suppose not. I just haven't been around a lot of men, and Oliver was, well, I suppose he was a bit conservative. He thought we should wait until after we were married to sleep together.''

Frowning, he slid his hands up her shoulders, then down her back. ''Oliver is an idiot.''

Surprised by Jacob's bitter tone, Clair lifted a brow. ''You don't even know him. Why would you say that?''

His dark gaze met and held hers for a long moment. She had the oddest feeling he was about to tell her something, then suddenly he flipped her onto her back.

''Let's just say I know his type,'' he said tightly. ''And anyway, he'd have to be an idiot to let you go.''

It was the nicest thing Jacob had ever said to her, Clair realized. She had to swallow the thickness in her throat before she could speak. ''He didn't let me go,'' she said quietly. ''I ran away and left him standing in the church. It must have been awful for him.''

Jacob's mouth pressed into a hard line and his eyes searched hers. "Are you having regrets?"

"Guilt, maybe." She reached up and touched his lips with her fingertips. "But no regrets. There isn't one thing I would change that's happened to me since I left that church."

"Not one thing?" He took her hand in his, kissed each fingertip. Every soft press of his lips sent sparks of electricity buzzing up her arm. "You sure?"

It rushed through her like a warm wind, the need, the heat, the desire. Her heart began to pound; her breath caught. "Well...maybe one thing..."

He hesitated, lifted a brow as he glanced down at her.

"I would have preferred four children instead of two," she said thoughtfully. "Little Jake and the baby—oh, dear, I can't remember, is it a boy or a girl?"

It was easier, Clair thought, to let herself tease, to be playful rather than discuss Oliver. Her ex-fiancé was the *last* person she wanted to think about right now. And certainly the last person she wanted to talk about.

One corner of Jacob's mouth curved. He turned his attention to the inside of her elbow. "A boy. Trevor."

"Of course, Trevor." She sucked in a breath when his teeth nipped at the sensitive skin. "Well, Jake and Trevor are getting older and with my disease—what was it again?"

His hand moved up her belly, his knuckles brushed the soft underside of her breast. "Myopia infarction."

"That's it." She gripped the bedclothes in her fists and hung on. "Well, I keep forgetting where I've put the children, so it would help if we had a couple more so they could all keep an eye on each other.'' She arched upward when his thumb brushed back and forth over her nipple. "And you...know...how much I want a little girl."

"Soon as I get my job back at the fertilizer plant,'' he said hoarsely, "we'll talk about it."

He moved over her, his hands, his mouth, brought her to the brink slowly this time. Mindlessly, breathlessly, they held on to each other, then once again slipped over the edge.

She was already in the shower when he woke the next morning. *His* shower, he noted, opening first one heavy eyelid, then the other. He blinked hard, then glanced at the nightstand clock.

7:00 a.m.?

With a groan, he slammed his eyes shut again. The woman got up too damn early.

He rolled away from the bathroom door and pulled the covers over his head, but he could still hear the spray of the water and the sound of Clair singing. Something familiar, though he couldn't place it or make out the words. He dragged the blanket down and listened, then opened his eyes again and flopped onto his back. She was singing in French. Something from an opera, he guessed, though he wouldn't know one from the other.

Thank God.

He could picture Clair, her back perfectly straight as she sat in one of those private theater boxes. She'd be dressed in sleek black, her shiny, dark hair pulled up in a knot on top of her head, exposing that long, regal neck of hers.

That was her world. The only world she knew.

She'd have her adventure, mix with the common folk for a few days, then she'd go back to that world. Where she belonged.

And he didn't.

Furrowing his brow, he sat and scrubbed a hand over his face. Where in the hell had *that* thought come from?

He and Clair both knew that they would go their own ways once they got to Wolf River. Last night hadn't changed that.

He glanced at the bathroom door and frowned. It *hadn't* changed, he told himself. The only thing it changed was that they'd be sleeping in one bed until they got to Wolf River. Now that he'd had a taste of her, there was no way he could keep his hands off her.

He couldn't remember when he'd ever been so hungry for a woman before.

So *desperate*.

When he heard her voice crack on a high note, Jacob shook his head, then tossed the covers off. Naked, he headed for the bathroom.

She'd switched from opera to country-western, he noted, a Dixie Chicks tune about wide-open spaces, though she wasn't quite getting the words right.

Her song was cut off abruptly by an explosion of cursing.

Lifting a brow, he inched the door open. "Clair?"

When she didn't answer, he stepped inside. On the other side of the blue plastic shower curtain, all he could see was her head stuck under the shower, her face lifted to the spray. He moved beside her.

"Something wrong?"

She squeaked, grabbing the shower curtain and hiding behind it. "Jacob! You scared me!"

"I thought you were hurt." He tried to peek around the curtain, but couldn't see a thing. "First all that caterwauling, then you're cursing like a truck driver with a loose wheel."

"Caterwauling!" She stuck her head out. Her face was wet, her cheeks flushed. Her eyes dropped to his naked body, widened, then she snapped her gaze back up. "First of all, I got shampoo in my eyes, and second, I'll have you know I studied with Mademoiselle Marie Purdoit for three years. She said I was a natural."

"Maybe she meant your hair," he teased.

Frowning, Clair swiped a hand over her face, flicked the water at him, then ducked behind the curtain and started to sing "Love Me Tender" in a deep, exaggerated off-key voice.

So she wanted to play, did she?

Grinning, he ducked back into his room and grabbed his camera, then slipped back into the bathroom and took aim.

"Clair," he said loudly. "I'm sorry if I hurt your feelings. You sing very well for someone who's tone-deaf."

"Tone-deaf!"

As she stuck her head out again, he clicked the picture. Shocked, she stood there for a moment, her mouth and eyes open wide. He took another shot.

With a shriek, she disappeared behind the curtain.

And cursed profusely.

Laughing, he put the camera aside. "Make way, Mademoiselle Beauchamp. I'm coming in."

"Jacob Carver," she yelled as he stepped inside the shower, "if you dare to—"

He cut her words off by taking hold of her shoulders and dropping his mouth on hers. She drew in a startled breath, then her arms came around his shoulders.

In spite of the busy night they'd had, the need rose instantly, heated his blood and made his heart race. He turned his back to the hot spray as he deepened the kiss and pulled her against him. Her skin was hot and smooth and wet. Her breasts flattened against his chest as she rose up to meet him; her arms tightened around his neck while she curled one long, smooth leg behind his.

Gasping, she dragged her mouth from his and looked up at him, her eyes filled with desire. "Tell me what to do."

He slid his hands down to her bottom and lifted her. "Wrap your legs around my waist."

He entered her quickly, pressed her back against the cool tile, was deep inside her when he began to move. Her moan echoed off the shower walls.

When her head fell back, he dragged his mouth and teeth along her jaw. Her long, sleek, wet legs tightened around him, intensifying the pleasure until it became unbearable.

"Jacob…hurry…"

Liquid fire raced through over his skin, pulsed through his veins. He felt the bite of her fingernails in his shoulders, then the nip of her teeth. He thrust deeper still, felt her tighten around him, tremble.

Her shudder rolled through him. With a moan, he followed.

Barely able to breathe, he eased her down his body,

felt her body sag against him when her feet touched
the tub floor.

Steam swirled around them and the hot spray bat-
tered their bodies. Still dazed, he gathered her close
for a moment, then turned off the water and took her
back to his bed.

Eight

"Coffee?"

"Hmm." Afraid she might fall off the cloud she was presently floating on, Clair did not turn her head at Jacob's question or even open her eyes. Since the shower incident almost two hours ago, she and Jacob had made love, dozed off in each other's arms, then made love again.

She had a bruise on her hip, knots in her damp hair, and every muscle in her entire body ached.

Smiling, she slid deeper under the sheet covering her and burrowed into the mattress.

"I take it that's a yes." He touched his lips to her bare shoulder, nibbled for a moment, then rolled off the bed. "I think we're both going to need it black and strong today."

Slitting one eye open, Clair watched Jacob drag a pair of jeans up his long, powerful legs, then tug the denim over his tight, firm butt. His waist was narrow, his shoulders wide, his arms muscular. He seemed completely at ease with his body, naked or clothed, and completely at ease with himself.

She envied him that. She'd always felt awkward with her body. Her arms and legs had always seemed too long, her breasts too small, her shoulders too bony. Well, at least until last night she'd felt that way. Now she felt…just right.

Not perfect, as everyone had wanted her to be, but just right.

"Thank you," she said softly.

"You can thank me when I get back." He pulled on a long-sleeved navy-blue shirt and waggled his eyebrows at her while he closed the buttons.

As spent and consumed as she felt, her body still tingled at the thought. Rolling to her side, she propped her head up in the palm of her hand and smiled at him. "Not for the coffee, for last night." She felt a blush work its way up her neck. "It was wonderful. You were wonderful."

Grinning, he sat back down on the edge of the bed and brushed his lips over hers. "You were pretty damn wonderful yourself, Miss Beauchamp."

"Why, thank you, Mr. Carver." She laid her palm on his knee. "How kind of you to say so."

He leaned into the kiss, increased the pressure of his mouth on hers. "Don't mention it."

She felt his thigh muscles tighten and bunch as she moved her hand up his leg. When he pressed her back onto the mattress, she forgot every ache, forgot her exhaustion. Pleasure heated her skin, her blood, made her heart pump furiously.

Jacob moved his mouth down her throat, blazed hot
kisses while his hand tugged the sheet slowly down—

The phone on the nightstand rang.

"Dammit." Jacob lifted his head and frowned at
the phone. "That will be Odell. I was supposed to be
at the garage thirty minutes ago to help drop the radiator back in my car."

Clair slid her hands smoothly down his chest, lingered at the open snap of his jeans. "You should
probably answer it."

She watched his gaze darken and his eyes narrow
when she traced her fingertip down his zipper. Her
boldness shocked, yet thrilled her at the same time.

"You answer it," he said roughly, then lowered
his head to her neck while his hands tugged the sheet
away. "Tell him I'm on my way."

Breathless, her head spinning, she answered the
phone on the fourth ring.

"Clair?"

Her heart, which had been pounding so fiercely,
stopped.

"Oliver?"

Jacob went still, then lifted his head and met her
startled gaze. His mouth pressed into a hard line, and
he rolled away.

"Why are you answering Carver's phone?" Oliver
demanded. "Put him on the line."

"How did you know where I was?" Clair pulled
the sheet up to cover herself, watched Jacob yank a
pair of socks out of his bag, then grab his boots and
sit on the edge of the bed.

"It doesn't matter how I know," Oliver said irritably.

In spite of everything, Clair was certain her mother

hadn't given the number to Oliver. "It matters to me."

"I just happened to see the number written down in your mother's office."

"You went through my mother's office?" She sat, stared at Jacob's stiff back while he pulled his boots on and laced them.

"You've forced me to resort to underhanded measures to find you." Oliver's tone was pious. "Clair, you're jeopardizing your reputation by gallivanting around the country with this Carver fellow. He's not to be trusted."

Clair frowned at the phone. "Why would you say that?"

"Men like Jacob Carver have no sense of ethics or scruples. They'll say and do anything to get what they want. He may even attempt to seduce you by telling you lies about me."

"I assure you, that has not happened." If anything, the opposite was true—she'd seduced Jacob. But Oliver didn't need to know that.

"I insist you come back home immediately." His irritation snapped across the line. "We can be married in a quiet ceremony."

"Oliver." Clair reminded herself that after everything she'd done, the way she'd left him in the lurch, he deserved her patience. "I know my parents explained to you I'm going to meet my brothers in Wolf River. I don't know when I'm coming home."

"You're being ridiculous," he said with more than a touch of arrogance in his voice. "There's still time to repair the damage you've done to our social standing. It's understandable that you've had a temporary breakdown from the shock of learning about your adoption. Just come home, Clair, and I'll forgive you everything. I love you.''

She'd thought he had, but the words sounded empty now. It seemed to Clair that Oliver's ''social standing'' was what troubled him the most. She knew she should be hurt, but the fact was, she was relieved.

When Jacob stood and strode across the room, Clair reached a hand out to stop him, but he didn't look back. The chain beside the door rattled when he slammed it behind him.

With a sigh, she laid back on the bed and stared at the ceiling.

''Clair?'' Oliver's impatient voice came over the line again. ''Answer me. Are you there? *Clair!*''

''I appreciate your magnanimous offer,'' she said evenly. ''But my answer is no. I did not have a temporary breakdown, I am not coming home, and I am not going to marry you. Goodbye, Oliver.''

''Clair—''

She hung up the phone, then took it off the hook. When she heard the phone ringing from her room, she groaned and put a pillow over her head.

Furrowing her brow, she pulled her head back out from under the pillow and listened to the persistent ring.

Why had Oliver asked the motel desk to connect him with Jacob's room first? she wondered. He'd obviously been surprised when she'd said hello, so he hadn't expected her to answer the phone. And he'd asked her to put Jacob on the phone.

Why had he done that?

Maybe Oliver had thought he could convince Jacob to bring her back to South Carolina. Perhaps offer him a reward for her return.

It didn't matter, she thought, thankful when the phone finally stopped ringing. Whatever Oliver's reasons were for wanting to speak to Jacob, she simply didn't care.

She knew that Jacob would be headed back to New Jersey soon, if not immediately, after they arrived in Wolf River. They might have slept together, but she wasn't so foolish as to think that last night had changed anything for him.

And she certainly wasn't so foolish as to tell him that she'd fallen in love with him. No doubt she'd be left standing in a spray of gravel and a cloud of dust if she did.

With a sigh, she looked at the nightstand clock, watched the time change from 9:02 to 9:03. She had no intention of pining away the precious minutes and seconds they had left together. Whatever time they had, she was determined to make the most of it.

Sliding out of bed, she hurried into her room and dug through her suitcase. She pulled out the leopard print thong, smiled slowly, then headed for the shower.

Two hours later, covered with dirt and sweat, Jacob came back to an empty, quiet motel room. Disappointment stabbed at him that Clair wasn't exactly where he'd left her—in his bed—but he supposed it was for the best. It was nearly noon and if they were going to make any time on the road at all today, they'd need to get a move-on.

Unbuttoning his shirt, he headed toward her room and stuck his head in. "Clair?"

Her room was empty, as well. His disappointment

turned to irritation. Where the hell had she taken off
to now?

Her bed was neatly made, the nightstands clear.

And her suitcase was missing.

His heart slammed against his ribs.

Oliver.

A muscle jumped in the corner of Jacob's eye. He
shouldn't have left her alone, dammit. Especially after
last night. Clair was vulnerable, maybe having regrets. That idiot Oliver had probably bullied her,
played on her guilt and talked her into returning to
Charleston.

He'd strangle the bastard.

Clair was too damn trusting. Maybe he should have
told her about Oliver messing around with that blond
bimbo, that the two of them had been at the Wanderlust Motel the night before the wedding and the
night before that, too.

That certainly would have blown all her wide-eyed
innocence to hell.

Which was exactly why he *hadn't* told her. He
couldn't remember when he'd met a woman with
such enthusiasm for life, such honesty. A woman who
blushed so easily, laughed so heartily and trusted
without question.

Fists clenched, he strode into the bathroom, looking
for something, anything, she might have left behind.
A brush, a tube of lipstick, a razor.

But there was nothing. Because she'd stayed in his
room last night and used his shower this morning,
even her motel soap was unopened, the glass still in
its plastic wrapper, the shampoo still on the counter.
As if she'd never been here at all.

She'd gotten to him, dammit. Gotten under his

skin. No woman had ever done that before. Not like this.

Dammit, *dammit.*

Well, fine, then. He set his teeth. He thought he'd seen beneath her submissive rich-girl facade and glimpsed a stronger, more determined, decisive woman. Obviously he'd been wrong.

Swearing under his breath, he tore at the buttons of his shirt and headed back toward his own room. If she wanted to go, then good riddance. He'd never wanted to go traipsing around these backroads, anyway. He hoped she and Oliver and his blond bimbo would be happy. *"Hasta la vista, baby,"* he said tightly. *"Sai la vie, Auf Wied—"*

"Who are you talking to?"

He turned so fast at the sound of her voice behind him, he whacked his elbow on the doorjamb. A jolt of numbing electricity shot up his arm. The single word he uttered was raw and coarse.

"Well, for heaven's sake." Key still in her hand, Clair stood in the open doorway of her motel room. "What's wrong with you?"

Momentarily dumbstruck at the sight of her, Jacob simply stared. She'd dressed to suit the hot day, a black tank top, tan capris and a pair of sandals with a white daisy between the toes.

Relief poured through him.

Followed quickly by annoyance.

"Where the hell were you?"

She lifted a brow, then closed the door behind her. "You didn't see my note?"

Note? He glanced back at his room. He'd been too busy ranting about her leaving to consider she hadn't actually left, or that she might have written a note.

"Obviously not." She dropped her black shoulder bag onto the bed, then crossed her arms as she faced him. "You thought I left, didn't you?"

"No."

"Liar."

"All right." He shifted awkwardly. "So maybe I did. Just for a minute or so."

"You really thought I would do that? Leave without saying goodbye?"

"You were talking to Oliver when I left." He defended himself. "Your suitcase is gone. What the hell was I supposed to think?"

"My suitcase—" she kept her gaze level with his as she walked toward him "—is right next to yours, in *your* room—the same room I put the note in."

When she moved past him and disappeared into his room, he shoved his hands into his pockets and followed.

Snatching a note off the bed, she stuck it in his face. "If you would have taken a moment to look instead of jumping to conclusions, you would have noticed."

Jacob, her note read, *Went to see Bridgette. Be back shortly.*

"Oh." Dammit. The only thing he hated more than being wrong about something, was having it waved under his nose. "Well, okay. I'll just take a shower and we'll hit the road."

"Not so fast, Carver."

"What?"

"I believe you owe me an apology."

There actually *was* something he hated more than having a mistake waved under his nose—saying he was sorry. "For what?"

She folded her arms and lifted her chin. "Based on erroneous information, you made an *assumption* that I'd packed my bag and left without so much as a thank you. That is a hardly a compliment to my character, and it speaks volumes of your faith in me."

"All right." He scowled at her. "I shouldn't have *assumed*."

She lifted a brow. "That's my apology?"

"Take it or leave it."

Rolling her eyes, she sighed and moved close to him. "Do you want to know what Oliver and I talked about?"

"No."

"Okay." She turned to walk away.

He grabbed her arm and dragged her back, though he was too dirty to haul her against him the way he wanted to. Damn her to hell, anyway.

"Yes," he said through clenched teeth.

"He said we could still get married in a quiet ceremony, that he would forgive me everything."

"What a generous guy." Jacob's voice was hard enough to cut granite.

"He said we could save our social situation if we told everyone I had a breakdown after I found out I was adopted."

"He's an idiot." Jacob decided he just might take a trip back to Charleston after all. He'd like to see Oliver's face just before he slammed a fist into his nose. "What else did he say?"

"That I shouldn't trust you." Clair dropped her gaze as she ran a finger down the front of Jacob's open shirt. "He said that men like you seduce women like me."

His pulse jumped when she tugged his shirt from

his jeans. "Maybe you shouldn't trust me," he said evenly. "Maybe I will seduce you."

His blood drained from his head and shot straight to his groin when she reached for the snap on his jeans.

"Too late," she all but purred as she tugged his zipper down. "I seduced you first."

"Is that what happened?"

"That's exactly what happened."

"Clair." He covered her hand with his to hold her still. "I need to take a shower."

She pressed her lips to his. "How long will that take you?"

"You know that town we were in two days ago?"

"Plug Nickel?"

"Don't Blink."

Careful not to brush up against her, he kissed her hard, nearly forgot his good intentions, then yanked his mouth from hers and headed for the shower, pulling clothes off on his way. The water was still cold as he soaped up, but it did nothing to cool the fire burning in his blood.

"Jacob?"

He smiled at her impatience, stuck his head out to tell her to join him if she couldn't wait.

The camera flashed.

He swore, reached out a hand to grab her.

She jumped back and the camera flashed again. Laughing, she hurried out of the bathroom before he came out after her.

He was going to wring her neck, he told himself.

Right after he'd made love to her.

Nine

The two-lane highway stretched long and flat under a hot sun. Fields of alfalfa on one side of the road gave the air a sweet, earthy scent. Until the breeze shifted. Then the pungent scent of cow from the dairy farm on the other side of the highway gained dominance.

Clair rested her arms on the door frame of the open car window and breathed in deeply. Cow or alfalfa, it didn't matter. With the sun on her face, the wind in her hair, and Jacob humming along with a Billy Joel song beside her, what could possibly matter? Nature was a beautiful thing. Even the dark, thick clouds gathering on the distant horizon didn't worry her.

Life was wonderful.

They'd been on the road for three hours since they'd left Liberty. To Jacob's annoyance, she'd made him stop several times so she could take pic-

tures: a white steepled church in a tiny town called
Hat Box; an abandoned tractor covered with moon-
flower vine in a meadow outside of Bobcat; an old
barn in Eunice. She couldn't wait to see them developed.

Especially the picture she'd taken of Jacob in the
shower this morning.

The expression of shock on his face, then anger,
had been priceless. Definitely a "Kodak moment."
Though he'd grumbled about the surprise photo, she'd
told him that turnabout was fair play. He'd taken two
of her; she'd taken two of him. They were Even
Steven, as the saying went.

Somehow, Jacob hadn't quite seen it that way, but
after he'd stepped out of the shower, they'd both forgotten soon enough about the pictures.

Their minds—and their hands—had been occupied
elsewhere.

He'd told her before that she was naive, but she
wasn't so naive to think that what she and Jacob had
shared wasn't something exceptional. Something special. She was certain she would never know another
lover like him. That she would never love another
man the same way she loved Jacob. Though her mind
told her she *would* love again, her heart wasn't so
certain.

The wind whipped at the ends of her hair and the
late afternoon sun warmed her cheeks. In spite of the
ache in her heart, she smiled.

There were no regrets. If their relationship was to
be no more than a physical one, then she would live
that. She would be *happy* with that. Well, if not
happy, then at least content.

Tucking her chin into her hands, she closed her eyes and let her mind drift.

What if it were possible that there *could* be more for them? she wondered. That maybe, just *maybe* Jacob had feelings for her that could take them past these few short days?

He'd been angry this morning because he'd thought she'd packed up and returned to Charleston after speaking to Oliver. Was he angry because he cared about her? She'd seen something in his eyes beyond anger when she'd come back to the motel room. Relief maybe? Jealousy?

She sighed, then shook her head.

She'd only make herself crazy if she tried to second guess what Jacob's feelings for her might be. She was having enough trouble with her *own* feelings, for heaven's sake. She knew she would only be setting herself up for disappointment if she let herself hope that Jacob might want more.

"So what's it gonna be, Clair?"

Startled by Jacob's question, she jerked her head around. "What?"

"We'll need to stop in an hour or so. Maybe sooner if that storm comes in." He picked up the map lying on the seat between them and held it out to her. "Where this time?"

"Oh." Settling back in her seat, she found where they were at the moment, then studied the towns lying ahead of them.

Forest Glen? No, too generic. Rolling Flats? A contradiction of terms if ever she'd heard one. Crab Apple? Too tart.

Gray Creek…Arrow Bend…Quartz.

No. No. No.

Fifty miles west, she found it.

Smiling, she looked up at Jacob and held out the map.

An hour later, Jacob pulled into the parking lot of The Forty Winks Motel in Lucky, Louisiana. Thick, dark clouds had already soaked up the light before the sun had even gone down. The air was hot and heavy and still, charged with electricity.

When thunder rumbled in the distance, Clair shuddered, then grabbed her purse and followed Jacob into the motel office.

The clerk behind the desk, an elderly woman with gold chains on her thick glasses and tight gray curls on her head, dozed in a corner chair. Curled in the woman's wide lap was a fat tabby cat, who opened one eye when Jacob and Clair walked in, then closed it again. From a small color TV, the sound of a popular game show blasted out questions in rapid-fire succession.

"...'Then there was bad weather'...was the opening line for this Hemmingway story..."

"Moveable Feast," Jacob muttered.

Clair glanced at Jacob, who didn't appear to be aware that he'd answered the question. When the game-show host gave the answer and Jacob was correct, Clair lifted a brow.

While they waited politely for the clerk to realize she had customers, the questions from the television continued. "This is the eighth planet out from the earth," the host said.

"Neptune." Jacob tugged his wallet out of his jean's back pocket.

Clair raised both brows.

"What is the square root of twenty-five thousand?"

"Fifty."

Her mouth open, Clair stared at Jacob, who tapped his palm down on the counter bell. The clerk came awake with a small snort. The cat tumbled off the woman's lap, then looked at Jacob and twitched his tail.

"Dear me." A hand on her ample bosom, the clerk jumped up and pushed her glasses back up her long nose. She wore a silver-metal name tag that said Dorothy. "I must have nodded off."

"We'd like a room for the night." Jacob slid a credit card across the counter. "King-size bed, non-smoking."

A room, as in *one.* Clair released the breath she'd been holding. Though they'd shared a bed last night, nothing had been said between them today regarding the sleeping arrangements for tonight.

How strange it was that she'd never checked into a motel room with a man before, and yet with Jacob it felt so comfortable, so natural to her.

The cat jumped up on the counter and glared at Jacob. Jacob glared back. A big, round blue ID tag on the cat's collar said Zeke.

When Zeke turned his back on Jacob and sauntered over to Clair to have his head scratched, Jacob scowled.

"Welcome to Lucky," the woman said with a friendly smile while she ran the credit card. "Where you and your wife headed?"

Your wife. Clair glanced sideways at Jacob, waited for him to correct the woman.

He simply signed the credit-card slip Dorothy

handed to him and slid it back across the counter.
"Wolf River."

"Why, fancy that." The clerk scanned two card
keys, then passed them to Jacob. "I have a cousin in
Wolf River."

Clair looked up sharply. "You—you have a cousin
there?"

"Why, yes. Boyd Smith. His wife's name is Angela."

Clair's heart started to pound like a drum. "Have
you been there?" she asked softly. "To Wolf River?"

"Used to spend every summer there on my aunt
and uncle's ranch outside of town." Dorothy's smile
widened. "'Course that was more than fifty years
ago, but I've been back to visit Boyd and Angie a
few times. Hardly recognize the town it's grown so."

"Clair." Jacob touched her shoulder. "Maybe you
should wait."

She looked at him, then shook her head and
glanced back at the clerk. "Do you...have you ever
heard of the Blackhawk family?"

"The Blackhawks?" The woman seemed surprised
by the question. "Well, of course. Anyone's ever
been to Wolf River County has heard of the Blackhawks. They used to own more than half the land
south of town."

"Used to?"

"There were three brothers when I was a teenager," Dorothy said. "William was the oldest. He had
a mean spirit, that one. Then there was Jonathan and
Thomas. Jonathan was the quiet one and Thomas was
the hothead. I used to fancy Thomas when I was a
teenager," Dorothy said with a bat of her eyes, then
leaned across the counter and pressed her lips into a

thin line. "Never believed he tried to kill that man, even though he went to prison for it and ended up dying there, poor man. Took almost twenty years to prove him innocent."

Her uncles, Clair realized. William and Thomas.

And her father was Jonathan.

"Did you—" Clair had to swallow the thickness in her throat "—did you know Jonathan?"

"Met him a couple of times one summer when I worked part-time at the hardware store. We were both teenagers back then." With a sigh, Dorothy scratched Zeke's head. "Angela sent me the newspaper article about the car accident. Killed his whole family—three little ones and his wife, though I can't remember her name."

We're not all dead, Clair thought. *We're alive.*

"Norah," Clair whispered. "Her name was Norah."

"That's right." Dorothy looked up in surprise. "You know the Blackhawks?"

"No." She shook her head. "I—I've heard of them."

"Far as I know, Thomas's son Lucas is the only one left now," Dorothy said sadly. "There was talk about William's boy, but the way I heard it, he ran off when he was a teenager and no one's seen him in years."

When the phone rang and Dorothy turned to answer it, Jacob took hold of Clair's arm. "We should go."

Outside the office, Clair sagged against Jacob. He circled his arms around her and held her close.

"I'd seen the documents," she said quietly. "Listened to my parents' admission. But, until this moment, it never seemed real to me." She curled her fingers into the front of his shirt and looked up at him. "That woman in there just made it real."

"Yeah." He tucked her hair behind her ears. "It's real."

"She met my father." The wonder of it had her smiling. And crying. "Knew my uncles."

A humid breeze blew over them; thunder rumbled, closer than it had been before. They stood there for a long, silent moment, then she touched Jacob's cheek, needed to know that he was real, too. His skin was warm, the stubble of his beard sent tingles up her arm. When he pressed his lips to her palm, butterflies danced in her stomach.

Something shifted. In the air. Between them. In the Universe, Clair thought. When Jacob's eyes narrowed and darkened, she thought he felt it, too.

But then he dropped his hands away and shoved them into his front jean's pockets. "There's a pizza place across the street," he said evenly. "Why don't we get something to eat?"

"All right." She forced her tone to be light and her smile to be bright. "As long as it's double pepperoni."

"Pepperoni was on the forbidden list?" Jacob shook his head in disgust. "That's downright cruel."

"Tell me about it."

They crossed the street to a two-story brick building—Earl's Family Pizza and Pool Hall. Make that *Pearl's* Family Pizza and Pool Hall, Jacob corrected himself when he noticed that the *P* had blanked out in the blue neon sign in the front window.

The aromatic scent of baking pizza dough and spicy herbs assaulted them when they stepped through the front door. The sound of Italian accordion music blasted from every corner speaker.

Pearl's was packed. Nearly every red-and-white-checked table was full. There was a line for takeout, a line for eat-in and a line for drinks. Servers shouted orders and filled beer and soda pitchers, the phones were ringing, and two men behind a glass counter flipped circles of pizza dough high up in the air, then caught it again.

"You go ahead and order," Clair said over the din. "I'll get us a table."

Several minutes later, Jacob joined Clair at a table beside the Family Fun Center, a room filled with video games and pinball machines. He nearly spilled the icy mug of beer and soda he carried when two young boys burst out of the room and exploded past him.

"Hoodlums," he muttered. He handed Clair her soda and a paper wrapped straw, then set a red plastic number card on the table that read 17.

"They're just little boys." Clair ripped an end off her straw's wrapper, then blew the paper sleeve at Jacob and hit him on the nose. "Don't you like children?"

Frowning, he crinkled the paper into a little ball and threw it back at her. "Sure. I used to be one. I was a hoodlum, too."

"I don't believe you." She took a sip of her soda, then set her elbows on the table and rested her chin on her fisted hands. "Hoodlums don't read Hemmingway or know the square root of twenty-five thousand."

"They might if they had a parole officer who believed in education."

"You were in *jail?*"

The shock in her eyes reminded him how little she knew about life outside her own secluded world. And how little she knew about him.

What would she think of him if she really *did* know him? Jacob wondered. Living in the slums of New Jersey was as far from South Carolina high society as a guy could get. Survival was all that mattered in the neighborhood where he'd grown up. When he'd been a kid, he'd seen things, even done some things, that would make Clair's skin crawl.

Hell, it made *his* skin crawl.

"Juvenile hall, actually." He could still remember the sound of the metal bars they'd slammed closed behind him. Could still feel the panic of being locked inside a cage. "I was fourteen."

"You were only a child."

"Where I grew up, fourteen is definitely not a child." He watched the two boys who'd nearly bumped into him run to a table across the restaurant where a man and woman were sharing a pizza. The quest for quarters, he thought with a smile. "And the man whose car I stole didn't much care how old I was."

"You made a mistake." Clair pressed her lips firmly together and lifted her chin. "You said yourself that your mother had abandoned you and your brother, and that your father was an alcoholic. Surely the judge took that into account."

"Sure, he did." Jacob stretched his long legs out under the table. "He sent my brother to a foster home, and me to a Newark boys' home."

"He separated you and your brother?" Indignation squared her shoulders. "That's terrible!"

"Turned out to be the best thing that could have happened." Evan had only been eleven at the time. Jacob remembered how hard those first few weeks had been for both of them. "It gave Evan a stable home with a decent family for four years and me a goal."

"What goal?"

"Not to end up like the rest of the kids I was hanging with, and definitely not to end up like my father. After I finished high school, I went to work for a bail bondsman and discovered I had a knack for finding people who didn't want to be found. Two years later I got my private investigator's license, then opened an office in Jersey."

"What about your brother?"

"He finished high school, then got a four-year scholarship to University of Texas." Jacob stared at the condensation on the mug in his hands. "Neither one of us has looked back."

Is that why Jacob had set no roots? Clair wondered. Why he'd chosen a job that kept him moving? Because if he was still for even a moment, he might look back and be reminded of what he'd left behind? Or of what he'd never had?

Strange, she thought. She couldn't remember her past, and he couldn't forget his.

"And Evan," she asked, "where is he now?"

"He owns a construction company about twenty miles outside of Fort Worth, a small town called Kettle Creek." Jacob shook his head. "A masters in science and he ends up swinging a hammer. Go figure."

There was pride in Jacob's voice, not criticism, Clair noted. "Why didn't you go to college, too?"

"Degrees are for nine-to-five people who like ladders and schmoozing with the boss.'' He crossed one boot over the other. ''My life is simple. No time clock to punch, no yard to mow, no quarts of milk to pick up for the little woman on my way home from work.''

Clair wasn't certain how the conversation had moved from getting an education to yard work, then to marriage, nor was she certain whether Jacob was trying to convince her or himself that he had no intentions of ever settling down.

She knew this was his way of letting her know he wouldn't be sticking around after he got her to Wolf River. His job would be over, mission accomplished. As hard as it was for her to hear it, she at least appreciated his honesty. There'd been far too many lies in her life.

More than anything, she needed the truth right now. She needed to know what happened twenty-three years ago. And most especially, *why.*

She knew the answers to her questions were waiting for her in Wolf River. That there were people waiting to give her those answers.

And she knew it was time to go there.

The call for order number 17 interrupted Dean Martin singing ''That's Amore'' and while Jacob went to get their order, Clair sat back and watched the families enjoying a night out. A blue-eyed baby girl two tables over rubbed spaghetti sauce into her blond curls while her older brother picked the cheese off his pizza, then—despite his mother's warning— crammed a huge bite of crust into his mouth. In the far corner, an extremely loud Little League baseball team was clearly celebrating a victory and at another table beside them, a little redheaded girl was having a birthday party with balloons and paper hats. A big pink candle on the cake in the center of the table declared that she was eight.

When she was a child, Clair's birthday parties had either been at the Van Sheever Yacht Club, the Four Seasons Hotel or Emily Bridge Rose Gardens. Never a pizza parlor. Josephine Beauchamp would have been appalled at the very thought.

Clair glanced around the restaurant again, felt an ache settle in her chest. Desperately she wanted to be a part of this. She wanted children and birthday parties and Little League games. A minivan or SUV. A white picket fence. Rosebushes. A dog.

And—she watched Jacob come toward her, holding the pizza high as he dodged children running underfoot—she wanted a man who would bring home a quart of milk on his way home from work.

They ate pizza, played video games and Skee-Ball, and that night, as the rain pounded the roof and thunder shook the motel walls, they made love with the same intensity as the storm overhead, both of them knowing their time together was growing shorter by the hour. By the minute. By the second…

Ten

"**W**elcome to Wolf River, Miss Beauchamp." Grinning broadly, Henry Barnes enclosed Clair's hand between both of his own. "You have no idea what a pleasure it is to finally meet you."

The silver-haired man, dressed in jeans, a white button-up shirt and cowboy boots, looked more like a rancher than a lawyer, Clair thought. His handsome face was tan, his years evident in the deep lines at the corners of his dark brown eyes and the brackets alongside his smile. The warmth in that smile took the edge off the icy fear in her blood and the tight knot in her stomach.

For the last twenty minutes, since she and Jacob had driven past the Welcome To Wolf River County sign, then parked in front of Beddingham, Barnes and Stephens Law Offices, Clair had not been able to put a coherent thought, let alone a sentence, together.

Gratefully years of etiquette now took over. "Thank you, Mr. Barnes. The pleasure is all mine."

"Just call me Henry. And you—" he released her hand and turned to Jacob "—are Mr. Carver, I presume. I'm not sure whether to label you a magician or a miracle worker, but as spokesperson for the Blackhawk family, I thank you for bringing Elizabeth—" Henry shook his head "—Clair, that is, safely to us."

Obviously uncomfortable with the compliment, Jacob shifted awkwardly, then accepted Henry's hand. "Jacob."

"I'll get us some coffee." Henry gestured toward two chairs opposite his large oak desk. "Make yourself comfortable and I'll be right back."

"I can wait outside." Jacob turned to Clair after Henry left the room. "This is private and I'm sure—"

"Would you stay?" She touched his arm. "I'm not sure I can do this alone."

I need you, she almost said, and would have meant it in every way. But that, she figured, was the last thing Jacob needed to hear. She would not cling, nor would she beg. It would only embarrass them both.

Hands folded in her lap and shoulders straight, Clair sat in the chair Henry had offered while Jacob studied a miniature train setup in the corner of the office. The detail in the old-time railroad display, right down to the shiny brass bell on the engine and an entire 1800s coal mining town was amazing. She watched Jacob glance at the switch that would turn the train on, couldn't help but smile when she saw the brief glimpse of childlike anticipation in his eyes

before he shoved his hands into the back pockets of
his jeans.

They'd both been unusually quiet since they'd left
the town of Lucky early this morning. She'd asked
for no side trips today, not even to take pictures.
They'd driven seven hours straight on the Interstate,
had stopped briefly for gas and fast food in Lampasas,
a small Texas town known for its mineral springs,
then were back on the road again.

She understood that the drive today—what might
very well be their last day together—was a transition
time for both of them. Though she had no idea *how*
her life was about to change, she knew without a
doubt it would.

And Jacob's would not.

"Here we go." Henry came back into the room
carrying a tray loaded with three mugs of steaming
coffee and a plate of cookies. "Judy, my secretary,
has the afternoon off for a PTA bake sale. We need
books for a new library at the elementary school."
He set the tray on his desk. "I made my donation
early and lucked out with a dozen of Angie Smith's
chocolate chip cookies."

"Angie Smith?" Clair glanced up sharply. "You
mean Angela Smith, married to Boyd?"

Lifting a brow, Henry sat in a brown leather chair
behind his desk. "You know Angie and Boyd?"

"No. I—she—" Suddenly she couldn't speak. She
felt as if her life had turned into a connect the dots
puzzle and with each new line drawn, she was closer
to a completed picture.

"We met her cousin Dorothy in Lucky, Louisiana," Jacob answered for Clair. "She told us to say
hello if we saw them."

Henry smiled warmly at Clair. "I'm sure you'll have a chance to do that, especially since Lucas's wife, Julianna, is best friends with Angie's daughter, Maggie."

Lucas, Julianna, Maggie. Clair knew she'd have to ask again later, but she was too dazed right now. Clasping her hands tightly together, she swallowed and leaned forward. "My family," she said quietly. "I need to know what happened."

With a nod, the lawyer leaned back. "We only sent the barest information for Jacob to give to you. Your brothers decided they would rather you heard the details in person, as they already have."

Your brothers.

Clair's heart started to pound furiously. A lifetime of learned patience flew out the window at the lawyer's words. "Please, Mr. Barnes—Henry."

"Twenty-five years ago," Henry began, "on September 23, you were born Elizabeth Marie Blackhawk to Jonathan and Norah Blackhawk. You had two brothers, Rand Zacharius, age nine, and Seth Ezekiel, age seven. Your parents owned a small horse ranch outside of town."

Henry pulled a document from a file sitting on his desk and handed it to her. Clair's hand shook as she stared at the birth certificate. She'd been born at 3:47 p.m., weighed seven pounds, three ounces. Twenty-two inches long, eyes blue.

"We always celebrated my birthday on August 29," she whispered, realizing the birth certificate she'd used her entire life was a phony. "I thought I'd been born in France."

"I already sent you a copy of the newspaper article about the accident." Henry slipped the original out of the folder. "Your parents' car went over a canyon ravine in a lightning storm and they were killed instantly."

"But the article said we were all killed." Clair looked at the article, but couldn't bear to touch it. "How is that possible?"

"The conspiracy was an elaborate one." Henry's expression was somber. "It was so unthinkable, no one suspected a thing."

"A conspiracy?" She shook her head. "I don't understand."

"The night of the accident, the first person to arrive on the scene was Spencer Radick, the sheriff of Wolf River. At first, Radick believed your entire family had been killed in the accident, so he called your father's brother, William. William arrived a few minutes later with his housekeeper, Rosemary Owens, and they discovered that you and your brothers were not only alive, but had suffered very few injuries."

Spencer Radick, William, Rosemary Owens. Clair struggled to keep the names straight, knew that each one was another number to help her connect the dots. "My uncle," she whispered. "He took us home?"

"I'm afraid not," Henry said sadly. "William was an angry, disturbed man. He'd been estranged from both his brothers since they married outside their own race."

Clair furrowed her brow in confusion. "But then what did he—"

The realization slammed into her like a two-by-four in the chest. She gripped the wooden arms of the chair she sat in, then said raggedly, "He *sold* us."

"In a way," Henry said, "though he saw no money himself. He split you all up that night, sent Rand with

Rosemary, Seth with the sheriff, and you with Leon Waters—a crooked lawyer from Granite Springs—a man who specialized in illegal adoptions. You were all adopted out, Rand and Seth each told their entire family had died in the crash. You were too little to understand what had happened.''

''But the newspaper article.'' Clair looked at Jacob, saw the rigid set of his jaw, then glanced back at Henry. ''The death certificates, children missing. Why wouldn't *someone,* a neighbor or another family member, have questioned or discovered the truth?''

''Your uncle Thomas and his wife were already dead. Their son, Lucas, was only a teenager. William's wife, Mary, was a weak woman. It was easier for her to pretend she didn't know what had happened. And their son, Dillon, was just a child himself.'' Henry sighed. ''Your uncle William was thorough and he had the money to pay off all the right people. Spencer Radick left town two months later and was never seen again, Rosemary Owens moved to Vermont shortly after that. Leon Waters closed his practice and disappeared.''

''Waters blackmailed my parents a few years ago.'' Clair remembered her mother and father talking about the lawyer. ''They paid him to keep my adoption secret.''

''Waters is the scum of the earth.'' Disgust filled Henry's voice. ''But if it helps you, the Beauchamps didn't know the truth when they adopted you. You were the perfect child, the right coloring and hair, healthy and young enough that you would forget your past.''

''They lied to me.'' She closed her eyes against the growing ache in her chest. ''Let me believe I was their daughter by birth. My mother even told a story about being in labor with me and how nervous my father was."

"Sometimes the line between the truth and fiction becomes blurry," Henry said gently. "What we're doing here now is making that line distinct and clear."

"Twenty-three years," Clair whispered, then glanced up sharply at the lawyer. "But how, after all this time, did the truth finally come out?"

"Rebecca Owens, Rosemary's daughter, found a journal after her mother died several months ago. I have copies of that journal in a file for you." Henry slid a thick manila folder across the top of his desk. "Rosemary had written in detail everything that happened that night, plus the names of everyone involved. Most likely it was to protect herself in case William ever came after her and threatened her. Rebecca contacted Lucas, your cousin, who hired me to track you all down. Rand and Seth were easy. You were not. If not for Mr. Carver here, I'm not sure we would have ever found you. We all owe him a debt of gratitude."

"Yes." Clair looked at Jacob, met his dark, somber gaze. "We do."

He'd saved her from a marriage she hadn't truly wanted, given her the courage to make decisions for herself, to simply be herself. The past few days had been the most important, most special, most exciting of her life.

When he left, he'd take much more than her gratitude, she thought. He'd take her heart, as well.

She turned away from him, couldn't think about him now, about his leaving. If she did, she was certain she'd fall apart completely. She'd come too far to allow herself to break down here.

Later, she told herself. After he was gone. Only then, would she allow herself to give in to the pain of losing him.

She forced her attention back on Henry and the reason she'd made this journey. The picture was beginning to take shape. Clair understood *what* had happened and *how*.

But there was one more question, possibly the most important.

"Why?" she asked quietly. "Why would anyone do such a horrible, cruel thing to three small children? We were family. Flesh and blood."

"For the same reason most men commit crimes." Henry opened the file and pulled out a thick, stapled document. "Your grandfather's original will. The one that left a very large estate to all three of his sons. Unfortunately, because William got hold of it before anyone else even knew it existed, he created a different, fraudulent will. One that left everything to him alone."

Clair was used to large amounts of money, had an extremely healthy trust fund of her own. Still, as she glanced through the papers, the size of the estate was very impressive.

It appeared that she was about to become five million dollars richer than she already was.

Her hand shook as she handed the will back to Henry. She didn't care about the money. She'd learned only too well that there were some things no amount of money could buy.

"William—" Just saying his name made her stomach feel sick. "Will he go to jail?"

"If he were alive, he would," Henry said. "He died two years ago in a small plane crash. His son, Dillon, left Wolf River when he was seventeen and no one has heard from him since. Your brothers are still discussing whether we should look for him. I believe they were waiting for you to help make that final decision."

Your brothers.

The last two dots to make the picture complete.

To make it whole.

She swallowed hard, drew in a slow breath. "When can I meet them?"

Henry sat back in his chair and grinned. "How 'bout now?"

"Now?" Surely he didn't mean *now,* as in right this minute. Breath held, she glanced at Jacob. He leaned toward her, covered her hand with his.

"They're waiting outside," Jacob said quietly.

"Here?" She glanced sharply at the door, felt her heart knock against her ribs. "They've been here all this time?"

"We all thought it best we didn't tell you until after you heard everything." He squeezed her hand and smiled. "You might have found it distracting."

Distracting? Good Lord, that was putting it mildly. Her stomach rolled, and it suddenly felt as if ice were pumping through her blood. She opened her mouth to speak, but couldn't force the words out.

Jacob looked at Henry. "Give us a couple of minutes, will you?"

"Take your time," Henry said kindly, then stood and left the room.

When the walls around her started to spin, Clair closed her eyes. "I—I'm not ready."

"Come here." He tugged her onto his lap, enclosed her in the warm comfort of his strong arms. "No one's rushing you."

"I'm scared," she whispered. She felt completely foolish, like a child, but she couldn't stop the shaking that had taken hold of her.

"It's all right." He pressed his lips to her temple. "Let yourself go with it."

She curled into him, felt the heat of his body warm her. Beat by beat her heart slowed and her stomach settled. He smoothed his hands over her stiff back, rocked her gently.

Muscle by muscle, she relaxed, melted into him while he tenderly, patiently held her close. The room no longer spun, it held steady and even. Secure. She thought she could sit here with his like this forever.

But there were no forevers with Jacob, she knew. What he offered was temporary. It hurt, but she could accept that.

She would have to accept that.

She eased away from him, touched his cheek with her hand, then smiled. "Thank you."

Drawing in a slow, deep breath, she stood, was thankful that the floor felt steady under her feet. "I'm ready."

When he moved toward the door, her pulse picked up, with anticipation this time, not panic.

Smoothing the front of her blouse with her damp palms, she stared, breath held, as Jacob reached for the knob.

The two men standing on the other side straightened as the door swung open.

Their eyes met.

She couldn't speak, wouldn't have known what to

say if she could. They were so *tall*. Dark hair like hers, the same dark blue eyes. They certainly looked like brothers.

They looked like *her* brothers.

Her neck began to tingle, almost as if someone were lightly touching her with their fingertips. *Strange,* she thought as both men rubbed at their necks.

Shoulder-to-shoulder, they stepped awkwardly into the room, seemed to fill it with their presence. Not knowing what to do with her hands, she folded them primly in front of her, swallowed back the thickness in her throat while she searched for something to say.

For what felt like a lifetime, they all stood there, silently staring at each other.

And then they smiled.

And she smiled back.

It was just that easy.

"Lizzie." The man on the left side held out his hand to her. Rand, she thought. She was *certain* it was Rand.

Tears streaming, she flew across the room and dived into both men's arms. They felt so familiar. They even *smelled* familiar. It didn't matter that she didn't know her brothers, that she couldn't remember them on a conscious level. She *felt* them in her heart, in her soul.

"You're Rand." Not even trying to hold back her tears, she kissed his cheek, then moved to Seth and kissed him, too. "And Seth."

Both of her brothers' eyes sparkled with moisture. She hugged them again, then eased back, struggling to find her voice. "It's so amazing, so wonderful."

"We were hoping you'd feel that way." Grinning,

Rand looked at Seth, then they both grabbed her again and squeezed.

The wonder of it, the magic, had them all laughing. They held on to each other, absorbing the moment and each other. She had no idea how long they all stood there. They felt solid against her. They felt *right.*

They formed a circle of three. The power of that circle coursed through her blood and pounded in her temples.

They finally eased back from each other, though still they did not break contact. "We weren't certain you'd come," Rand said, gazing down at her.

"I had to," she said softly. "But you know that."

"Yeah." Rand nodded. "I think I do."

Stepping back from Rand and Seth, Clair opened her mouth to introduce Jacob, then closed it again.

He wasn't in the doorway.

She glanced over her brothers' broad shoulders and looked into the outer office. He wasn't there, either.

He wouldn't have left without saying goodbye, she was certain of that. But he hadn't wanted to stay and be a part of her family reunion, either. One more way he was letting go, she realized.

Strange how her heart could feel so full, yet so empty at the same time.

"So, little sis." Seth took her hand. "You ready to catch up on twenty-three years?"

Turning back to her brothers, she smiled through her tears. "Yes," she said with a nod. "I am."

Down the street from Beddingham, Barnes and Stephens Law Offices, Jacob sat at a small corner table in the lounge of the Four Winds Hotel. The room was crowded with locals getting off work and—according to a welcome sign outside the lounge—an East Texas Cattle Rancher's convention. A sea of cowboy hats bobbed across the room like boats on Hudson Bay.

He drained the last of the beer he'd been nursing for the past two hours and did his best to concentrate on a baseball play-off game on the television over the glossy oak bar. He thought it was the seventh inning, but he hadn't a clue what the score was. In spite of the fact he was a die-hard baseball fan, he didn't much give a damn, either.

A cocktail waitress named Michelle came over after dropping off a load of drinks at the next table. The blonde picked up his empty glass, then set another beer in front of him and a fresh bowl of peanuts.

"On the house," she said, curving her lips. "I figure if it takes you as long to drink this one as it did the last, it'll be about the same time I'm getting off work."

"Thanks." He managed to work up a smile, knew that there was something seriously wrong with him when he couldn't even find it in him to banter with a pretty woman in a very short skirt. "I'm waiting for someone."

"Two hours is a long wait." Michelle rolled one shoulder in a disappointed shrug. "Let me know if she's a no-show."

"I'll do that." He lifted his glass to her, took in her long legs as she turned and walked away. And felt nothing.

Damn. Something was *definitely* wrong with him.

And that something was Clair.

He'd checked her into a suite at the Four Winds after leaving the lawyer's office. He'd figured after several days on the road sleeping on lumpy mattresses in backwater motels, she'd be ready for plush towels, soft pillows and room service again. He'd left a message for her with Henry telling her where he'd be, then had her suitcases taken up to her room by a bell cap. Jacob was smart enough to know that if he'd gone up to the room himself, the temptation to stay would be too great.

He stared at the white foam head on the beer in his hand, but all he could see was the image of Clair in Rand and Seth's arms, the joy and happiness on all their faces as they'd embraced.

In the past two hours, he'd asked himself where he fit into that scene—if he *could* fit in. And the answer kept coming back.

Nowhere.

What did he have to offer her? He'd made some healthy investments over the years, he didn't even have to work if he chose not to. Still, her bank account made his look like pocket change.

She had a loving family, *two* loving families now. Jacob realized he hadn't seen his brother in a year.

Or was it longer?

Hell, he couldn't keep track, he thought with disgust. He couldn't even remember the last time he'd seen his own apartment. Three months maybe? Like money, time had never meant a great deal to him.

He caught sight of her as she stepped into the lounge, and his heart jumped.

Dammit. No woman had ever made his heart jump like that before.

She made her way through the crowd and sat in the chair opposite his, then made everything worse by smiling. He had to take a drink of beer to wash away the sudden dust in his throat.

"I take it everything went well?" he asked when she just sat there and kept grinning.

"It was wonderful." She leaned across the table, her voice slightly breathless. "They're wonderful. We talked for two hours straight and barely touched the surface. Rand trains horses and he's remodeling our parents' ranch and Seth is, or was anyway, an undercover police officer in Albuquerque. They're both engaged, can you believe it?"

He listened while she told him how Rand had met his fiancée, and they'd rescued wild horses in a canyon, how Seth had met Hannah after crashing his motorcycle in her front yard.

Her face glowed; her eyes sparkled. He thought she looked more beautiful at that moment than any other.

"My cousin Lucas has invited us for dinner at his house tonight," she said, her blue eyes wide with excitement. "He's married and has three-year-old twins, a girl and a boy, and a brand-new baby boy named Thomas. Oh, and he owns this hotel we're sitting in, isn't that amazing!"

"Clair—"

"Oh, and Hannah, Seth's fiancée—" she couldn't sit still in her seat "—she has five-year-old twin girls, too. They're all going to be there. I don't know how I'll keep everyone's names straight." She tilted her head sideways and glanced at his wristwatch. "I need to go up and shower. We're supposed to be there in an hour."

"I can't go."

The smile on her lips froze. "You can't go?"

"I have a meeting in Dallas early tomorrow morning. I'll need to hit the road in a few minutes."

"Oh. Well." She stared at him for a long moment. "Okay."

Okay? He told himself it was good that she wasn't making this difficult, but still...a simple "okay" wasn't exactly what he'd expected.

Hell, what *had* he been expecting? That she'd cry or complain?

Maybe even ask him to stay?

No. That *isn't* what he wanted. Obviously it wasn't what she wanted, either.

He had no reason to feel guilty that he was leaving so quickly, he told himself. None at all.

"Clair." Though he knew it would probably be a mistake to touch her, he took her hand. Her fingers were warm in his, her skin smooth and soft. "I'm sorry I can't hang around for a couple of days, but—"

"Don't be sorry, Jacob." She squeezed his hand. "Please. These past few days have been wonderful. More than I could have ever hoped for. I realize you have your own life and you need to get back to it."

Dammit, it was one thing to make this easy, and another that she was practically holding the door for him.

He let go of her hand and pulled the hotel key card out of his shirt pocket. "I got you a room," he said, heard the annoyance in his voice and felt even more annoyed. "Your suitcase is already up there."

"Thank you." She stood, leaned down and touched her lips to his cheek. "For finding me. For bringing me here. For everything. It's been quite an adventure."

She turned and walked away, her shoulders straight and her chin level. Jacob frowned, wondered what the hell had just happened. His frown deepened as he watched several male heads turn her way as she passed through the throng of people.

And then she was gone.

It's been quite an adventure.

It sure as hell had.

He stared for a long time at the corner she'd disappeared around, then picked up the beer and practically downed it in one gulp.

The waitress appeared a moment later. "You want another?" she asked.

He didn't even look at the woman, just shook his head, then left.

Eleven

With a glass of icy lemonade in her hand, Clair stepped onto the patio of Lucas Blackhawk's house and soaked in the activity surrounding her. Children playing kickball on a thick, green lawn; Rand and Seth arguing over the outcome of a recent baseball game; Lucas standing guard over steaks sizzling on an open barbecue.

So familiar, yet so strange, she thought, watching Lucas studiously brush marinade on the meat with one hand while he fanned billowing smoke with the other.

"The resemblance between them is remarkable, isn't it?" Julianna, Lucas's wife, came out of the house carrying a bowl of macaroni salad. The stunning blonde hardly looked as if she'd had a baby only four weeks ago. "I nearly kissed Seth earlier when he came up behind me in the kitchen to sneak one of the cookies I'd just taken out of the oven.''

"Now *that* would have been interesting," Hannah, Seth's fiancée, said from the doorway. Her baby blue eyes sparkled as she stepped out of the house and set a basket of potato chips on the patio table. Tucking a loose strand of golden hair behind her ear, she gave a wicked grin. "But I have to admit, I almost pinched Rand on the behind a little while ago when he was searching for a beer in the refrigerator."

"I'd have paid good money to see his reaction to that." With a toss of her shoulder-length auburn hair, Grace, Rand's fiancée, joined them on the patio.

"I'm sure he'd be thoroughly appalled," Hannah reassured Grace.

The women all looked at each other and laughed.

Smiling, Clair glanced at her brothers and her cousin. The resemblance *was* remarkable. The distinct, angular features that declared the Native American heritage in their blood, their thick, shiny black hair and tall, muscular build. Even their gestures were similar, Clair thought, watching the men all turn their heads and frown with concern when one of the little girls—Lucas's daughter, Nicole—began to shriek at her brother, Nathan, for pulling her tennis shoe off. The crisis was quickly over when Maddie and Missy, Hannah's twin girls, snatched their shoes off, as well, and soon all the children were barefoot and laughing again.

All except for little Thomas. The sound of the baby's fussing came over the monitor sitting on a patio chair.

"May I?" Hannah asked Julianna. "I know I

hogged him all afternoon, but it's been so long since I've held a baby.''

''Be my guest.'' Julianna swept a hand toward the open door. ''Though I suspect you'll be holding one of your own before long.''

''Oh, I hope so.'' Hannah's eyes softened at the thought. ''I decided if our bed and breakfast doesn't succeed, we'll just fill all those bedrooms with children.''

''I've tasted your baking.'' Julianna slipped an arm through Hannah's and together they walked into the house. ''Trust me, you'll succeed.''

Clair felt an ache in her chest as she stared after the two women. They had everything she'd ever wanted: children, a home of their own, a man who loved them. Clair knew that she was now part of their happiness, part of all their lives, and for that she would be eternally grateful.

Yet still her heart ached.

How foolish she'd been to let herself hope, to dream, to believe that she'd finally met the man—the one man—who might share those hopes and dreams with her. She still didn't know how she'd ever managed to walk out of that hotel lounge without her knees crumbling, or without running back to him and begging him to stay, even just one more day. One more night.

She wouldn't have changed one thing that had happened between her and Jacob, unless it could be for him to want her, to love her, as deeply as she loved him. And no amount of wishing in the world could make that happen.

''Clair?''

Realizing that Grace had been talking to her, Clair

did her best to cover that she hadn't been listening. "I'm so sorry," she said, felt the heat of her blush on her cheeks. "You were saying?"

"Just how excited we all are to have you here." Grace tilted her head and studied her soon-to-be sister-in-law. "Is something wrong?"

"Of course not." Even as her eyes started to fill, she forced a smile. "Nothing's wrong."

"Baloney." Frowning, Grace took the glass from Clair's hand and set it on the patio table, then took her hand and led her inside the house. "Time for girl talk."

"I'm fine," Clair protested, but couldn't stop the tear that slid down her cheek. *Damn you, Jacob Carver.*

Grace took Clair to the den, then tugged her down on the leather sofa beside her. "Something's bothering you, Clair. Tell me what's wrong."

"Nothing. Really." How pathetic she must look, Clair thought miserably and struggled to hold on to her last thread of composure. "It's just that…so much has happened. I'm feeling a little emotional, that's all."

"How incredibly insensitive we've all been." Her lips pressed into a thin line, Grace shook her head. "So you *are* in love with him, then."

Shocked, Clair simply stared. Grace couldn't know. No one could know. It wasn't possible.

"All this talk about weddings and babies," Grace went on. "After what you've been through. I'm so sorry."

"You—I—" Completely frazzled, Clair didn't know what to say. "Please don't be sorry."

"We could invite him here," Grace said firmly.

"Maybe if he met all of us, and we could explain face-to-face, he would understand why you did what you did."

What I did? What had she done? And invite Jacob here? Clair thought. Good Lord, no!

"Grace," Clair said carefully. "I—I don't understand."

Grace took Clair's hands in her own. "Oliver."

"Oliver?" Clair frowned. "What about Oliver?"

"We know about the wedding," Grace said gently. "How you left the church."

Clair blinked. Grace was talking about *Oliver?*

In spite of the situation, in spite of the ache in her heart, Clair started to laugh. Startled, Grace stared in confusion.

"What's so funny?" A smile on her lips, Julianna came into the den and looked at Clair, then Grace.

"I have no idea." Grace shook her head in bewilderment.

Holding little Thomas, Hannah moved into the room. "Is Clair all right?" she asked, biting her lip.

"I'm not in love with Oliver," Clair managed to say between a mixture of tears and laughter. "I'm in love with Jacob."

Grace lifted a brow; Julianna and Hannah looked at each other, then back at Clair.

"Oh," they all said together.

"Julianna." Grace kept her gaze on Clair. "Go tell the men they can feed the kids and we women will be out in a little while. Hannah, let's you and me take Clair upstairs where it's quiet."

"Please don't fuss over me." Clair looked at all the other women. "I'm fine. I don't want to be a bother and—"

"You are no bother," Grace said while Julianna hurried outside and Hannah waited anxiously. "We're family now, Clair. We're here for you. All of us."

Upstairs, they all listened quietly while she poured her heart out, then each one of them hugged her in turn. It didn't seem to matter that she'd only just met these women. It felt as if she'd known them forever.

In the love and comfort they offered, Clair was certain that somehow, one day, her shattered heart would mend.

Family.

That single word made her throat thicken and the tears start all over again, but this time they were tears of joy.

Jacob slammed the nail into the two-by-four, then stood back and gave the window frame a solid shake. The house was a mere skeleton, but it was taking shape quickly; the first story was nearly complete and the sheeting for the roof was ready to drop in place. The sound of skill saws and men hammering from inside the framework mingled with the smell of freshly cut wood and damp concrete. Overhead, white puffy clouds floated on a deep blue sky.

With the hot Texas sun on his back and a hammer in his hand, Jacob moved to the next window frame. Sweat poured freely down his brow and between his shoulder blades, but he didn't mind. It had been a long time since he'd worked with his hands like this, even longer since he'd worked side by side with Evan.

Too long, he thought. Too damn long.

"You gonna stare that nail into the stud, or hit it?"

Jacob swiveled a look at his brother, then turned back to the window frame and drove the nail in with one powerful swing of his arm.

"Not bad for an apprentice." Evan stepped through what would be the back sliding door of the house, one of three custom homes, each on one-acre lots that Carver Construction was under contract to build. He opened the top of a large cooler sitting beside the house and pulled out two bottles of cold water.

"Apprentice, my ass." Jacob took the water Evan offered, then tipped his head back and guzzled half the bottle. "I taught you everything you know."

"You mean you taught me everything *you* know." Evan leaned one well-muscled shoulder against the bare wood of the doorjamb. "Which took all of five minutes."

Jacob shot a look at his brother that would have had most men backing up. Evan simply grinned, then took a long drink from his own bottle.

Evan was a man in his element, Jacob thought. Relaxed, confident, his dark, long hair covered with a thin layer of sawdust. The blue bandanna wrapped around his head gave him the rough, wild appearance of a desperado, a look that Jacob knew was popular with the ladies. Lord knew there'd been a steady stream of "friends," as Evan as called them, traipsing through the work site this past week.

"So when you gonna finally tell me why you've been hanging around here for the past week doing manual labor with those lily-white hands?" Evan wiped at his mouth with the back of his hand. "I figured either the law's after you or it's a woman."

Because Evan was too close to the truth, Jacob turned his back on his brother and slammed another nail into the window frame. "Can't a guy visit his brother without accusations and the third degree? You want me gone, say so."

"Ah, so it *is* a woman." Evan ignored Jacob's attempt to start a fight. "So what's the deal? She start looking at wedding rings and cooing over babies? That would send you running."

"Evan, just shut the hell up." Jacob dropped the hammer into the work belt slung low around his waist, was furious he couldn't stop the twitch tugging at the corner of his eye. "And I'm not running, dammit. It just wouldn't work, that's all."

It *wouldn't*, he'd told himself a thousand times over the past two weeks. How could it? With her background, her money, all the people who loved her and cared about her, worried about her, what was left for him?

"Well, I'll be damned." Evan's jaw had gone slack. "My brother, the Great Jacob Carver, the man who stands as an icon for the rest of the single male gender, has finally fallen."

"The hell I have." He might have pulled off the lie if he hadn't denied it so hotly. "She got under my skin for a few days, but that's behind me."

"Yeah, I can see that," Evan said with a grin. "That's why you haven't gone back to Jersey and you've been busting your butt pounding on nails. Because it's all behind you."

"That does it." Jacob unbuckled his work belt and threw it at a pile of scrap wood. Pieces of two-by-four went flying. "I'm outta here."

He stomped off, got maybe ten feet, then whirled around and stomped back. "She went to *Cotillion,* for God's sake!"

Still standing calmly against the doorjamb, Evan frowned in confusion. "She went to where?"

"Never mind." Jacob dragged a hand through his hair and shook his head. "It just wouldn't work."

"I believe you already said that." Evan pushed away from the doorjamb, then stepped back from the house and called up to his foreman. "Hank, pack it in. Full day's pay for the crew and first round of beer at The Bunker on me."

The men scrambled at their boss's generous offer. Within minutes, the site was cleared, leaving Jacob and Evan alone.

"So." Evan folded his arms and faced his brother. "You gonna tell me, or do I have to beat it out of you?"

"As if you could," Jacob said irritably, then sighed. He nodded at the cooler. "Got any beer in there?"

With a grin, Evan opened the lid again, dug through the ice to the bottom, then pulled out two cans and tossed one to Jacob.

Jacob popped the top and stared at the foam rushing out. "It's complicated."

Evan shrugged. "Since when did you ever do anything that wasn't? Why don't you just tell me her name."

"God, even *that's* complicated." He blew out a breath, then decided he might as well start at the beginning.

"Twenty-three years ago…"

Pappa Pete's sat on the corner of Main and Sixth. The '50s diner had been there since…well, since the '50s. It was glass and chrome, white Formica counters and red vinyl booths. The food was good, the prices fair and the service terrific.

"You gonna finish those?"

Clair polished off the last bite of hamburger she'd ordered, then glanced up at Seth. His expression was hopeful as he stared at the French fries still on her plate.

"Yes, I am," she said evenly. "And don't think I didn't notice there were some missing after I returned from the ladies' room."

"That was Rand." Seth looked at his brother, whose handsome, rugged face suddenly turned innocent.

"Not me." Rand held his hands up, then looked past Clair's shoulder and lifted his chin. "Hey, do you know that woman over there? She's trying to get your attention."

"What woman?" Clair turned to look, but didn't see anyone. "I don't see—"

The fries had been cleaned off her plate when she turned back. Folding her arms, she sat back in her seat and frowned at her brothers. "That was rude and unforgivable."

"One chocolate shake with extra whip cream, just like you boys ordered for the little lady." Madge, the middle-aged platinum-blond owner of Pappa Pete's, set the shake down in front of Clair.

"Forgive us now?" Rand asked, lifting one brow.

Clair smiled and reached for a spoon. "Absolutely."

The past week had flown by. There'd been two meetings with the lawyer to finalize the paperwork for the estate, a bridal shower for Grace and Hannah and a christening for baby Thomas. Her head was still spinning from all the activity, but she'd been thankful for the distractions.

Anything to keep her mind off Jacob.

It had helped to share her heartbreak with Julianna, Grace and Hannah, but Clair knew that she had a long, long way to go before the pain of losing him eased. And in spite of everything, in spite of the emptiness in her soul, she still cherished every minute they'd shared and grieved for what might have been.

"I say we go find him and kick his butt."

Startled, Clair looked up at Rand's words. His eyes were narrowed in anger, his gaze locked on Seth. *Darn it.* Her brothers knew exactly where her mind had drifted, and the person she'd been thinking about.

"No argument from me," Seth replied tightly.

Clair had been careful not to let her feelings show this past week. Though Rand and Seth had no details, they were well aware of the fact that their sister had fallen in love with Jacob.

"I'm fine," Clair insisted and squared her shoulders. "I appreciate your concern, but really, I'm fine."

Rand shook his head. "She said she was fine twice in the same sentence."

Seth nodded. "Doesn't sound fine to me."

It hardly seemed possible that in such a few short days these two men could come to mean so much to her. Twenty-three years had slipped away and they were family again. Yesterday the three of them had gone to the ravine off Cold Springs Road where their parents had lost their lives, and where their own lives had been torn apart. They'd held hands there, stood as one, and felt the peace fill them, felt the broken bond heal and grow strong in the love surrounding them.

Their parents' had been there, as well, watching them, smiling. Clair had felt their presence, knew that they were happy now, that they could finally be at rest.

When her eyes started to tear, the heat in Rand and Seth's eyes cooled.

"Dammit," Seth muttered. "He made her cry. Now I really am gonna go find that jerk and kick his butt."

"I'm not crying over Jacob," she said, shaking her head. He was part of her tumultuous emotions, Clair thought, but only a part. "I'm crying be-cause…because I love you both so much."

Though they'd shown each other how they felt over the past week, she was the first one to say the words out loud. It threw Rand and Seth a curve ball.

They were silent for a long moment, then Seth said, "So can I have your shake, then?"

"Touch it—" Clair pulled her glass closer "—and you'll see whose butt gets kicked."

They all grinned at each other, then Rand cleared his throat and reached across the table to take her hand. "I love you, too, Liz."

Rand and Seth both had been careful to call her Clair all week, but every so often, the name they'd always known her by—Lizzie—would sneak out. Every time it happened, she'd feel a little catch in her throat and a hitch in her chest.

"Me, too," Seth added, then hugged her.

It felt so good, she thought.

Almost whole.

She'd booked a flight out tomorrow morning for

Charleston, was anxious to see her mother and father and begin to rebuild their relationship. Though they'd talked on the phone every day, Clair hadn't told her adopted parents yet that she would be moving to Wolf River. She thought she should do that in person, knew that they were not going to easily accept her leaving South Carolina.

"Sorry, boys, but I've got to get back to the hotel." She slipped out of the booth and gave both Rand and Seth a peck on the cheek. "Grace and Hannah are meeting me there so I can try on a bridesmaid dress."

"Someone getting married?" Rand asked.

Clair rolled her eyes. In one week, Rand and Seth were having a small double ceremony in the same church where their parents had been married. Clair was flying back to Wolf River the day before the wedding, and if all went well with her parents this week, she intended to ask them to come with her.

"Adagio's at eight tonight," she reminded Rand and Seth of the reservations she'd made at the hotel restaurant. "My treat."

The day was pleasant, warm with a soft breeze and the scent of fall lingering in the air. Scarecrows and cornstalks decorated the windows of the local merchants and banners announced a Halloween Festival in three weeks. Julianna was in charge of the dime toss booth and Clair had already been recruited to help.

She couldn't wait.

It was a short walk to the hotel and Clair strolled casually down Main street. People passing by smiled and waved. Sylvia, a waitress from Pappa Pete's honked as she drove by in a blue pickup. Everyone in Wolf River knew who she was, knew how she and her brothers had been adopted out and were now all back together. There had even been an article in the local newspaper detailing what had happened. The town had welcomed them all with open arms, offered sympathy and support.

In the few short days she'd been here, Clair knew this was where she belonged.

If she couldn't have Jacob, couldn't be a part of his life, or him a part of hers, then she'd make a life of her own. It certainly was time, she thought. It was *past* time.

She started to pass the drugstore across the street from the hotel when she remembered the roll of film she'd dropped off earlier in the week. When she'd first pulled the plastic cylinder out of her suitcase, she hadn't wanted to see the pictures. She'd even tossed it in the trash can, determined to put the past week behind her and move on.

But in the end, her heart won the argument with her head and she'd retrieved the roll of film from the trash, then taken it to be developed, cursing her weakness the entire time.

Just one look, she told herself as she ducked into the drugstore and quickly paid for the developing, then she'd throw every picture away and move on with her life.

She *would*.

Five minutes later, sitting on the sofa in the living room of her motel room, her hands shaking, she opened the package.

The first few pictures were the ones she'd shot on the road—the barns, the fields, the abandoned tractor. The memories of every moment came rushing back and made her smile.

Her heart skipped as she stared at the picture Jacob had taken of her in the shower—just her startled face, thank goodness, then came the pictures she'd taken of him. Remembering that moment made her laugh out loud, but it blurred her vision, as well.

There was a shot of Jacob sitting in his car, frowning at her—she certainly didn't need a picture to remember *that* look. A picture she'd taken of Dorothy, the motel clerk who had told them to say hello to her cousin Angie in Wolf River. Two more pictures of Jacob she'd snapped when they'd stopped along the road, both of them candid.

She was nearly to the end of the roll when she realized there were other snapshots on the roll that Jacob must have taken. They were slightly dark, obviously taken at nighttime. A man and woman coming out of a motel room. She looked closer, then gasped.

Oliver and Susan?

Her gaze darted to the date and time in the corner. The picture had been taken the night before the wedding!

Oliver and Susan?

Jaw slack, she quickly went through the rest of the pictures. Oliver and Susan kissing outside the motel room, another one with the two of them embracing and Oliver groping Susan's bottom. There were three other shots, all showing her fiancé and best friend being extremely intimate with each other.

Good God, what an idiot she'd been!

She was torn between wanting to laugh at the absurdity of it, her outrage at betrayal by two people she'd trusted, and her ultimate relief that she hadn't gone through with the wedding.

Her eyes narrowed slowly.

Jacob had known.

With something between an oath and a groan, Clair tossed the pictures on the sofa. Fisting her hands, she stood and began to pace, muttering to herself as she strode back and forth across the living room of her hotel suite. Jacob had been fully aware of the guilt and shame she'd felt at running out on her wedding the way she had. She'd felt as if she'd let everyone who loved and trusted her down.

He'd known how miserable she'd been, and still he hadn't told her!

Well, she had a few things to say to Mr. Jacob Carver. She'd track him down like the dog he was and then she'd tell him he could go straight to—

The knock on her door had her whirling. Grace and Hannah were going to get an earful about his, Clair thought as she threw the door open.

"Wait until you—"

Her mind went blank when it was Jacob standing there, not her future sisters-in-law.

He lifted a brow. "Until I what?"

"You."

Jeez. Jacob had imagined several different scenarios of how Clair would react when she saw him— anger, joy, even a cool calm—but *this,* this wild fury caught him completely off guard.

"Clair, is something—"

She started to slam the door, but he managed to get his boot in the way before it could close. She'd already turned on her heels and stomped across the living room to the sofa. She picked up a handful of pictures, stomped back toward him and threw them at him. They fluttered to the ground.

"What in the world is wrong with—"

He caught a glimpse of one of the photos that had landed faceup.

"Oh."

Dammit, dammit. He'd completely forgotten about the pictures he'd taken of Oliver and the blond bimbo. He never would have given her that roll of film if he had.

No wonder Clair was so hot.

Crossing her arms, she faced him, her lips pressed into a thin line. "Why didn't you tell me?"

So much for the carefully thought out speech he'd prepared driving here. In the blink of an eye, he and Clair were running in a different direction than the one he'd planned.

And why did that not surprise him?

Closing the door behind him, he squared off with her. "Because after you ran out of that church, you had enough to deal with," he said simply.

She lifted her chin and pointed it at him. "You knew, had *pictures* of my fiancé having an affair, and you kept it from me."

"I just told you, I didn't think—"

"You certainly didn't think, buster." She jabbed a finger at his chest. "You let me wallow in my guilt, worry that I'd left poor Oliver standing at the altar, when all along he was sleeping with Susan—my best friend, for God's sake!"

"And if I had told you that the jerk was cheating on you," he said irritably, "do you really think you would have felt better? You'd just found out that your parents had been lying to you your entire life. Did you really need to know that the man you nearly married and your so-called 'best friend' were lying, as well?"

"It isn't a question of whether I'd feel better or not. It's about the truth. I needed the *truth*." She flounced away from him, throwing her arms out in frustration, then suddenly she turned back, her eyes wide. "Oliver knew you knew, didn't he? That's why he called your motel room before he called mine. He wanted to talk to you before me, so he could find out if you'd told me."

"I have no idea why he called." Lord, she was beautiful all riled up like this, Jacob thought. Her cheeks were flushed, her eyes flashed blue sparks. "You spoke to him, remember? Not me."

"I'll just bet he offered you money not to tell me, didn't he?" She moved close, the expression on her face daring him to lie. "How much?"

He was getting angry now, the last thing he'd come here to do. But she wanted the truth, so he'd give it to her. "Twenty-five thousand dollars."

She went still at the figure, then her mouth dropped open. "Twenty...five...thousand?"

"And another twenty thousand to bring you back to Charleston."

Because her knees were too weak to hold her, Clair stumbled backward to the sofa, then sat. It felt as if all the blood had drained from her face, and with it, some of her fury. She was simply too stunned to be angry.

"You didn't take it," she whispered. She knew he hadn't, could see it in his eyes, could *feel* it in her heart. "Why?"

"He tried to buy you back," Jacob said tightly. "Like you were a car or a goddamned watch. He put a price tag on you, and that just ticked me off."

She stared at him for a long moment, then carefully

asked, "Is that why you came back?" she asked. "To tell me about Oliver?"

"No." He moved in front of her, reached for her arms and pulled her up from the sofa. "I spent the past week with my brother in Kettle Creek, working on one of the houses he's building there."

"You said you had an appointment in Dallas. That's why you—"

He laid a finger on her lips. "I did have an appointment. A referral from Henry. But I turned the job down and somehow just ended up at my brother's. He's swamped with work and I hung around to give him a hand."

She was glad he'd gone to see his brother. She really was. Maybe they'd talk about his visit later. But right now it was not the most important, the most crucial subject on her mind.

"You didn't answer my question, Jacob." She refused to let herself hope, refused to throw herself in his arms and beg him to stay. But her voice wavered as she asked, "Why did you come back?"

"For you, Clair. I came back for you."

Her heart started to pound fiercely. "Why?"

His thumbs lightly brushed her collarbone. "With every yard of cement I poured, every nail I drove in, I thought about you, here in Wolf River, with your family."

Thrilled by his words, but still cautious, she searched his face. "What about my family?"

"I realized that while you were trying to find your past, I was running away from mine." His dark gaze held hers. "And that I was running away from what I wanted the most, which was you."

When she opened her mouth to speak, he shook his head.

"I couldn't see any way around our differences. Money, social standing, family." Lightly he traced his knuckles along her jaw. "You deserved so much more than I thought I could offer. Then I—"

"Jacob—"

"Don't you know it's rude to interrupt, Miss Beauchamp?" he said with a frown. "Now be quiet."

She pressed her lips firmly together, thought she might burst if he didn't hurry and get out whatever it was he was trying to say.

"Then I stood back and looked at the house I was pounding nails into. There was a lot of finish work to do—walls, roof, plaster—but it had a solid foundation and a strong framework." He cupped her chin in his hand. "I figure if I can't give you all those other things you deserve, I can at least give you that. A solid foundation and framework. If you'll have me, we'll work together on the rest."

If she'd have him? The flutter of hope she'd felt a moment ago took full flight. "You—you want me?"

He smiled, then brushed his lips against hers. "I don't just want you. I need you. I need you beside me when we go to bed at night, in the morning when we wake up. I need the sound of your laugh and the enthusiasm in your eyes when you experience something new. I love you, Clair. I want to marry you. I want babies and a house with a white picket fence, Little League games and piano recitals. God help me, we'll even do that cotillion thing if you want."

Her knees turned to water and Clair was certain if he hadn't been holding her, she would have sank to the floor. "You love me?" she whispered. "You want to *marry* me?"

"I love you," he repeated. "I think I've been in love with you since the moment you turned toward me in that church and asked me for a ride."

He loved her. Wanted to marry her. The joy of it swelled in her chest and tightened her throat. When she said nothing, just stared at him, she saw the panic settle in his dark eyes.

"I know I was a fool to let my pride get in my way," he said urgently. "But now I'm asking, I'm begging, please marry me. God, Clair tell me you love me, too."

Laughing, she threw her arms around his neck, then kissed him. She felt the relief shudder through him as he circled his strong arms around her and kissed her back. "I do love you," she gasped, dragging her mouth from his. "And yes. Yes, I'll marry you."

"Thank God," he muttered, closing his eyes. "I was afraid I'd lost you."

"You didn't lose me, Jacob," she whispered against his mouth. "You found me, remember?"

Lifting his head, he grinned down at her. "I guess I did. So, can I keep you?"

She smiled back at him through her tears. "I'm yours, Jacob. I always have been. I always will be."

He kissed her again, a deep, soulful kiss. A kiss filled with promise. With truth.

They were both breathing hard when he finally pulled away and looked down at her. "I don't care where we live," he said raggedly. "I'll build you a house, a big house. We'll fill it with babies and a couple of dogs and a hamster or a fish. My brother wants to bring me in as a partner, expand his business outside of where he is now. I could set up an office anywhere.''

"Jacob." He'd be the first person she'd tell, she decided. The first person to know what she planned to do. "I want to live here, in Wolf River," she said, her voice shaking. "I'm going to buy The Four Winds."

"The hotel?"

"I know that Lucas has wanted to sell it for a long time, but he's been looking for the right buyer. *I'm* the right buyer." Her smile widened. "I know I'll have a lot to learn and I'll have to work hard, but I can do it, Jacob. I know I can."

"No doubt about it, sweetheart." He slid his hands down her back and tugged her close against him. "No doubt at all."

The thrill of his touch, the joy of the kisses he trailed along her jaw, overflowed her heart. To love that one special man, to be loved back, it was everything she'd ever imagined. She took his face in her face and looked up at him.

"I have to fly back to South Carolina tomorrow and see my parents," she said softly. "Will you come to?"

"I have a better idea." He pressed his lips into her palm and gazed back at her. Her smile widened.

And together they said it.

"Let's drive."

*   *   *   *   *

0808/25/MB151

Queens of Romance

Uncertain Summer

Serena gave up hope of getting married when her fiancé
jilted her. Then Gijs suggested that she marry him instead.
She liked Gijs very much, and she knew he was fond of her –
that seemed as good a basis as any for marriage. But it
turned out Gijs was in love…

Small Slice of Summer

Letitia Marsden had decided that men were not to be trusted,
until she met Doctor Jason Mourik van Nie. This time, Letitia
vowed, there would be a happy ending. Then Jason got the
wrong idea about one of her male friends. Surely a simple
misunderstanding couldn't stand in the way of true love?

Available 1st August 2008

Collect all 10 superb books in the collection!

Queens of Romance

Bedding His Virgin Mistress

Ricardo Salvatore planned to take over Carly's company, so why not have her as well? But Ricardo was stunned when in the heat of passion he learned of Carly's innocence…

Expecting the Playboy's Heir

American billionaire and heir to an earldom, Silas Carter is one of the world's most eligible men. Beautiful Julia Fellowes is perfect wife material. And she's pregnant!

Blackmailing the Society Bride

When millionaire banker Marcus Canning decides it's time to get an heir, debt-ridden Lucy becomes a convenient wife. Their sexual chemistry is purely a bonus…

Available 5th September 2008

Collect all 10 superb books in the collection!

This proud man must learn to love again

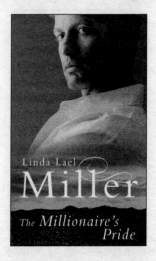

Successful, rich widower Rance McKettrick is determined that nothing is going to get in the way of his new start in life.

But after meeting the sweet, beautiful Echo Wells, Rance finds her straightforward honesty is challenging everything he thought he knew about himself. Both Rance and Echo must come to grips with who they really are to find a once-in-a-lifetime happiness.

Available 18th July 2008

www.millsandboon.co.uk

M&B

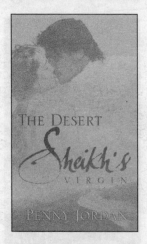

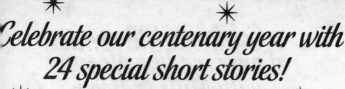

Celebrate 100 years of pure reading pleasure with Mills & Boon®

To mark our centenary, each month we're publishing a special 100th Birthday Edition. These celebratory editions are packed with extra features and include a FREE bonus story.

Plus, you have the chance to enter a fabulous monthly prize draw. See 100th Birthday Edition books for details.

Now that's worth celebrating!

July 2008

**The Man Who Had Everything
by Christine Rimmer**
Includes FREE bonus story *Marrying Molly*

August 2008

Their Miracle Baby by Caroline Anderson
Includes FREE bonus story *Making Memories*

September 2008

Crazy About Her Spanish Boss by Rebecca Winters
Includes FREE bonus story
Rafael's Convenient Proposal

Look for Mills & Boon® 100th Birthday Editions at your favourite bookseller or visit
www.millsandboon.co.uk